I0760756

the NEVERSEEN KING

the NEVERSEEN KING

THE NEVERSEEN KING

www.AnastasisBlythe.com

Hardcover ISBN: 978-1-960606-10-5

Jacket Cover design by Saint Jupiter.
Laminate Cover and Interior Design by Dragonpen Designs.

FOR LEISA

A toast to book rants. Thank you for being such a wonderful writing buddy and internet bestie.

1

THE NEVERSEEN KING

TODAY IS MY wedding day.

I had hoped to never think those words again. At first, because I was starry-eyed and stupid, believing Liliana would be my only wife—believing I could trick fate and prove I would be the first Neverseen King to not sacrifice his human bride. Then, because I was committed to surviving on my own.

Alas, here I am.

Sitting on the floor outside Nadira's room, leaning my head against the wall. I alternate between staring at the unlit brass sconce on the opposite wall and closing my eyes. My body might be healed from last night's arrow wounds, but the use of magic left me so drained I can hardly stand.

So I sit. And I listen.

"Ugh! It's too sloppy!" The voice that drifts through the walls belongs to Eshe, nimble-fingered thief and Nadira's best friend. "Look at that smear!"

"It doesn't matter," comes Nadira's much softer reply.

"Of *course* it matters! You cannot be a bride without *mehndi*! It's such a grievous sin that this crucial job is left to me. I steal art, not make it. It doesn't even help that you're holding so still; my hands are shaking enough for both of us! Sands, this is a travesty! Look at that blotch on your wrist! It looks like a wart."

"It's fine. Truly, it doesn't matter to me."

"I should have known you would be the most insufferable bride in existence."

At that, I give a slight huff of amusement, my lip curling up.

"This isn't a normal wedding, and I'm not a normal bride," replies Nadira. "Nothing about this is traditional, so there's no need to lose your sanity over this minor bit of tradition."

"This is exactly *why* we need this bit of tradition. Otherwise, this marriage of yours will be the most scandalous thing of the century."

"*Mehndi* on my hands fixes the scandal?" There's a note of humor in Nadira's low voice. "Then by all means, continue."

Eshe grumbles something in reply that I cannot make out. With each passing moment, I expect Nadira to pick up paper and ink and scrawl one simple note.

I've changed my mind.

She must be considering it. She's already run away from the palace once—and she'd be right to do it again. If I close my eyes, I can almost see her there in the gown I'd made for her, staring at a piece of parchment while Eshe clucks over her like a hen with her brood.

The torture of wondering if Nadira will decide against our marriage is almost more than I can bear. At least in my current weakened state; perhaps I would have handled it better if I possessed my usual vigor. If she says the word, I'll let her go without hesitation. It would be better for her if she left. I won't stop her. To the very moment our vows are exchanged, I'll let her go.

I won't make her my captive bride.

Footsteps from down the hallway alert me to my steward's approach. Part of me considers climbing to my feet and hurrying halfway down the wing to feign checking a portal lock.

I cannot bring myself to move. So I stay where I am, leaning like an invalid against the wall and waiting for him to come find me eavesdropping on my soon-to-be wife.

The footsteps grow louder, until at last he comes around the corner and into view, his long severe face unreadable, as always.

"Emin," I say quietly in greeting, not wanting Nadira or Eshe to hear me.

He inclines his head toward me. "Master. Would you care to refresh yourself and prepare for this evening? The afternoon is quickly passing."

He's right. It's the prudent thing. I ought to get up, bathe, dress—probably even sleep, if I can manage it. But the moment I do those things, it'll start to feel more real. It won't just be a moonlit dream that she said she'd marry me. It will be reality. Then, if she backs out, it will be that much more painful.

I shouldn't be afraid of pain. I've faced the deepest rages of pain, yet I am still here.

"Thank you. I would like to prepare for this evening, yes." With those words, I clench my fists, gathering the last reserves of my strength, and get to my feet. Emin comes to my side as I stagger, ready to help support my weight. It's almost laughably ridiculous. I must weigh twice what he does. If magic wasn't so draining at the moment, I'd abandon my physical body altogether, slip into the dream realm, and make my way to my quarters. Alas, it takes all my strength to maintain the spells hiding my face.

I really should rest. A little rest and I'll have my strength back.

It just seems impossible to rest today.

ANASTASIS BLYTHE

Emin walks with me back to my chambers, pointedly ignoring my heavy breathing. When we finally arrive, he pushes the double doors open for me. The familiar setting hardly registers in my mind as I make my way straight to my bedroom. Just an hour or two of rest and then I'll be good as—

I push open the door and freeze.

There is my bed, with its four great posters, its plush cushions and coverings. Just as it has always been.

Nadira will be here tonight.

I turn away quickly, swallowing around the sudden tightness in my throat. She might still change her mind. There's no guarantee she'll be here in a few hours. I tell myself it's more likely that I'll face this empty chamber again, like I have for the last ninety-nine years.

I'm not sure which option will be more difficult.

"The bath is drawn, my lord." Emin's grounding voice pulls me from my thoughts. "If you care to bathe before you rest."

I clench my jaw, step out of the bedroom, and pull the door shut behind me. "That would be wonderful." Maybe by the time the sun goes down, I will be prepared to do what must be done—to take Nadira as my bride.

When did my most treasured dream and darkest nightmare become the very same thing in my heart?

THE MOURNER

Darkness spreading across my skin catches the tail of my eye. I startle sharply. My mind screams that my hands are covered in blood. My reaction is frantic, desperate, flinging my arm away from me as though I could lose it entirely. Then my vision clears, and it's only the complex whorls of black *mehndi*. I immediately chastise myself. How many times have I done this already today? I fight the instinctive urge to rub away the stain.

Eshe will shriek at me if I destroy her careful work.

The hours have dripped by like blood through fingers. They've given me time to reconsider the declaration I gave the Neverseen King last night, after I'd slaughtered the army led by Jabir to take over the palace. Those words had been given in the wake of an unexpected kiss, fueled by emotions and adrenaline both. I hadn't been thinking straight. I'd been fighting for my life, for Eshe's life, for the Neverseen King's life. I was exhausted, stupid.

Yet, somehow, I cannot bring myself to pick up a scrap of paper and write those very words. If I say no now, it'll be the end of us—of whatever has been growing between us. If I take back my declaration, those words will be my goodbye to him.

Forever.

I can't.

So I sit still at this vanity while Eshe bends over my hair and meticulously applies my cosmetics. A handheld copper mirror rests near my hand, but I'm too terrified to pick it up and see what strange face looks back at me.

At the back of my mind, a familiar grating voice repeats.

"You'll find you're not rid of me so easily."

I want to completely dismiss Jabir from my mind. He's dead. He cannot hurt me anymore. That chapter of my life is behind me. I can shut it up in the recesses of my inner self, lock it away, and pretend it never happened. I can believe my parents' forgotten surname was al-Risya and that I've borne that name from birth.

But there was something Jabir said before I killed him that I cannot forget.

"Not if there was someone else who wanted the Neverseen King's position."

Jabir made a deal with a fae. He would take Arbasa, and the fae could have the Neverseen King's position. Someone was trying to backstab the Neverseen King. The question of *why* is beyond me, but that isn't pressing right now.

It seems like the most unromantic thing to inform my sultan of the plot against his life and throne on our wedding day. But nothing about this wedding day is romantic. It's just . . .

"Perfect!" announces Eshe, stepping back and clapping her hands. "Not to pat myself on the back, but considering that you looked like you'd been dragged through hundreds of miles of mud and then hung upside-down to drip dry in a sandstorm, it is *quite* impressive that I've managed to make you look like a queen."

"There's too much jangling," I say, frowning as bangles clang together when my arms move just slightly. Even a mere turn of the head results in a symphony of tinkles from all the ornaments on my hair, my throat, my ears.

"You're not an assassin tonight. You're a bride," Eshe replies stubbornly. "Besides, you can't *not* wear jewelry in a gown like that! I must say, for all his faults, the shadow freak has fabulous taste in fashion."

I glare at her, but then my attention is snagged by the gown. It is, indeed, *very* lovely. It's dark blue, with a fitted, beaded bodice. The sweetheart neckline and cap sleeves leave far more golden-brown skin on display than I'm used to, but it's still tame enough that I don't feel entirely vulnerable. The fabric of the billowing skirt has a beautiful sheen to it, and it falls in a flattering silhouette.

My favorite parts, however, are the cleverly hidden places for knives. There are two decorative sheaths at my waist that perfectly fit my larger blades. Smaller knives fit into built-in sheaths on the inside lining of the bodice. Not to mention two more pockets in the skirt just over my hips.

Whoever tailors for the Neverseen King clearly received very specific instructions to custom make this gown for me. It's almost uncomfortable, the knowledge my bridegroom has of my preferences.

"Don't you want to look in the mirror?" asks Eshe, indicating with the way she bounces on the balls of her feet that I'm to look and praise her handiwork. "I'm *waiting* for your compliments."

I smile. Then, before I can second guess myself, I grab the mirror and hold it up.

Khol-lined eyes blink back at me, the cosmetics making them appear shockingly large. An unfamiliar mouth with full, tinted lips purses in the reflection. I don't know who that is, but it's not me. Quickly, I angle it up to my hair, away from the unsettling image of not-my-face. I inspect the sparkling strings draping across my hair and winding down the long braid. "That's a lot of gold."

"You're impossible!" bursts Eshe. "I spend all day trying to make you—"

"It is impressive work, indeed. I never thought you capable of such a feat."

She glares at me, but the familiar teasing glint has returned to her eye.

A knock on the door makes us both jump. We glance at each other, sharing a look. Neither of us has fully recovered from last night, despite the attempts to rest. Eshe scampers to the door, her own beautiful turquoise skirts kicking up behind her. She opens the door just barely and sticks her head out. "Who is it? I won't have the Neverseen King taking sneaky peeks of the bride!"

"It's me, the steward," comes Emin's smooth voice. "The Neverseen King is ready for Lady Nadira."

"Ready as in . . . *ready ready*?" asks Eshe, tightening her grip on the door. "As in, time-to-get-married, ready?"

"Indeed. He is ready for the wedding."

My hands go suddenly sweaty. Eshe glances back at me, and I hope whatever cosmetics she applied to my face hide the way the heat has drained from my skin. It's not too late to turn back. I can spin on my heel, throw these bangles off my wrists, and escape. I've been a free woman for not even a full day, and I'm already binding myself again.

You can still get out of this, her eyes say. *You don't have to do it if you don't want to.*

I draw in a deep breath. I'm not running away. This is my choice, and if it kills me, it kills me. Maybe once I'm dead, I won't be so afraid anymore.

Eshe, reading my expression, opens the door wider. "Then here is the bride. Ready to marry the shadow freak."

CHAPTER 2

THE MOURNER

MY HEART POUNDS as I follow the steward out of the safety of my room.

Eshe is silent behind me, saying nothing as we step onto the staircase and descend to the lower level. I reach out one unsteady hand and rest it on the banister. Its warmth flows into my fingertips, the sentience of the House reacting to the thoughts swirling in my head.

I'm afraid, I whisper to it. *I don't know how to not be afraid.*

I won't let him sand you, comes the House's fierce reply. An echo of a promise I once gave it.

I almost smile. *I need to teach you some more phrases, don't I?*

Don't I? it replies, which I take to be an agreement.

The staircase spills into the lower hallway, opening into the wide doors leading to the courtyard. Early evening light pours like melted butter onto my face. The courtyard itself is still barren from the ravages of Crenfyre, the parasitical mist that nearly swallowed me and Eshe both last night. Sad and empty as the courtyard is, my chest tightens as we walk past it. Even if I am afraid, this strange place has become almost . . . *comforting*.

We encounter no human servants as the steward guides us through the labyrinth of corridors until we turn a corner, and suddenly the steward stops. I glance at him uneasily, my fingers twitching. Eshe's feet come to a halt at my side, and the shuffle of her slippers echoes down the empty, shadowy corridor before us.

"Why are we stopped?" I ask.

"The Neverseen King wishes to speak with you." When I don't respond, the steward inclines his head toward the corridor before us and enunciates, "*Alone*."

Oh.

Eshe lifts her chin and folds her arms over her chest. "Absolutely not. He cannot see the bride until the—"

"Where is he?" I ask. Eshe huffs.

The steward gestures toward the hallway with its pilasters framing the lattice windows on one side. Evening light spills like liquid gold through the lattice and casts a pattern across the opposite wall. A mosaic floor depicts a geometric arrangement of sunroses.

He's not here. He cannot be far away, however.

"Very well," I mutter under my breath, picking up my skirt and slipping into the hallway. Behind me, my awareness of Eshe and the steward fades away. I'm on my own.

My jewelry gives soft tinkling sounds with each step. I try to ignore the way my pulse picks up its pace. I haven't seen the Neverseen King since last night, since I cut those arrowheads out of his chest and told him I would marry him. Not since he helped Eshe and I get safely back to my room.

It feels like it's been years.

When I'm halfway down the corridor, the air shifts. My exhalation leaves me in a gust as gooseflesh rises on my neck.

A slight draft blows in my face as the shadows deepen at the end of the hallway. They come closer, the air warping and twisting with each step.

The Neverseen King comes to a stop a few feet from me, just beyond the center pilaster. He stands there, not speaking a word, hardly visible to my eye. My awareness of him, however, pounds through my veins. He could be completely invisible, and still, I would not miss his presence.

"Neverseen King," I say. The title sticks in my throat, almost as familiar as a name. I fight the urge to hide the *mehndi* design on my hands behind my back. Standing here, it suddenly seems presumptuous to have worn the ceremonial ink as though I am a normal bride. As though I hold dreams that this is more than a necessary contract between the two of us. The cosmetics and jewelry itch against my skin. I should have just worn my normal clothes instead of pretending to be something I am not.

"Mourner," his deep voice rumbles back. It isn't a cold greeting, but the formality of my own title only serves to make my gown feel all the more ridiculous. The passion with which he kissed me last night is swept away, likely never to be indulged again.

I don't think I can bear to have him speak the words aloud. So I clear my throat and say briskly, "If you have come to remind me that this is a transaction and nothing else, have no fear. I remember quite clearly."

He doesn't answer for one long, excruciating moment, but his careful study burns me from head to toe. Then, very softly, with the tone of an admission, he says, "You look beautiful . . . Nadira."

My chest thuds painfully as heat licks up my neck to my cheeks. I clear my throat again, glancing away. My earrings tinkle in harmony with my wrist bangles at my subtle movement. "I wish I could say the same to you."

Amusement hums in the air between us. For that brief moment, I don't feel like a snake needing to shed its skin. Maybe I want to belong in this skin, this dress, this beauty.

The moment passes.

I'm back to wanting to scrape off my *mehndi.*

"You haven't changed your mind, then?" A thread of vulnerability weaves through those words, tentative and ready to snap.

Not trusting my voice, I shake my head.

Was that a quiet sigh? Impossible to know for certain. When he speaks, his voice is brisker than before. "In that case, I wanted to prepare you for the ceremony. It differs from most fae weddings, due to my role as the Neverseen King and your role as my human wife. There must be witnesses—fae witnesses. They are sent by the High King of the Fae to confirm everything goes as intended. As for the ones he sent . . . well, they are not your friends."

I search in the shadowed air for the telltale glimmer of his eyes. There's none. It's the tickle of warmth washing over me that tells me he's stepped closer.

"Stay by my side. Don't speak to them. They will try to catch you alone and make bargains with you. Do not. No matter what they offer you or how tempting it sounds."

It's a little difficult to imagine what a fae could offer me that would tempt me to trust enough to make a bargain with them. I keep this thought to myself and merely nod.

He takes another step closer, until he seems to be standing not even a foot away, looking down at my face. My lips part as I stare up at the arched ceiling, the air darkening enough for me to make out his silhouette.

"I . . ." He stops. Hesitates.

I hang suspended in the moments between his words.

He tries again. "The . . . ceremony. Since there will be witnesses, I must give you something first. Something you must say during the ceremony—but very quietly. The witnesses will hope to hear it, and with it, gain power over me."

"Hear what?"

"My name."

The sun stops its descent, the wind stops its song, and both of our hearts stop beating.

"Your name?" I croak, suddenly dizzy with anticipation. I've wanted to know his name for what seems like forever. He's known my name. What there is to know of it, that is. But when I asked him for his name, he wouldn't give it. He said he would never risk giving such a thing to a human, that we were too careless with the power names hold.

Perhaps that is why he hesitates now. He's entrusting me with something—something that seems to have far more value than I can comprehend at the moment.

He bends his head toward mine, coalescing into something much more physical as he does so. He's close enough to draw me into his arms, to set his mouth against mine. Even as my body prickles with the awareness of his nearness, he doesn't touch me. Not even as he brings his lips just above my left earring.

"My name," he murmurs, his breath tickling my ear, "is Kaladen Ashrift Felladyr."

The name rings, striking a chord inside me.

"Kaladen," I whisper.

He hasn't pulled away, his mouth still hovering at my ear, above my shoulder. When I say his name, a tiny shiver seems to race through him, but all he says is, "Yes. My name is Kaladen."

Has it been ninety-nine years since someone called him by his name? I say it again, just to make sure I have it right. "Kaladen Ashrift Felladyr." The syllables are unfamiliar to my tongue. I struggle the most with *Felladyr.*

He only says softly, "Very good, Nadira al-Risya."

Something about the way he says my name in that deep voice of his makes my knees turn unsteady. I retreat a step just as the Neverseen King—*Kaladen*—pulls back. Then we're staring at each other. Him, nothing but shadow, and me, in full bridal regalia.

Kaladen. Kaladen. Kaladen.

I lick my lips. "May I call you . . . by your name?"

"Yes. Just—not the full name in front of others, if you please."

I nod. "But . . . why?"

At first, he doesn't seem inclined to answer, as though uncertain whether he should trust me with such information. Then, he tells me: "Names among the fae have binding power, like a bargain. With them, you can be called across vast spaces. You can also be made to do many things you do not wish to."

"Oh."

"Indeed. And one other thing." He lowers his gaze from mine, and it's not until he continues that I understand why. "I will need a drop of your blood."

"For what?"

"For the bonding."

Bonding. It sounds so much more . . . *constrictive* than the word *marriage*. Which is probably silly. Marriage is just another contractual bond. So why does this feel like more than promises and vows?

"I didn't want to startle you during the ceremony by bringing out a knife."

It's surprisingly sweet. And yet, it makes my insides sink. The memory of broken ribs, of him hovering over me, of the way I once panicked when he brought out a knife washes over me. I wish he hadn't seen me like that. Choking and terrified. I lower my gaze.

"If you give me a drop of blood now, I will save it for the ceremony."

"You can do that?"

He shoots me a look. "I *do* usually offer to do things I'm physically incapable of doing."

I cannot help my tiny snort. "I was just surprised."

When he doesn't respond, I realize he's waiting for me. To give him a drop of blood. I glance down as my right hand instinctively wraps around the hilt of a knife in my belt. Before I can second guess myself, I unsheathe it, bring the glittering tip to my lip, and prick.

When I draw the blade away, a faceted jewel of blood gleams on the tip. I offer it to the shadow before me.

He reaches out, the outline of his strong hand meeting the tip of my knife. My blood vanishes into thin air.

I lick my lip and taste copper. "Anything else, Neverseen King?"

"You still intend to marry me?"

"Asking me more times will only make me dig my heels in deeper."

I expect him to chuckle, but he doesn't. It's only the memory of his kiss last night that keeps me from spiraling into doubt. Unless I dreamed that moment of fervent longing. Perhaps I imagined it in between bouts of sleeplessness.

Maybe I was wrong to think his desire for me outweighed his fear.

"Then come with me," says the Neverseen King, and seems to offer his arm.

Last chance, the terrified part of me screams. *Run away while you still can.*

I hook my hand in the crook of his elbow, just as he coalesces into a tall silhouette made of darkness. Smooth fabric slides beneath my hand, and I take a deep breath as the Neverseen King opens a door I hadn't seen and guides me through.

CHAPTER 3

THE MOURNER

THE ROOM WE step into is mostly dark. I blink into the dimness, trying to make sense of the surrounding space. Small purple globes float in midair, casting an eerie hue across the darkness, bobbing around like fireflies.

By their light, I can make out a few shadowy forms. They meander through the gloom like phantoms, their whispers carrying like a chorus of secrets.

"There you are. *Finally*," drawls a male voice. "And with *it*."

I must be the *it* this fae refers to.

"Such a shame you must bring it to the ceremony," comes a low, melodic, and distinctly feminine voice. "Really, this whole bonding is a shame." A delicate sniff follows this statement. "The human stench gives me a splitting headache without fail. How you put up with it, Kaladen, is beyond me."

"Be seated," the Neverseen King growls, tension radiating up his arm. "You were invited as witnesses, not commentators."

My fingers twitch on his elbow, uneasiness spilling down my spine to my toes. Now I wish more than ever that my jewelry didn't give light tinkling sounds with each movement. My free hand finds my knife hilt and clutches it, ready to draw.

A purple globe wafts toward my face. I duck away from it, leaning closer to the Neverseen King. In response, he drops his arm, forcing me to let go of his elbow. A sharp bolt of fright cuts through me, replaced by something entirely different when he doesn't pull away, but instead wraps his hand around my waist, drawing me tight against him.

An almost silent gasp escapes me.

Then we reach what seems to be the center of the room. The Neverseen King swats at one of the purple globes floating toward us. It bobs away, illuminating a pair of hairy goat's legs, complete with cloven hooves, emerging from beneath fine robes. I shudder.

"Kneel with me," his deep voice rumbles in my ear.

With my back to the cloven hoofed fae? My chest clenches so tightly I can barely breathe. Just as quickly, a large, warm hand lands on my shoulder and a thumb presses against the hollow of my throat. His magic surges through me, opening my airways and loosening my lungs. He ducks to whisper to me. "I'm right here."

I lift my eyes to his, barely able to discern anything. Strangely, his reassurance is enough for me. I . . . *trust* him. He won't let harm come to me here.

I kneel as instructed, my skirts swishing quietly as they land in a circle around me. The Neverseen King doesn't let go of me for one instant as he kneels across from me, sliding his hand down from my shoulder to my fingers, leaving tingles in its wake.

It has gone eerily silent in the room.

My back burns with the gaze of the cloven hoofed fae, my awareness sparking of him and at least two others besides the Neverseen King.

I want this to be a moment just for us. I wish I could pretend for the span of this ceremony that this bond is more than magic and portals and palaces.

It's impossible to forget, however, with the prying and antagonistic gazes studying me.

The Neverseen King takes my wrist, gently angling my palm up to face him. Somehow, it comes as a surprise when he presses his own palm against it. A jolt spasms up my arm, but his fingers close around mine—keeping me from jerking away.

I don't want to jerk away, however. At least, not until the fae behind me speaks.

"I, Eldreth of the Star City, am here to bear witness to the Neverseen King's bonding to . . ." He trails off with a lilt.

"Nadira," the Neverseen King replies irritably.

"To Nadira," Eldreth finishes.

The female voice chimes in. "I, Yirmuth of Ildreer, am here to bear witness to the Neverseen King's bonding."

"To Nadira," growls the Neverseen King. "You must say her name for the spell to work."

"Maybe I'm wishing your bonding *wasn't* to . . . *that*."

"Maybe you should cease wishing for fairytales and face reality. Say her name."

A sigh of long suffering. "To Nadira."

The third voice is so crackling and ancient I cannot tell its gender. "I, the Eye of Baltor, am here to bear witness to the Neverseen King's bonding to Nadira."

Finally, the last voice, painted in colors of boredom, drawls, "I, Prince Trenian, heir to the throne of the High King of the Fae, am here to bear witness to the Neverseen King's bonding to Nadira."

"I, the Neverseen King, accept Eldreth of the Star City, Yirmuth of Ildreer, the Eye of Baltor, and Prince Trenian, heir to the throne of the High King of the Fae, as witnesses to my bonding with Nadira."

My name sounds so barren next to all those titles, though it's not as if I want him to attach *The Mourner* as my title.

Am I expected to say the same thing? Accept these strange witnesses to my bonding with the Neverseen King? I prepare to, running their unusual names over again in my head. The Neverseen King resumes speaking again, this time in a language I'm unfamiliar with, and I take that to mean the human bride isn't required to accept the witnesses.

As he speaks, light suddenly glows from his chest. I almost startle, and then stare enraptured as a silver thread grows from his heart, illuminating the silvery embroidery on the collar of his black tunic and casting a glow upon the skin of his throat, but no higher. The tendons in his neck move and flex as he speaks, his voice washing over me like rainfall. The silver thread keeps growing, winding around his sleeve, all the way down to our joined hands. He says my full name like a murmur right as that silver wraps around our fingers.

"Nadira al-Risya."

I feel my name on his lips in my very soul, something catching and . . . *binding.*

There is something that strikes me as very solid, very unmovable, very permanent about this. Fear thrills through me, and I look up to catch the Neverseen King's gaze. It's not there, not visible. The potency of it, however, almost undoes me.

He feels it too, then.

He is afraid also, isn't he? Of what this means for us and our future.

"Repeat after me, creature," sniffs the female fae—*Yirmuth*.

I don't deign to respond. Not until she mutters unfamiliar syllables, barely giving me time to repeat them. What comes out of my mouth is a jumbled collection of sounds that cannot be even remotely accurate. Will the magic work if I'm not pronouncing it correctly?

As if in response to my concern, the Neverseen King issues a correction, his low voice carrying to me over the higher timbres of Yirmuth. I repeat the word, then struggle to catch up until he barks, "Great Kings, slow down or I'll do it and report your insolence to the High King."

"I wouldn't do that," says Prince Trenian with a dark chuckle, his shadow leaning back cavalierly. "The High King has been in one of his moods for the last century. But I can always *accidentally* lop off someone's head if she isn't behaving properly."

My rational mind knows he's referring to Yirmuth, but I cannot help the spike of anxiety that insists it's *my* head that is at risk.

"I'd prefer to make it through my bonding without a decapitation," says the Neverseen King.

Sharp teeth flash in a grin as Prince Trenian replies, "It doesn't have to be now."

Yirmuth sniffs. "I will continue if certain people would stop *interrupting* me."

"Please do," the Neverseen King growls.

Yirmuth does indeed continue, though only slightly slower. I firm my spine, glaring into the darkness as I force my tongue to keep up. At some point, however, everything changes. It starts slowly, too slowly for me to notice, until my gut is icy, and the cold spreads like spider veins through my body.

For the first time since last night, I reach down into that sleeping well of power inside me. It churns at my touch, like a barely chained monster ready to be loosed. Ready to devour.

My lips keep moving of their own accord, my eyes closing. The spell wraps around me like a familiar embrace, like the greeting of a friend. These words are familiar—my soul echoes them in response to the promises spoken by the Neverseen King. I sink deeper into the awareness of that icy world of my magic, into the spell dancing through my body, reaching into my heart, drawing something out of me.

I bind myself to you. All that is myself, I give to you. Everything I treasure is yours.

Now I know why it felt like his eyes were boring into mine. The pulse of magic under my skin throbs with something between glory and pain, rejoicing and heartbreak. It is as though I am taking my deepest loves, my darkest fears, the kernel of truth that is my very soul, and holding it out in my hands to—

"Speak his name," Yirmuth says.

I open my eyes, and the glow between me and the Neverseen King is brighter—so much brighter from the light of my own blue strand tangling with his silver one, binding our hands together. There is a gleam like diamonds beyond them. Pinpricks of light.

I meet his gaze and breathe the smallest whisper: *"Kaladen Ashrift Felladyr."*

Our strands twist, binding us together in a way that is beyond words. It doesn't feel like we are kneeling across from each other, our hands clasped, but instead wrapped in an embrace so tight we cannot be separated.

And for the first time in so *very* long, a core belief I've treasured flips on its head. For the first time since I was a tiny child, I know what it is to belong.

I'm not alone anymore.

Tears spring to my eyes, and I cannot care that there are witnesses. A bright grin bursts across my face. It's all I can do to keep from laughing with joy.

This is what it is to be happy.

Happiness is glorious, and I want to have it forever.

The Neverseen King has gone very still, the dark shroud across his face untouched by the brilliant glows of our twining soul-threads. Then, his fingers move, sliding between mine and clasping my hand tightly. I can almost hear his silent voice as his mouth forms my name, *"Nadira."*

He brings his free hand above our clasped ones and tilts it. Two drops of blood fall on the glowing threads, and—

Mama screams. "Give her back! You can't have—"

A scimitar stabs through her chest. Blood gushes everywhere. I scream, struggling to get away, begging her to get up as she falls in a heap to the ground. "Mama! Mama!" Blood runs down cobblestone, coming like a monster to eat me.

Get away, away, away—

"Liliana!" Panic blinds me, strips my throat raw, as I surge toward her.

Her bright blue eyes pierce mine. I can reach her in time. I can—I will!

I reach out—

Her white-knuckled grip gives way. She falls.

"Liliana!" I scream.

The images flash before me. Stunning. Discombobulating. Horrifying. Paralyzing. I'm lying on a frozen lake—Jabir's leering face blurring in and out of my vision. Everything pounds. Noise, noise, *noise*. A screeching, high-pitched note that won't stop, won't stop, won't *stop*.

The monster inside me surges.

The resounding screams might belong to me, to my memories, or neither.

I'm beating like a drum. Falling like a bird shot out of the sky. Sinking like a stone in an oasis.

It's too much. The pressure building inside me. It's too much.

The dam breaks.

Ice floods from me in a torrent. I scream, my back arching with strain. It's going to break me. It's going to overwhelm—

Something warm flares, cutting through the ice. Something that reaches out to me, calling my name, burning like a torch into my awareness. I cling to that warmth with a grip made of sharp fingernails.

Slowly, the world of ice and blood fades, replaced by dimness and hazy purple lights. I'm breathing so hard I can barely form a cohesive thought.

I lie on my back, staring up at a floating orb. And a dark-as-night shoulder. A great weight presses into me, restraining, but also comforting. Shielding.

Kaladen.

His name enters my mind like a beacon of hope. His arms are around me, and he's saying my name, over and over again. Asking me if I'm alright, if I can hear him. The questions are urgent, but not nearly as shrill as the voices beyond the Neverseen King's circle of warmth.

"It sliced open my leg! And you're not going to execute it for—"

"Maybe it would be best to report you to the High King after all, Yirmuth, if you cannot put up a shield against a mere mortal's magic. Quite humiliating." That drawl—Prince Trenian. "And all that blood is everywhere now. You'd best be careful the Eye doesn't steal any of it."

"The Neverseen King cannot take a bride so volatile! It's obscene!"

Suddenly, the Neverseen King surges upright, taking me with him, his arm pressing me to his chest as he wheels back and throws something straight into . . . the wall? It hits with a sharp thud, and Eldreth barks a startled protest. "Don't you dare leave," he snarls. "Sit back down. I won't have you making merry with my Bridge and this city while I'm supposedly distracted. As for the rest of you, you've witnessed our bonding. Like it or not, by law and magic, Nadira is my wife now. Report to your High King as you see fit. Now, I recommend you take the door out to Valehaven before my House turns. It doesn't like the smell of fae."

Something presses into my hand. It's so thin and delicate I wouldn't have felt it except for the hot fingers shoving into mine. But the moment I do feel it, a voice speaks in my head. Guttural, ageless. The Eye's voice.

"Bargain with me, human girl. Give me what I want, and I will grant your thief friend immortality."

The Neverseen King yanks the frail string from my grip a second later with another low snarl. "What have I told you about giving strands of hair to my brides? My patience is wearing thin. I suggest you leave before I have none left."

"Come now, my friends," chirps Prince Trenian in that sarcastic tone. "We best not tarry. The wrath of the Neverseen King isn't to be trifled with, now is it? Have a delightful wedding night with your little ice explosion, Kaladen. See you shortly in Valehaven."

CHAPTER 4

THE MOURNER

THE NEVERSEEN KING lifts me up as he stands, cradling me to his chest. I sink into his arms, my gaze snagging on long bolts of sparkling ice protruding from the walls and ceiling. They glow blue and purple in the light of the floating orbs. Perhaps part of me would deny again that this came from me, but there's no denying the lack of strength in my limbs. I wince and close my eyes again.

I will grant your thief friend immortality.

What does the Eye—whatever the Eye *is*—want from me? And how does it know about Eshe?

The Neverseen King dodges around my death spikes of ice and carries me out the door we entered, leaving behind the chaos of the fae witnesses.

I want to insist I didn't mean to lose control again. I want to apologize. Instead, I turn my face into his tunic and search for that spark of happiness that had been mine only minutes ago. I dig into my memories of that freshly soldered connection between us.

There. There is the thread binding my soul to his. It anchors in my heart, tying it to his.

But where is the happiness?

It slips through my fingers like water, leaving me with nothing but those horrible memories. My mother's death combined with his previous wife's death. I blink repeatedly, trying to shut out those memories forever.

If I return to them, I'll lose control of my magic again.

I grit my teeth. One way or another, I need to find some way to subdue this force inside me.

Last night, I killed the boy who used to sneak into my room and give me kisses after my jobs. The boy who betrayed me for the sake of his little sister. *Kolb.* I didn't mean to kill him. If Eshe hadn't been hiding behind a pillar when I released that blast last night, she would have died too. All because I couldn't control my magic.

There is no option. I *must* learn to master this.

The Neverseen King's footsteps increase in speed, his chest heaving harder than it should, and I have the awareness to peel my head away from him and glance out at the world beyond the cocoon of his embrace.

Daylight is almost gone.

Night nearly engulfs the eerie, silence-shrouded palace.

Eshe is—thankfully—nowhere to be seen. Neither is the steward or any of the other servants. The Neverseen King's boots click on the polished floor, a pace just shy of a run.

My throat tightens despite myself. I should find the strength to swing my legs out of his grasp, plant my feet on the floor, and carry my own weight.

Then he stops before a pair of double doors. With a muttered word under his breath, the doors fling open on their hinges. He hurries me inside, then speaks another word—and the doors slam shut behind us.

He releases a great sigh of relief, his shoulders dropping.

I fist my fingers into his tunic, lifting my head and peering at his shadowed face.

He isn't looking at me. "Can you stand?"

I nod without considering the question.

He gently lowers me to my feet, but waits until my knees steady themselves before withdrawing his arm from around my waist. Then he steps back, putting distance between us.

Yellow-warm globes on stands, not candles, illuminate the room we stand in. It appears to be a sitting room of sorts, with dark, comfortable upholstery arranged in the center. Several doors line the walls, only one of which is open. Smaller globes light that door and shine from the interior. Is that . . . a *bed*?

Suddenly, Prince Trenian's parting words hit me.

Have a delightful wedding night with your little ice explosion, Kaladen.

"Those lights are magic. We call them lumiral globes," says the Neverseen King, apparently thinking those are what have made my eyes bug. "They are much more efficient at lighting spaces than candles—*and* they have a purifying influence on the air."

I don't *care* about the lights.

These are the Neverseen King's personal chambers.

This isn't . . . this marriage isn't . . . it's not *real*. Not in *that* sense of the word. Unless . . . is it? The Neverseen King only said this wasn't to be a *sentimental* marriage. It is merely a transactional, mutually beneficial arrangement.

I don't pretend to understand how fae marriages work. What if consummation is part of the transactional aspect of this marriage?

Cold washes over me. I'm not prepared for this. If I'd had time, I could have made a plan. A plan for what? A plan to manage whatever happened the first time we kissed? When I'd panicked and nearly passed out?

I want to groan.

If I couldn't handle a kiss, then how can I handle more than that?

The same way you've handled everything else.

I take a step back, matching his retreat. My hand lands on the back of an upholstered chair, catches hold, and clings. In the flickering globe light, the Neverseen King remains a tall, dark shadow. One that continues to not meet my gaze or say a word.

My husband.

The word bolts through me, shattering my composure in its wake. I *married* the Neverseen King. He's my husband. I'm his wife.

I knew this. This is what I decided.

And yet, somehow, it finally hits me—the full magnitude of what I've done. I've bound my life to his. The freshly forged connection shimmers in the air between us.

Still turned away from me, he breaks the silence. "Will you not say anything?"

"Will *you* not say anything?" I croak back, wrapping my arms around my middle. I feel myself slipping back into antagonism. It's not where I want to be, but it's safer than anywhere else.

"What am I to say?"

"What am *I* to say?"

He lets out a long, frustrated breath. "This is going about as well as I expected."

I shoot him a scowl, drawing my own irritation around myself like a cloak. Why am I still so afraid of him? Am I afraid he will—what? Force himself on me? Even I cannot believe that. Despite his scars and the secrets he still hides from me, that's not who he is.

In that case, I should just tell him. Ignoring the creeping heat into my cheeks, I square my shoulders and say, "If you'd intended to touch me, you should have warned me in advance."

Finally, his head swivels toward me, puzzlement thickening in the air. "It was to save your life. And to pull you out of . . . the memories. I didn't think you would mind."

We're talking about two different things. My flush deepens as I reach up to tuck an invisible strand of hair behind my ear and end up scratching my neck instead. How can I say this?

Then his words turn over in my mind again, and I shoot him a look, alarm racing down my spine. "Did . . . you see them too?"

He looks away.

I swallow the lump in my throat and seek the floor. With much more difficulty, I find my voice. "What I meant to say is that I won't sleep with you tonight." Hopefully he hears the words as I mean to say them: firm and final, without the barest waver.

"You must."

Alarm flashes through me. I retreat another step, barring my teeth. "I won't."

Shocked silence falls like a thunderclap. Then he whirls toward me, hands outstretched, and quickly sputters, "That's not what I—I didn't mean it . . . like that. Not like that. I wouldn't—that is, I meant it in the literal sense." He rakes a hand through his hair, cursing. "Forgive me. I thought I'd made it clear that our marriage . . . that it isn't . . . that I have no intention of . . . I didn't mean to frighten you."

The nearest globe flickers in my vision. I cast a glance toward the bedroom. My lungs loosen. Somehow, my fist ended up clenched over my chest. I lower it hesitantly.

His voice drops, his eyes sparking as they find mine. "I'm not going to hurt you, Nadira. Please believe that."

I do believe it. More than I wish to.

"There is much I must explain about magic and how it works," he continues. "But do you remember the dream you had before our dance? You'd gone to sleep in the afternoon, and I'd been nearby. We met in the dream realm. You . . . asked me for my name."

I freeze. "That was real?"

"It was."

"Not just a dream?"

"It *was* a dream. But a real dream. The dream realm is where I do much of my . . . work. It's where you will work too. Because of my fae blood and magic, I can slip in and out of it as I like. You cannot."

The puzzle pieces fit together in my brain, even before he continues and explains, "If you fall asleep near me, you can be drawn into the dream dimension. This is what I meant about . . . sleeping together."

If I didn't know better, I'd guess he was turning red along with me.

We both go quiet, and suddenly I become aware of something very faint pulsing in the air. Something that is linked to me. Is it . . . his heartbeat? My eyes widen. It *is*. That's his heartbeat, connected to mine. Is that due to our bond? Or does the fact that I have magic play a part?

His heart is beating rapidly.

"Are you hungry? Thirsty?" he asks abruptly, stalking past me to a table against the far wall. "I had Emin leave refreshments. The bathing chamber is through that door, should you have need of it. I keep magic regulating the temperature of the bath, so you only need to speak for it to be hotter or colder. I had Emin bring whatever cosmetics you've been using—though I suspect they're mostly Eshe's. Hopefully she won't be angry when she discovers their absence. There's a wardrobe with your clothes. If you need more, inform me and I'll take care of it. That room—the door's closed, I know—is for your leisure. You can do with it what you like. I wasn't sure what you wanted, so it's mostly empty. But tell me what you want and I'll have it set up however you like."

I exhale slowly through my nose, my eyes darting over the space, following each door he points to. He's saying that this is my new home. My old room isn't mine anymore. His chambers are mine now.

He keeps prattling on, and eventually I find the courage to put him out of his misery. He stops talking the moment I open my mouth. "I would like to change, if that's alright."

"Yes, yes, certainly."

He abandons the table spread with food and drink, marching to a door and shoving it open for me. This chamber is similarly lit, giving it a strangely intimate atmosphere as I slip past the looming tower of the Neverseen King. It's very spacious, with one side occupied by an enormously long vanity.

"There are soaps and oils and towels." He points to a low shelf situated beside a deep, in-ground pool. The water has a gentle current to it, though where it flows from or to, I cannot begin to guess. "Your wardrobe is there, beyond the vanity. The mirror isn't copper—it's fae-made. It reflects much clearer."

I blink, following his gesture. *That* is a mirror? It could be a window for how clear it is! It's also very large, like the vanity. How can I dodge something that big? It'll be impossible to be in this room and not look at myself!

He catches hold of the doorknob and closes the door behind me. It shuts with a click. "Call if you need anything."

I stand where I am, still in my ridiculous wedding finery. What does it matter that the dress is beautiful? The ceremony was in the dark.

One thing is for certain: I'm not bathing. The last thing I need is to submerge myself in all that liquid and have no one but the Neverseen King to help me when I inevitably panic. With a grim set of my mouth, I slip past the bath, intent on getting to the wardrobe.

My reflection appears in my periphery. I stop.

A shudder slipping down my spine, I force myself to look.

I almost startle at the face staring back at me.

She's surprised, her dark eyes enlarged with kohl. The narrow line of her jaw, the long oval of her face, the gold-draped column of her neck, the bronze skin, the painted mouth—all the features of a stranger. She reaches up one patterned hand to the ornaments in her ear, her hair, and flinches.

I drag my eyes away, to the tall wardrobe which is my destination. I skitter forward, hating the loud sounds that follow my every movement. With a wrench, I yank off the bangles on my wrists, then set to unclasping and unhooking every piece of jewelry. They clatter against the polished marble vanity. When I'm finally free of them and the only sound I make is the swish of my skirts, I pull open the wardrobe and rummage through it until I find what I'm looking for: an earth-toned tunic, sirwal, sash, and a pair of stockings.

The last thing I'm wearing tonight is one of the nightgowns stacked so neatly to one side.

With a paranoid glance around the room, I find a screen to change behind. I strip quickly, my hands trembling as I pull all my knives out of their hiding places. As fast as I can, I redress, replace my knives in their usual sheaths, and then stop. Breathe.

Only then do I step out from behind the screen and dare a glance back at the mirror.

The young woman staring back at me is more familiar than the bride from a few minutes ago. She looks at me with disgust, and I'm reminded of all those nightmares, of being a child and running from the same face that stares at me now.

"He won't let you kill me," I whisper at the young woman.

Then I tear my eyes away, slip around the pool, and march back to the door of the washroom. I pause at the handle, heart thumping. When I reach out in my awareness of the Neverseen King's heartbeat, I cannot find it. I'm not surprised; it was so faint even when I was near him.

You have nothing to fear here, I tell myself. *You're not afraid of him.*

My hand still trembles on the knob when I turn it.

CHAPTER 5

THE NEVERSEEN KING

I PACE BACK and forth in front of my bed, trying to get a grasp on my rattled composure. So many things spin through my mind, ready to tear me into pieces. The High King will know about Nadira's magic now. It's not that I could have hidden it much longer; if anything, this was probably a good way for him to find out. Still, I don't like the idea of the High King having her in his thoughts, however briefly. I don't want there to be anything remarkable about my newest human bride. She's just another human woman. Just another soul to keep close and then lose.

What did the Eye put in that strand of hair?

I grit my teeth. The vision, the voice, the feeling—whatever it was—was already gone when I touched the hair. I'll have to ask Nadira about it. I want to believe she would tell me of her own accord, but

I cannot believe it. Not yet. The trust between us is still tentative and only extends so far.

Yirmuth and Eldreth are also clearly on a mission to dismantle my authority and power whenever they can. Neither of them is especially dangerous. Not on their own, at least.

It is a relief the Wolf wasn't sent to witness this ceremony. I expected the High King to delight in sending my long-time nemesis for this task.

Two-faced though he may be, Prince Trenian isn't my enemy. *Not yet.* Perhaps when he ascends the throne, we'll be enemies then. High Kings and Neverseen Kings don't get along. It doesn't matter that I answer to the High King; he knows that with the Bridge, I'm the only one with enough power to dream of overthrowing him.

As if I would ever have such aspirations. The Bridge is enough responsibility on its own. I am not inclined to add the rest of Faerieland to my shoulders.

I continue my pacing back and forth, trying to look anywhere but the bed. The floor has been extremely compelling for the last several minutes. How long is she going to take in there? Is she avoiding me?

It wouldn't matter if she was. My life would be easier if she was determined to avoid me.

I just can't handle this *suspense.* This *waiting.* I endured it all day. Even when I slept this afternoon, she was there in my dreams. Leaving me, running back to me and kissing me, then leaving me again, until I was so emotionally exhausted, I could barely open my eyes when Emin woke me up to finish dressing.

I abandon my pacing before I wear a tread in the floor. In a huff of frustration, I drop to the bed and sit. Forcing my muscles to be still. I need to preserve my energy. Despite my earlier rest, despite the strength returning to my limbs, I'm still not back to my full capacity.

And I have a long night ahead of me.

I close my eyes, drop my head in my hands, and let out a deep breath. In the darkness against my eyelids, she's there again. Blue light illuminates her beautiful features, and I cannot stop playing that moment over and over again when she looked up at me and smiled. Smile isn't even strong enough to describe her expression. She was beaming. Her happiness had spilled down the connection between us, and I wanted to bottle it up.

It was the most exquisite glimpse of all she is beyond the fear and darkness clouding her soul.

Then our blood had hit the forging bond, and her whole body jolted, her eyes flying wide as though she'd been stabbed. I saw nothing more before the memories overtook me, too. Not until they rolled past, leaving me shaken, did my vision clear enough for me to recognize the swelling power in the air that had nothing to do with our binding.

She needs to learn to control her power. It cannot continue to be an unconscious defense when she's afraid or overwhelmed. It'll make her a liability to herself, to me, and to Eshe. But tonight isn't about that.

Those memories flash before me once more, dark and searing. I shove aside my own, focusing on hers, on the sound of her young screams, the way her world had tilted on its axis in a way reminiscent of how mine had when Liliana died.

My blood simmers beneath my skin. I almost wish Jabir was still alive so I could tear him to pieces for what he did to her. Every instinct inside me demands justice, vengeance. I want to make him pay tenfold for every way he hurt her. But I cannot. I don't have time for vengeance, anyway. The Bridge needs every ounce of strength and attention I have, and now that Lulythinar is only three weeks away, I must do everything I can to prepare Nadira.

My shoulders sink lower, my gut plunging despite myself. There's no way she can survive. It'll be too much. I just don't know if I can bear the loss a second time.

But I'll have to. There's no choice. Maybe in a stroke of fortune, I'll die too and then the High King will be forced to appoint a new Neverseen King. I will, at long last, be free of this life and this ache.

My ears prick. The washroom door just opened. My heart picks up its rhythm. I give myself one moment to squeeze my eyes shut, to build up every mental and emotional fortification I can manage.

I will not be undone by her.

When I open my eyes, she stands in the bedroom's doorway, silent as a wraith. She's fully dressed in dark colors, her face an impenetrable mask. The cadence of her pulse thuds through the distance between us, tangling with mine until they are the only sounds filling the room.

I'm not sure what I expected her to wear, and if someone had forced me to make a guess, this is what I would have predicted. And yet, it stings. After everything, she still doesn't trust me.

Small steps, I remind myself. Trust isn't earned in a day. Especially not Nadira's. Hardly a few days ago, she wouldn't have willingly walked into a room alone with me. Not without bargains and cajoling.

I celebrate this one small win. I suspect there will only be more losses ahead of us tonight.

All of these thoughts rattle around my brain, giving me very little space to think about the fact that she will lie down beside me tonight, and many nights in the future. With Liliana, it had been so natural. There had been no kidnapping, no desperate measures, no futile attempts to forestall disaster. Just a love match between two starry-eyed idiots.

This is different in every way.

I hardly know what to do. If I was more at ease, perhaps I could be a more welcoming and relaxing presence. I could calm her fears and nerves. I could be what she needs right now.

Instead, I'm too caught up in the pounding of emotions at the sight of Nadira standing there in the doorway. *My wife.* I swore never to take another wife, and yet here she is. Lovely, the very picture of my own destruction and dearest hope.

I force down the desire to draw her into my arms and kiss her slowly, to show her how much I long to discard everything I've said about the nature of our marriage. To take her to my heart and let her ease the ache of a hundred years of soul-crushing loneliness.

No.

I will not be undone.

I will remain steadfast in my resolve.

If I let myself love her, then losing her will break me. I barely survived losing Liliana. I *cannot* go through that again.

CHAPTER 6

THE MOURNER

HE SITS THERE on the far end of the bed, a great mass of darkness. I stay where I am, my tongue sticking to the roof of my mouth. What am I to say? Ought I to go to the other side and slip in as though it is entirely normal for us to sleep in the same bed?

I cannot help the subtle drop of my stomach when his shadows cling ever tighter to his body, his face. I may have his name, his name that almost no one else knows—and yet I am not permitted to see him?

When he says nothing, I make my way to the empty side of the bed, the path illuminated by glowing lights. He doesn't turn to look at me, but his awareness burns into me like a desert fire. I dare not steal a glance at him, so I focus instead on sliding my hand beneath the cool sheets and peeling them back. I take a seat.

He could be a statue on the other side.

Drawing in a deep breath, I pull my feet up and slip them beneath the covers. Then I sit there, my sweaty hands folded into the soft fabric, and I stare straight ahead of me. My eyes glaze over as I stare at one small globe hanging from the ceiling, casting its warm light in a small sphere.

"Are you feeling better?" he says at last, his voice rough. "After your magic use?"

My limbs remain a little unsteady, but I don't feel as weak as I did when I killed Jabir's army last night. I nod. Then I brave a question of my own. "Have you recovered from last night?"

The hesitation that answers my question tells me more than his reply of, "I have."

Only a partial recovery, then.

The hum of his heartbeat becomes the only sound. I scrape my mind for other small talk to make. Small talk isn't my forte, which hasn't mattered for much of my relationship with the Neverseen King. And yet, here we are: like fresh-faced fifteen-year-olds having their marriage arranged the first day they meet.

Perhaps I should forgo the small talk and bring this back to business. When I open my mouth, I first intend to say *Sultani*, but then attempt his name. Sultani is too formal and distant, but his name feels so much more intimate than I'm comfortable with. So I say neither and jump straight to it.

"Jabir told me last night that he made a deal with a fae that he would rule Arbasa, and the fae would rule the Bridge. I thought you should know."

Did his shoulders just relax slightly?

"I figured as much."

"You know who?" My mind returns to the four witnesses at our wedding. One of them in particular made unease crawl down my spine. "Is it one of those who came tonight? Prince Trenian?"

A quiet snort echoes from the other side of the bed. "Definitely not Prince Trenian. He will be High King one day. He cannot take my position."

I furrow my brow, even as the tension slowly uncoils from my body. "Because it is too much for one person?"

"Yes. One person can barely contain the Bridge, and certainly not while ruling all of Faerieland."

Or apparently, even Arbasa.

He seems to be relaxing slightly, enough that he tilts his head toward me. The lilt at the end of his statement makes me pause, waiting to see if he'll continue. Eventually, he does. "The Bridge wasn't always here. Not as it is now. Not with so many portals."

Something is there, behind his words. Something unspoken. I search for it, picking apart the words, but I cannot find it. A history I don't know.

More mysteries to unravel.

I'm suddenly too exhausted to think of more questions to ask. I sigh, shut my eyes, and rub the back of my hand against them. "We just . . . need to be close when I fall asleep, right?"

"Yes."

He's like a wall of stone, closing off to me. I try to ignore my disappointment at his coldness as I twist away from him and scoot fully under the covers. My heart flips over itself when I do, the vulnerability of my position cutting me like a blade through the lungs. My back is to him, my fingers slipping beneath the head cushion for a knife. Of course, there isn't one. I clench my hand into a fist, breathing out through my nose. Forcing myself not to grab for one of the hilts digging into my waist.

He won't hurt you. Stop being a coward.

Maybe if I wasn't a coward, I would flip over and face him.

Instead, I stay where I am, staring at the wall and the globe-illuminated tapestry of a crystal-blue waterfall in the middle of a forest. A sight I have never seen before, surrounded as I've always been by sand and desert.

My awareness prickles when the Neverseen King's weight finally shifts in the large bed. We're not in any danger of touching, and yet my heart jumps straight to my throat when he pulls his legs up, lying down and situating himself comfortably.

The glowing orbs all snuff out at once, plunging the room into darkness.

Is he facing me? Or the opposite direction? I cannot know without looking, and I cannot look without betraying my curiosity. So I stay where I am, trying to coax my pulse down to a more manageable and less incriminating rate.

I slam my eyelids shut, determination keeping them closed. At least, until the Neverseen King shifts again, and my eyes fly wide open. He settles. I attempt to settle my nerves in response.

This is going to kill me.

I won't be able to fall asleep. It's impossible. There's no way I can sleep in this bed, with him mere feet away. I force my breathing to even.

By habit, names spring to my lips, ready to be spoken. It was my routine when I was Jabir's slave to repeat that growing string of names until I fell asleep. I dare not say them out loud, but in hopes that it might lull myself into a false sense of routine and normalcy, I silently shape the syllables with my lips.

Murtadi, Shawar, Tibon, Azim bint-Abaas.

The names roll off my tongue, as familiar as my own name. I abruptly stop.

Kolb.

My chest hollows out.

"The names of people you've assassinated?" the Neverseen King asks, startling me.

I freeze. He couldn't have heard me. I wasn't making a sound! Biting the inside of my cheek, I debate denying it. No, there's no use in that. "They're dead. They don't deserve to be forgotten, too."

"And it's your job to remember them?"

I bite my cheek harder, my thoughts returning to the curly-headed, gangly boy. One of my only friends. One of the only people who had ever cared if I lived or died. "Some of them didn't have anyone else to remember them."

I stare into the darkness in the direction of the tapestry, waiting for sleep to take me. Maybe the Neverseen King ought to just knock me out. He should use one of those spells to put me to sleep.

"How old were you?"

My body tenses. I force it to relax a fraction. "When I was taken?"

"When you first killed."

I find the edge of the sheets with my finger and trace along it. "Eleven."

Shock pulses through the air. The bed shifts as he sits upright, his gaze burning into my shoulder blades. Is he angry? Disgusted? Didn't think I was capable of it?

"Your first assassination," he enunciates carefully, "was at eleven?"

That is rage coating his quiet words.

A shiver slips down my spine. I lick my lips. "No, I didn't assassinate until I was fifteen. But Jabir wouldn't send me as an assassin if I hadn't killed before." I turn slightly, enough for my head to tilt in his direction. "You cannot be that shocked—I'd bet good money you've killed more than I have."

"I wasn't a *child* when I had my first kill."

My lips twist ruefully. "Neither was I."

Our gazes meet, the invisible connection between us pulling taut.

"I know he was yours to kill," the Neverseen King says, turning his face away. "But if you had left him for me, I would have made what he did to you look like mercy."

My hair stands on end. He means it.

And yet, even while part of me reels from his dark words, another part of me eases. As though my body sinks a little lower into safety.

He cares about me. I knew this, but it still hits me afresh. Will it ever not?

When I speak, my voice is very soft, underscored with earnestness. "Thank you . . . Kaladen."

He flinches at the sound of his name, but doesn't retreat. "I will avenge anyone who hurts you. You are my wife, Nadira. I will not tolerate ill treatment of you. *Ever*."

It's at those words the certainty hits me: *I did the right thing marrying him.*

I'm almost overcome with the desire to roll over completely, to scoot closer to him and burrow into his chest. To spend the night wrapped in his arms.

He wouldn't want that, though.

I let out a soft sigh and pull the covers higher. "I also have no tolerance for the people who would hurt you."

That rush of ice whirls in my memory, the overpowering acidity of my fear when those arrows had struck him last night. In response, my gut churns, flaring to life. I chain it quickly, breathing to pull it back under control.

It scares me the things I would do—*have done*—for him.

"I know," he whispers.

"Goodnight, Sultani."

"Goodnight, Nadira."

At first, I think I'm actually about to fall asleep. The drowsiness pulls me deeper, deeper, deeper. Then, suddenly, it's like I'm wide awake—as though I never fell asleep at all. I sit up in the darkness, and blink.

Did it work? Am I in the dream realm? Or did I just wake myself up before I finished falling asleep?

"Sultani?" I whisper.

"That was easier than expected," comes the Neverseen King's reply. "How do you feel?"

I frown, rolling my shoulders. "Fine? Perhaps a little disoriented? How am I supposed to feel?"

"You seem in your right mind, which is good." When I turn toward his voice and frown again, he adds, "Because last time you acted like you were drunk."

I shake my head. "I didn't think it was real."

"So it seemed. I'm glad you're acclimating well. Sometimes the magic can act . . . finicky. It'll simplify things if it gets along with you."

I pat my thigh, almost surprised to find myself wearing the same clothing I wore to bed, complete with my knives. I draw one out. The blade catches a scrap of light, flashing in the blackness. I can almost make out the outline of the tapestry against the wall, the outlines of the dark orbs that glowed when we first entered this room. "Why do I need to be in this . . . dream realm?"

His voice is *much* closer when he responds. "You're safer here. You cannot be hurt like you can be in our dimension. Injuries will still hurt—you'll feel everything as though you are in your body—but they won't be sustained when you wake up, since your physicality is only an illusion."

A small light flickers, slowly growing and brightening until it illuminates the calloused edges of his hand. He stands only a pace from where I sit on the bed.

"I have a lot more questions," I say, searching in the shadows for a glimpse at his face.

"Come, ask them as we begin our rounds."

To my surprise, he holds out his free hand to me. An invitation. I hesitate only a moment before placing mine in his. That spark of contact, the warmth as his strong hand closes around mine, goes straight to my core. He pulls me to my feet, and suddenly we're very close. Close enough for me to thread my fingers into his hair, close enough for him to bend down and claim my lips as he's done twice before.

We might not be physical here, but I bet kisses would feel the same.

He drops my hand and turns away. His voice is much rougher than it was a second ago. "This way."

I lick my dry lips and follow him and his bobbing light. My own voice is more difficult to find than I expected. I clear my throat as he leads the way out of the bedroom. "Does not being physical prevent us from running into the House's defenses?"

Last night Eshe, Safya, and I had been forced out of our rooms by the parasite Crenfyre, only to discover the House was full of traps and monsters set on destroying us. I have no interest in experiencing that again.

"You are a sharp pupil," he says, sounding pleased. "It does. In this dimension, the House slumbers. Which makes it possible for you to aid me. It can pose issues, however, if one of the various peoples attempting to break through their portals is clever enough to come through this dimension instead. That is always very headache-inducing."

He opens the main door and walks right out into the palace hallways, motioning for me to follow. I tamp down on my impulse to hang back, on the sudden burning inside me insisting that I don't know what we're doing, where we're going, or how any of this works.

Calm down, I tell myself. *You're learning how it works. It's just . . . the magic version of scouting.*

"Does it happen often?" My tone pitches higher than I intend as I leave the safety of the Neverseen King's chambers and slip into the hallway after him.

"No, it's only happened a handful of times in the years I've been Neverseen King."

The hallway is dark as night, with only the smallest slivers of moonlight coming through cracks in shutters. My scalp prickles, but I hurry after the bobbing light following the Neverseen King. He moves quickly, as though worried about how much we must accomplish tonight.

"What are we doing?" I ask, rubbing my arm.

"The first task is to check each door and see which ones are breaking down. If there are any that require immediate attention, we stop and address it. Otherwise, we make a note and come back to it after we've finished the rounds. Once you're comfortable, you'll have your own patrol each night. Until then, I want you at my side."

He tries to keep his voice even, but I sense the underlying strain. He's trying to stay rhythmic and methodical, no matter how much he might want to sprint from one crumbling portal to the next.

I glance at his turned back, the breadth of his shoulders, his massive height. He appears very physical here. He said that he could come and go from this realm at will. Was his slipping back and forth between them what gave the illusion of his invisibility? When he seems like shadow, it's because his body is in the dream realm, isn't it?

"What makes the portals break down?" I ask, following as he turns a corner.

I stop short.

It's a hallway of doors before me—and they're all *glowing*. Their glows mingle, creating a tunnel of rainbows, but mixed into an exquisite chaos. My jaw drops to the floor as I behold blues and pinks dancing together, with rays of gold and silver twining with violet and emerald.

It's iridescent majesty.

"Oh," I breathe.

The Neverseen King's smile warms the side of my face. "I thought you would like it. I've wanted to show you this for some time."

"Magic is beautiful," I whisper.

"Many people use it for evil, but that is because they care only for power, never beauty. Never goodness. They miss the heart of magic."

Colors tangle before my eyes in a dazzling array, but somehow, I find the strength to pull my gaze away, up to the dark silhouette beside me. "What is the heart of magic?"

A pair of glittering diamond eyes meets mine. "Awe."

Awe.

I cannot help the small smile that twists my mouth. I take a step closer to the beautiful colors, then huff a quiet laugh and say over my shoulder, "And you complain so much about your job."

"If the entirety of my job was admiring rainbows, I assure you I wouldn't be complaining." He stops, tilts his head, then adds, "Well, I might get bored."

I chuckle again, reaching one hand into the mixing of pearlescent white and indigo. It's difficult to imagine ever getting bored with such beauty.

That's when something catches my eye. I draw back my hand and cock my head. "Why does it look like there's a bloody thumbprint at the center of each door?" Now that I've noticed it, the bursts of scarlet glare at me like a dozen bloodshot eyes, piercing through the swirling color.

"I must give your keen observation credit. It looks that way because there *is* a bloody thumbprint. It's the seal."

"The seal?"

"A lock. To keep the door shut. This is where you will come in. It only lasts so long with my blood, but with *your* blood, it'll hold much longer."

"Why?"

"Well, no one is completely sure why—it was an accidental discovery a few millennia ago—but what we know for sure is that it has to do with harmony. Magic is always seeking balance. As it turns out, the instability of these portal locks, which are full of wild magic, is balanced by human blood. Use blood from a female, and the stability doubles. Use blood from a human female who is bonded to a fae, and the stability doubles yet again. Don't ask me why because, like I said, I don't know. All I know is that it *works*. It's the best counterbalance we've discovered so far."

That is . . . strange. A dozen more questions build up inside my brain, clamoring for release, and it's quite the effort to sort through and pick a couple to ask without losing the rest. "Will my magic affect anything?"

"Almost certainly. In what matter, and to what extent . . . that is what we will discover. I doubt it would make the seals *less* secure, but either way, it'll be more secure than what I've been doing."

"Do they break open often with your blood?"

He draws a deep breath between his teeth, stepping to my side and motioning for me to follow him down the hallway—right through the midst of the beautiful chaos of colors. He moves swiftly, not allowing us to linger. "I try not to let them get so far as breaking open, but it's . . . it's a lot of work. The seals break down so fast that by the time I'm finished checking them all, the first ones are already weakening. That is . . . what happened with Mahja. She must have been near the Crenfyre portal when it started breaking down."

A memory flashes before me, of nearly walking straight into a pale-faced Mahja—one of the other women competing for the position of Queen of Arbasa—her eyes vacant just a moment before she collapsed to the ground. I can still hear the Neverseen King's panicked shouts for his steward to come that moment.

From what I've surmised, Crenfyre is one of the most dangerous portals here.

If not the *most* dangerous.

"What makes the portals break down?" I ask, scurrying to keep up with the Neverseen King's tall, black-as-night shadow as he marches through the magic glows of the doors.

"Natural degradation mostly," he replies, glancing at each door as we pass, "but sometimes creatures on the other side like to try to break through. Goblins, for example, are the *worst*. They're always chewing through my seals. I reseal their door every single night."

For some strange reason, this strikes me as funny. I force my mouth to stay in a straight line—

He stops abruptly, turning toward me. "Did you just snicker?"

"Absolutely not," I say quickly, pulling my rebellious face under control. *Almost* under control.

He stares down at me, cobalt blue swirling over his hooded head. His voice is dryly amused when he says, "Perhaps I should leave *you* in charge of the goblin door."

"I'm sure I don't have your vast skill at magic and magic bindings."

"Was that an attempt at flattery?"

He steps closer, tilting his face toward mine. My mouth suddenly goes dry, my heart picking up its rhythm as he leans over me. Bringing his warmth nearer, nearer, blocking out the light around us.

"It cannot be flattery if it's true?" It comes out like a question rather than a statement, and his rumbling chuckle washes over me in response.

He gives my chin a little chuck. "I rather like putting you on the defensive."

He's walking away before I can react, leaving me a dizzying mix of flushed, surprised, and even more defensive than before. I lower my brow at his back, then increase the length of my strides to catch up with him. "I can make you regret those words."

Kaladen only chuckles again. "I'd like to see you try."

He wants to goad me, does he? Well, I can—

He turns his head toward me, just barely, but it's enough to catch the sapphire twinkle in his eye. Is he smirking at me?

Fine, he can think he's winning right now. I'll get him back. I'll put *him* on the defensive and chuckle at *him*, and then I'll laugh when he glares at me.

He stops abruptly. My gaze shoots to him, then follows the direction of his attention to a door that pulses waves of lilac and mauve. Its thumbprint seal isn't a vibrant crimson like the others, but a muted brown, and it almost appears like it's been slashed through, leaving bits of brown flaking off.

"Is this seal breaking down?" I ask, creeping only the tiniest step closer to peer around the Neverseen King's bulk.

His voice isn't light and playful like it was a minute ago. Not one bit. "It's been tampered with."

Ice churns in my gut, a shiver slithering through my body. "What do you mean?"

Beneath the darkness of his words runs an undercurrent of something almost *frantic*. "The witnesses. One of them sabotaged this seal—and maybe others. *Gravbaks*," he growls furiously. "Mountains of Ildrid, when did they even have *time*?"

I stay silent, trying to shove away the heaviness creeping up my limbs.

He glances up and down the hallway, as though searching for more browning seals. "Nadira, I'm sorry, but I must—"

Like a candle being snuffed out, the colors suddenly vanish. The entire world around me is gone in an instant. The Neverseen King, my knives, the hallway, the portals. *Gone*.

I blink against the darkness—only to have it be instantly replaced by near-blinding light.

The sun is shining. A hot wind rearranges my unruly hair as I scurry barefoot across the dusty floorboards to where Jabir sits sharpening his knives. My fingers are wrapped around a small length of rope that I proudly hold up, barely restraining my grin.

No.

"I did it," I say, my missing front teeth making the words come out with a lisp. "I figured out how to undo the knot you gave me."

No, no, no.

Jabir doesn't respond for a long minute. He continues sharpening his knives, ignoring me. A bolt of fear hits me. Did he not want me to interrupt him? But he said to tell him as soon as I finished it. Besides, this was the first time I'd figured out one of his knots without asking for help. For once, I thought he might . . . be glad?

At last, he looks up. There's not a hint of pride in his dark eyes. Not a word of praise on his lips. He just rolls his scrutiny over me, over my dusty and torn clothes, over the unraveled rope in my hands.

Please no.

"Come here."

Those words slither around me like a constricting snake, cutting off my air and filling me with dread. I know what he's going to do to me. But *why*? I did what he said—I succeeded! Why isn't he pleased with me? What have I done wrong?

I want to whimper, but that will only make things worse. So I tamp down on any sound that might escape my throat. I do as he says, my whole body trembling.

Not this. Not this.

"Hold out your hands."

I obey, fighting to stay still as he takes the rope and ties my wrists to a ring in the wall, using the very same knot I'd just labored to solve. He grabs a long, thick cut of leather and winds one end of it around his fist.

"Solve it again," he says.

Then the blows begin.

CHAPTER 7

THE MOURNER

"WAKE UP, NADIRA! Wake up! Wake *up*!"

I'm being shaken. Hands grip my shoulders, knees straddling my hips as someone growls into my face. My eyes open to a room dimly lit by floating globes. Not the hallway of rainbow colors. Not that hut out in the desert—

I heave for air. My stomach turns upside down. Panic runs like sweat down my body.

Someone is restraining me. Someone is pinning me. A hand cups the side of my wet face. I dare not scream, but I throw my weight, wrestling to get my knees up—

"Nadira! It's me, Kaladen. It's me. It's just me!"

"Let go of me!" I gasp, and the moment those hands release my shoulders, I stumble out of bed, hurtling for the far wall. My palms hit the tapestry I'd been staring at earlier, and I hardly recognize it.

You're awake. You're not there. That's in the past. It's done and gone.

My shoulders heave, my hands fisting in the tapestry as I bow my head. The moment I close my eyes, those images flash before me again—of my bound hands chafing until they bled as I gnawed the rope with my teeth. The memory nearly swallows me again, and I open my eyes. I dare not even blink.

"What was that?" I croak, my throat raw. I repeat the words, demand lacing my tone. "What *was* that?"

He sounds far away, his voice muffled, as if I'm still not fully in the room with him. There's no shock in his voice like there is in mine. "I don't know. Sometimes . . . sometimes it does things like this."

"What?"

"The magic. It . . . doesn't always work as intended. I was about to pull us both out of the dream, and then it . . ."

He said it was finicky—he had *not* said I would be reliving nightmares. Nightmares that should be dead and buried. I clench my teeth. "Why didn't you tell me?"

"I didn't know it would do this."

"But you knew it *could*."

His growl tightens. "I didn't have reason to believe it would, considering how you reacted to it last time."

I let out a long, gasping breath, shuddering against the wall. *Pull yourself together, Nadira. You're stronger than this.* The sting of those lashes fades until at last I can close my eyes and meet only darkness. Darkness and relief.

"Are you alright?" he whispers, a depth of concern in his tone I haven't heard before. As though he was genuinely frightened for me. Perhaps he still is.

I swallow, burying my sweaty forehead into the tapestry. Then, I tighten my fists as hard as I can . . . and let go. I turn around and say without the barest quaver: "I'm fine."

He stands by my side of the bed, tension radiating from every pore of his body, one hand partially outstretched toward me. He withdraws it and clenches it into a fist. "We're done for tonight. I'll—"

He turns to leave, but I dart forward and catch his forearm. The tautness of his tightly coiled muscles radiates into my grip, but I don't let go. "I want to try again." The words are out of my mouth before I can stop them, though it's impossible to know which of us is more surprised by the declaration.

He shakes his head too vigorously. "This is enough for tonight. You need time to adjust to the magic, and it needs time to adjust to you, and *I* need to go investigate my slashed seals before a portal breaks—"

"Then trying again will make it go faster, right? I won't bother you. I'll just trail along behind and be quiet."

"Not . . . necessarily."

I frown, very aware of his urgency to inspect the damaged seals, but not quite willing to back down. *Yet.* "Then how do I make it accept me faster? What does it want from me?"

The muscles in his forearm ripple in my hold, and he seems to struggle with the need to pull away from me. "It's not sentient, with desires and wants. It's more like water running down a hill, looking to fill the lowest spots first. It is always searching for balance. Harmony. Where it is lacking, it seeks to fill."

I twist my brow into a knot, trying to make sense of this. "Are you saying . . . that it finds me misbalanced?"

He doesn't answer, which is answer enough.

"But it accepts you as balanced?"

"Not at all," he says with a tinge of dryness. "It has simply adjusted to me and found a way to compensate."

Well then, it'll have to compensate for me too. "I want to try again."

He pulls his arm out of my grip and paces toward the door. "No more tonight."

"Why not? Do you think it'll happen again?"

"I don't know *what* it'll do," he growls. "I *do* know what will happen if that portal opens, which is why I must leave—"

"Just let me come and watch! I didn't handle this one well, but now that I know what to expect, I'll handle it better. I promise." I bite my tongue before I resort to begging; I won't beg. But the force of my desire to try again almost shocks me, the desire to *prove* I can master this. To prove I'm not still that small, frightened child I was in my nightmare.

I want to earn his respect.

To prove that he wasn't wrong in taking me as his wife.

To be, in this small regard, worthy of him.

He's silent, his teeth grinding audibly in the dim light. At last, he opens his mouth. "You're not the reason I don't want to try again. It's because I can only control so much fury in one night, Nadira. *And* because I don't want to bring you into this before I know the extent of the sabotage."

Fury? At . . . me? For not—

He saw it.

Again.

He saw exactly what Jabir did to me when I was a child. Ice stirs in my belly, and I swallow obsessively, as if that will suppress it.

"I have precious little self-control when it comes to him," he whispers, deathly quiet, confirming my fears. "To have to watch over and over again the things he did to you, and not be able to stop it—to not be able to protect you. It kills me, Nadira."

I stop breathing. "Oh."

He shoots those jewel-like eyes at me. "You understand now?"

I nod slowly, once. "I would still like to try again. If I'm to have any hope of surviving Lulythinar, then I need to master this. Fast."

He puffs air out of his nose, turning away from me once more. The fact that he doesn't fight me tells me I'm right: he cannot afford to dally. Both of us need me to be strong. And that means facing difficult things.

But just when I think he is about to open his mouth and tell me I can join him, he marches to the door, abandoning me.

“Get some rest,” he whispers, and each soft word is like a nail through my flesh. “You won’t be pulled into the nightmare if I’m not nearby. I will see you at breakfast.”

Then he leaves, drawing the door of our bedroom shut behind him.

Chapter 8

THE NEVERSEEN KING

BEING DRAWN INTO Nadira's flashback was not the same as the burst of memory that overcame us during our bonding. It was longer, more real and I was physically present for it—not experiencing the trauma through her body but watching as a separate entity in that dusty hut. I was *there* when the small girl came prancing out of the adjoining room, her hope and pride gleaming in too-large eyes as long curls bounced around her shoulders. I watched that hope die, watched as cold-knifed terror and dread replaced it.

I witnessed the heart of that little girl die.

No one was there to protect her, to let her be the child she should have been. She ought to have been playing games of hide and seek among the stalls of the bazaar with other children, with two parents to love her and welcome her with open arms.

It makes me angry.

Beyond angry.

It makes me *furious*.

But what good will my fury do for her? It won't help the situation. It won't calm the raging storm inside her.

Besides, I must get to the bottom of this sabotage immediately.

I'd rather stay here, in this bedroom. I'd rather try to soothe her, to get past the determination to succeed and survive, to the vulnerability beneath. What I *want* is to take her into my arms and vow that no one will ever hurt her again.

But to make that vow is to promise things I cannot give, in an attempt to hold close what I cannot have.

It is better to face reality.

So I leave, and despite my rational mind insisting that I *must* leave her to protect her, her friend, and her people, I cannot help but feel that I am running away from the one thing that matters.

Three seals have been slashed. All on opposite sides of the palace, which should have been impossible with the amount of time the witnesses had between when I left them and when the House's defenses were activated.

Breathing hard, I slam the door to the Wendlier portal, pressing my bleeding thumb to the seal and the burning phoenix feather I stole. The seal brightens, successfully reinforced. I yank my finger back, throbbing from the burn of the feather, and don't take a second to watch the House's healing magic begin restoring the tissue. This portal is near my chambers, but Crenfyre is on the next floor of the House, and Salvatar is in an antechamber near the gates.

The threads of connection between me and those portals tremble, ready to snap at any second. I grind my teeth against one another. It's not a choice—I've got to deal with Crenfyre. Which means Salvatar is going to break open.

"Sorry, citizens of Risya," I mutter under my breath as I step into the dream realm, lose my physical projection of my body, and hurry toward Crenfyre.

THE MOURNER

I toss and turn, plagued in sleep by nightmares and plagued in consciousness by the absence of the Neverseen King.

I want to rationalize everything, to order each event into a neat little row. But I can't. Not in the darkness. The empty, all-consuming darkness is nothing like the shadows my new husband wears.

There is no reprieve in sleep. Only ravaging nightmares that leave me sweating through the sheets. I kick them off only to wake up too cold. Then I imagine every manner of enemy lurking in the corners of this unfamiliar bedchamber.

Safya comes back with her unflinching ruthlessness. "If I hadn't died," she says in that even tone of hers, "he would have picked me. You know he should have picked me."

Raha, wreathed in black with eyes like angry, glowing embers, prowls to my bed where I'm pinned. "At last, vengeance for what you took from me." She stabs me in the gut, and I gasp, the pain like a brand through my entire body.

Then her face morphs, splits, until all the faces of the people I've killed are above me, but it's Kolb's mop of curls that frightens me more than anything, as he lifts a knife along with the rest, ready to finish—

My eyes flutter open.

Screeches fill the air.

I'm out of bed the next instant, sleepy fog vanishing from my mind as I catch myself against the windowsill and peel back the curtains. It's hard to see in the night outside, but I can still make out small, dark *things* flying through the sky.

That's no earthly creature of Arbasa.

A portal must have broken open.

I unlatch the shutters and swing myself out the window. The screeching only intensifies. I check my knives as I break into a run—though a few knives are paltry against what sounds like thousands of airborne creatures. Beneath the screeching, there is a low humming, like the beating of wings.

Something dark and small zips in front of my face. I yank back, then pull my scarf up and wrap it over my nose and mouth. Are these creatures poisonous? Do they bite or sting or kill? My mind begins inventing all manners of horrors—creatures that inject venomous larvae into their victims, creatures that swarm and sting until the victim is dead, or creatures that are so deadly a mere brush against a victim's skin is enough to kill them.

"What *are* these things?" cries Eshe from somewhere to my left. "Get *away* from my *face* or I'll *eat* you, you disgusting creatures!"

"Eshe!" I follow her voice and find her in the courtyard with the empty, cracked fountain, both relieved to have her near and terrified for her safety. "We need to find out if they're confined to the palace grounds or if they've gone into the city!"

Another creature zips past Eshe, but her hand shoots out and catches it.

"Eshe!" I choke. "That might be poisonous!"

She brings it close to her face and opens her palm. Her lips wrinkle. "Eww! What a gross . . . thing!"

"Put it down!"

"No, come look at it! It's like a worm with wings! A worm with little pincher claws! See, it's trying to pinch me. You little stinker—knock that off!"

I start to speak, to reiterate my command to let the creature go, but then I stop, tilt my head, and step closer. The creature's wings join the humming cacophony around us, but Eshe keeps it secured as she holds it for me to look.

Her description is apt. It's smaller than I expect, but large for an insect. The body is the size of half her palm, fat and slug-like. It has a row of ten thin, short legs that separate into teeny pinchers at the end. Its face is very insectile, with small black eyes and long antennae. The wings are glossy and white, more flexible than a moth's. They reflect a slight blue in the moonlight.

"Actually, it's kind of cute," says Eshe. "I think I'm going to make it my pet."

I shake my head. "We need to make sure the city isn't being overrun!"

"Let me find a safe place for this little guy and then I'll join you."

Sands preserve me. I break into a run, leaving her and her insect-monster-pet *thing* behind. It reminds me of all the jobs we did together before the Neverseen King came into our lives. All the times I created a meticulous plan only for Eshe to immediately ignore it and do whatever she wanted.

Somehow, we still always succeeded. I just nearly lost my mind every time.

Like now.

I don't know what I'm expecting to find when I dart through the sets of arches leading into the courtyard by the palace gates. Part of me hopes there will be some magical forcefield keeping all these creatures in—some creation of the Neverseen King's to protect the city.

But we have no such luck.

Instead, swarms of the horrible flying worms come from one of the windows on the second story nearby, and they fly in every direction. Including the city.

I duck just before one of them hurtles straight into my face. I glare up at the sky as the swarm covers the moon. Cursing under my breath, I get a running start on the gates, leap, catch the top spokes, and vault to the other side. They're tall enough that I roll when I land to avoid jarring my knees. Springing up to my feet, I survey the situation.

Candles and torches flicker to life inside the city. Then people start screaming.

I curse again.

There is no plan in my head when I plunge into the streets of Risya. There is only the certainty that I know more than nothing about these creatures, which is not something that can be said about these poor people.

I'm hardly a few steps into the main street of Risya before city guards appear, armed with torches and scimitars. The sight of them makes me duck inside an alleyway by instinct. I watch as the creatures dive-bomb the guards and anyone unfortunate enough to be left on the streets. Heavy thuds of windows being boarded up combine with the shrieks of those whose houses are being swarmed.

The guards slash into the air, lobbing creatures in pieces that fall to the earth. One guard fights particularly hard and somehow manages to not look completely ridiculous in the process. "Tariq!" calls one of the others as he's overwhelmed. The first guard runs to his aid at once.

I wait where I am, every muscle in my body tensed for the second guard to fall dead and prove these creatures are lethal. But once the guards have fought off this particular swarm, leaving bits of sliced wing and slug-like body on the ground, the targeted guard shows no sign of injury.

I dig my fingernails into crumbling plaster as I hug the alleyway, my attention darting over what must be *millions* of creatures filling the air now and darkening the sky blacker than midnight. Even if they're not dangerous, how can I possibly help the situation? Surely there must be *something*.

"Hey! You there!"

I freeze at the guard's voice. It's the proficient one—Tariq, was his name?—come close to my alleyway. His gaze is on me even as he slashes the air anytime a creature ducks low enough to be in range of his scimitar.

"Get out of the streets! This is no place for a maiden!" he shouts at me—just before he is swarmed.

I take his moment of distraction and sink deeper into the shadows of the alleyway, backing up slowly until I can turn and break into a run. My breath comes in short pants, but I get away from that guard as fast as I can. I cannot help my paranoid fear that one of these guards will somehow recognize me as the Mourner. Especially after my last assassination of Lord Kishon went so terribly wrong.

The screeching penetrates even in the depths of the alley, among rubble and old ripped sacks.

And a small group of dirty-faced urchins.

One of them, a little boy, is rolled in a fetal position on the ground as the creatures swarm him, while the other children use sticks and broken pieces of brick to smash the creatures.

Knives have a fraction of the reach of a scimitar, but I yank them out anyway. "Get back!"

The children don't obey, not until I reach through the swarm of beating wings to grab the boy's arm and try to yank him out of it. They come with him like they are glued to his ragged clothes. I hack them off one by one. He covers his face, not making a single sound.

The little boy I uncover beneath the swarm is sweet-faced, with large lips and even larger ears. He looks up at me in a mixture of pure shock, adoration, and fear.

I must be terrifying with my dark clothes and my scarf covering all but my eyes.

"Thank you!" an older girl cries, holding a toddler close to her chest. She looks like the oldest of all the children, but she cannot be even sixteen. Her crooked front teeth remind me of Eshe, except this girl is nothing but a thin layer of skin over bones.

Screeching overhead nearly drowns out my voice when I shout: "You need to find somewhere safe to be for tonight!"

The older girl looks at me blankly. The boy scurries to her side, poking out behind her tattered skirt. The other children huddle nearby, glancing between me and the sky. There must be ten of them all, with enough distinct faces that I doubt almost any of them are related. Is . . . *this* one of the bands of orphans?

It's so small.

Eshe wasn't lying when she said things had gotten so much worse.

"We don't have somewhere else," the oldest girl says at last.

The screeching becomes ear-piercing. I whirl, only to discover a fresh swarm breaking free of the larger group and diving between the buildings for us. "Get back!"

I have no idea what the children do, because the next second, I'm utterly enveloped. Little pinchers grab hold of my clothes, my scarf, sluglike bodies wrapping around my wrists, wings beating in my face so fast I can barely draw breath.

My knives slice through soft, oozing flesh and papery wings that disintegrate into dust. I catch a glimpse of small hands grabbing hold of a creature and yanking it off me—and then suddenly I'm afraid of using my knives and hurting whatever children are trying to help me.

I kill the ones near my face to regain my eyes.

And there's Eshe—having apparently followed my trail—helping the children pull the rest of the creatures off me. One of them pins a creature while the little boy jumps on it until it's nothing but a pile of goo.

"I changed my mind," chirps Eshe. "These would make horrible pets. But wing dust becomes you."

I swipe at my face, which became exposed during the attack. My hand comes back dirty. "We need to get the children to the belltower. The creatures seem to like attacking visible targets. The children should be able to hide there."

"But the belltower is haunted!" cries the boy with big ears. "If you go in, the djinn will eat you and ring the bell to tell everyone you're dead!"

Eshe chortles. "The lot of you together would hardly be enough to fill the belly of a djinn."

I elbow her. "Not helping!" To the children I say: "Come along now! And what's your name?"

The oldest girl looks up when I address her. She still holds the young toddler who sucks vacantly on his fist, caring not a whit for the teaming monsters in the sky. "Zara," she says softly.

"Are you afraid of djinn, Zara?"

She glances between me and Eshe, then down at the children clinging closely to her. It's as though I watch the argument in her head play out in her eyes—the superstition of a child with the responsibility of a girl grown too early into the cares of adulthood. She lifts her chin firmly, the latter having won out. "No."

I gesture ahead. "Then follow me."

THE MOURNER

"ARE *WE* THE reason the belltower is considered haunted?" Eshe asks as we herd children through the broken doorway into the small, confined world of dust and stone beyond.

"*You* are the reason," I correct.

We hid here once before a job and when I wasn't looking, she rang the bell.

She grins. "I had to see if it still worked."

Jabir nearly flayed us alive for that, but that one was one of the few times it was worth it. I still remember that moment of pure horror and shock when that eardrum-splitting gong rang out right by my head and how fast we ran from the tower . . . and how hard we laughed when we escaped.

The stairs are so broken and rickety that no one risks climbing them. They do, however, make a good shelter from the sight of the creatures. Zara firmly orders all the younger children to squish together beneath them. She slides in last of all, still holding the little one that probably isn't her blood relative.

"My name is Abbi," says the little boy with the big ears, apparently having forgotten everything about the city's peril.

"That is a very handsome name," says Eshe.

He puffs out his chest. "I picked it out myself!"

Her expression doesn't falter as she bends down to ruffle his hair. "Excellent choice."

Meanwhile, I am forced to turn around and stare out the shambled excuse of a door. Of all the things I have lost, of all the things that have been taken from me, I'm glad I still have my parents' gift of a name, even if it's incomplete. *Nadira*.

I wrap my scarf around my face once more. "I'm going back into the city."

It starts so slowly at first, I don't notice it. I'm busy finding more clumps of terrorized orphaned children and moving them to even the most temporary of shelters. It starts with one creature falling to the ground, vibrating, and then going still. Then another, and another.

The first hints of sunrise turn the sky purple, and more creatures fall from the sky. The city guard aids those whose homes weren't prepared for such an onslaught and killing any who swarm in the streets. I stay away from them, as do the children I help. It's infuriating that the most vulnerable people in the entire city are the ones most ignored during a crisis. I let that fury swirl in my gut, turning colder with each second.

But then the sun rises in earnest, and the drip, drop of falling creatures like light rain turns to a torrential downpour as creatures hit the dirt, vibrating in their death throes, before *finally* going still.

When golden rays sear my eyes, I look around. Not a single creature flies in the sky. Instead, there are piles upon piles of wormy bodies and what remains of their filmy wings filling the streets, covering the roofs.

My lip curls in disgust.

The exhaustion of the night seeps into my bones, and I'm suddenly so tired I could collapse right here in an alley. I make it back to the belltower, only to find Eshe doing the same thing, coming from the opposite direction. When she spots me, she taps her temple and gestures to mine. "Look at us. Same brains."

"What's the status on the north side of town?"

"It doesn't look like anyone is dead. The guards are a little worse for the wear from a night doing something besides sitting on their backsides. The orphans got the worst of it, but as far as I can tell, no one is seriously hurt. Do you think these things will rot? If so, this place is going to stink to the clouds. By the way, where is the sultan? Shouldn't he be helping us with this? And I suppose I ought to be asking how your *wedding night* was. Or, at least, what little there was of—"

I'm about to step into the belltower to avoid answering her questions—questions I've been wondering, save the last one—when a chorus of male voices make me go stiff. Eshe ducks deeper into the alleyway by instinct. My thoughts go to the children still crammed in the belltower. I don't want the guards to find me either. Not because I'm doing anything wrong, but how am I supposed to explain what I'm doing without explaining that I'm the Neverseen King's *wife* now?

They would laugh me into the stocks for being a suspicious liar and throw dead insectile monster bodies at me. And I couldn't blame them.

Where *is* the Neverseen King, anyway?

As long as the children don't make noise, the guards won't find them. I slip into the opposite alleyway and crouch behind the crumbled remains of a barrel.

". . . came from the palace. I'm sure of it. Tariq was the one on scout duty and he saw them like a dark cloud rising from the palace gates," says one of the guards. He sounds like he might be a little younger than me. There's something slightly shrill in his voice, as though he hasn't fully calmed down after the adrenaline rush of the attack.

"That place is more haunted than this belltower," growls his companion with a voice roughened by frequent use of cigars. "Hey look—there are footprints. Little ones."

"I thought the urchins didn't come around here," says the first guard.

I stay in my hiding place, hoping against hope that they'll move on. But the second guard stops and pokes his head into the tower. "There's a whole passel of 'em in here. One of them has a pretty face. Come out, little girl. Put that baby down and come with us. We won't touch the others if you're quiet."

Zara.

The blades of my knives catch sunlight as I slide out of my hiding spot, my whole body suddenly icy with rage.

But it's Eshe who beats me to the guard. I didn't even know she had a knife on her, but she has it against the second guard's throat, her voice a soft purr. "Leave the girl if you value your life."

Both guards freeze even before I have my blade against the first one's throat, even if I'm not sure he's much of a threat. He's short and scrawny, with an uncertainty hovering around his shoulders, whereas Eshe's quarry is stout with a large beard and arms the size of her legs. The brawny one's hand strays to his sheathed scimitar. Eshe presses the blade tighter against the underside of his jaw. "Mmm, I love a good bad decision, but don't you dare."

"Zara," I call, not daring to take my eyes off the two guards for even a moment. "Get the children out of here."

The line of them scurries out of the doorway, Abbi leading the way and Zara taking up the rear, the toddler clutched tightly to her chest. She looks once at me, then at Eshe, but refuses to let her gaze meet the grizzled guard's as it wanders over her.

"Who are you two?" the brawny guard asks. He still doesn't move, but I can see him weighing his options as he surveys my blade against his comrade's throat.

"They are my wife and my friend," growls a new, low voice from behind me. "And you will do them no harm."

I nearly drop my knife in sheer relief.

The Neverseen King has come at last.

"Neverseen King?" croaks the brawny guard.

Eshe seems to get a signal from Kaladen, because she releases the guard and steps back. I do the same, but do not sheathe my knife.

The Neverseen King is a mass of black shadow in the early morning sunshine. He inclines his nearly invisible head to me. "Is there a problem?"

"Not anymore," I say, not bothering to hide the disgust I shoot at the brawny guard.

"Good. Then you two"—he gestures at the guards—"can clean up the mess in the city. And *you* two"—gesturing at me and Eshe—"can return to the palace."

The guards quickly leave. Eshe catches my eye and jerks her head in the direction the orphans disappeared. She peels off to ensure they're safe before she returns to the palace. Leaving me momentarily alone with my new husband.

"*Beechka* are disgusting pests," he says by way of greeting, kicking a dead creature out of his way. "Fortunately, they cannot tolerate the sun."

"What happened?"

"I had to choose between this one opening or Crenfyre."

"Oh."

He regards me. "You look exhausted."

I poke my tongue into my cheek and drag my eyes up to his. I'm not expecting his hand to land on my shoulder and give a gentle squeeze.

"Get some rest back at the House. I've got more to do."

Then he's gone, and I trudge across the sandy cobblestones, kicking aside *beechka* bodies as I make my way back to the palace.

CHAPTER 10

THE NEVERSEEN KING

FIVE SEALS WON'T make it to dusk—likely others, as I'm not inspecting as close as I usually do—so I will have a long and grueling day ahead of me. Exhaustion flags my steps as I finally reseal the last portal with my blood.

When I finish and impending doom has been forestalled another few hours, my shoulders hunch in weariness. I sag against a wall, and find myself staring at the door to Nadira's old room.

What a night.

I have enough work to do without dealing with saboteurs from the High King.

Nevertheless, it's been almost impossible to focus my mind on the present, instead of processing the things I saw of Nadira's past.

And my own.

Resolve firming within my chest, I stay in the dream realm as I slip into Nadira's old room. There's the settee and chairs arranged near the window, the large bed to one side—reoccupied to no one's surprise by a sprawling, snoring Eshe, with her streaks of light hair tangled with the dark strands, her clothes filthy from fighting *beechka* in the city, and her slender, short frame taking up little space—and the vanity against the wall to my right. I ignore all of it, going straight to the painting on the wall.

Curious, sparkling blue eyes meet mine.

I'd been such a lovesick fool when I'd had these paintings done and hung in so many rooms in the palace. Then, after I'd lost her, I'd ordered Emin to have coverings made for each. Something to hide those blue eyes that pierced mine with their laughing warmth. I couldn't bear to have them taken down, but neither could I look upon her face.

Now I do.

I don't let myself flinch away. Not from the memory of her, and not from what I believed about myself after her death.

Nothing but a failure.

I'm nothing but a failure.

I sit with those words. The same words that echoed through my mind only hours ago, watching the light go out of Nadira's young eyes and being helpless to stop it. And then again, when I had no choice but to allow the *beechka* to overtake the city.

The strength of midmorning's glow fall across the roofs of the palace complex and the city beyond.

Dawn will come again.

Those were the words I said to Nadira before her magic manifested. It was only darkness after that moment. Do I still believe my own words?

Is it time to stop mourning the past?

Maybe it's time to wake up. To allow dawn to come instead of clinging to night.

No, part of me insists frantically. *You cannot let her go. It's betrayal. How dare you let yourself love again? Do you think you deserve happiness after how deeply you failed Liliana?*

But what if it isn't betrayal? What if clinging to the dead isn't justice, but bondage?

Liliana doesn't need me anymore.

You deserve to suffer for how you failed her.

Perhaps I do. I've been suffering for ninety-nine years now. I've been punishing myself for nearly a century.

It's . . . *enough.*

Everything holds still in that small moment of forever. That truth permeates to the very depths of my being. Then it floods me like a tidal wave, breaking on the edges of shore and overcoming everything in its path.

It's enough.

It's time to let Liliana go. Forever.

A sudden upswell of grief makes me stumble backward into one of the chairs. I'm still in the dream realm, so I don't disturb Eshe as I bow over my knees, gripping my head in my hands.

The tears come, ugly and loud. It hits me afresh, the reality of her loss. The loss I haven't accepted. My heart breaks open, and I let it. I savor the pain. This is what I should have done decades ago.

"I release you, Liliana," I whisper between ragged sobs. "I'm done holding on to you. I'm done denying that you're gone. I release you—and I release myself. Enough is enough. Be at peace."

It feels so final, this last severing. This giving up. Part of me wants to fight it, to cleave to her memory just a little bit longer. To hope for just a few more minutes—to deny reality for one last second.

But I won't.

Those years that our stories overlapped were wonderful. But I'm done believing that they will be the only good years of my life.

I'm done spending my life mourning the dead instead of *living.* Instead of being *with* the living.

Liliana doesn't need me anymore. She is at rest, at peace.

But Nadira?

I've spent so much time these last several days being angry at Jabir, hating that I cannot avenge his abuse of Nadira. But what does *she* need? She doesn't need revenge, much less me exacting it for her.

She needs healing.

I cannot heal her, but I can do what I am able to create space for her to heal. I can open my arms to her.

My heart.

She might not want my heart. She might be too wounded to ever trust and feel safe with me. Or maybe we can find each other after all. Maybe, with her magic, we can both survive Lulythinar.

The sun's golden rays cast across the brightening sky outside the window. I pull my gaze from the portrait to the painted colors of morning.

Dawn will come again.

It's time for me to stop withholding myself—protecting myself—from Nadira.

It's time for me to truly and deeply love my wife.

CHAPTER 11

THE MOURNER

SOMETHING YANKS ME from my deathlike sleep. Midday light streams across the damp, matted sheets tangled with my legs. The curtains are pulled away from the open window. An azure sky greets my blurry gaze, and my whole body relaxes.

No more *beechka* nightmares to wake up to.

I let my head fall back against the cushion as a sigh of relief gusts from me. I should go to Eshe, see how she's faring. The Neverseen King probably won't—

Another knock sounds on the door.

That's what woke me up. Someone's outside the room. Needing me.

I shove aside the covers and swing my legs over the side of the bed. My clothes are sticky and damp and still dirty from last night, but my knives are all in their proper places. I'm not even halfway to the door before it opens, revealing a tall shadow carrying what seems to be a breakfast tray.

"What are you doing out of bed?" he asks, a frown emanating from his wreathing darkness.

I blink twice. "It's very late."

"Yes, and you had a very long night. And I am bringing you breakfast."

I open my mouth, only to close it again. Why does he act as though these are antithesis to each other?

"Back to bed with you. I can't serve you breakfast in bed if you are, in fact, *not* in bed."

"Oh. I . . . um, we could eat in the sitting area?" I'm not sure why I suggest it, or why my face colors at his words. He acts as though nothing happened last night, as though we are truly a new bride and groom. I scratch behind my ear, more than a little confused.

"Come now, indulge me." He holds up the tray as though it's a peace offering. "You don't need to look so suspicious. There's no ulterior motive. I'm only bringing you breakfast. It's a thank you for doing an excellent job managing the *beechka* infestation while I resealed the portals."

I glance away from him, from the tray he carries, studying instead the little, unilluminated globes hanging from the ceiling. In the morning light, they look like large, crystalline bubbles.

I turn on my heel, shuffle to bed, and climb back in. My cheeks only grow hotter when the Neverseen King strides confidently to my side and sets the tray on my lap. Then he marches to the other side of the room, grabs one of the two chairs near the window, and drags it over to my side of the bed.

I watch him without making a sound, without so much as touching the steaming tray of food in front of me.

He sits in the chair, facing me, with his hands steepled beneath his chin, and announces, "Neither of us is leaving this room until you finish everything on that tray."

"What?" I burst, surveying the glass of goat's milk, cup of qahwa, several salted and stuffed dates, an assortment of cheeses, sausages, flat bread and humus, *and* a sesame-studded kaek sandwich filled with cheese, za'atar, and baked eggs. "Do you think I'm an elephant?"

"Do elephants eat sausage? No." He seems to arch a brow at me. "Do you need more proof?"

"We're going to be here all day!"

"If worst comes to worst, I'll just spoon-feed you. Come on, eat."

"You are *not* spoon-feeding me."

A slow, curving smile. "Then *eat*."

I pick up a slice of cheese, eye it, then set it back down. "Your scrutiny is making me nervous."

"You think I can't tell by now when you're lying?"

"I'm not lying!"

"You are on dangerous ground, Mourner."

"And why is that?" I demand, folding my arms across my chest.

He leans forward just an inch, the edges of his darkness coalescing into something that is almost fully corporeal. "Because I am *this* close to spoon-feeding you."

I pick up the cheese and take a bite, chewing and swallowing deliberately. All while fixing him with a potent glare.

His teeth flash in a grin as he sits back, linking his hands behind his head. "Well done. At this rate, we'll only be here until dusk."

My glare deepens, but there's no true irritation behind it. It's all I can do to keep from smiling as I eat in earnest. Kaladen sits quietly, watching me, and whenever I slow down, his gaze sharpens. An intangible threat that I'd better finish.

Well, I can't finish this whole tray. I force myself to eat until I'm bursting at the seams, and I haven't even touched the sandwich. Truly, he *must* have mistaken me for an elephant if he thought I could eat everything he served!

When I shake my head, Kaladen crosses his arms over his chest and says firmly, "All of it."

"If I eat one more bite, I'm going to throw up and I don't want to do that to your nice coverlet," I protest.

"How sweet of you. Keep eating."

I push the tray back and shake my head again. "I'm done."

"Am I going to have to feed you?"

"I'll throw up in your *face*!" I'm not teasing either. He can spoon-feed me all he wants, but there's no way I'm choking down another bite.

A low chuckle rumbles out of him, a warm sound that is nothing like the version of him that left me alone last night. "Very well, I'll let this pass only for today. Tomorrow you're eating the whole tray."

"Are you trying to fatten me up?"

He grins at me. "Absolutely. You claim to be an assassin, yet I could snap one of your arms in half with hardly a thought."

"Are you bored?" I ask instead of responding. "Are those seals too easy for you?"

"Hardly! I was just taking a little break before I returned to them. You continue to be a problematic distraction for me."

I lift one eyebrow. "Is that an attempt at flirtation?"

"Oh come now, I know you're not wholly immune to my charms."

This is definitely not the same Neverseen King as last night. I narrow my eyes at him, crossing my arms over my chest. "Do you want something from me? Are you trying to make me feel better about what happened last night? Or are you trying to make up for the fact that I spent hours chasing tiny monstrous creatures all over the city?"

The glimmer of his eyes narrows right back at me. "Must you always accuse me of ulterior motive?"

"You have one. I can smell it."

He gives a little snort at that and leans back in his chair, legs spread wide, as he regards me. "And if I do?"

"Then spit it out!"

"Definitely not."

"Kaladen!"

He waves a hand at me, amusement sparking in the air between us. "Say my name again, very sweetly, and maybe I'll tell you."

"Kaladen," I growl.

He shakes his head. "Not sweet enough. Try again."

"Why are you goading me?" I half-demand, half-whine.

"I'll tell you if you say my name. Sweetly."

I don't want to play his stupid games, but I also want answers. And . . . it's possible I enjoy the attention. Infuriating as the attention might be. With a wince, I attempt a higher-pitched version of his name. "Kaladen."

He chuckles. "Not quite, but better."

"Kaladen!"

"You're regressing."

I huff, turning my face away from him. "I don't know how to say things sweetly! I'm not a sweet person!"

"Sure, you're sweet. Killing all those people for me was sweet. Taking care of the city was sweet."

"Your ulterior motive is making you too desperate."

"Don't you wish you knew what my ulterior motive was?" He baits me again, refusing to fall for mine. "Just say my name sweetly. It's not that difficult."

"Kaladen," I grumble.

"Should I make this easier for you?"

"Please!" I say with a groan, and when I shift in the bed, the porcelain on the tray rattles. "Give me something a little easier. Sweetness isn't my strength."

Suddenly, he's crouched over me, his hands planted on the bed on either side of me, his shadowed face only inches from mine. Energy pulses through me. Shock, yes, but something else too. Something equally electrifying.

"Say my name now," he breathes, his mouth hovering above my temple. "Say my name, Nadira."

It's as though he knows his soft uttering of my own name would be my undoing. I collect my breath, swallowing against the sudden palpitations of my heart.

"Kaladen?" It comes out as a question. Not sweet, but low and undulating.

His nose slightly brushes my hair, and I have the impression that he closes his eyes. "Yes?"

"Is . . . that . . . good enough?"

His smile radiates into my skin. "For now."

But he doesn't pull away. He stays where he is, bowed above me, his lips hovering over my hair, my skin, like clouds above the surface of the earth. Close enough to dream of touch, but always just out of reach.

"Will you . . ." I swallow, finding my voice with difficulty. ". . . answer my questions now?"

"Hmm, you'll have to remind me," he murmurs. "I seem to have forgotten what they were."

I should be concerned about how I smell after that long, sweaty night. I should push him away, say something grumpy and snappish. But I can't care, not when I feel starved for his closeness.

I turn my head toward him, just slightly, so his mouth hovers above my forehead instead of my temple. "I asked why you were goading me," I whisper, a tad breathlessly. "And what your ulterior motives are."

"Ah yes." He leans his weight on one hand, lifting the other to tuck a wayward strand of my mussed hair behind my ear. "I goad you because it's fun. As for the other . . ." He hooks his finger under my chin so lightly I could ignore it if I wanted. Instead, I follow his prompting and lift my face toward his. Instinctively, my lashes flutter closed. "I think I'll keep my motives secret a little longer."

His words process belatedly. My eyes fly open just as he withdraws his hand, chuckling, and picks up the tray. I've hardly had time to react before he's halfway across the room, like a butler carrying away my unfinished breakfast.

"What?" I demand, coming to my senses and flinging the covers off, scrambling after him. "You said you'd tell me!"

"I said I *might* tell you," he tosses over his shoulder.

I run the conversation back through in my brain, then shout, "You!" just before he kicks the door open and saunters into the main chambers.

"I will be busy for the next hour or two," he calls out. "Portal business. But after that, we will be traveling, so make yourself presentable. I had clothes made for you for the occasion. You can find them in your wardrobe if you want them. I'll see you later!"

"Kaladen!"

But he's already marching into the hallway and shutting the door behind him.

I stare into the emptiness of the main chamber, the bedroom door still lightly listing on its hinges. This is not the same person who reinforced the boundaries between us last night.

"It doesn't mean anything," I mutter, trying to ignore the memory of his closeness, the warmth of his breath on my forehead. "You're not going to care. You're going to focus on upholding your end of this bargain and keeping Eshe out of trouble. If you don't master this portal magic nonsense, she'll be in danger."

Or have to go back to the streets.

With that, I glance down at my sticky clothes, a shudder running down my spine. I'm disgusting. I'll have to bathe. Am I brave enough to get into the pool in the bathing chamber to wash? I don't *always* black out when I immerse myself.

Steeling myself, I march out of the bedroom, into the main living area, then pull open the door leading to the bathing chamber. Sunlight pours into the white marble space, bouncing off the bubbling water and the enormous reflective mirror. It's almost blinding. In a beautiful sort of way.

The Neverseen King said he'd be busy and that I wouldn't see him, but I cannot help my paranoia that he *might* walk in while I'm bathing. I grab the screen, drag it across the chamber, and set it up beside the pool, facing the door, so I can hide behind it.

Then I peel off my sweat-soaked garments, leaving them in a pile next to the screen. My knives are set down with much more reverence. Maybe once I've finished here and met up with Eshe to see how she's doing, I'll sharpen them. It feels as though ages have passed since I've completed that ritual.

Crossing my arms over myself, I face the pool. It's not that deep. I could comfortably stand in it and the water would reach my shoulders. The light current makes the morning sunbeams reflect like sparkling jewels. When I dip my toe, the temperature is pleasantly warm. Kaladen said it was regulated by magic.

"Hotter," I say, half-expecting nothing to happen.

But the water does, in fact, heat. Not too much, just enough for it to be noticeable. My lips part, even though I shouldn't be surprised.

"Cold," I say, like a child that has just discovered a fascinating new toy. The water turns to ice around my toe, and I yank it out with a stifled yelp. "Back to warm."

It obeys.

A ridiculous grin spreads across my face. I can do this. I won't faint.

I stick my foot in, planting it on one of the stone steps. My vision speckles slightly, but nothing terrible. "Warmer," I say to distract myself with the amusement of playing with the water's magic as I step my other foot into it.

I can do this.

Water swirls around my calves. Liquid sloshing, warm, dark—

"Cold," I bark, grabbing onto the lip of the pool. The water turns to ice around me, bringing me back to the moment. A miserable, shivering moment. But I don't faint.

If ice-cold water is how I can keep from fainting, then I will endure all the shivering I must. When I get waist deep, my body locked up and tense, I break down and stutter, "A little warmer?"

It's not much, but it's better.

I wash myself quickly, shaking like a leaf, and then grab hold of the edge as I step my foot on the lowest stair.

I pause.

What if I could inch my way back up to warm? Maybe I can cure myself of this stupid limitation. With the sun shining, and the buzz of my success so far, I find enough boldness to say, "Warmer."

Subtle heat flares in the water, making my body relax. It's not a threat, only a relief.

"Warmer." My vision remains clear. "Warmer."

I get all the way back up to the heat it was at the beginning, my body almost drunk with the soothing temperature and my mind spinning from the thrill.

I'm standing in a pool of water without Eshe, and I'm . . . fine.

A tiny, incredulous laugh builds up in my chest. I don't want to push my luck, though, so I climb out of the tub, grab a towel, and set to drying myself off.

That's when I feel the slide of those warm droplets down my bare skin.

It's not water anymore. It's blood. So much blood. I'm covered in it, drenched from head to toe. It drips from my hair, slides down my face, runs down my back, my arms, my legs.

It's Baba's blood. Kolb's blood. The blood of Dabria's uncle. Raha's father. Lord Kishon's blood.

Jabir's blood.

My vision tunnels, my heart beating frantically, my airways closing.

"Get it off! Get it off! *Get it off!*" I choke, swiping blindly at the blood. But now it's on my hands, staining them red.

There has always been so much blood on my hands.

The monster inside me rears its head, ice shooting to the ends of my fingertips. Blood and ice, everywhere I turn—

"Squeeeeee!"

In a sudden burst, my awareness returns to me. I flail my ice-cold limbs, only to find them bound tight by thin, green rope, stretching my arms apart and keeping my ankles bound. An inarticulate cry rips from my lips, but as quickly as a blink, the rope—the *vine*—retracts, loosening my limbs.

I lay on the polished floor of the bathing chamber, sparks of blackness dancing across my vision. Coolness leaks into my back, my legs, my shoulders.

I roll onto my side, swallowing and gasping to keep from throwing up that massive breakfast the Neverseen King forced me to eat. The cold of the mosaic beneath me soaks into my bare torso. I shiver anew. At least my magic didn't break through again and decimate the Neverseen King's bathing chamber.

"Urggg?" comes a squeaked question from a few feet away.

I blink open one eye, still quaking on the ground, and find a curling vine tip hovering near my face. When I don't respond, it puts forth a bud that bursts open and twirls in front of my face.

"Grrrrp!" it says, then it shoots away, darting to wrap around a chunk of . . . towel.

Gently, it drapes the towel over my shivering body, arranges it neatly, and then peels away—only to shove its flower back in my face.

I wince and bat the flower away, but I don't snap at it. Despite the part of me demanding that it helped Safya, that it strung me up like a slaughtered lamb before the palace gates, I don't protest about the towel. Instead, I wrap it up tightly in my fist and cling to that scrap of security.

"Prrr?" the vine asks, magenta pistils bobbing up and down. It hovers above me, as though it's worried. When I don't respond, it reaches out a leaf like a hand and pats my shoulder.

"I'm fine, Badh-a," I croak.

It jerks back, half-startling me. It vigorously shakes its blossom at me.

"I *am*," I grumble, my teeth chattering. "I know it doesn't look it, but if you would give me a minute or two, I'll be back to normal."

That flower continues shaking at me. One of its leaves points to the door.

Now it's my turn to vigorously shake my head. A sudden surge of energy has me sitting up, clutching the towel to my chest, and blurting, "Don't tell the Neverseen King! I promise I'm fine!"

The flower folds back into a bud, the rest of the vine sagging in a huff.

"I'll prove it to you!" I say, pushing up on wobbling knees to get to my feet. Keeping the towel close to my vulnerable body, I make my way to the screen. For a heartbeat, I close my eyes, exhaling through my nostrils.

Don't count it as a defeat. You got farther than you normally do. It's a success.

It's hard to count anything as a success when my muscles are quaking like leaves in a gale, but I pull my clothes on without falling. They're not the special clothes he'd left in my wardrobe, but rather a much simpler outfit of brown with subtle gold detailing. I'll change when it's time to go. Wherever he's taking me.

The vine pokes its bud around the corner of the screen, then lets out a high-pitched squeal and darts away when I shoot a look at it.

"Don't tell him," I say, using the same stern tone I once used with the banister when I first arrived here. "See? I'm completely fine."

You are *completely fine*, I tell myself, shoving away the continued pounding of my heart in my chest.

The vine huffs in response.

I avoid looking in that massive mirror as I pull open drawers in the vanity and find a comb to rake through my hair. I've spent most of my life avoiding bright colors—they're too conspicuous and hard to keep clean in my line of work—but Kaladen has left a simple dark blue scarf in the wardrobe on top of the other dark-colored ones. I'm not sure what makes me select it today. Probably the fact that it is on top.

I arrange my scarf over my hair, double-check my knives are all where they should be. The vine has curled up by the screen, watching me without eyes. Does it see via scent? Sound? Or is it just some inexplicable magic?

I glance at it sidelong. "Why did you help Safya?"

It shoots upward about a foot, bursting out its flower and shaking it vigorously.

I lift an eyebrow. "You *didn't* help her?"

It shakes its flower, adamant.

I pull one blade out of its sheath and inspect the tip. "So you're a traitor *and* a liar."

"Graaaah!" it cries in protest.

"Sure."

"Wheeee!"

"Likely story."

It spews out air and flops back to the ground, stuffing away its flower.

"You don't have to sulk," I tell it. "I'm not going to hurt you. Not after you were kind to me just now. But that doesn't mean I trust you."

"Grrr," it growls in reply.

I roll my eyes and step out of the bathing chamber. The trembling in my limbs has eased, my heart rate has come back down to normal, and I can almost believe nothing happened in the bathing chamber at all.

A pounding knock sounds on my door. Loud and desperate. A servant girl's voice echoes through the solid wood. "Lady Nadira! Come quickly! It's Lady Eshe!"

CHAPTER 12

THE MOURNER

I THROW OPEN the door of the Neverseen King's quarters and rush out into the hallway. The servant girl is pale, her hands wringing in front of her.

"What's wrong?" I demand. "Where is Eshe?"

"By your old room! The Neverseen King told me to get you!"

I'm already running before she finishes. Have Jabir's men come back to attack the palace again? Or is it the fae who sabotaged the Neverseen King's portal?

Stay alive, Eshe. I'm counting on you.

I swear, if someone so much as lays a hand on her—

My whole body is tuned to any sight or sound besides my own pounding footsteps, the rush of blood in my ears, and the play of sunlight and shadow across the palace walls. Each second is torturous, my chest constricting as my mind conjures image after image of every terrible thing that could have happened.

Cold floods down my arms, throbbing into my fingertips.

I reach the main hallway of the palace and fling myself up the stairs, leaping three at a time.

Please be alright. Please don't be hurt.

I dare not call out to her and potentially put her in more danger. But when I round the corner, I cannot restrain a gasping, "Eshe!"

Relief hits my body before the horror. She's standing against the wall, her face buried in her hands, which are slitted enough for her to peer out of. There's no blood on her dust-orange clothes, no apparent injuries in how she holds herself.

Then I take in the rest of the scene.

Someone lies on the ground—and the Neverseen King bows over him, his voice frantic, his hands moving quickly over the man's chest.

There's blood on the floor.

I stumble back a step, hit the doorframe.

It's the steward. Emin.

"Work!" the Neverseen King growls. It almost sounds like tears choke his voice. "Work, you stupid magic. Work!"

Eshe bows her head, a sob shaking her shoulders.

Kaladen's healing magic doesn't work on people already dead.

He knows it, too.

As though hearing my thoughts, his arms go lax, and his head falls. Those powerful shoulders bow, his whole body sinking lower. How many decades—or longer—has Emin served him? How many losses must Kaladen bear? Tears prick my eyes, but I swallow them. "Who did this?"

The Neverseen King's hand on Emin's still chest clenches into a fist. "I am going to find out. And when I do, I will make what he did to Emin look like child's play."

I should be used to his dark and vicious threats by now, but my stomach still quivers. Eshe peeks between her hands, something between horror and relief warring on the scant bit of her face I can see.

I go to her side, rest my hand on her shoulder. She leans into the touch.

"You found him?" I ask quietly.

She nods, drawing a shaky breath.

She's so valiant in every other area, so unshakeable, even saying how thrilling it is to dance close to death. And yet, there's something about being confronted with the stark reality of it that rattles her to the core.

Bravado cannot change a soft heart.

I squeeze her shoulder. "I'm sorry."

She gives me a sad, watery smile.

Then I let go and walk to Kaladen's side, kneeling next to him. My vision darkens at the sight of blood seeping into the rug, but I focus my attention on the shadow beside me.

"The House's defenses killed him," he growls under his breath. "Emin would never have left his room or ventured into the hallways after dark. He knew there was no surviving the House's defenses."

"Someone forced him into the hallway?"

In response, Kaladen swipes his thumb on Emin's pale cheek and brings it to my nose. "What do you smell?"

I lean forward, take a whiff, and sit back on my heels. It's subtle, mingled with Kaladen's own scent, but . . . "It smells sweet. Fruity."

"Faerie fruit."

"What is that?"

Kaladen's shoulders raise and lower with a deep breath. "Fruit that grows on trees in Faerieland. Fae enjoy it just as you enjoy pomegranates and figs. For humans, however, it . . ." His voice cracks, and he pauses, composing himself. I almost reach out to touch him, to give him that scrap of comfort like I gave Eshe, but I can't quite bring myself to do it. After a moment, he continues. "It has a strong effect on humans. They lose their minds, and will do anything they're told."

Cold floods my limbs, my magic seeking an outlet for the anger building up inside me. "Someone poisoned him—with this fruit. And then told him to go out into the hallway after dark." My mind spins, the consequences of this unfolding before me. *Oh.* I straighten, and Kaladen's eyes shoot to me. "How long does the influence of this fruit last?"

"Hours."

I finger the hilt of my knife, certainty forming in my chest. "Emin slashed that seal."

Kaladen's attention sharpens on me. There's a wildness in the air around him—grief, fury, a need for retribution. Still, he holds himself in check, and I can almost see his mind catching up with me.

"You said the witnesses didn't have time to do it between the end of the ceremony and the House's defenses activating," I say.

"Because they didn't do it at the end of the ceremony."

"They poisoned Emin *before* the ceremony."

Kaladen nods and keeps nodding, as it all fits into place. He clenches his fist even tighter. "They told him to slash the seals during the ceremony, and then hide most of the night in one of the rooms. Then, likely just before daybreak, when I was finishing my rounds and you two were out in the city, he was instructed to leave his room and enter the hallway."

He shoots to his feet, pacing as he rakes a hand through his hair.

"The wound was still fresh when I found him," Eshe says softly from where she stands against the wall.

"And I wasn't going to know of this *murder* until now—long after the witnesses have all left," the Neverseen King growls, turning on his heel and pacing back toward us.

Suddenly, the blood drains from my entire body. I catch my weight on my hand before I fall forward. My mouth fills with bile.

Eshe was the last person with Emin. The fae could have decided to use her instead.

She could be next.

Strong, warm hands grip my shoulders. I jolt. *It's only Kaladen.* I relax.

"They aren't going to touch her," he vows, his voice soft and deadly against my ear. "I have extra wards around her room."

I nod—the only response I can manage with how much my body shakes.

"After we parted ways last evening," he says to Eshe, letting go of me and continuing his pacing, "what happened?"

She's chewing on her knuckle, but at his question, pulls it out of her mouth and says with only the slightest tremor in her voice, "He escorted me back to my room. I gave him some trouble and . . ."

"And what?"

Eshe winces. "I threatened to eat both of his ears if he didn't let me attend the wedding."

Kaladen's pacing stops for just one heartbeat. Then he resumes. "He convinced you to go back to your room, then?"

"Eventually. He left after I closed the door, but didn't say where he was going."

I close my eyes, which only makes it harder to stop myself from imagining all the terrible ways last night could have gone.

"One of the witnesses must have intercepted him then." Kaladen stops pacing, and I look up. His tall silhouette cuts the morning light in half, and I wish we could rewind time just a little bit—just to the moment he'd nuzzled close to my face, teased me, and urged me to say his name.

"Which witness do you think it was?" I ask, getting to my feet and putting a few steps' distance between me and the corpse.

Kaladen lets out a wordless snarl under his breath. "I intend to find out. Today. Now."

"Now? How?"

"We're going to Valehaven."

"What's Valehaven?" I ask.

"The High King's Court. The witnesses will all be there."

"I'm coming," says Eshe.

"No, you're not," Kaladen and I both say at once.

"Will it be too conspicuous?" I ask, drumming my fingers nervously on my crossed arms. "They'll know why you're there. When was the last time you even went to the High King's Court?"

"What in the Great Desert is a High King?" asks Eshe.

"Doesn't matter," says Kaladen at the same time I say, "The fae king."

"Fae?" Eshe wrinkles her nose. "Like . . . djinn?"

"This is the only time visiting the High King wouldn't be conspicuous," Kaladen says to me, ignoring Eshe. "Because I have a new wife I haven't presented to the High King."

"You have to present me to the High King? Of the fae?" I sputter.

He cringes. "I . . . yes."

That's why he had special clothes made for me.

"I was going to take you later, after I'd finished . . ." He trails off, glancing around the palace hallway. "I need to reseal two more before we go."

I shoot a look at Eshe, who leans against the wall with her arms crossed over her chest. She's recovered from her shock, but the spark hasn't returned to her eye. It's disconcerting to see her so serious.

"Reseal whatever you need to," I say to the Neverseen King. "I don't want anything breaking open while we're gone."

He nods. "Get ready to leave. Have you eaten, Eshe?"

She shakes her head.

"Then I'll have the staff bring you something in Nadira's new room. And I will have them . . ." He swallows, seems to have to recollect himself. "I'll have the staff come and prepare Emin's body for burial. We will honor him when we return."

The dress Kaladen has ordered for me is nothing like anything I've worn before.

It's a rich, royal blue, floor-length gown with wide sleeves that fall to the skirt's hem. It isn't belted around the waist, falling naturally over my form, toning down the harsher lines of my shoulders and emphasizing softness and femininity. Orange crystals adorn the shoulders and bodice of the dress, forming a V shape down to my naval. The design motif echoes on the edges of my sleeves and the skirt's hem. It's beautiful. It's also rather striking—*and* very womanly.

He said I don't have to wear it if I don't want to, but after a moment of hesitation, I oblige. It seems too petty a thing to argue about with all that is happening right now. So I don the dress, curse the amount of beading, and murmur a word of thanks that the long sleeves and full skirts provide ample room to conceal my knives.

Eshe is uncharacteristically silent, sprawled on one of the settees in the main room of our chambers. Her eyes rove over the space, frowning at the mural of a nebula in a starry midnight sky on the ceiling. I cannot think of anything to break the silence, so I let it linger as I join her, sitting on the other end of the settee.

Eventually, she speaks. "Do you ever stop, look at your life, and wonder how in the Great Desert we ended up here?"

"Every day."

That pensive furrow remains between her eyes. "Where would I be if my mother hadn't been caught running from her owner? If I hadn't had to learn to pick pockets to survive?" Her mouth twists. "Where would I be if we hadn't run into each other that night?"

The foul memory of our first meeting returns, and I keep my posture upright and sharp. "You would have carried on, as strong as always."

She shakes her head. "No, I wouldn't have."

"You're the strongest person I know."

"Obviously," she retorts. The sparkle of her saucy confidence fades slightly. "Though, I think there just aren't that many strong people in the world."

I reach across the distance between us and clasp my hand in hers. The grip is familiar, warm, full of the strength we forged together.

"We've faced many things, separately and together. In the wild turns of fate, we found ourselves here. There is much we have lost along the way. People we've loved, parts of ourselves."

Eshe bows her head, squeezing her eyes shut.

"But this isn't the end," I say, my throat clenching and aching. "There is a future for us. What we gain will be all the more precious for what we've lost."

I don't know where these words come from. They don't feel like mine—like something I believe. They're wisps in the wind, promises of comfort that the harsh realities of the world will blow away.

And yet . . . I hope they're true.

We squeeze each other's hands at the same time. Eshe gives me a misty-eyed smile.

"Pretty words coming from you," she says dryly.

"I hope you don't want more; I think they were my entire lifetime reservoir of pretty words."

She rolls her eyes with a huff, a more genuine smile playing across her features. It quickly morphs into something devious. "Does the shadow freak have pretty words for you?"

Say my name, Nadira.

"When he does, they're usually sarcastic," I reply, hoping the heat in my cheeks doesn't give me away.

She arches an eyebrow at me, obviously unconvinced. With a forceful scoot, she closes the distance between us, sitting on her hands, and whispers, "*So,* how was last ni—"

A knock sounds on the door, and I try not to sound too desperate when I call for whoever it is to come in. A maid with puffy, red eyes enters, bearing a large, steaming tray of food. She bobs a curtsy without a word, sets down the tray, and leaves.

"Poor thing," Eshe says after the door closes. "The steward's loss must come as an enormous shock to the staff. Who knows just how much he did to make this palace run smoothly?"

Those words make something snap together in my brain. I shoot up, and, abandoning Eshe to her breakfast, chase after the maid. "Excuse me?" I call to her back as I shut the door to Kaladen's chambers behind me.

The girl turns, eyes a little wide as she sniffles. Is she afraid of me? Do all the staff members know about when I nearly choked another maid when I woke in a panic on my first day here?

I stop a good distance from her, not wanting to frighten her. "I'm . . . sorry," I begin, and curse myself for the awkwardness of the statement. "About Emin. You must be devastated."

Her shoulders drop—not in dejection, but a release of tension. A tear drips down her cheek, and she gives a single nod.

"I don't want to bother you," I say as gently as I can, "but when you have a moment, I'd be grateful if you—or another staff member—could give me a list of Emin's duties?"

Kaladen has enough to worry about. Maybe there are some small burdens I can take upon myself, so he isn't too overwhelmed by the loss of his right-hand man.

She nods again, a little more alertness coming into her eye. Perhaps she's glad for the small distraction. When I expect her to turn and leave, she instead opens her mouth. "H-he managed the household staff and took orders from the Neverseen King . . . so we didn't have to. He also tried to help with the kingdom's most pressing issues when the Neverseen King couldn't."

He was the one trying to resolve the kingdom's issues when Kaladen was occupied? Wouldn't that make him acting regent of Arbasa?

"Do you know where Emin used to conduct his work?" I ask, my mind already spinning. Maybe if I took care of these things, Kaladen can stay focused on the portals and preparing for Lulythinar.

"Yes, my lady! I could take you there. If you like."

My lady.

I nod once. "Lead the way."

CHAPTER 13

THE MOURNER

EMIN'S STUDY IS spotless. Not a speck of dust has collected on the neat, labeled piles of papers or the books on the shelves built into three walls. Light comes from the skylights, though there are candles throughout the room. A little cot is tucked into a corner, out of the way, perfectly made.

"Was this his bedroom, too?" I ask the servant girl before she leaves.

"Oh, no, my lady. He had a much nicer bedroom. He just kept the cot there for nights . . ." Her voice breaks, but she presses on. ". . . when he was working after dark and couldn't return to his room."

I thank the girl and she shuts the door, leaving me alone.

Unusual and ornamental as my dress is, it moves silently and easily, so I am not encumbered as I go to the shelves and read the labels.

Emin has volumes upon volumes of financial reports, both of the palace itself and of Arbasa. He has ledgers of staff members, their duties, their wages, the circumstances surrounding their hiring and, in some cases, their dismissal. He even has an entire manual on the running of the palace, down to the most minute detail.

"Sands, he was organized," I breathe, moving from the shelves to the stacks of paper and missives on his desk.

I find a tome filled with his precise handwriting, detailing every decision he made for Arbasa, his reasoning behind it, with accompanying dates. My respect for this man I hardly knew is the size of a mountain by the time I look up and realize from the slant of the sun that over an hour has passed.

Eshe would be disappointed in how engrossed I am in this detailed log of resourcing notes. Apparently, the steward knew all the best places to buy food and trade goods, varying by season. It's utterly fascinating.

"Found you," hums a deep voice from behind me.

My body reacts before I have a chance to think. I whirl, my knives out and slicing instinctively toward his neck. Both my blows are blocked, and my wrists snatched in an iron grip before I process that it's only Kaladen.

"You scared me!" I gasp, sagging in relief. He hasn't released my wrists, standing almost near enough for an embrace.

"I didn't think it was possible to sneak up on the Mourner."

I tug at my wrists. "Don't tease."

He doesn't let go—instead pulling me so we're almost chest to chest, him towering over me like a pillar of night. "I'm not teasing. I didn't mean to startle you."

He says it so forthright that I immediately know something's wrong. I trail my gaze up his chest to the shadows shrouding his face. "Kaladen?"

He steps forward, his leg brushing mine. I retreat by instinct—and hit the table behind us. I don't mean to gasp, but a tiny one escapes me. He takes another step, until he has the back of my legs pressed to the table, and he is almost flush with me.

Then he gives one last pull on my wrists, and the distance between us is gone.

My breath comes faster, the counter beat to the raging thump of his heart in the air.

He leans his head down toward mine. "Am I frightening you?"

"N-no." The denial is out by habit, and my grip on my knives goes sweaty. I can't bring myself to sheathe them, which is more telling than any words I manage. "I don't know."

"You frighten me," he whispers, so quietly I barely hear it. He leans more of his weight into me. "You frighten me more than anything else I've faced. And yet there is nothing I want more."

I shiver, his grip on me the only thing keeping me upright. "You don't want me," I say, though the words hardly make it past my lips. "You're just . . . tired."

He lets go of my wrists, but I don't have time to feel bereft. His hands slip around my waist, crushing me to his chest as he buries his face in my shoulder.

Rational thought flies out of the window, replaced by an overwhelming flood of sensation. Only my death grip on my knives keeps any part of my mind anchored to my body as his lips move against my shoulder.

"I *am* tired," he whispers. "So desperately exhausted." One of his arms unwinds from my waist, and his hand slides up to cup the back of my head, tugging it backward as he tilts his lips toward my ear. "I'm tired of fighting. I'm tired of loss. And I'm tired of resisting you."

With that, he presses a soft kiss to my jaw. My lashes flutter, my vision swimming in and out as though I'm drunk. "You n-need a nap."

"I need you," he insists against my neck.

"I promise to do what I can to—"

"Not your skills or your human blood. I need . . ." He trails off, his weight becoming heavier against me. "I need . . ."

"Kaladen?"

He slumps against me. And that quickly, my senses return. Dropping my knives in a clatter, I catch him with a loud "oof!", and with every ounce of my strength, carefully lower his enormous body to the ground.

Then I get on my knees beside him and run my hands over him, searching for any secret injury or a reopening of his recent wounds. Nothing.

It seems like he's overextended himself again.

That would explain the things he was saying. And . . . everything else.

My skin is hot and sticky as I hurry over to Emin's old cot and commandeer the head cushion and blanket. I'm still blinking away the memory of that one tiny, electrifying kiss as I drape the blanket across him—it doesn't cover his feet—and situate the cushion under his heavy head.

It's probably good for us to delay the journey to the High King's court.

I cast a glance at the sky above me, noting the angle of the sun. If worst comes to worst, I'll let him sleep and then wake him shortly before evening.

I pick up my knives and inspect their tips. The damage could be worse, but one of them now has a dent in the tip I'll probably never get out. I climb to my feet, resolving to continue looking through Emin's records. My knees still haven't steadied. My skin hasn't stopped tingling. And I'm not sure I'll ever be free of those words now rattling around in my head.

I want you.

THE NEVERSEEN KING

My eyes peel open slowly, painfully. Sunlight burns into my pupils, searing into my brain.

Ugh.

"You're awake!" comes Nadira's low-toned voice from somewhere above me. "I was afraid you'd sleep the whole day away and then I'd have to wake you up."

Sleep? What is she talking about? When—how did I . . .?

I'm covered by a blanket, my head propped up by something soft. A distinct scent tickles my nostrils.

Emin.

Everything hits me like a boulder. The horror of finding Emin's body. Spending all that healing energy trying to revive a dead man. Then going to reseal the worst of the portals and draining my already exhausted body to its dregs.

Searching the palace for Nadira.

Finding her here.

Pressing her against—

My eyes widen. A face comes into my view, hovering over mine with a concerned brow. What did I say to her? I don't even remember. I remember her closeness, though. I remember the kiss I gave her.

Horror pools in my stomach. What was I thinking, moving so quickly? Nadira needs time, space, not me practically forcing myself on her. She doesn't need proclamations of love. She needs to be shown, slowly and delicately.

"Are you alright?" she asks, her chin puckering. "You probably should rest more. It's only midafternoon."

Midafternoon? I push up on my elbow, and for a split second, my glamours fracture.

"Emin has many notes on the running of the palace. I was thinking Eshe and I could go over them and see what we can do to keep everything running smoothly," Nadira says, returning a book to its place on a shelf while I blink against the bright sunlight and yank my glamours back in place. *She didn't see*. I breathe a sigh of relief. "Not that Eshe is organized at all, but she's smart and eager to learn. Besides, it'll give her something to do. You have so much on your shoulders already, I figured this would be a way we could take some of the burden."

My eyes adjust slowly until I can stop wincing enough to look at her. At the beautiful, royal blue gown she wears with its brilliant gold accents. It would be lovely to just sit here on the floor and watch her move around the room, that little furrow between her eyes as she scans the contents of another book. The dress doesn't make a sound, just as I ordered. If I'm going to take her to Valehaven, she needs to be—

Valehaven.

Great Kings—*Valehaven!*

I shove to my feet in a burst of panic. "You said it was midafternoon? We should have left hours ago!"

Nadira swivels her attention toward me, lifting one eyebrow and appearing otherwise unphased as she slides the book she was reading back onto the shelf. "I didn't think it would be a good idea to go to the High King's court, weakened as you were. Are you feeling better?"

"I . . . do feel better," I admit with a grumble, trying to calm my racing heart. Sleeping—even just for a few hours—does wonders at rejuvenating my strength and my magic. Unfortunately, I don't have much time for it. Even without trips to wretched Valehaven.

"Good." She puts her back to the shelf, facing me. Her eyes arrest me, and I wonder—not for the first time—if she has any clue how forceful, striking, and beautiful they are. "Do you want to go today or tomorrow?"

"Today," I answer immediately, climbing to my feet. "Eldreth and the Eye are bound to leave Valehaven soon, maybe Yirmuth too."

The Wolf will also be in Valehaven.

I shake away the tightness that returns to my shoulders at the thought of his name. "Before we leave, you must tell me what the Eye of Baltor showed you."

She blinks in surprise before her gaze shifts away from me, her jaw tightening. "There were no images. It was a voice."

My muscles tense, my voice dropping. "What did the voice say?"

The question feels like a test of our relationship. To see if she trusts me enough to tell me, or if she will protect her secrets. I wait for her answer, running my eyes over her face, down to the nervous twitching of her hands, as if I can read exactly what she's thinking.

"He said he would bargain with me." Her voice is a low whisper, and if not for my fae senses, I wouldn't have heard what she says next. "For Eshe's immortality."

The air leaves my chest in a sudden gust. Mountains of Ildrid, I want to strangle the Eye.

"Does the Eye even have the power to grant that?" she scoffs. "I can only imagine how furious Eshe would be at me for securing such a thing for her. *Immortality is so boring,*" she mimics in her friend's tone.

She says it lightly—as if it's preposterous that the Eye could grant such a thing. "I'm afraid the Eye can, indeed, make Eshe immortal."

Her voice rises in pitch. "It can? And what would a feat like that cost?"

"Something you won't want to pay."

"I'm sure," she says, a bit too casually. As if she wants to continue scoffing at the idea, but maybe just a tiny part of her is intrigued.

She's a human. The extent of her experience with Faerie has been here, in my palace, where the rules are very, very different from the rest of Faerie. She doesn't know that the named price of a bargain is only a fraction of its cost. The bargains I have made with her are nothing—*nothing*—like the bargains other fae set up. I never tried to trick her or take advantage of her.

"It will cost you vastly more than you think," I say, endeavoring to snip any curiosity in the bud, "and the payoff is often a trick, anyway. You may think you're purchasing Eshe's immortality, but if you aren't careful with how you bargain, that eternal life may be as a rock—or a tree. Or youth might not be part of the bargain, so she ages like any regular human, until she is nothing but a bedridden shell racked with pain, and is never allowed the final rest of death. Whatever he offers you, no matter how good the prize and how small the price, you will regret that bargain until the day you die."

She shrugs. "That doesn't surprise me one bit. What else do I need to know before we get to Valehaven?"

"The first rule is to never, ever, under any circumstances, make a bargain with a fae."

She huffs. "So you have already made abundantly clear."

My lip twists. "Good."

CHAPTER 14

THE MOURNER

KALADEN TAKES ME to a door on the first floor of the palace, not far from the secret chamber we were married in yesterday. The door itself is made of carved oak, inlaid with gold filigree depicting an enormous tree with a root system even more expansive than its network of branches and leaves.

"When I present you to the High King," Kaladen says, casting a backward glance at me before drawing his shadows tighter around himself, "you won't have to say anything. I will do all the talking. And please do not take offense at anything I might say. I despise politics, but we both have too much to lose for me to disregard them."

I nod, but he doesn't see it. I miss having my belt of knives, and unease slithers down my spine every time I reach for their comforting hilts, only to find they're not there. Most of them are hidden in my floor-length sleeves and are still very accessible. It's just not what I'm used to.

Cold prickles beneath my skin, stirring in my gut.

Kaladen stops before the door, his hand inches away from the golden handle, as though he senses the tide of magic rising in me. "I wish we had an entire month to set aside for you learning to control your magic."

I wish we had an entire month for many things. With Lulythinar only a few weeks away, we have time for almost nothing.

"The High King will have heard of your power," Kaladen continues, dropping his voice. "It is better he doesn't see it, however. Better he sees you and forgets about you."

"I don't know how to stop it. When it comes, it just . . . *comes*."

He lets out a long, deep sigh. "I know. But one of these days, you'll learn how to call it and restrain it at will. When you do, you'll be formidable even to a fae warrior."

Is that . . . *pride* in his voice? Suddenly, beyond even my own motive to survive and protect the people I love, I desperately want to master this magic of mine.

I want Kaladen to be proud of me.

He continues, oblivious to the unexpected rush of energy inside me. "You should know something about magical suppression before we go. I've observed that your magic surges when you are afraid. This is logical, as it is part of your body's survival instinct. In order to control your magic, then, you must control your fear."

I lift an eyebrow. He might as well have commanded me to breathe underwater.

"Don't give me such a dubious expression. Something that greatly helps is for you to have a mental grounding. A place in your mind where you feel safe, calm, and relaxed."

I'm about to open my mouth to say that there is no place in my mind that I feel calm, but then I stop.

There *is* a place I have often retreated in my worst moments. It was not where I felt safe, but it was where I was in control, and it had never occurred to me to go there of my own volition. It had always just . . . happened.

"Did you think of something?"

"I . . . yes."

"Good. Now, think of something you're afraid of. Not your deepest fears. Just something that—"

He warns me too late. The image of Emin's dead body in that hallway assaults my mind's eye, but instead of Emin, it's Eshe. Her face contorted, blood pouring from multiple wounds.

Ice floods my entire body.

Fury and pain and deep, soul-wrenching—

"Easy, Nadira," Kaladen's sharp voice cuts through the sudden knife-sharp terror. "Go to that place in your mind. The safe place."

I'm sitting on my ragged quilt in my old prison-room. My knives are arrayed in a semicircle in front of me, my toe catching in one of the quilt's holes. I move my hands rhythmically, sharpening a blade on a wet pumice stone.

One, two, three, four, five.

It wasn't Eshe last night. She's fine. Kaladen has wards around her room. She's smart and capable.

Six, seven, eight, nine, ten.

The ice recedes, washing away from the cliff of my control. It doesn't vanish completely, but it's not at the tips of my fingers anymore, ready to explode into the world with torrential vengeance.

"Good," Kaladen whispers. His hand hovers at my back, not touching me, but near. Present. "Very good. If you are afraid while we are in Valehaven, return to that place in your mind. It's better the High King doesn't see the extent of your power. But also . . ." His voice changes, and darkness tints his tone. The darkness that I knew so well when he first brought me here. "If you need to use your powers to protect yourself, then use them. Use them, and do so without regret."

His intensity makes me swallow and my fingers twitch for my blades. "Is the High King our enemy?"

A grimness hovers around his cloaking shadows. "In a word, no."

So . . . basically, yes. "How are we going to find out who killed Emin?"

"I will ask."

"Won't they just lie?"

"They can't."

I blink, caught off-guard. "What?"

"Fae lies smell—and taste—like iron. If they lie to me, I'll know it."

"You've lied to me." It comes out as a statement, but it's really a question.

"Not exactly, no. But the fae rules are different for me. As the Neverseen King, living and working with such an enormous concentration of magic, I'm often outside its restrictions. I'm *part of* the magic that keeps Faerieland in balance."

I search for his gaze and find two pinpricks of light amid his pillar of darkness. "So, our suspects will truthfully deny or evade your questions."

"Some of them will evade even though they didn't do it, which will complicate things. Either way, we should be able to make progress."

"Anything else I need to know?" I ask as the Neverseen King's hand reaches for the golden knob once more.

"Don't let yourself be separated from me under any circumstances."

Then he turns the knob and opens the door.

The room beyond the door is dark. At first, I almost lose sight of Kaladen after the door closes behind us, shutting out the light of day beyond.

It's not completely dark, however, and my curiosity gets the better of me. I take several steps into the room, trying to discern what great, tall thing lies in the center and fills the arched ceiling.

Kaladen says nothing. He moves with the grace and confidence of a prowling lion, stalking to the center of the room. I pause, hesitating by habit. Then I continue forward, slower than Kaladen, but I don't stop until I'm at his side.

He pulls a knife from his person, and I startle. *Calm down,* I tell myself. *He isn't going to hurt you. You know that.* He cuts open his finger, and with a quick flick, sends a drop of blood flying to the ground beneath us.

It sparks when it lands. I hold my breath.

It starts as an ember, a small, glowing pinprick of light. Then it spreads like a liquid, golden spiderweb. Climbing across . . .

Tree roots.

The streams of gold grow, climbing upward, illuminating the massive trunk of the tree, and reach higher to its wilted, barren branches.

I step a little closer to Kaladen, my mouth open as the golden light spreads farther. It reveals the full height of the enormous tree—even bigger than I realized. We're dwarfed now, and I cannot tear my gaze away as I stare with a slackened jaw as the entire tree turns the color of a new day's sun.

Then the tree bursts forth leaves in a sudden, spectacular explosion of color. Sapling green morphs into a deeper, mature emerald. The branches darken from gold to garnet, though light still shines through every crevice in the bark.

I'm not sure when I slip my hands around Kaladen's arm. I become aware of it only when his biceps twitch, and I feel his gaze burning into the top of my head.

That's when I register exactly how close I am to him, and exactly how large and muscular this arm I'm clinging to is. With an undignified, wordless "Uhh!" I let go and force my hands to my sides. "I . . . Sorry."

He smiles at me.

It's the last thing I expect. There's no withdrawal from me, from my touch. It's only the tree's golden light reflecting off teeth, enough that I can just barely make out a pair of full lips stretched wide.

Every thought eddies from my mind.

"You can cling to my arm. I don't mind," he says, those lips twisting into a smirk.

"I didn't mean to," I say stupidly, wishing I had enough control over my magic to cool the flush of traitorous cheeks.

Leaves fall in a sparkling shower, and when they reach the ground, they turn to silver. Kaladen doesn't stop me when I give into my curiosity once more, bend down, and pick one up. It's pure silver, the detailing as fine as an eyelash, and is weightless in my hand. Vanilla perfume wafts from the tree's trunk, and I close my eyes, breathing deeply.

Kaladen's heart is a faint pulse at the edge of my awareness. It beats faster than normal. It brings me back from the distraction of the beauty before me, back to the reality of where we're going. What we must do. Is he afraid?

The tree's trunk twists, and its entire canopy of leaves twists with it, until a glow emerges from the center of the trunk.

"Is that the portal to Valehaven?" I ask.

Kaladen nods. Then, to my surprise, he bends down toward me. Hooks a knuckle under my chin and lifts my face toward his.

He's going to kiss me.

It's like lightning hits me—so unexpected, I don't know how to react, whether to pull away or lean in closer. In the end, I hold deathly still . . . as his lips ghost across my forehead. Barely there, and then gone.

"Stay at my side, my wife," he whispers, and it's a request—almost a *pleading*—instead of an order.

Perhaps it's the magic swirling around me like wind, tugging at my hair and ruffling my skirts. Maybe it's his almost-kiss and the tone of his request. Or maybe I'm just losing my head altogether, because I don't hesitate to accept his offered hand, and answer, "Always."

His fingers lace with mine. It's familiar and fresh all at once. It's *right*. The warmth of his hand, the roughness of his calluses, the strength of his grip—it weakens my knees and straightens my spine.

If Kaladen had picked any other moment to pull a golden circlet dripping with diamonds from his cloak, I would have balked. I would have utterly refused. After all, I'm nothing but an orphaned cutthroat. No part of me belongs on a throne.

But for some reason, in this second, despite my shock at seeing the crown, I don't protest. I don't fight.

I don't resist as the Neverseen King places the crown atop my head. It is a comforting weight, despite the monumental responsibility it represents.

His gaze meets mine, burning like sapphires. "Come, my queen. Let us face our enemies."

And find a murderer.

CHAPTER 15

THE MOURNER

VALEHAVEN, AS IT turns out, is a magnificent white palace set into a sheer, rocky cliff overlooking a vast sea.

It's nothing like Arbasa.

The air is warm, but far more temperate than the scorching sun of the desert. It tastes of salt and something else that tingles my tongue and tickles my nostrils.

Kaladen walks to my side over the rounded stones of the seashore. I peer up at him—and find him completely corporeal. It's almost startling to not have his outlines be made of shadow and dust. The charcoal gray tunic, the wide leather belt, the long, dark trousers, and tall black boots are all visible. Even so, his heavy black cloak swallows the sunlight. He wears a long pendant with a great crest hanging to his navel. Black gloves conceal his hands and the hue of his skin. I've always known he was a large man—larger than any human man I've ever known, both in height and sheer brawn—and yet I feel almost ridiculously mouse-like at his side now.

He wears a low hood and a wreath of shadows like a mask.

Not an inch of his face is visible.

I turn my back to him, fixing my gaze instead on the gardens spilling like waterfalls over the edge of the palace's many tiers. Maybe if I don't look at him, he won't sense my disappointment.

"Have you ever been outside the desert?" the Neverseen King asks.

I focus on the uneven terrain of large, smooth stones. This seems like a perfect place to roll an ankle. "No. Though I wouldn't say I've always lived *in* the desert. I've spent most of my life on the edge of one. Only when I was very young, and Jabir was training me, did I live in the desert."

It's clear to me now that Jabir took us there to keep me from running. And to keep others from hearing me scream.

I tuck away my shiver and, ignoring Kaladen's penetrating gaze, wince against the sun reflecting on the white palace. "Are we on the beach of a sea? Is the river saltwater too?" I follow him as he steps onto a long, sturdy bridge. One could lead a herd of camels across this thing, and it wouldn't break.

"The river is freshwater," he says, surprising me.

"All of it?" I stop where I am, halfway across the bridge, and peer down into the rushing water as it floods into the sea. If this was Arbasa, not a drop of this water would make it into the sea. We'd redirect it, use it to nourish our crops, wash our clothes, clean our streets.

But if we had this much water, Arbasa wouldn't be a desert, now would it?

"Of all the things I've shown you," Kaladen says, and there's a smile in his voice, "I think you might be most astounded by this river."

I roll my eyes and push off the railing of the bridge. We make it to the palace steps a moment later, and I'm struck by how *green* this place is. So very green and white. Plants seem to grow into the walls themselves, dripping over windowsills and the stairs. They're not low to the ground and thin like back in Arbasa—they're lush and brilliant, like I would imagine in a jungle.

Sensing Kaladen's attention on me once more, I grumble, "I'm not gawking."

He doesn't reply. Only smiles. Which is far worse than anything he could have said. I give a silent huff and force my gaze to focus on my feet. *There*. Now I'm *actually* not gawking.

My sense of ease is fleeting. The fragrant white flowers we pass seem to turn and follow us, as though they are hundreds of pale little eyes. I shift closer to Kaladen as we take a path skirting around the edge of the palace, climbing up stairs lined with more curious flowers and following uncovered walkways.

The first living thing we encounter is a guard—but at first I assume he's a statue. He stands as though carved from granite, his white, feathered wings tucked in close to his back. He wears a breastplate of gold, a contrast to his pale skin and hair. In one hand, he bears a mighty, terrifying spear—and probably many more weapons I cannot see. My knives seem suddenly like such a paltry protection.

But then again, I am the wife of the Neverseen King.

I'm just not used to depending on someone else for safety. I force my hands to my side, refusing to even touch my hidden knives. No matter how much my fingers itch for that comfort. I look instead to the large, gloved hand swinging at the Neverseen King's side, so close to mine.

Close enough I could reach out. Take it.

Instead, I let my attention travel up his strong arm, his broad shoulder. He walks purposefully, confidently, like someone who knows what he is capable of, and knows he has nothing to fear. If I didn't know him as well as I do, I would think he was, indeed, fearless.

He's still far more fearless than I am.

Maybe if I stand by his side long enough, part of that confidence will rub off on me.

Shouting pulls me from my musings and admiration of a well-muscled arm. I look up quickly, my body tensing.

"Seems like someone is having a grand time," Kaladen says dryly as we finish climbing a staircase and turn the corner. "The parties are usually just beginning now."

We stand at the entrance to a very green and very full lawn, punctuated by towering oaks that fade into a forest. Creatures in various shades of humanity are scattered across grass, lounging on blankets or in low-hanging branches. A dazzling array of colorful food and drink adorns the tables. More creatures—fae, I presume—dance in circles to strains of strange music. Music like nothing I've heard before.

The creatures vary dramatically from each other. Some are more humanoid than others, where the only giveaway is their height, tremendous beauty, and long, pointed ears. Others have goat's legs and horns and hair the color of a desert sunrise. Some have webbed fingers, gills flaring beneath their jawbones. Rat tails and butterfly wings.

I'm suddenly glad that this is my first time seeing a fae. I don't think I could have focused on fighting them as well if I was so stunned by how . . . *strange* many of them look. Or how beautiful others are.

I steal a glance at the Neverseen King and his shadows. He watches me—judges my reaction, maybe. Does he have gills and strange ears? Purple hair or gray skin? Or is he one of the beautiful ones? Perhaps he is both beautiful and strange.

Maybe that is why he wears those shadows.

I quickly look away, and am just in time to watch as a tall fae woman approaches us. Her focus is on the Neverseen King, with not even a single glance my way. She stops before us, and I have to force myself not to retreat a step or get my hand on the hilt of a knife.

"Here at last to present . . . *that* to the High King?" The fae woman shivers her delicate shoulders and tosses locks of glossy, moss green hair. Her eyes are long, sleek, with startlingly green irises, a deep blue mouth, and seaweed wrapped around her neck like a string of pearls.

"Yirmuth," Kaladen says, and I think he addresses her for my benefit. It wasn't necessary though, because I hadn't forgotten that low, silky voice. "I see you remember Queen Nadira of Arbasa. I must ask you a question."

She puckers her blue lips at the mention of my name, but steps closer to him. Her eyes search his, drop to the shadows where his mouth is, and lift once more. "Yes?"

Desperation doesn't look any better on fae than it does on humans. I realize I'm crinkling my nose and quickly pull my face back under control.

Kaladen doesn't move a muscle, and his tone is flat when he asks: "Did any of my servants speak to you while you were at the Bridge?"

"I'm certain none of them did. Why?"

"Did you see any of the other witnesses interacting with one of my servants?"

"If I did, I thought nothing of it. What's the matter, Kaladen? Is there any way I may be of aid to you?"

"I'll be sure to tell you if there is."

With that, Kaladen's hand lands in a barely-there touch on my elbow, guiding me away from that seaweed hair and blue lips. I might have been glad, except that he takes me deeper into the lawn of fae enjoying their drink and dances.

"I have some questions," I begin as we pass by a table of multicolored drinks. He takes one, and it fizzes as he lifts it to his lips. I take his grunt as permission to continue. "Is she in love with you?"

He immediately spits his drink out and sets into a fit of coughing.

"Are you alright?" I ask at once, my hand unconsciously landing on his forearm as he nods, clearing his throat.

He pulls his composure back under control, as if he didn't just water the lawn with something the color of a strawberry mixed with ocean water. "That's just how fae act. Both the men and women, with few exceptions."

"I do believe you just dodged a question."

Kaladen, who has been searching the greens, swivels his head down to me, and I don't need to see his face to know his brows just pulled together in a taut bundle. "That's"—he stops himself, gives an impatient huff, and deposits his empty glass on the nearest table—"I don't know how much of her attention is for show, and how much is honest. It is true she once endeavored to wed me, but in Faerie, that hardly equates to sentiment. It certainly had more to do with being the High King's nephew than anything."

"You're the High King's nephew?" I hiss under my breath, trying to stay quiet despite my shock. "You didn't mention—"

"It wasn't important. My current appointment is much more important than any royal blood I might have."

I step to one side as a bat-winged creature runs past me on all fours, a wild and wicked smile on his face. I don't relax until he's on the other side of the lawn, and I can finally collect my reply. "But could you have been High King? If he hadn't had an heir in Prince Trenian?"

The Neverseen King doesn't give the surrounding wildness a second glance. "Most definitely not! I would need to be a direct descendant to qualify for the throne. Now come, here's Eldreth."

"But I have more questions! Like why you didn't ask Yirmuth—"

"Eldreth!"

I don't see who he's calling to at first, because the group we're approaching has their backs turned to us, and I am searching for cloven hooves. What I find, instead of cloven hooves, are long, rich mantles. One fae in particular has a huge rack of horns protruding from his head. Long, silky black hair, and pointed ears. His royal blue mantle has an upturned collar embroidered with stars.

He steps out of the group and turns toward us. My breath catches in my lungs at his sheer magnificence. Without the antlers, the

Neverseen King is taller, but the antlers make Eldreth far taller than anyone else present. His face is narrow, long, with a sharp, disinterested gaze. His robes are elegant, shiny like silk but far thicker. When he takes a step, he doesn't move like a human, and peeking beneath those robes is the tip of a single cloven hoof.

He inclines his head toward us in a shallow nod—and I think he must have neck muscles of steel to support those antlers.

"You remember my queen, Nadira," says the Neverseen King, introducing me as if we are sipping qahwah on a hot afternoon. Am I supposed to bow? I blink twice, then offer a return nod. Eldreth's gaze drifts to me, and returns almost immediately to the Neverseen King.

He is far more magnificent than he sounded at our wedding. Darkness doesn't do him any favors, apparently.

"I remember," he says. "What is it you wish to discuss with me?"

"It is a matter of curiosity and some concern," the Neverseen King replies. "When you were at the Bridge, did any of my servants speak to you?"

Eldreth taps one finger on the stem of the glass he holds, then releases it. It breaks into a cloud of shimmering dust as it falls to the ground, which sinks into the earth—as if it never existed. My eyes bulge. He brushes his fingers together, as though to clean them. "I know what matter you speak of. It was not I who poisoned your steward, but I saw who did it. Get me three or four beautiful human girls—the more different the girls are from each other, the better—and I shall tell you what I saw."

Human girls? I barely remember to click my jaw shut so my mouth doesn't fall open in horror.

"Would three more be enough to satisfy you?" Kaladen asks, disgust heavy in his tone. My stomach revolts at what he implies.

Eldreth's mouth quirks in the first semblance of an expression. "You've been away from Valehaven too long if you believe satisfaction is what I crave. You've forgotten how good it feels to be ravenous."

That is enough for me. I don't want to hear another word out of this fae's lips.

"Very well," Kaladen says. Apparently, he is done, too. "Enjoy your evening. I will come to the Star City if I deem your bargain worth taking."

Then he's marching away, and I scramble to keep up with him. "You're not going to—"

"Of course I won't take his bargain. I hope you wouldn't think so little of me by now."

"Certainly not!" I say quickly. "I am merely surprised that you allow him his bargain. He has the information we need. Why not threaten to set one of your portals on his Star City if he doesn't comply?"

A surprised chuckle bursts from deep in his chest. "Sometimes I forget how bloodthirsty you can be."

"I'm not bloodthirsty!" I cry, indignant. "You're the bloodthirsty one, with all your dark and unsettling threats! I'm simply surprised that you use force and threats sometimes, but not here. Why not?"

He stops, pausing his search for who I assume is either the Eye of Baltor or Prince Trenian. "The Bridge is my domain. I am its master. To a certain extent, I can do whatever I please there, as can any Neverseen King before or after me. But we are no longer at the Bridge. I am not the master of all Faerieland, and should I endeavor to make myself as much—even in small ways—I will make an enemy of the High King. Which I am not inclined to do shortly before Lulythinar. So I will let Eldreth do as he pleases. I've gotten the information from him I wanted anyway: that he didn't do it."

Something prickles the back of my spine. Just before I'm about to turn, Kaladen's hand lands on my low back. His fingertips press into the fabric of my dress, and when I look up at him, the shadows around his face have darkened. My hands catch hold of air when I reach for my knives.

"Is this your lovely new human bride?" comes a voice that is both cheery and roughened. "Just in the nick of time, hmm?"

We both turn, and I don't miss how Kaladen's already protective grip turns possessive, wrapping around my waist and pulling me against his side.

In other circumstances, I might have reacted to his touch, whether to pull away or lean closer, whether to feel threatened or safe. Instead, my mind becomes fully occupied by the fae standing before me.

He's not big like Kaladen. In fact, he might be one of the first fae I've encountered that isn't especially tall. Still, there is no denying the strength cording his lean limbs, as if his body is made purely of tightly coiled muscles. Thick hair coats what I can see of his chest, arms, and the bare, clawed feet sticking out from beneath the long animal skin he wears. His face is just as hairy as the rest of him, though his beard is bushier rather than long, and it cannot hide the elongated canines protruding from between his thin, grinning lips. Or the yellow cat's eyes staring back at me.

"You must introduce me, Kaladen," says the fae, running his eyes over me in appreciation that I doubt is honest. Or perhaps he appreciates the dark skin of my bare throat.

"It has been some time, Wolf," Kaladen replies instead of introducing me. "Are you well these days?"

Wolf's smile only grows, the slits of his eyes dilating as he shifts them to Kaladen, and then back to me. "Oh, extremely well. Now, pretty girl, tell me your name."

I say nothing. My glare is enough of a response.

"Brr!" he says, chuckling. "The ice makes sense, doesn't it? So, where did you find this one? Does she know about the other one? Oh, I see she does! Did you tell her you have me to thank for finding the love of your life?"

Kaladen is stiff and unforgiving as iron beside me. It radiates through his side, in his hand still on my back.

"I know about his previous wife," I say coldly. Because I suspect he already knows, I answer his earlier questions. "My name is Nadira. He found me in one of the human cities."

Kaladen's hand tightens on my waist, and I can almost hear him growling: *You don't need to talk to him.*

I lean into his touch, just slightly. *I know.* My heart spikes when his thumb, resting on my back ribs, lightens and gives a subtle caress.

Wolf's eyes dilate once more. A short, goat-horned servant comes by, his hooves making soft *pats* on the grass. He carries a tray of golden fluted glasses on one hand. Wolf takes one, his attention never straying from me as he sips. "So, Nadira. Are you—"

"We must be going," Kaladen interjects.

"I'm having a conversation with the lady!" The Wolf gives a bright laugh, licking his drink off his sharp teeth. "Do you drag her off because you are frightened that I might charm her?"

At that, Kaladen actually smiles. "No. Charm doesn't work on this one."

Oh, doesn't it?

Stars and sands, I wish it didn't! My mind goes back to his breath on my cheek, his low voice in my ear. *"Say my name, Nadira."*

Wolf sniffs his drink, frowns. "This is cold." He looks up, flags down the servant who just served him. The little goat man comes quickly, bowing.

"How may I—" the man starts to say.

Wolf pounces. It happens so fast I wouldn't have been able to scream even if I wanted to. His face shifts to a long snout, and his long teeth rip out the servant's throat. Blue blood runs down Wolf's face as it morphs back into something more humanoid, and he grins while licking his teeth. "That's better."

Kaladen yanks me away, physically turning me so I cannot see the horror. My vision tunnels, blocking the death on its own. None of it helps, because that image is forever seared into my brain.

Kaladen's hand is on the back of my neck, his voice spinning around my ears like a swarm of flies. It takes me a minute to recognize the command in his voice, and another to register that he is telling me to breathe.

My lungs squeeze painfully. Am I not breathing at all? I try to obey, but it's not until his magic rushes into me like a balm that my chest fills and the panic subsides.

When I look up, there are no crowds of people gasping or staring in horror at the corpse behind me. Everything is as it was when we arrived. Fae mingling, eating, drinking, laughing, dancing. As if nothing happened.

I hate Faerie.

I hate Valehaven.

And I really hate Wolf.

"I will get you out of this," Kaladen is growling. "The moment after I present you to the High King, we're leav—"

"Jabir al-Risya."

The name rings out in the air, clear and rough. Piercing and serrating.

I stop in my tracks. Ice floods my body to my toes. I think of what Kaladen said earlier, about how I should go to the place in my mind where I can control the fear response of my ice.

I don't want to do that.

In this moment, I savor the burn of the cold as I turn around. As I lock eyes with Wolf. "How do you know that name?"

"Nadira," Kaladen growls, his warm hand hovering over my elbow, as though he considers dragging me away before I do something we'll both regret.

But I cannot think about Kaladen right now. I take another step toward Wolf, and I don't stop the ice that fills up my fingertips, ready to be released. "Answer me."

Blood drips out of the corner of Wolf's mouth as he grins. He is so very pleased to have my attention. "An old friend of mine. I heard he lived in the same part of the human lands as you did. Do you know him?"

He knows very well that I do. From the cruel tilt of his furry brow, he also knows exactly what my relationship with him was.

A hand wraps tightly around my elbow. I react, startling, and almost draw one of my hidden knives before his touch registers. It's Kaladen. He pulls me away from Wolf, not giving me the chance to respond, or unleash my ice on him. At first, I try to yank away.

Then his thumb gives me another soft stroke, even as his grip is unfaltering, and the blinding, frightened rage calms. He leads me out of the palace greens, up a grand staircase, into a palace of white marble.

There's no blood here. It's clean. White. With glowing statues, full of natural light, and vegetation spilling over railings and coiling around pillars. It soothes me enough to find my senses, to go to that place in my mind where I sharpen my knives, one by one, on a patchwork quilt.

"I assume it's no coincidence that he had your same surname?"

Kaladen's voice startles me out of my focus. It takes me a full minute to understand his question, and when I do, a pang hits my chest. My gaze shifts from a patch of small, pink flowers clothing a winged statue to the floor. To my silent slippers that peek out beneath my skirts with each step.

"I don't remember what mine was," I say, trying to keep my rising emotion out of it. *It was so long ago,* I tell myself. *You don't care anymore.*

I do, and nothing will convince me I don't. But the lie is soothing in its own way.

"I always knew my first name—that, I still have. The surname, though . . . Jabir made me take his. Truly, I forget it was his. It's been years since I've heard someone call him that."

We come to a halt in front of two great double doors. Silent guards stand at attention, their strange, shiny breastplates attest to the lack of battles they've been in. Or perhaps it's one of those fae glamours that keeps them so bright and spotless.

Kaladen glances back at me, and something potent swims in the darkness around his face. Is he afraid to take me to the High King?

Is he angry about Wolf and Jabir? Is he frustrated I almost lost control of my ice?

When he speaks, it's about none of those things. His voice is quiet, cognizant of where we are. "If you wanted it, you could have my name."

"I—what?" I stammer. Do fae treat surnames like humans do, where the wife takes her husband's name? I assumed they didn't, since Kaladen had never mentioned it.

The weight of his gaze, the unexpected softness that comes with it, roots me to the spot. I barely remember to follow when the guards open the doors and Kaladen strides inside.

"The Neverseen King!" the crier announces. The rabbit-faced fae looks at me, a little puzzled, until Kaladen nods at him. "Queen Nadira of Arbasa!"

Though Kaladen has repeatedly called me thus in the last hour, hearing the title from the lips of a stranger makes me wobbly on my feet. It feels so . . . *wrong*. I want to shudder away from the words. My crown turns heavy.

"High King Faradir," the Neverseen King booms, his powerful voice carrying through the vast throne room.

At the center of the marble room is a cut stream of rushing crystal water, a circle of pillars, and a throne on which sits a small sun. A golden sun with glowing skin, radiant blue eyes, and long, luminescent hair like liquid.

The High King's beauty rocks me like a blow. I don't want to look anywhere but at him, and yet there's something about his straight white teeth, revealed in a dazzling smile, that reminds me of a predator.

He's not the only person in the room, however. A sizeable gallery of what I imagine to be low-ranking fae and diplomats of all shapes and sizes fill much of the room. It's not them I notice, however. They might as well not be here, with their whispered murmurs of *"Neverseen King,"* and *"Queen Nadira of Arbasa."*

No, the person who snags my interest is the tall, dark-haired fae who leans against one of the pillars at the foot of the High King's throne. He wears a roguish smile, and light sparks in his cunning eyes. Every bit of his posture is irreverent, and I don't need Kaladen or the crier to know exactly who this is.

Beautiful as he is, with his sculpted face and glittering eyes, I think I like him even less in the daylight.

"Crown Prince Trenian," says the Neverseen King with a nod to the prince.

"Neverseen King," he replies with a smirk. "And the lovely Queen Nadira."

The High King leans back in his throne, his smile much less snake-like than that of his son's. And yet, somehow it is even more cruel. "It has been such a long while since we've had the honor of your presence, Neverseen King. I take it you've been busy?"

"You hope I have," Kaladen replies.

The High King's smile retracts a fraction. Ice stirs in my gut. As if sensing it, he turns his arresting gaze on me. "And you brought your new human wife. Queen Nadira. That is a pretty crown."

Is this the real reason the Neverseen King is required to present his human bride to the High King of the fae? So I can be paraded around, pointed at, and called adorable? So that I know I am so far beneath them?

I don't like Faerie. Don't like Valehaven. I'm beginning to think the only good-hearted fae in existence is Kaladen, and that he's only that way because he married a human woman and lived in her world.

Behind us, the crowd stirs. The crier announces: "The Wolf!"

I grind my teeth even as my scalp prickles. Why must he follow us? Can't he leave us alone? Or does he love the idea of tormenting me more about Jabir?

The Neverseen King lets out a quiet exhale that tells me what *his* thoughts are of this interruption. He doesn't step closer to me this time. Doesn't put his hand on my waist protectively. Maybe he is trying to avoid revealing his hand in front of the High King too much. Maybe it would be a liability for him to express too much concern for my safety.

Or maybe he's trying to tell the High King that I don't need protection.

Whatever the case, I try to keep my face under control, and when a chill tickles my skin at Wolf's approach, I try not to let it show.

He steps right next to me. I refuse to look at him, but in my periphery, I watch him turn to me and give a big, bloody-mouthed grin. "Neverseen King. Queen Nadira. High King Faradir. Prince Trenian."

"Ah yes, Wolf," the High King says with a wave of his fair hand. "I'm glad you're here. I sensed a few Bridge breaches the other night, Kaladen. Are you having trouble managing the Bridge? Should I appoint a substitute?"

"Appointing a new Neverseen King this close to Lulythinar would be a catastrophe, my liege," Kaladen replies with measured patience. Only slight threads of ire slip into his tone. "As you see, I have fresh blood to use now."

All eyes turn to me. Wolf's gaze is the hungriest, burning into the side of my face. I don't allow the faintest shred of emotion to be revealed in the creases and crevices of my features. So *this* was the sort of thing Kaladen warned me about beforehand. It almost makes me chuckle. I've been called so much worse than merely fresh blood.

"Well, if you ever find yourself getting overwhelmed, Wolf here can take your place." The High King's tilted head, his cocked eyebrow, all tell a different story from his pleasant words.

Don't cross me, or else I will make you pay, he is saying.

"I hope he knows how to contain Crenfyre," Kaladen replies coldly.

Prince Trenian grins where he stands, leaning against the pillar, thoroughly enjoying the scene playing out before him.

The High King narrows his eyes and shifts his attention to me. "Now, come closer, sweet girl. I want to get a good look at you."

Absolutely not, I want to snap back.

"I must admit, Kaladen, you have an eye for beauty. But what is wrong with her skin? It's all mottled around her jaw."

"Those are called scars, Father," says Prince Trenian brightly. "Humans have a lot of them."

"I know what a scar is," the High King snaps.

I just want to go home. My feet itch to put distance between me and every unfamiliar fae in this room.

The High King shifts his ire from his son to me, then back to Kaladen. "I do not know why you put up with such a flaw in a wife. There are plenty of humans without so many scars. Here, have her turn around for me."

Quiet fury laces Kaladen's voice, as though he is barely controlling himself. "I brought her here to present her, not for you to conduct an inspection of what is mine and scatter your ignorant opinions like seeds to be sown."

Oh, so he *isn't* controlling himself.

The room goes silent. Prince Trenian raises his brows, as though entertained by an interesting plot twist in a story.

Wolf's open-mouthed breathing quickens, like a predator excited to strike.

The High King smiles slowly. A smile that sends a tremor straight to my bones. "Ignorant, am I?"

The Neverseen King holds his ground, not wavering for a second. "Queen Nadira is suitable for the purpose I have for her. Her physical characteristics were not part of my consideration, nor should they have been."

Wolf chuckles, and steps forward to interject. I still pointedly keep my gaze fixed in front of me. "I must explain, Your Majesty. Kaladen here believes in a partnership between the Neverseen King and his human bride."

"It is better that way," growls Kaladen. "The magic is stronger, and the work is done faster."

"Eventually. But your lovely queen doesn't have experience with portal magic, correct? Which means there must be training. Your Excellency, I do believe the reason for the recent breakouts has to do with this process. It takes time for someone to learn portal magic, even longer for a human. The Bridge is less stable during this interval."

Wolf's words crawl up my spine like a spider with legs like knives.

"I take it you have a different philosophy?" the High King asks Wolf, leaning back in his throne.

Beside me, Kaladen is tense as a rod.

"Indeed, my lord. The human wife must be viewed as a commodity. She is only valued for her blood—and beauty. Should I have one, she would be well taken care of, her blood extracted, and her beauty there to be enjoyed as a reprieve from the hard work of managing the Bridge."

It suddenly hits me how terrifying of a position I could be in now if someone else besides Kaladen was the Neverseen King. How terrible things could be for Arbasa. Bile burns in my throat.

The High King gives an acknowledging nod, stroking his chin. His eyes shoot to Kaladen. "Dismiss your human. I wish to speak to you privately. Everyone—out!"

Chaos immediately ensues as the viewers in the gallery hurry into motion. Kaladen's voice rings out above the noise: "I will not dismiss her. She stays by my side."

Once more, everything in the throne room stills. I glance halfway to him, stopping before I draw too much attention to myself. *You don't need to protect me. I will be fine,* I wish to tell him. Even though it's a lie.

I don't want the High King to give the throne of my kingdom, of my people, to Wolf.

"You are insolent today," the High King muses with eerie calm. "I could have you killed for refusing me. Or I could give your position to someone worthier."

Wolf smiles.

The Neverseen King doesn't back down, even though I'm gnawing anxiously on the inside of my cheek. "If you wish to speak to me privately, I will oblige. My wife will remain at my side, but I can put a glamour on her, so she hears nothing. You must understand, however, that it would be foolish of me to let her out of my sight. And our conversation must be quick. I am needed back at the Bridge. Crenfyre is unraveling, and I would hate to see it break free across all Faerieland."

The High King's expression darkens at the mention of Crenfyre. Is the parasite that feared across all the worlds? It should be, but somehow, I didn't think names of particular portals would be well known among the fae.

Remembering that creeping white mist, the way it curled around Gaya and sucked her life out in a flash, fills me with dread.

The High King opens his mouth to reply—

But at that very moment, the entire throne room goes black as midnight.

Something cold and spiced clamps down over my mouth and nose. My body screams in sudden panic. Only a second later, my limbs turn to liquid, and I fall into the darkness.

CHAPTER 16

THE NEVERSEEN KING

THE SHEER MAGNITUDE of the magic momentarily blinds my senses. The darkness lasts only a few seconds, but those seconds are long, agonizing, where I frantically try to recover my bearings. *Nadira, Nadira, Nadira.*

The disorientation fades to an eardrum-exploding amount of screaming and shouting. The High King's roars of fury rise above the rest, yelling demands of his guards. His own light-filled glamours cut through the darkness first. They don't help as I grope through nothing, grabbing thin air in my search for Nadira. I don't stop, even though I know she's gone. That someone took her.

That someone planned this.

Whoever it is, I'll kill them. And if someone so much as leaves Nadira with a scratch, I will make them beg me to kill them.

Just as expected, Nadira is nowhere to be found. I scan the room for familiar faces, noting who is present and who isn't. It quickly becomes apparent that she is not the only person missing. There is one other very notable absence.

I break into a run, shove aside those in my way, and force my way past the guards out the door.

THE MOURNER

The first thing I'm aware of is my dry bottom lip. The second is that my hands are tied.

My senses return to me in a rush. I'm sitting in a chair, my ankles bound to either leg, my wrists bound behind the back of the chair. My head is foggy, my nose tingling with the aftereffects of whatever drug was used on me.

In front of me is a wide, wicked grin set in a handsome face. A silver circlet crown rests just above one cocked eyebrow.

"Good morning, lovely. I have a bargain for you," Prince Trenian says.

I can't get to my knives. I can't *move*. "No bargains," I croak.

"Easy there," the prince says, stepping toward me. I react, trying to jerk away from his outstretched hand. In the process, I nearly knock myself over. He catches the back of my chair, steadies me, and doesn't flinch when I bare my teeth at him. He dodges my feral attempts to bite and places two fingers at the base of my throat. Immediately, a wretched calm comes over me. I try to fight it, try to force myself to reject the magic.

It doesn't work.

I calm down. I breathe. And the ice I hadn't noticed rising inside me sinks back beneath the surface. My lips pull back in a furious snarl that he can control me so easily.

"I don't need you exploding on me," says the prince with another smirk. "As I was saying. A bargain—"

"No bargains!" With the forced calm I now have, I fiddle with the bonds, trying to discern what type of knot he used.

"It'll be mutually beneficial. I promise."

"I don't believe you."

"I cannot lie without consequence."

Which tells me he can and absolutely *does* lie. I take a minute to note the room we're in. It appears to be some sort of private quarters, with a comfortable living room for hosting—where I am tied up as a hostage. From this vantage point, I can make out what appears to be a dining room, set with a crystal chandelier, and a hallway that likely leads to a washroom, bedrooms, and so forth.

My wrists ache from the effort, but I forget the pain the moment I figure out which knot this is. Then the pain comes rushing back. I *hate* this knot. It'll take me a few minutes to get out of it. I must keep him distracted. "What do you want? Did you kill Emin?"

"Emin? The starched, boney-faced man with the pocket-watch?"

I narrow my brows at him.

Prince Trenian takes a coin out of his pocket. Tosses it up in the air. Catches it. Tosses it again. "I know who killed him. I'll tell you if you bargain with me."

My jaw clenches, both from irritation and from the tension shooting up my forearms as I work the rope. "What do you *want*?"

A sudden *bang!* resounds from the door. I crane my neck, trying to get a glimpse, but my chair is tilted too far away. Is that Kaladen? Or someone else? Hope wars with dread in my chest.

A mechanical break sounds. Prince Trenian lets out a sigh of long-suffering. "A pity. I'd hoped for more time for just the two of us. Do pardon me, my lady." He grabs the back of my chair, tilts it to its hind legs, and drags me away from the door. My stomach shoots into my throat.

Then everything stills as two deadly sharp knives press against me—one against my throat, the other at my heart. I freeze. My hands halt their progress on the knot.

The door breaks in a cloud of splintering dust. A darkened, furious silhouette fills the entrance. And immediately stops.

My breath is both shallow and heavy as the knives press harder, threatening the Neverseen King to come closer.

"Must you break the door like a wild animal? My servants will be furious with me." Prince Trenian tsks his tongue, his voice so very near my ear as he makes me his living shield. "Watch your step. I don't want to hurt her."

"Are you hurt?" the Neverseen King asks me, his dark gaze searching mine, running over my gown, my bound ankles, my heaving chest.

I dare not answer him.

Prince Trenian's knife slides up to my chin, tracing my jaw to my ear. "You can tell him, Queen Nadira. You can tell the Neverseen King you're not hurt."

I find my voice with difficulty. "I'm not hurt."

Shadow and living embers curl out from the Neverseen King. The heat of his fury billows across me, a contrast to the rising ice of my own, and still, I nearly panic from the flood of helplessness overtaking my blood, the tingling of my fingers and toes.

"I mean her no harm," the prince says, returning his knife to my throat. "I just want a bargain. I know who is working to overthrow you. I know who killed Emin. And . . . well, I have your pretty wife. All good reasons to bargain with me, no?"

"What do you want?" Kaladen demands.

"A favor. From you. To be redeemed at any time and any place of my choosing."

"Do you even know what you're asking for?" Kaladen snarls, stepping closer.

Trenian responds, pressing the knives sharper against my skin. "Of course I know what I'm asking for. You know the High King will kill me the moment I have a son to replace me as heir."

"Is this about a woman? A woman you're pining for and need a bargaining chip against the High King to have?"

Trenian's dry chuckle grates against my ear. "Wouldn't that be nice? But no, dear cousin. Rather, the opposite. I'm trying to avoid such a disaster. And to do so, I need collateral. So, which will it be? The information you've come to find, and your sweet wife, or—"

The frozen lake inside me surges like a tidal wave. My back arches under the sudden strain. Trenian drops one knife, presses his fingers quickly to my throat, even as Kaladen demands: "Breathe, Nadira!"

It's like trying to swallow against the urge to vomit. I'm losing, losing—and then suddenly it recedes.

I gasp, my eyes watering.

"Or you can give up your favor," Trenian finishes. The crinkling of his wicked smile sounds in my ear. As if I didn't just nearly kill us all. "Your choice."

The Neverseen King is quiet for several long minutes. Minutes where I throw caution to the wind and resume—oh so carefully—trying to undo my bonds. If I can get myself out of this position, Kaladen won't have to bargain at all. He won't have to give up something that could be used against him. So I hurry, even as I try not to let my movements give me away to Trenian.

"Tell us who killed Emin now, Prince Trenian," the Neverseen King says finally. "Or I might just let Crenfyre loose on Valehaven for a few hours."

"She has the answer in her pocket," Trenian replies glibly. "The ink will only show up in the light of the human sun."

I reach the worst part of getting out of these bonds quickly. The part where I have to dislocate a finger. I take a deep breath in through my teeth. Can I do this without crying out?

Just as I brace myself, Kaladen's voice drops to a low seethe. "And why, pray, would you want me to be so far away when I found out who killed Emin?"

"Maybe she knows," Trenian replies, smirking.

Kaladen takes several aggressive steps forward. "*You* killed him! It was you, wasn't it?"

"Stay where you are!" Trenian barks. His knife presses against my jugular, sharp and threatening. "Don't make me hurt her."

"You are a coward, hiding behind a woman."

"I know the rules of the game, Kaladen. It appears you've forgotten them in your time away from Valehaven."

Enough. With a quick jerk on my bonds at a gruesome angle, pain rips up my finger, up my arm. A sharp, short cry bursts through my lips.

That's when the world turns blinding white with magic.

CHAPTER 17

THE NEVERSEEN KING

I HAVEN'T SEEN this version of Prince Trenian before. The Trenian I knew as a boy wasn't like this. Yes, he was a mischievous troublemaker, too smart for his own good, but he never betrayed me. Not like this.

I want to call his bluff. I'll not let him hold his knife to Nadira's throat while keeping her bound—bound like Jabir had. Part of me hesitates, insisting I don't know this version of Trenian. Maybe he *will* hurt my wife.

But then she cries out, and I cannot hold back any longer.

I launch myself at Trenian. He reacts, shoving aside Nadira's chair as he flings up an arm, shooting a glowing ball of magic from his palm. I counter with my own, and they meet in an explosion of light and force.

When the light settles into a shower of sparks, Nadira has freed herself from the chair and runs past me, out of the way.

Good, clever girl.

"I had orders!" Trenian shouts over the ruckus. "From the High King. He got the idea from the Wolf. It was a test to see how well you could control the Bridge!"

"A test?" I roar, stalking toward my cousin in his crowded living room. "Haven't the last two hundred years been test enough?"

Both our hands are upraised, ready to hurl magic again, but neither of us attacks yet as we circle one another. Trenian's brow hardens, burning away his perpetual cavalier smirk. "I told you; it is the Wolf trying to undermine you. He's been doing it your entire reign, but these last few years, with your increased number of breakouts, the High King has finally been listening to him."

I tighten my fist and take two aggressive steps forward. "You are just a victim, then? Just a loyal son carrying out his father's despicable orders? Murdering my good steward, kidnapping my wife?"

"The High King had nothing to do with me kidnapping your wife." Trenian, backed into a corner, lifts one side of his mouth as his eyes darken. "I may have been ordered to kill your steward, but I enjoyed it."

The sudden, almost overwhelming stench of iron assaults me. Trenian barely reacts, as though he's desensitized to the taste of his own lies.

"Liar," I snarl.

I rush forward, grabbing his wrist and a shoulder as I slam him backward into the wall, tipping over furniture. The chair Nadira was tied to crashes to the floor, breaks a leg. My face is only a few inches from Trenian's.

"You're wasting your time with me," he growls, barely fighting back. "All I want is your debt. I want to know that if I need your power to help me get my throne, I can have it."

"It's unfortunate you lost your bargaining chip. You underestimated my wife."

"A mistake I will not make again."

"You will not touch her again, or lift a finger toward her in harm."

"I'm not your enemy," he says, his bright eyes sharpening, narrowing.

I let out a dry, brittle scoff.

"I'm *not*," he insists. "Focus on the people who want you and your wife dead. People like the Wolf who are determined to turn those in high places against you."

"I will deal with them. After I deal with you."

Trenian, lax in my grip, shifts his gaze from me to behind me. If he's about to trick me to get Nadira back in his power to force me to bargain with him—

"You might want to turn around," he says, turning up one brow. I'm not about to fall for his tricks. "Since you smashed my door, there is nothing keeping the riffraff from entering. Someone is about to bargain her soul away to the Eye of Baltor."

That makes me release him. I whirl on my heel, spring across the room.

Because he's telling the truth.

There, by the doorway, is Nadira in her beautiful fae-styled gown, speaking to a hunched creature covered in tattered cloaks, with only a long, thin ghastly nose protruding from its hood. It says something in its creaky, ageless voice that I cannot discern.

"My magic in exchange for Eshe's immortality?" she says, eyebrows rising in surprise.

"No bargains!" I roar.

"I wasn't going to!" Nadira cries.

The Eye's voice rises above the din. "A strand of your hair, Queen Nadira, in exchange for your true surname!"

Nadira flinches. Her attention shoots back to the Eye—just before I rip her away from the Eye, and put myself between them, as if distance will prevent her from making the worst decision in her life thus far.

"I wasn't going to!" she insists again. Is she angry at *me*?

"You were tempted!" I shoot back. "Don't lie to me. I know that look on your face."

She takes a step back from me. That's when I realize she's cradling her left hand close to her. She quickly shifts it to her side, the hurt in her expression shifting into an ice-cold mask.

"We're leaving," I say, and even though I know she doesn't want me to touch her, I need to keep track of her so no one tries to kidnap her again. I rest two fingers between her shoulder blades, trying to keep my touch light—even though I'd rather scoop her up and carry her all the way home—and guide her back out of Trenian's chambers.

"We can still bargain," he calls out after me, a dark smirk twisting his voice mischievously.

"Be glad you're the High King's heir and I cannot avenge either my steward's death or your treatment of my wife like I want to," I snap back at him.

Nadira looks back at where he leans against the wall amid the wreckage of his living room, his arms crossed over his chest as he quips, "Oh, I am glad indeed."

I've had enough of his cocky, self-assured voice today.

We leave Valehaven just as the sun is setting. My mind is a whirling, reeling mess as we take the portal back to Arbasa. Nadira is silent, but the swift thump of her heartbeat in my ears tells me how rattled she is.

I want to reach out to her, to apologize for snapping at her, to ask if she's alright. Yet every time I open my mouth, nothing comes out. It's like the wind has swept away my voice, carried it away across the ocean's tides.

I told you, I want to say as we return to Arbasa, and the evening light casts shadows in the hallways. *I told you that you shouldn't marry me.*

The thought of making rounds tonight exhausts me. Each night is so important, but I'd rather Nadira rest after today. Besides, I just *know* the magic will find both of us more misbalanced tonight than usual. I don't want her to have to endure another flashback.

As shadows darken around us, I steal a glance at her walking beside me. She thinks I'm not looking, and I catch her flexing her hand a few times.

"Is your hand hurt?" I ask, breaking the silence.

She slips it back to her side. She looks up at me, but before her eyes quite meet mine, she glances away again, looking forward. "It's fine. I dislocated one of my fingers to get out of the bonds, but I popped it back into the socket. The pain will go away soon. I had to act fast to keep you from making that bargain."

I shouldn't be surprised anymore, but the shock flares bright and red. She did that to herself to protect me? To think that she could be tied to a chair, likely half out of her mind in fear, with an enemy's blade at her throat, and she was concerned about *me*.

Wordlessly, I stop in the hallway and take her hand. Gently, so as not to hurt her. She starts to pull back, opens her mouth to protest. As though to tell me this isn't worth the drain of my healing magic. I tighten my grip, just enough that she cannot withdraw. She looks up with her big dark eyes and meets my gaze.

I return my attention to her hand in mine, the swollen joint, the calluses of her palm. When I send my awareness into her hand, I find strained tendons and ligaments. Reaching into the part of me that is connected to the Bridge, the incredible well of magic, I siphon it through myself, filling her hand up with it, speeding up the healing. Reknitting tissue, soothing inflammation, aligning the bone and tendons.

It's a small wound to heal. There is little strain, and it won't keep me from working tonight as I should.

Our eyes meet once more, and the dying sunlight streaming through the designs in the architecture cast the outline of a star on her forehead. Her heart beats faster. I haven't let go of her hand. I don't want to. Maybe I won't. Maybe, instead . . .

Slowly, I lift her hand. Her pulse is a pounding rhythm in my ears, increasing with each second. It's electrifying to hear how I affect her. It emboldens me to bow my head, to not look away as I bring her knuckles to my lips and press a kiss to them.

She lets out an involuntary shiver, averting her attention, and slips her hand out of mine. Her heart doesn't slow a fraction. Will she draw back if I take a step closer to her?

"Kaladen," she says, still not looking at me. That is how I like my name on her lips: breathy, soft.

"I'm sorry for what I said in Valehaven," I whisper. "It was cruel of me."

She swallows, shaking her head. I want to catch her chin, tilt her face up to mine so I can better read the complex layers of emotion flashing across her features. But I don't. I wait for her to speak.

"None of them wore shadows," she says at last, her voice so soft I can barely discern the words. At first, I'm puzzled, unsure what she means. Then she clarifies: "I saw their faces, Kaladen."

Everything in me goes still.

"Why do you still hide from me?" Her pleading is soft, and that makes it so much worse. "After everything?"

The stillness after her question swells like a brewing storm, and search as I might, I can find no answer to give her.

The truth is, I'm afraid. No matter how much I try to protect Nadira, to draw her out of her shell, to care for her like she deserves, I carry my own scars. I want to be completely open with her. I don't want to be hindered by fear.

But I have worn these shadows for almost two hundred years. In that time, the only person who saw my face was Liliana. And she died—as Nadira might.

Nadira nods slowly, her throat bobbing up and down. Her voice cracks. "I'm going to go see Eshe." She turns and heads down the hallway to the room that used to be hers.

I hate myself for letting her go. I hate that I cannot give her an answer, or even an apology.

As she reaches the banister, I almost call after her to tell her to be back in my room by nightfall. But I clench my jaw, biting back the words. She knows the risk. And if she doesn't want to spend the night with me, I won't force her to.

Either she will be in my room before nightfall, or she won't. I must simply wait . . . and hope.

Despite everything.

CHAPTER 18

THE MOURNER

"YOU'RE FINALLY BACK!" Eshe cries, throwing herself into my arms the second I open her door. "I have been bored out of my wits with nothing but a tremendous amount of food to keep me company! Ooh, what a pretty crown! Tell the shadow freak I want one, too."

I smile, disentangling myself to shut the door. The evening sun is sinking into the horizon—counting down the seconds until I must either return to Kaladen . . . or stay here. "Then you got enough to eat?"

"I'll say! Come, I couldn't even finish my supper. You should eat the rest; from the looks of it you haven't had a moment to spare."

The smell of roasted meat and fragrant rice fills my nostrils, my empty belly reminds me I haven't eaten anything since breakfast.

"I'm not hungry," I tell her honestly. "But I must speak with you before I have to go back. I need your help with something."

She plops down on the settee near her tray of food and nibbles on a pistachio as I speak. "What is it?"

I sit down across from her. When my hand finds the armrest, I'm forced to be grateful for the healing the Neverseen King provided me. Popping my finger back into its socket was even more painful than dislocating it, but no one was paying attention to me while the prince and the Neverseen King were fighting. Not at first, at least.

Give me your magic.

That ageless voice crawls down my back like an army of sand beetles. I look at my friend, with her crooked teeth, rosy cheeks, and the beautiful sun-bleached highlights in her hair. Guilt gnaws at the base of my neck, that I was far more tempted by finding out my lost surname than I was by protecting Eshe. I know Kaladen was right that it would be a trick in some way or another, but it certainly didn't seem like anything could go wrong with the second bargain.

I'm sure the Neverseen King is right. In some way, shape, or form, I would have regretted either bargain. Despite whatever my face said, despite how much part of me wanted to take the bargain, I *wasn't* going to. I still won't.

Though the second one seemed very harmless.

Still, for all our fights, I trust that Kaladen cares about me and knows more about the ways of the fae than I do. Maybe I *shouldn't* trust him, but I do.

"With Emin gone," I begin, "this palace needs to be taken care of so things run smoothly. He has been the one ruling Arbasa in the absence of the Neverseen King."

She cocks her head to one side. "Are you asking *me* to rule Arbasa?"

"Well, not by yourself. I'm asking if you will help me carry these responsibilities."

She leans forward on the settee, a piece of flatbread sticking out between her teeth. "A couple of street urchins are going to run this kingdom? I am *so* excited!"

I laugh, surprised by her reaction. "What makes you so excited? It's not as though you love the topics of trade and tariffs."

"We can finally do something about the orphans! And the city guard!" She shoves to her feet, cheeks rosy, hair blowing around her face from a breeze whistling through the open window. "We'll create something for the children. A way for them to be safe and their bellies full when they go to sleep at night."

"The coffers are running low. How are we supposed to feed and protect hundreds of orphans—of all ages—this close to Lulythinar?" The boy Abbi's too-large ears flash through my mind. Zara's thin, weakened frame and the haunted darkness in her eye. There are so many besides them. "I also want to help them, but—"

"You wouldn't do it all on charity. We'll give them work. Easy work for the younger ones, harder work for the older. *Some* of it would have to be charity, because I'm sure not all of them are capable of working. But most of them are able-bodied, and with regular meals they'd be strong."

I nod, still frowning. "But no one will hire them. Are we supposed to make a law that tradesman and craftsman must hire any street urchin that comes knocking?"

She drops herself back onto the settee, propping her jaw on her fist. "*We* could hire them?"

"To do what? What can they do?" Anything we do will have a cascade of consequences, and I want to make sure that what we do will *actually* benefit the orphans. There are the gangs to consider, the varying physical abilities of the orphans. We cannot have the stronger turning on the weaker, robbing them of their money. We cannot have them dependent on me and Eshe, such that if something happened to us, things would slide back to how they are now.

"We'll think of something. A way for them to get food. A way to keep them safe. And we'll need accountability for the city guard."

The sun is dangerously low on the horizon. I nod as I rise. "I'll think, and do some research. You keep thinking, too."

She leaps out of the settee. "I won't do anything *but* think!"

I laugh as she kisses me on either cheek, and we share a quick embrace before I hurry out the door, glancing at the lowering sun every few seconds.

I greet the banister with a gentle touch and a soft, "Hello, my friend."

It replies: *Hello, my friend. Didn't I tell you I'd come back?*

I laugh. "Well, technically I came back, not you, but I'm sure if you had legs, you would come to me often."

You would come to me often?

"Of course," I reply, and give it a long, good scratch before time forces me to say goodbye. My heart picks up a staccato rhythm as I hurry back to the Neverseen King's room. I'd rather stay with Eshe. I don't want to go back to him right now, with the strangeness between us.

But I refuse to abandon my responsibilities.

The shadows are long and sinuous when I reach his door. I reach for the handle. My fingers stop, hovering just above the cool metal. I close my eyes, take a deep inhale. Then I grasp the handle, open the door, and slip inside.

I freeze on the threshold, barely remembering to close the door behind me.

Because sitting there on his own settee, staring at me, still wreathed in shadows, is the Neverseen King.

Why do I feel like I'm in trouble?

"I didn't think you'd come," he says.

I didn't want to. I decide to keep that thought to myself. Instead, I walk past him, take the lopsided crown off my head and set it on the table beside him. It clatters. Then I make my way to the washroom. "I know my duties. Do you mind if I wash first?"

"Go ahead," he replies, and there is something in his voice I cannot unravel.

I feel as though I should respond. A thank you? My tongue catches in my mouth, so I simply enter the washroom without a word and shut the door behind me.

Back in my regular clothes, with my knives all in their proper place, I brace myself to return to the bedroom.

I never should have mentioned the shadows to the Neverseen King. He's made it clear how things are between us, even if it often seems like he forgets the boundaries himself. Things between us will only be awkward if I make them so. I'll pretend everything is business as usual. I can handle that.

Lifting my chin, I walk briskly out into the main rooms and zip straight to the bedroom. My determination falters at the sight of that grand bed, the softly glowing lumiral globes. But no, I refuse to let it get the best of me. I march to my side of the bed, peel back the covers, and, after kicking off my slippers, slide beneath them.

He's still in the main living area.

He might be too far away for the magic to work if I fall asleep now, but if he is, he can wake me up and we'll start afresh.

"Goodnight!" I call, mustering as bright of a tone as I can.

"Have you eaten?"

My stomach clenches. I cannot stand the thought of food. "I ate with Eshe," I lie, and pull the covers up to my chin. Every inch of my body is tense. I'm not sure what I'm waiting for, what I'm bracing against.

Sleep is impossible to find.

Eventually, the soft swish of the Neverseen King's robes reaches my ears. He shuts the bedroom door, and I shut my eyes, even though he must know I'm not asleep.

He climbs into bed beside me. My heart flies to my throat as the mattress dips and rises with his adjustments. Then he goes still, his pulse a harmony to mine in the quiet chamber.

"Nadira," he whispers.

So much for *business as usual*. My shuddering breath is my only reply. My throat is too thick to construct even a single word.

"I will show you my face," he says softly, gently. "But I do not feel ready yet. I am still fighting to overcome my own demons. I do not mean to shut you out. I ask only for your patience, as I endeavor to give you mine."

I want to begrudge him his answer, but search as I might for anger, I find only understanding. Do I not also withhold pieces of myself from him? Did he not say that was how things would be between us?

I debate saying nothing and holding still. But there is this growing urge inside of me that I cannot suppress. I roll over, toward him—and find him shockingly close. Immediately, I suck in a quiet breath and nearly lose my courage. The twin pinpricks of light where his eyes are arrest me so suddenly I forget what I was going to say. It was going to be something much prettier than the awkward, "Very well," that escapes me now.

"Your crown suited you today," he says, and the sound of his voice confirms he's smiling just a little bit. "You were clever with the bonds."

I roll my eyes, but my cheeks still heat. "I learned how to dislocate a finger to get out of bonds quickly. Jabir hated it. He would make me start over if I did it because he wanted me to undo the knots themselves, not cheat."

"Sometimes a quick cheat is the difference between life and death. Or freedom and a binding bargain. Though I'd rather you didn't hurt yourself like that in the future if it can be avoided."

"Why would I avoid it when I have a husband who can heal it?"

He goes quiet suddenly, and if I didn't know better, I'd think he was the one flushing now. Sometimes I forget how satisfying it is to put him off balance, like he so often strives to do with me. Was it the word *husband* that did it?

"Why?" he answers, at last. "Because I don't like seeing you in pain."

With that and nothing more, he turns over, his back a great wall between us. But it doesn't feel like he's shutting me out. I'm almost tempted to slide closer, to see what he would do if I touched his back, if I laid my palm between his shoulder blades.

I blush at the thought and quickly turn over so I don't give that impulse any opportunities.

CHAPTER 19

THE MOURNER

THIS CONTINUES TO be very strange to me—the way I fall asleep and then almost instantly wake up again. While still being asleep.

"How do you feel?" Kaladen's deep voice almost startles me.

I swallow, rub my arm. "Fine. Cold."

The pace of his footsteps toward me sounds almost concerned. "Is your magic swelling?"

"I . . . no, no, I don't think so."

"Is this better?" His voice is behind me, very near and very low. I'm not sure what he means until his hand lands on my shoulder. He gives me a single tug, pulling me so my back rests against his chest.

I'm so surprised, I barely keep myself from leaping away. His warmth washes over me like a hot wind in the desert. I both desperately want to stay and cannot bear to.

"I'm warm now." It comes out high and squeaky, but it's true.

"Good," he says, squeezing my shoulders, and turns to leave our chamber.

I follow, the heat of my skin scalding into my bones. "What are we doing tonight?"

"If the magic behaves, you'll make your first seal tonight."

"Should I be nervous?"

He glances back at me. "If you'd like to be."

"I forget sometimes how hard it can be to get a straight answer out of you."

"It's the fae blood, I'm afraid."

I learned a lot about fae blood today. "Do we have to go back to Valehaven?"

"Someday, perhaps. If I had any say, then never."

That sounds good to me.

Shortly, we reach the hallway of rainbows with its dazzling array of colors. I cannot help slowing down just slightly, marveling at how wondrous it is. I wish I could take a glass jar and scoop up the swirling colors to keep close to me. To remind me in the darker moments that there is such beauty in the world.

Kaladen's keeps his brisk pace. "There are several seals close to breaking down. One is down this hallway. If you are ready, I'd like to try using your blood tonight."

"You can have as much as you want," I say absently, only to realize a second later what I've said and add hurriedly: "within reason, of course."

It sounds like he's holding back a chuckle when he replies, "Of course."

He stops in front of a door with a dull, crumbling seal. The door itself, though hard to distinguish from its radiant glow, is dark, as though covered in a thick paint. I squint to get a closer look at it, but just then, the seal flares like an ember and blackens around the edges.

"This is the Olata Portal," Kaladen says. "The part of Olata we will be entering is a swamp and—"

"We're *entering* the portals?"

"Not for long. Ten paces from the portal is the anchor. We need something from around that anchor—it doesn't matter what; it could be a blade of grass or a rock or dirt—to pair with the blood to reseal the portal."

"Ten paces . . ." I muse aloud, tilting my head to one side. "So how long it takes depends on what is on the other side of the portal. And if they want us dead."

He taps his temple, grinning. "Smart girl."

"How do you close Crenfyre then?"

"Crenfyre . . . is a challenge. A challenge for another night. Olata is not a terribly difficult seal, but it is dark and swampy. Sometimes there are snakes."

"Snakes?" I cry.

"Don't worry, they can't kill you if you're in the dream realm. If you get bitten, it'll sting, but the moment we leave the dream realm, you won't feel a thing."

I edge back a step. "You are incredibly nonchalant about this."

"I promise it sounds more frightening than it is." The jewel-like glimmers of his eyes wink at me. "There's a reason I wanted Arbasa's most notorious assassin at my side. Now, get ready."

I grab hold of his elbow frantically. "Wait! What am I supposed to do? Do I find the anchor?"

"I'll find the anchor for this one. You'll stand guard at the door and make sure nothing tries to get through the portal. And then you'll seal it with your blood."

"I'm not sure I'm ready for this."

"Of course you are! Now, get ready in three, two—"

"Kaladen!"

"—one!"

He throws open the door and runs inside. Not wanting to be left alone, I dive after him, my grip on his sleeve the one thing keeping us connected as pitch blackness swallows us whole.

"You said it was dark!" I hiss. My feet sink into something sludgy and gluey. Disgust shivers my shoulders. I tense, my legs prickling with the expectation of a stinging, painful snake bite at any second.

"Yes? Is this not dark to you?"

"You didn't say it was like drowning in ink!"

His only reply before he pulls free of my fisted grip on his sleeve is an easy, "You'll get used to it."

My jaw falls open. "I'm going to murder you!"

His voice sounds from further away as he replies, "Best keep quiet. The snakes love two things: light and sound."

I clamp my mouth shut, silently fuming as I pry my eyes open wider to catch any speck of light. At some point, I grabbed my knives. They are a comforting weight in my palms as I stand beside the closed door—which I've already lost in the darkness. I wriggle my toes, shiver again as globby goo holds them prisoner.

What a horrible portal.

Suddenly, a pinprick of light cuts through the heavy darkness. It's straight ahead of me, glowing a soft, eerie green.

"This is the anchor!" Kaladen calls. "Usually it's partially buried, like this one. Now, get your blood ready because—Great Kings, that was fast!"

The light winks out, but not before a sharp movement throws a sinuous creature back into the darkness. All the breath steals from my lungs as I choke back a gasp.

"Get ready!" Kaladen's voice comes hurrying toward me, little grunts punctuating the squelching of each footstep. But that isn't the only sound coming toward me. Low, softer noises come from the ground, like something gliding through muck.

I bite my tongue to keep from letting a single sound out of my mouth. Quickly, I swipe my blade against my thumb and try to take a step backward.

That's when I realize in a horrifying moment of clarity that all this time, I've been sinking into the mire.

"Kaladen!" His name is out before I can help it. I try to grab hold of something to yank myself free, but there is no handhold within reach. *Sands and stars,* I curse inwardly. Then I freeze—because something slick just brushed against my ankle.

I move before a rational thought can enter my brain. I grab my sharpest knife and slice it across the thing touching me. A hiss pierces the darkness. I have no idea if I cut off the thing's head or just sliced it clean down the middle, but my fear gives me the strength to yank my foot out of the sludge. My shoe sticks behind, and I couldn't care less.

Then Kaladen is here, forcing open the door, pushing me out of it, and slamming it shut behind us. "Hurry! The blood!"

I find my balance, my eyes adjusting to the sudden overwhelming light, and blindly shove my bloody thumb onto the seal. It sinks into a small ball of muck—what Kaladen must have smeared on top of the dull brown, pulsating glow.

We both wait, breathlessly, as I pull back.

My bloody thumbprint flares a bright red, and the rainbow colors of the door swirl back to life.

"Excellent work!" Kaladen cries. Is that . . . excitement in his voice? I'm not sure I've ever heard him *excited* before.

"We did it!" I find myself grinning, equally excited, even though I did almost nothing but get stuck in goo and bleed a little. I feel like I shouldn't be excited, considering I've essentially learned how to do a dangerous chore that, if all goes according to plan, I will have to perform hundreds, maybe thousands more times in the future.

Even that thought doesn't dampen the thrill filling my chest.

"How many times did you get bitten?" I ask, glancing over the shadows that conceal him. He fades to my vision until he's invisible, but it's only a second and then he's back. "It sounded like it hurt!"

"Oh, it was only four or five times. Not bad."

I shake my head, still grinning despite myself. Kaladen has an adventurous streak, doesn't he? Not long ago, that sort of thing would have frightened me. Now I find it strangely exhilarating.

Maybe it's the idea of being useful to someone in a way that doesn't involve killing that makes me blurt: "Can we do the next one? I want to find the anchor this time."

Kaladen laughs, and the sound is so rich, so warm, I think I could get drunk on it. "We can do this all night if you'd like."

I nod eagerly.

We set off for the next seal.

"Will I be able to sense them breaking down like you do?" I ask.

"I think you will. If you spend enough time working the magic, your attunement to it will grow. By the time she died, Liliana could sense them about half of the time. I suspect it will happen faster for you, since you possess your own magic."

He doesn't sound sad at the mention of his previous wife. Even so, I'm not sure what else to say, so I keep my mouth shut as we turn down a new hallway of rainbows.

The skin on the back of my neck pebbles.

I pause, look over my shoulder. Only a darkened corridor meets my gaze. I suppress a shiver and catch up to Kaladen. "You mentioned before that I would have my own routes to walk at night. Will I be sealing portals on my own?"

"If you have enough of a knack for the work, I'm sure you'll be doing it by yourself in no time. Not *any* portal, mind you, but about a third or so would be manageable with your skill level."

I could swear eyes burn into the back of my neck. Once more, I turn. Once more, nothing is there. *Stop inventing frights,* I tell myself. *You're just recovering from how dark it was in Olata.*

"You'll find the anchor on this one," Kaladen continues. "It's much brighter in this one, though the anchor is ten paces *behind* the portal instead of in front of it."

Ice fills my stomach.

There *is* something behind us.

Dread crashes over me like an ocean's wave. I reach out instinctively and catch hold of Kaladen's arm. He looks down at me. "Are you alright?"

I swallow hard. My hand is trembling. No matter how hard I try, I cannot shake the dread. "I think someone is following us."

He stills. "That's impossible."

"Didn't you say occasionally creatures will come through the dream realm?"

"When there has been a breakout, yes, but there isn't a breakout. All the portals are closed—at the moment, at least."

I cannot explain it. All I know is that my intuition is honed for danger, and every part of me screams that a malicious presence follows us.

"Do you hear something? Tell me. You've gone pale as a lily. Do we need to stop? Where is it?"

I don't want to stop. I don't want be a failure, and I *really* don't want to go back to our room by myself while this dread rolls over me.

Gooseflesh erupts across my whole body. I draw a knife with one hand and point it back the way we came. "Something is there."

"Stay right here," Kaladen says. He pries my hand off his arm and marches straight into the darkness, leaving me surrounded by rainbows.

I draw my second knife and hold them both—as if they are my shields. With every step he takes, every step that puts distance between us, the alarm in my mind rings louder. What if it's the Wolf? What if Prince Trenian has come for his bargain? What if Kaladen gets hurt protecting me—again?

I open my mouth to call after him.

A cold, grating voice sounds right in my ear. "There you are. I've been looking for you."

I cannot even take a breath before hands clamp down on my throat and shove me face-first against a wall.

"This is going to hurt, but I only do it because I love you," Jabir purrs as he chokes the life out of me, as he pins me with his heavy weight so I cannot angle my knives for his ribs. "I am making you stronger, little one."

Then he thrusts his knee shockingly hard into the back of my thigh. I'd cry out if I could take a single breath. The world before me is red-hot, the world inside me made of nothing but pure panic, coursing blood, and pain.

"Let her go!" Kaladen roars. He's so close, but he feels a thousand miles away. My life is ebbing, washing away like street dust in a rainstorm. "Get off her!"

But Jabir doesn't listen. My limbs freeze entirely, so I cannot move when he shifts. He lightens his grip on my throat so he can grab the collar of my tunic and rip the back open to expose my scars. I don't fight him. I can't.

I have fought him so many times, and no matter how hard I tried—

I never won.

I will never win.

He will flay open the skin of my back like he's done dozens of times before. And this time, he doesn't need to tie my wrists.

"Nadira!" Kaladen's scream echoes through the pain, the terror. "Hold on for me! Hold on!"

I hear the snap of Jabir's whip. I cannot cry, cannot scream, cannot fight or run. The world shifts around me, and I don't see nightmarish rainbows but the muted colors of a patchwork quilt. I'm holding my knives, sharpening them. I'm safe here. I'm in control here.

The counting begins.

One.

I don't even feel the pain anymore.

Two.

I will stay here on my patchwork quilt. Here, where I am safe.

Three.

Suddenly, my patchwork quilt is gone. It's replaced by a much finer quilt. My knives aren't in my hands anymore. They're sheathed at my belt. The pain is gone. Every last speck of it.

And Kaladen's arms are around me, crushing me to his chest, rocking me. "I've got you. I've got you. You're safe now. Can you hear me?"

"I can hear you," I reply, my voice a dull monotone. My body is stiff against his, and part of me feels like I'm not here with him in this moment. I don't know where I am.

"I couldn't get to you!" He sounds distraught. "I couldn't touch him—couldn't touch you. I had to come back and wake you up to make it stop. Nadira, are you hearing my words? Are you alright?"

I plant a numb hand against his chest and push back enough so I can make out the outline of his head and shoulders in the darkness. "I'm fine."

"You're not fine!" he bursts, catching me by the shoulders. Are those tears glimmering on his cheeks? "You're not fine, and you've never been fine! Do you not remember what just happened?"

"I was sharpening my knives."

"He was flogging you!" His voice breaks, turning even more ragged as twin jewels of light drip down his cheeks.

I look up at him. I still feel so distant, so far away. It's like he's behind a wall of ice.

The pain on his invisible face shifts. His frantic hands calm, turn gentle against me. His fingers tilt my chin up. "Where are you?"

"I don't know," I reply hoarsely.

"Breathe with me." He lets go of my face, takes one of my hands in each of his. Warmth floods into my cold skin. A fraction of the tension eases from my muscles. "I want you to match your breaths with mine. Inhale, long and deep. Then exhale. Slow, controlled. Can you do that?"

I nod.

He inhales, and I follow. We exhale. Inhale. Exhale. That's when I realize just how fast my heart is beating. We keep breathing, and the tempo of my pulse slows. His words rumble over me, soothing. "Now feel my hands in yours. Notice how warm or cold they are. Whether they're big or small, soft or rough."

I close my eyes, still matching my breathing with his, and focus on his hands, the strong twine of his fingers through mine. I've always loved his hands. It's easy to think about them, how wide and square and solid they are. His calluses are rough and sometimes sharp, but I like them. I like how his hands have wielded weapons. It makes me trust him more, to know that he doesn't only care about me but is capable of protecting me. I haven't felt protected since I lost my baba. But I feel safe when I'm with him. Even when Prince Trenian captured me, I knew Kaladen would come for me.

I move more by instinct, lifting one of his hands with mine, pressing his palm to my cheek and leaning into its warmth, its strength. I keep breathing, falling into the rhythm he sets for us.

His thumb begins slowly caressing the apple of my cheek, in time to our breaths.

An eternity passes. The darkness is a warm blanket, his touch a soothing balm, the sounds of our breathing like a small symphony. It is like sleeping in a cocoon.

"Where are you now?" Kaladen murmurs, brushing my cheek with his thumb once more.

"Right here with you."

He gives my hand a gentle squeeze. "Good."

"Kaladen?"

"Yes?"

"Jabir . . . wasn't real, was he?"

"No, he wasn't. It was a waking nightmare."

"Because of the magic?"

He nods, heaves a deep sigh. His hand falls from my cheek, leaving a cold imprint behind. "I've never heard of it doing something like that, much less separating us."

Shivering, I wrap my arms around myself, and when I close my eyes, I have to fight the urge to weep. It's like my anger ripped away when Jabir's scratchy voice filled my awareness. My anger is my refuge, and without it, without its wall between me and pain, I feel about as strong as a newborn kitten. Another shiver ripples down my spine. "Kaladen?"

"Yes?"

"How long is the magic going to do this to me?"

His head drops, his great big shoulders sinking. "I don't know."

My throat stings. My eyes burn. My lungs ache. When the tears build up to a painful pressure, I can do nothing but swallow obsessively to keep from releasing them. No matter how hard I search for that shield of rage, I cannot find it. Maybe I've let Kaladen too deep into my heart and trust, and that is why I am so vulnerable.

His hand lands on my arm, covering one of the small knives in the sheath at my biceps. "Let it out, Nadira. You've held it in for far too long."

"Don't say that!" I cry, but it's too late. The dam breaks and the torrent of tears bursts free. I cover my face, bowing my head. My shoulders shake, and the tears that stream down my cheeks aren't quiet, tame little drops of salt.

"Oh, Nadira," Kaladen groans. He pulls me to his chest, wrapping his arms tightly around me. My legs are tucked in close, becoming a little ball in his lap that he holds close.

"I don't understand," I gasp between ragged sobs. "I don't understand!"

"Shh." One of his hands slides into my messy hair, his callused fingertips against my scalp. "I want you to breathe."

"I need to understand!"

"What don't you understand?"

The words are physically painful to get out, as though I wring them straight from my grief-stricken chest. "I killed Jabir . . . but I am still not free of him. I'll never be free of him. He will haunt me, and I will be a slave for the rest of my days. I just want to be free!"

He holds me closer, his breath on my forehead, my ear. "You *will* be free. But Nadira, I don't think you realize how terrible the things were that you endured. You aren't going to be past it in a day. It is often the aftermath of horrors that proves more difficult than the horror itself."

"I don't want it to be harder. I don't want to *remember*. I just want to forget!" This cursed, wretched magic refuses to let me have the one thing I crave: peace, oblivion. Every time I take a step forward, this magic rips me back, shreds me to pieces.

"I know, darling, I know."

At his words, a surge of anger—blessed anger—returns to me. It fills my gut until it's molten. Still, I cannot lash out. It stays inside me, melting my ice, birthing a river of tears I cannot control. My awareness shifts from the iron-hard grip I have on Kaladen's robes, his arms around me and my head hitting his chest as I rock back and forth—shifts to the agony in my lungs. My tears turn soundless, as though they come from a knife in my heart, as though they're too painful even for weeping. Everything insides me builds up, up, up, until my sobs aren't enough. Not nearly enough to let out the storm gathering in the deepest parts of my soul.

My jaw clicks, open and closed, rapidly, uncontrollably. I tremble violently, fighting against what is rising in my throat, what is shoving aside the sobs, pushing against my teeth, until—

That first scream wrenches from my body. It tears through me like the serrated edges of a blade, slicing into the darkness.

It should make Kaladen flinch away. He should go back to his seals, leave me behind to work this out on my own. He should let me scream myself hoarse into the depths of his empty palace.

But he doesn't. He doesn't let go. Even when my screaming turns to thrashing like a wild animal, he holds me. He doesn't say a word, doesn't try to rub my back or trace his finger up and down my arm as though to comfort or tame me.

He lets me hurt. He lets me rage. He lets me break open into a thousand tiny shards. He is the boat that carries me through the raging tempest, sheltering me from the highest waves and the most terrifying depths.

My hands shake violently. My hands, which have dealt so much death. My hands, forced to wield a blade, forced to learn to kill before I'd even had my first bleed.

I let myself fall into the tremors of my body and soul. I let the pain ravage me.

Then, as suddenly as a storm relents, like stars breaking forth after a final burst of lightning, calm—*blessed calm*—washes through me.

I sag forward. My forehead hits the hollow of Kaladen's throat. All strength evaporates from my body. Little shudders break out in my hands, my jaw, my whole torso—like the death throes of a monster.

His arms pull me closer, until we're nothing but two shadows, rocking in tandem.

He says nothing. I say nothing. There's no need for words when peace I hadn't known I lacked settles inside my heart.

I feel . . . safe. Not just safe from harm.

But safe to feel.

So I let myself feel. The breath coming in and out of my body. The heat of his skin radiating into mine. How solid he is. How grounding his heartbeat is in the quiet air.

My limbs are simultaneously airy as a cloud and heavy as a stone wall. My words come out slurred and half-dead: "I hope there are no enemies to fight, because right now, I don't think I have the strength to draw a knife."

He brushes the hair back from my face, takes my heavy head, and tilts it back so he can look at me.

When he says nothing, I murmur a stupid, "Hello."

He leans forward, still holding my face. Warm, pillow-soft lips brush lightly over my forehead. All the breath leaves my lungs, and I sit suspended in this little eternity. Then he pulls back.

Our eyes meet.

I crave the comfort of his lips on mine. I want his hands in my hair again. If I ask, will he oblige?

But I don't want him to oblige. I want him to crave me too.

He shifts on the bed. I remember I am still arranged in his lap. I hardly have the thought before he lifts me, lays me down. This time,

I sink deeper into the mattress, and I wouldn't mind if it swallowed me whole.

He covers me with the quilt. My eyes close despite themselves. "Are we going back to work?" I yawn.

"You're going to sleep the rest of the night. And you're not going to fight me on that."

"Yes, Sultani."

"No mocking either. I've told you not to call me that."

I smile. "Yes, Sultani."

He huffs, but there isn't an ounce of malice in the sound. He places one hand on the crown of my head, ruffles my hair slightly. "Goodnight."

CHAPTER 20

THE NEVERSEEN KING

I STAY THERE with Nadira as her breath steadies. My mind spins. Reels. I rake a hand through my hair and let out a low exhale.

It's as though I stand between a fire-breathing dragon and Crenfyre's death-laced mist. This magic is so much worse than I expected it to be. How am I supposed to ask Nadira to continue her work with me? And if she cannot help me, then have I risked her life over and over again for nothing? Will I continue to put her at risk for nothing?

I will not put her blood in a bottle to use like past Neverseen Kings. Not unless she agrees to it, and we have no other option.

But even if I did, I still need her to be able to seal her own portals by Lulythinar, or else this city will be razed to the ground. The *beechka* outbreak is child's play compared to what will happen.

Carefully, I ease myself away from her sleeping body, from her fanned lashes, slightly parted lips, and mussed hair. I dare not enter the dream realm so close to her. The last thing I want is to bring her back for the magic to torment. So I try not to rouse her as I take myself off the bed and slip out of the room.

What we need is *time*.

We don't have it.

But I know a way to get it.

It's just . . . I close my eyes. Green branches of rich foliage flash before my memory. It's accompanied by a smiling face, long blonde curls, shining blue eyes. I haven't gone there in so long. If anything, this last hundred years, I've wanted nothing but for time to speed up. No matter how exhausted and ragged I grew, I never wanted time to rest. Rest meant time to think, to remember, to be miserable.

This is the first time I've wanted time, and now that I want it, it's slipping through my fingers.

But there is a place. I won't let myself avoid it any longer.

I will take her there tomorrow, after we honor Emin's loss.

With a sigh, I slip back into the dream realm. I may crave rest and a chance to calm my racing thoughts, to process the growing number of horrors I've been forced to witness. But there is no time for that.

"If you work quickly enough, maybe you can return to Nadira before she wakes," I tell myself, trying to motivate my limbs into motion.

It works. I find a renewed burst of determination and set off to address the remaining weakened seals.

I am only a few minutes into my rounds when I encounter Nadira's favorite banister. I intend to climb it like I always do, refusing to touch the wood.

Then I stop. I reach out. Let my fingers brush the wood.

You need to behave, the wood tells me. Because, unfortunately, that is one of the only things I've said to it.

I'm sorry I've snapped at you, I tell it. *I should be kinder.*

I'll sand you, it replies, echoing my favorite threat.

Don't get cheeky.

Don't get cheeky, it immediately shoots back.

I sigh. I suppose I ought to give it something nicer to say. Should I compliment it? My nose wrinkles at that thought. What sort of compliments does one give a banister? *Your finish shines like the stars.* Absolutely not. I'd sooner let the Wolf take the Bridge than let those words out of my mind.

Maybe saying something nice about something else—

I stop. A small, slow smile tilts my lips. I know what I can say to it.

Nadira is beautiful, don't you think?

Nadira is beautiful, it agrees, even though it possesses no eyes and is no judge of beauty.

I like her very much.

I like her very much, the banister agrees.

My smile widens. When I climb up the stairs and reach the top, I lay my hand down once more. Instead of its insolent quips, it says at once: *Nadira is beautiful.*

I nod, pleased. *Yes, she is.*

Then I return to my work.

THE MOURNER

Sunlight turns the inside of my eyelids red. My head feels like a swirling mass of sand on a hot dune, and yet when I blink my eyes open, there is a lightness about the way I lie beneath the heavy quilts of Kaladen's bed. I'm so warm, but it's a pleasant heat.

I draw in a deep lungful of crisp morning air. The curtains waft from the breeze slipping in through the open window. Birdsong sounds from outside. The corner of my mouth twists upward.

Then my gaze snags on something very unexpected.

Hardly three inches from my stomach is a hand. Resting on the mattress. It is a large, square hand. White threads of old scars crisscross golden skin and curled knuckles. The hand is attached to a thick wrist, and a corded, muscular forearm that rests on the dip between my hip and ribs.

That's when I process exactly *why* I am so warm. There is a heavy weight situated just behind me that radiates heat into every pore of my being.

Shock thrums through me, stripping every thought from my mind except a repeated chorus of: *he's cuddling me, he's cuddling me, he's cuddling me.*

Except . . . his breathing is still very even. His heartrate is slowed in repose.

He's still asleep, isn't he?

I nearly whimper aloud. I cannot get out of this bed without moving his hand—and likely waking him up. If I wake him up, we'll both be flustered and awkward. But the alternative is to just lie here, pressed up against him, and wait until he wakes up—in which case, I will have only delayed the inevitable.

Do you really want to leave? a small part of me asks.

The answer that immediately rises from my gut almost terrifies me. It's too overwhelming to stay, to feel how his knees fit against mine, to let the rise and fall of his chest burn into my back.

I'm still debating what to do when he shifts. I tense. His sigh stirs my hair, sends shivers down the back of my neck. His hand drags from the mattress to my stomach, where it splays out across my tunic. Even though his breathing remains steady, I could swear his heartrate picks up. Those long, golden fingers of his begin tracing patterns across my midsection, gently, softly.

It is confirmed: I will never breathe again.

His heartrate continues to climb, and his gentle touches shift to something firmer, more possessive. With a grip on my waist, he pulls me back into him so there isn't even a whisper of air between us. A gasp catches in my throat, while he lets out another long, satisfied sigh.

He's still asleep! He doesn't realize what he's doing. He probably doesn't want this. Maybe he is confusing me for his previous wife. Maybe—

His nose nuzzles into my hair, his breathing picking up, his pulse increasing its rhythm. Meanwhile, my heart stops completely. His breath caresses my ear, warm and electrifying.

It's all so overwhelming. Thrilling and unsettling at once. I hardly know what to do with the way my stomach keeps flipping over itself, or the way my instincts war inside me to nuzzle back or to flee.

"Kaladen!" I gasp, and it comes out in a high-pitched squeak.

"Nadira," he rumbles in reply. His grip on me tightens as he burrows his face deeper into my hair. "You smell so good."

"Kaladen!"

He freezes. I freeze too. My eyes squeeze shut of their own accord, as if that will shut out when he flies back in horror.

"Nadira?" Kaladen's voice is extra deep from sleep. He sits upright, quickly withdraws his hand from my waist. "Did I—? Great Kings, I didn't mean to force myself on you! Are you alright? I never meant to make you uncomforta—"

"It's fine," I say quickly, sitting up. I cannot bring myself to look at him. Not while my face is red as a pomegranate. That'll give away my lie when I say: "I wasn't uncomfortable."

He goes quiet, but the air thrums with energy.

"You finished everything?" I ask, still facing the window, staring at it as though my life depends on it.

"The seals are all reinforced at the moment, yes," he replies, drawing a deep breath. "I finished early this morning and came back to get some sleep before the sun rose, if I could."

"Did you sleep well?"

"I cannot remember sleeping better," he admits, and his honesty only renews the flush of my cheeks and neck. "How did you sleep?"

I reach up and begin combing my tangled hair with my fingers, fiddling to feign nonchalance. Because my answer is the same as his. "I slept well."

"Good."

Then, not able to bear it any longer, I shoot to my feet and practically hurl myself out of the bedroom to get to the bathing chamber. There, I set the water to just above freezing and try to cool my raging heartbeat and the memory of his arm around me, tracing patterns on my stomach. It's misery, but a misery I gladly embrace to keep from fainting in such a compromising situation. I towel myself dry and pull on a fresh sirwal and tunic. The sunlight pours through this window, sparkling on the water and warming the pebbled gooseflesh of my skin. As soon as I'm dry—except for my hair, which I simply tie off in a quick braid—a flood of frantic, ravenous hunger barrels into me. I nearly fall backward and collapse into a pile of quivering bones from the force of it. I catch myself on the doorframe of the bathroom, my eyes wide. So maybe a full day is too long to go without food, but I've often gone that long or more without a proper meal.

Yet I am more certain than ever that if I don't get food in me within a few minutes, I will pass out.

My hand fumbles with the latch on the door, but I swing it open and croak desperately into the ether: "Food!"

Kaladen is there in a second, the glimmer of his eyes blinking quickly as he takes me in, mewling like a kitten, clinging to the doorframe of his wash chamber.

"I need food," I gasp.

"I will get you food right away," he replies, catching my upper arm. "Sit down before you fall and smash open your head! Mountains of Ildred, you're shaking!"

"I need food." It's apparently all I'm capable of saying as he sets me down on the settee.

"Hold on for just a few moments. I'll be back as quickly as I can be," Kaladen says, the shadows around his face shifting and lightening as concern and some other emotion overtakes his invisible features.

I wait for him to return. My fist clenches around the armrest of the settee, as though that will make the cavernous pit of my stomach and the weakness flooding my limbs vanish. I don't think I have ever been so hungry in my entire life! It's like Eshe's appetite suddenly was thrust upon me.

When Kaladen returns, a steaming tray in his hands, I nearly collapse in gratefulness. "Thank you!" I gasp. I throw myself into the meal with vigor, and every mouthful is exquisite.

Kaladen sits across from me wordlessly. I don't pay any heed to his focused attention until, at last, every single crumb of food is licked clean from the tray. It's only then that I become aware of how intently he watches me.

"Do you need more?" he asks.

I pause, taking a deep breath. And actually . . . I am quite satisfied. I shake my head, gasp another, "Thank you!" and flop back against the settee. "That was the most delicious meal I've ever had."

"I will give your compliments to the cook," Kaladen replies wryly, cocking his head to one side. "You didn't seem to think so fondly of the meal yesterday."

"I wasn't as hungry as I was today," I reply at once. There is something so full yet so light about my entire body now. It is like I fly among the clouds while still being fully anchored to the ground.

He shakes his head. "You are such a liar, telling me you ate with Eshe last night."

I cover my mouth with my hand, suppressing a giggle. "Sorry."

The shadows around his face shift once more. He props his chin up on his fist, and that might be a smile his darkness is trying to hide. "I'm never believing another word out of your mouth."

"Your loss," I reply tartly.

"That does not make any sense."

"I don't really care if it does. It just sounded like a good thing to say."

"What?" The word bursts out of Kaladen in a confused laugh. His laugh will forever and always send my stomach tripping over itself.

I lean forward on the settee, hardly able to control the sudden flare of energy inside myself. "Can I go to the bazaar? I won't be long."

"In the city? You can go wherever you like. You do not need my permission."

I know that. I do. But it goes against every instinct to just *decide* I want to go somewhere . . . and just *go*. My body tells me there will be consequences. Consequences I will not like.

That's not true, though. At least, not anymore.

"In about two hours, we will lay Emin to rest. You do not have to be there, but I thought you should know about it even so."

Emin. A pang of guilt rips through me that I've already forgotten about him. "I want to be there," I assure quickly. "I won't be long at the bazaar."

I don't leave immediately, though. I head to the washroom. The moment I walk in, my eyebrows go up and I call back: "Kaladen? Why is the pool . . . boiling? I didn't set it that hot!"

"Did you leave your clothes on the floor?" he calls back.

I glance down. They are indeed in a pile where I left them, beside the screen. I scoop them up, and immediately the roiling of the water smooths out, the steam fading into nothing.

"It's one of the few things the House is extremely particular about," Kaladen says, his voice suddenly very close behind me.

"Sorry, House!" I call to the ceiling, walls, and floor.

The water splashes in reply before settling down once more.

"It appears you are forgiven." He's smiling again. It doesn't last long, however, because I find what I came back for: a small, folded piece of paper rests in the pocket of my clothes from yesterday. It crinkles as I unfold it and hold it up to the light. At first, there's nothing across its creamy surface. Behind me, Kaladen has gone quiet.

Then, like a snake slithering across the page, the writing appears beneath the light of the sun shining through the window.

"It was a very large dose," I read aloud. I open my mouth to read the second sentence—the rest of the note—and immediately close it again. I swallow hard around the rock in my throat. It feels impossible to get these few simple words out.

He felt no pain.

A hand lands on my shoulder. "It's alright. I see what it says."

I nod, grateful as I blink back the sting in my eyes.

"Go to the bazaar," he says softly. "I'll be here if you need me."

Here—resealing portals. Forever and ever. Always behind and never truly caught up.

I close my eyes, breathe deeply, and wait until the emotion fades just enough for me to speak again. "Very well. I'll be back within the next two hours."

Then I escape into the sunshine.

The streets of Arbasa are dusty and loud. It's a flood of smells, from mounds of rich, brightly colored spices to the donkey excrement I dodge. A patchy black cat lies on her belly in the mouth of an alleyway, situated in the single sunbeam that cuts through the torn awning above it. Shopkeepers bargain loudly with their customers, insisting their rugs are the best woven on this side of the sea.

I do not wear my normal belt of knives. I have only the smaller, hidden ones. None of them are technically necessary. I just . . . couldn't leave them behind.

"Here, kitty!" Eshe tsks beside me, taking a hunk of flatbread she apparently brought with her out of her pocket. I roll my eyes and keep walking while she tosses scraps to the cat.

The sun burns my face in the most glorious way. Hot and purifying and energizing. With my full belly and a complete night's sleep, I'm not sure I've ever felt so good.

I'm still not comfortable walking the streets of Arbasa, though. At any moment, I expect someone to jump out of the shadows and scream my name, exposing my identity and bringing the city guard down on my head.

Kaladen wouldn't let them hurt me. *I* wouldn't let them hurt me. But being hurt isn't what I'm afraid of in this moment.

Children's laughter punctuates the rolling of rickety wheels down the street and bazaar bartering. I look up as a little boy and girl chase each other between stalls. They kick up a cloud of dust and angry stall owners behind them. But the children don't care. Even when their mother pulls them aside and scolds them, they pretend to behave for all of thirty seconds before they're running again, right past city guards. One of them I recognize as the brawny one from the morning after the *beechka* infestation. He doesn't give a second glance at the two children.

It's just the ones without protection you target, I think bitterly.

"Children with parents have no self-preservation instinct," Eshe observes as she catches up to me. She doesn't notice the brawny guard, and I'm not about to point him out. With a winsome smile and a coin purse I've never seen before, she walks up to a stall, begins bartering, and shoots me a wink. *I have friends in high places now,* she says with that wink.

I shake my head. Involuntarily, my attention returns to the children. Their mother has each of them by the ear and pulls them along while they protest.

My mother used to do that, too.

The memory hits me out of nowhere. Of all her scolding, and the way Baba let me get away with anything. I haven't thought about that in ages. It's not like I *forgot* it. I simply . . . didn't remember.

The returned memory brings a host of emotions. A pang to my chest, pressure behind my eyes, and yet it is the beginnings of a smile that curves my mouth.

"Look at how big these dates are!" Eshe exclaims, back with her sack of food. "It's good they're big because they're expensive. Everything is expensive! Even though the Neverseen King gave me ten silver fals, I think spending money will always kill me."

"I thought you were more resilient than that," I say. "To be killed simply by the exchange of tender for goods."

"You will be the death of me."

"I'm glad the feeling is mutual." A sharp whack hits my arm, which I probably deserve. I grin at Eshe, who only arches one cocky eyebrow in return. "I'm going to scout now, so you can scout with me or do whatever you planned to do with those dates."

She grins and pops one in her mouth. "They're all for me," she lies blatantly.

I sigh, shaking my head, and after pulling my headscarf over my mouth, I slip into the nearest shadowed alleyway. There's no telling what I will find at the end of this alley, whether it be more starving urchins or bandits ready to rob me. I keep my senses alert as I hurry deeper into the shadows, and peel into the next alleyway on my way to the abandoned belltower.

When I arrive, I don't bother going through the broken doorway. I don't trust an inch of what remains of the stairs. Instead, I pull out my *jurbah* rope from my sash, glance over my shoulder to make sure no one has followed me, and tie a quick knot to my little anchor. This is the shadowed side of the tower, so no one sees me as I throw my anchor, hook it inside the window, and climb up the side of the wall.

I haul myself onto the sill, pull up my rope, and slip along a rafter until I'm out of sight of the window. The massive, rusted bell fills much of the space.

I loop my rope around one of the highest rafters, test my weight, and then pull myself—fist over fist—up until I can perch on the enormous beam that holds the bell. One day, this beam will rot through, and this bell will crash to the ground below. Thankfully, that day is not today.

From here, I can observe most of the bazaar below. I can see the flow of foot traffic and animals, as well as which shops are frequented the most and which are overlooked. Which shops people put the most money on the table for.

A few members of the city guard stroll through the market, and the few visible urchins immediately pull back into the shadows. A growl rumbles in the back of my throat, but I suppress it. Figuring out how to get the urchins off the street will help the problem of the city guard.

I sit, my legs dangling near the side of the bell, and I scan like a vulture on the scavenge. Last night's conversation with Eshe runs in the back of my brain. My intuition tells me that if we are to set up a system to help the urchins that would be effective, it needs to be sustainable. Sustainable means it needs to fit into the existing market we already have. It should be able to run on its own, no matter whether Eshe or I am available to help, no matter if Arbasa has money in its coffers to spare.

I don't want a solution that will temporarily patch up a dire situation, so we are only kicking the real problem down the road. No, I want to *truly* address this. I want to reverse it.

And I want to be careful about this because there will be unforeseen effects. I don't want to set up something that will fall to pieces the moment Eshe or I are not there to facilitate it.

So I sit, and I watch, and I think.

I become so absorbed in my thoughts that I completely lose track of time. It's a crested lark flying and landing next to me on the beam that suddenly yanks me out of my mind.

"Oh, sands!" I cry, scrambling up to my feet. "Emin's memorial! Cursed, wretched sands!"

CHAPTER 21

THE NEVERSEEN KING

THE SUN ARCHES overhead. I stand gripping my wrist behind my back, wearing so many glamoured shadows I must look like a black void in the sunlight. But the staff of my palace stands all around me, their heads bowed, ready to honor our faithful steward and friend. His body lies in the middle of the cracked flagstone of the barren courtyard, wrapped in linen.

Still, I delay.

Because Nadira said she would come. I do not know whether to take her delay as a reflection of her changing her mind, or her getting into some kind of trouble. Or perhaps she simply lost track of time.

A tiny, insidious part of me whispers: *Maybe she ran away.*

I shake my head. I'll wait a little longer, and if she still doesn't come, we will begin without her. If she isn't back by the end of the ceremony, I will go looking for her. Since we are now bound as husband and wife, I expect the bond between us to alert me if something is truly wrong. Right now, when I search the tie that binds our heartbeats together, there is no panic or terror.

The moments trickle by, until at last I give a great sigh and lift my head. "Thank you, people of my House, for leaving your tasks to honor our beloved steward, Emin bint-Sarbas."

A thread anchored inside me twinges suddenly. I stop and look up. Someone—no, two people—have stepped through my gates. Briefly, I allow my eyes to close, my tense shoulders to relax. *She's home.*

I continue speaking, my voice louder than before, as I list a few of Emin's many virtues. Around me, servants of all ages nod in agreement. Some shed the tears I hold back, while others smile sadly.

When a dark, hooded head slips into the crowd, followed by Eshe, I relax even more. Nadira's gaze immediately finds mine as she pushes back her headscarf. She gives me an apologetic wince, and I incline my head to her in the smallest of acknowledgements. My chest fills with a comforting warmth—one I have missed for ages. I've forgotten how much easier it is to bear burdens when you do not carry them alone. Perhaps I should feel more grief in this moment than I do, but as I speak, the emotions that fill me are courage, gratitude, and hope. As the tears flow around me, I can think only that I am glad to hold my people in their grief, and be held in return.

Every minute, I am achingly aware of Nadira's gaze, of the way her mere presence gives me the strength I need to press onward. When I reach the final part of the ceremony, I look up, catch her eye as I flick a blade across the pad of my thumb. *"Solnir,"* I breathe, as I let a drop of blood fall onto the linen covering Emin's heart.

The blood seeps into the fabric, and then flares. One or two people gasp, but most don't flinch. Eshe's bright eyes are wide as full moons in the crowd as the light brightens, spreading into the sky above the body. One of the gasps was definitely hers. The portal will not be as brilliant, competing as it is with the light of the sun, but it is still no less magical when it winks open like an eyelid. A world of stars and nebulas and multi-colored clouds fill the portal above the body. Some staff members take a startled step backward. Others lean closer, trying to take in more of the beauty. Nadira is one of the latter.

I pause. Emin's wrapped body lies before me. It strikes me again how permanent death is, a truth I have faced so many times before. It never gets easier to bend down, lift that body, and feel the lifeless shell of what a person once was. But most important things are not easy.

So I bend. I lift my old friend.

"I've got you," I whisper through my thick throat. "I will miss you. Thank you for all that you were. To me, to these people gathered here, to Arbasa and Faerie. Now be at rest, my friend."

I slide his body through the portal. Stars bend to accept him, wrapping him in a crystalline shower of color and light. It is the highest honor I can give, that he will become one with the sky and from him, a new constellation will be born. Then, at night, there will always be a reminder of him.

This is what I've always wished I could have done for Liliana, but I didn't have her body. Perhaps Emin's constellation can shine enough for them both.

A murmur rises from the people. Their final farewells. My voice joins them.

Then, because of my fae hearing, I can discern what Eshe says when she leans over, tears pouring down her cheeks, and whispers to Nadira: "Why am I crying so hard? I barely knew the man!"

Nadira's dark eyes shoot to mine. *I understand,* that look says. Then she wraps an arm around her friend's shoulder and pulls her close.

As the view of Emin fades in the portal, I let the wave of sadness wash through me. And then I step forward, focus my attention on the portal itself. It's time to close it and lay this all to rest.

Closing portals I opened is much easier than closing those that break open, unless something escaped that needs to be contained. But that is never the case with this portal. I reach out, grab the edges of the great eyelid before me, and wait until it firms into something tangible.

Then I pull with all my might. Slowly, bit by bit, it collapses into smaller and smaller orbs. Until, at last, it finally, completely, winks out.

CHAPTER 22

THE MOURNER

THE CROWD DISPERSES as everyone returns to their duties. I stay where I am, watching the great shadow that is the Neverseen King after the portal vanishes. He stands amid the courtyard. His gaze seems to have latched onto the space where the Emin was only moments ago.

"I have some things to get to this afternoon," Eshe says beside me. She wipes her face off with her sleeve, and when I expect her to turn tail and retrace her steps to the market, she follows the servants inside the palace.

Leaving me alone with the Neverseen King.

I step to his side.

We stand there quietly for several minutes before I say, "Is the fountain broken beyond repair? After Crenfyre?"

"No, but it'll need more than repair. Crenfyre takes life force, and even things that aren't *alive* still contain life force."

"So . . . magic can restore it?"

"If the amount of life force is small enough, yes. But I don't like wasting magic on such things."

"Because it is exhausting, like healing?"

"Indeed. Anything that restores life takes a great deal of magic."

I nod, surveying the barren courtyard, the dead husks that were once palm trees, the cracked stone of the lifeless fountain. "I don't like seeing death win."

His head twists down toward me. "Is that a request?"

"Merely a statement," I reply, arching one eyebrow.

Then, slowly, I overcome my hesitancy and lift one hand. I gently touch his arm. It is too insignificant a thing to offer words of comfort. Nothing I say will ease his pain. But perhaps my presence, the knowledge that I am here with him, will do something.

His shoulders loosen. His right hand covers mine and gives a gentle squeeze. As if he knows exactly what I am thinking.

We stand like that for some time, the sun beating down on our heads.

"I have a secret I've been keeping from you." His voice startles me. I look up, hoping he cannot read the embarrassing turn of my thoughts on my face. "Will you come with me?"

"A secret? About what?"

He takes me back to the palace, not answering until we reach the second floor. "It's not some terribly dark secret, but it is a very powerful tool you should know about. No one else does, except for me. And now, you."

He brings me to a wing I haven't visited before. The door is made of polished wood carved with a rushing waterfall. When I stare at it too long, it almost seems like the water in the carving begins moving, flowing toward me as though to sweep me away. I take a step closer, and my slipper lands in a puddle of water. I startle and look down.

Sure enough, water drips from the carving straight onto the floor, pooling around my slipper. I turn in shock to Kaladen.

"It must like you. It doesn't do that for everyone," he says, smiling. "Come now. I remember your fascination with freshwater."

He rakes a fingernail over the new cut on his thumb and presses a fresh drop of blood to the doorknob. A click like a lock sounds. He pushes the door open—

The roar of a waterfall and chorus of birdsong hits me even before the spray of foam does. My mouth opens, but Kaladen grabs my hand before I can decide I'm too afraid to continue. He pulls me after him, straight into a lush jungle.

My eyes bug out at the avalanche of green. The air turns cool and heavy. It coats my mouth and nose when I breathe.

"The secret is most enjoyable barefoot," Kaladen says, kicking off his boots and leaving them in a pile beside the shut door. He looks at me, and I think he might be grinning at my disbelief. "Nothing here can hurt you. Except maybe a sharp rock, but there are few enough of those. Come now, don't look so tongue-tied, my desert princess. I promise, you'll enjoy this."

"Are we working?" I ask dubiously, taking off my slippers and leaving them with his giant boots despite my hesitancy. The ground is cool, rich, solid beneath my feet. It doesn't shift like sand or fly up in my face like dust. It's dark and rich.

"We are training your magic." With that, he takes my hand once more and pulls me down a small footpath amid enormous trees, wild ferns, and multi-colored flowers blooming on branches.

"But there is a tremendous amount of work to be done!" I protest. "The days are slipping by and there is much to be caught up on with the kingdom's rule. I need to search Emin's library because there are things I need to understand about how markets work—"

He is suddenly right in front of me, pressing a long finger to my lips. "Our priority is preparing for and surviving Lulythinar. So, I want you to forget the rest for the next few hours—"

"*Hours?*" I exclaim.

"—because time moves differently here," he finishes with a stern look at me. "An hour here is roughly equivalent to a minute back in Arbasa."

I blink. "What?"

"When you are here, time stands still." He draws his finger away from my mouth. "So, you see, there will be plenty of time to accomplish your many tasks. But right now, we need time to practice your magic. And if that is not a sufficient reason for you, I do believe it will benefit our work at night if we are . . . closer."

"You want to train me to get to know me better?"

"Your magic could be the difference between death and life, Nadira. Not just for you, but for many others. Especially those in the city. It is imperative you know how to control it properly."

I scowl, but because I know he's right, I give no further protest. A second later, I forget about my anxiety over my work when I spy a strange, colorful bird in the tree above me. It has an enormous beak, with a beautiful black and yellow pattern on its feathers. Kaladen keeps dragging me along, so I don't get to stare at the bird as long as I would like. A second, different bird replaces it a few moments later. This one has tail feathers nearly as long as I am tall, and they are a brilliant turquoise.

"What kind of fairytale world is this?" I ask, stumbling along after Kaladen because I cannot be bothered to look where I am going. "The green is blinding!"

He laughs. "It was once part of the human world. Did you know there are places like this not tremendously far from Arbasa? But this particular jungle got folded into Faerieland by accident one Lulythinar. Now it is here, its own little part of the worlds that runs at its own time."

"Why don't you come—" I stop myself before I finish the question. Of course he must have come here with Liliana. Why else would he never rest even though he has a place he can go to rest without wasting time?

Kaladen doesn't seem bothered when he answers my inappropriate question. "I didn't feel ready to come back. I am ready now, though."

I've almost forgotten the roar of water because it surrounds us so completely. The spray becomes more insistent, however, drawing my attention back to it. At first, it's fine, soothing even. But when it becomes so heavy it beads into droplets, my gut clenches in dread. *Don't pass out, don't pass out*. He doesn't know about my issues with water, does he? I *refuse* to ruin this moment by collapsing into another flashback or faint.

Quickly, I close the distance between us and position myself on Kaladen's side, so he shields me from the worst of it. When he glances curiously at me, I feign interest in the giant leaf we pass that is at least twice the size of my face. My interest quickly becomes genuine, and the more I look around us, the bigger the leaves seem to become. "That leaf is as big as my entire torso!"

Kaladen gives no reply, only smiles. As if I am hilarious. I frown at him. "You can wear all those shadows, but I can still tell when you're trying not to laugh. What is so funny about me experiencing something new? I bet you were just as overwhelmed when you saw this for the first time. Whenever that was. Five thousand years ago or something."

"Five thousand?" He chokes on the words. "How old do you think I am?"

I squint. "Four thousand?"

"I am not even five hundred years old, you goose."

"So what does that make you in human years? A twelve-year-old?"

He stops walking. Turns to me. Levels an extremely rewarding glare down at me. I grin back. He shakes his head and continues on his way.

I cover my mouth in feigned shock. "Younger?"

His pinch is swift and sharp, but there is no edge to it. I rub my arm and try not to giggle.

"In human years, I would be something like ten years older than you, if you *must* know."

"Will you live forever?" I ask.

"Do you have any other questions? I'd rather you got them all out at once so I can answer them in bulk."

"No," I immediately lie. He knows it's a lie too, because he gives me another firm glare that tells me my questions don't bother him at all.

"I will not live forever. If I live long enough to die of natural causes, I may live to be thousands of years old. It's rare to find a fae who lives to be ten thousand, but they do exist. I doubt in my line of work, however, that it will be natural causes. Now, I see you opening your mouth to ask another question. No more until we arrive, understand? Don't make me gag you."

I close my mouth like a good little girl, and wait until we've hit our stride once more before I ask: "Why?"

His arms wrap around my waist so unexpectedly I let out a sharp squeal. He lifts me straight off the ground so my feet dangle in midair. "Kaladen!" I shriek, trying and failing to peel his arms from around me. "Put me down!"

Now he's the one grinning as he shifts his grip to one arm and keeps walking. As if I weigh nothing. As if I could struggle for hours and it wouldn't wear down his strength.

Fine. I've got other weapons at my disposal. I reach for the knives hidden in my tunic. My belt is still in our room since I didn't have time to collect it after my visit to the market. But I have these other—

My hands find empty sheaths.

"Looking for this?" In his other hand, Kaladen holds up one of my small knives. I lunge for it, kicking to give me leverage. He just holds it high, his long arm far above anything I could dream of reaching.

"That isn't fair!" I cry.

He brings the knife down, gives it a toss, and catches it out of the air before I can reach it. "So you can tease me, but I cannot tease you? Interesting rules you've set up for our relationship. You know what I always say about unfair rules? It's better to cheat."

"You want to cheat?" I say, lifting my brows. "I can show *you* cheating."

"What are you going to do? Choke me? Gouge out my eyes? Ram those sharp elbows of yours between my ribs?"

"Don't make me hurt you."

"Ah yes, and the more I taunt you, the closer you get to making me regret it. Except you"—Here, he bops me on the nose—"are much sweeter than you like to let on. And to prove it, I'll even give you your knives back."

He whips each out of his belt and offers them to me. All while still holding me against him, my feet dangling. Begrudgingly, I accept my weapons back and sheathe them. Because he's right. I can't do anything but threaten him with them.

Or rather: I *won't*.

But that's alright. I can avenge myself later.

"Such a good little assassin," he teases with a grin, patting me on the head before putting me back on my feet.

"You'll regret that," I say darkly.

"I'm sure I won't."

I roll my eyes, but I keep to his side and ignore my hot cheeks as we come to the end of the trail.

We step out of the trees into the most magnificent oasis I've ever seen.

CHAPTER 23

THE MOURNER

A MASSIVE WATERFALL spills into a pool as transparent as glass, which empties into a stream that threads through the trees. Moss covers the rocks lining the waterfall and pool. Jungle trees, ferns, and shrubs fill my view, blocking out the sky. The dirt beneath my feet is damp and cool—not hot and dry like sand. It smells earthy and wet, like the stones at the bottom of the pool.

"The problem with jungles is that they tend to have a lot of insects," Kaladen says beside me. "I would recommend closing your mouth."

My wide-eyed wonder turns into a glower in one second. Kaladen just grins at me, and I decide exactly how I will get him back. Still, I bide my time.

He steps several paces away from me, planting his legs wide. "Let's get to work. We've already discussed strategies for keeping your magic from exploding when you are afraid. We will keep working on that, but for now I want to spend time on honing your ability to summon your magic when you *do* want it."

"That's easy," I reply. "I want it when I'm scared. It comes when I'm scared."

He shakes his head. "True mastery of your magic will happen when you can control it regardless of your emotional state. Try to summon it now."

He stares at me. Waiting. I bring one arm around my middle, slightly tilting my body away from him. I've never tried summoning it randomly. I don't even know where to begin.

"That's alright," Kaladen says, as though he reads my thoughts. He comes back to my side. "Where does your magic lie within you?"

"Where?" I repeat.

"Does it reside in your hands? Your chest? When it feels like it's going to explode, where does it feel like it's coming from?"

"My stomach."

He nods, then steps behind me. I start to turn, following him, only to find that he is right at my back—unnervingly close. "May I touch you?"

The question startles me so much it takes me a second to remember to answer. I opt to nod instead of giving my voice a chance to shake.

His warm hand slides over my belly. I keep myself very still so I do not flinch. His voice is a little lower than usual when he speaks again. "What do you feel?"

I do *not* want to answer that question.

"If you breathe into my hand, do you feel your magic rising?"

Oh.

I breathe into my core, and feel his hand rise with it. All I can feel is the heat and weight of his palm. Not a stitch of ice is available to me. *Worthless magic*. And why am I struggling to think straight while he's completely focused on what we're trying to do?

"If you cannot feel it, I will use a little of my own magic to amplify yours."

Was that the tiniest thread of strain in his timbres? If so, it's probably just from the magic.

A second later, the skin beneath my tunic tingles slightly. Kaladen doesn't move or make a sound. The tingling seeps into my skin, sinking deeper and deeper, until—

There.

There is the pinprick of ice. "I feel it."

"Excellent! Now I want you to focus on that awareness. Think of its shape, its size, its location. I want you to memorize those things. Nadira?"

"Yes?"

His hand shifts slightly on my belly. "Are you paying attention?"

My eyes fly open—when did I close them? "Yes! Why?"

"You . . . don't have to lean against me. That is, *I* don't mind, but you don't have to for the magic to work."

I stand up straighter, the resulting flush nearly erasing my awareness of my magic. I nearly offer an apology, but the word sticks to my tongue, and I decide to keep my mouth shut, lest something even more incriminating escapes me.

Kaladen clears his throat. "If you think of the magic as something with a specific location, a specific shape, and so forth, you can call it easier, even if you don't feel it. You can focus your awareness on where you know it is, and the more you expect to feel it, the more it'll answer your call."

I force my awareness past his hand to the light stirrings beneath it. Now that he says it, the force within me feels like a sphere, with a smudged, soft outline, settled right beneath my ribs. "I sense it."

He slowly removes his hand, but stays at my back. "Do you still feel it?"

I nod.

"Now think of it like a fire, and of each breath like brush to fuel it. If you expect it to rise, it'll come."

"This seems like too much effort for this power to be useful."

"We are training its dexterity. When you were a child, something as simple as fastening a button was difficult, yes? Now you can do it in a second. That is how your magic is. It is a muscle that must be trained and honed. It is awkward and tedious now, but it will be as simple as swallowing once you've mastered it."

Something about the way he speaks makes me turn my head. He's so close behind me, his head bowed toward mine. He catches my eye—and quickly looks away. The next second, he steps backward. Giving me space. Putting distance between us.

"I'm afraid much of your training will be tedious exercises of calling and restraining your magic. Learning how to keep it simmering and waiting for your bidding, learning how to never let it get beyond your control."

He takes another step away from me as he speaks. It's one step too far. I want to bring him back.

Time for my revenge. We can finish practicing later. I imagine releasing my magic from my grip, and my awareness of it fades away. I search the vicinity, quickly spotting exactly what I need.

I point to a flower floating on a wide green leaf at the edge of the pool. "What is that?"

He cranes his neck to see it. "That is a waterlily and its lily pads."

I don't look back at him, afraid my face might give me away as I ask: "Could you . . . bring it to me? I want to see it closer."

"You could walk over to it. It's right off the bank."

"I don't want to get wet," I say honestly. *Think innocent thoughts.*

He turns toward it, holding out an arm. "You won't get wet. It's just—"

I throw my entire weight at him. He lets out a grunt when my shoulder collides with his impassive frame. I catch him off-guard. He stumbles, his arms flying out—

He makes a massive splash as he hits the surface of the pool. I scurry backward, dodging the worst of it, and burst into laughter when his head emerges from the water. His glamours shudder, as if they nearly break, and his cloak floats around his shoulders as he fixes me with a look I do not need to see to read.

"You look a little wet," I say, grinning smugly. "I never took you as clumsy."

The water soaking his clothes slows his swim toward me. I scurry backward even more, hiding behind the trunk of a massive tree. My eyes widen a little when he stands—the water up to his waist—and his dark tunic clings to an extremely well-muscled torso.

"Don't hide behind that tree like a coward," he says.

"When the odds are in your favor, I must do what I can to cheat. Do you regret picking me up and stealing my knives now?"

A slow smile breaks through his glamours. "Definitely not."

He leaps out of the pool with uncanny agility and surges toward me. With a shriek, I turn to dodge into the forest and run. But I'm not used to this world, and I don't get two steps before I trip over a root sticking up—why are there roots sticking out of the ground?—and would fall flat on my face.

Except Kaladen's arms scoop around my waist and lift me right off my feet again. I let out another shriek, kicking and trying to pry his arm off me. But like before, I cannot bring myself to *actually* hurt him, and thus, I can do nothing as he carries me to the edge of the pool.

"Don't you dare!" I shout, kicking more violently as he steps into the water. "Don't you *dare* throw me in the water, Kaladen!"

"I won't," he says with a self-satisfied chuckle.

But then he jumps. I let out a scream like I haven't screamed since I was a child, my arms flailing and nails scrabbling for purchase as if I can climb on top of his head to keep from being submerged.

Then I'm falling into the water. It closes over my head. My eyes turn to ice in their sockets as the light above me grows dimmer. Everything is so cold—so, *so* cold. And I need to breathe!

The arms around me tighten, and suddenly we're shooting upward. We break the surface of the water with a splash. I gasp for air, spluttering through wet lips.

Kaladen holds me tight against his chest, his chin at my eye-level. "You cannot swim, can you?"

"Nobody who lives in the desert can swim!" I splutter.

He chuckles against my wet head as I fight to get all my hair out of my face. The only warmth in this freezing water comes from his body, pressed against mine. I suddenly become aware of just how close we are—just how close he holds me in the water. My legs kick instinctively, and I find myself holding on to his shoulders, my fingernails digging into the wet fabric of his tunic.

"You're shivering." The smile still hasn't left his voice. "I can warm the pool up for us."

"We're staying in the water for longer than ten more seconds?" I blurt.

His low laughter is warm. His hand on my back slides to my waist. "I find it pleasant. Do you?"

I suck in a breath, forcing my gaze to the waterfall behind him instead of watching as his head dips closer to mine. I am freezing and I cannot stop shaking, but it would be a lie to claim I want to leave this instant.

The water warms around me. I nearly flinch. "Don't make it warmer!"

He tilts his head to one side. "But you're cold."

I don't want him to see my eyes roll back in my head in a dead faint. He's seen *enough* of my issues. "I like the cold."

"If you don't tell me the real reason, I'll make it warmer."

My mouth drops open.

He arches a brow at me. Then he leans down, brings his mouth to my ear. "How many times must I tell you I know when you're lying?"

"But I don't *want* to tell you!"

"Why not?"

"Because I don't want to," I reply stubbornly, tilting my face away from his. It makes me feel like a petulant child, but I don't know how to describe the crawling pressure up my back when I think of telling him.

"You don't have to tell me anything you don't want to," he says, his tone turning gentler. In the water, with our clothes wet, it feels like there is so little between us. And yet, it is as though I am still a mile away. "But I want you to acknowledge that there is nothing you can say that will make me think worse of you."

My eyes snap to his. "That's not true."

"Tell me how it isn't true. Tell me what would make me think less of you."

"You told me you would kill me like you killed Dabria and Fathuna if I betrayed you."

He lets out a long sigh, which warms my wet hair. "Do you want to know a secret?"

"What?"

His fingers wipe away water droplets from my cheek. I don't breathe. Not as his touch skims to my neck. "I could never hurt you, Nadira. You could betray me to my worst enemies and devote your life to my destruction, but I can never lift my hand against you in harm."

I don't realize my lips have parted until his thumb wipes a bead of water off them. Heat crawls up my neck into my cheeks. I cannot bear the weight of his gaze anymore. I look away.

"I don't think I ever could have hurt you, Nadira." His voice is a low, soft murmur that brushes against me like the kisses of a long-lost lover. "I used to believe I could, but I think I was lying to myself. Trying to make myself believe I wasn't in danger of . . . falling . . . again."

I'm breathing hard now, and so is he. He presses me against his chest, one hand smoothing down over my wet hair. Confusion fills me from head to toe, turning me upside down and right-side up again. "I don't know what you're saying. I don't know what that means."

"It doesn't mean anything you don't want it to," he replies gently. "Now, do you want to get out of this cold water? Or do you like shivering?"

The words are out before I can stop them, propelling forward as though by some invisible force I cannot control. "It feels like blood." He stops, but as soon as the words are out, I realize how little sense they make. "Warm water—it feels like blood and it makes me feel like I am drowning."

He's quiet for a minute, his scrutiny so intense I'm forced to look away again. Then, slowly, he nods. "That makes sense."

"What? How does it make sense?"

He waves away the question before lifting me a little higher. Now we are eye-level, and it's more difficult to avoid his attention. He has one arm wrapped around my waist, and his other hand slides up to cup my leg. "When did it start?"

"My first kill," I manage to answer around the sudden dizziness of his touch. Then I frown. Images flash before me suddenly. Sharp and terrifying, washing down my spine like an electric shock. "No . . . it was earlier."

How have I forgotten? It's like this entirely new memory captures my mind—except it's not new at all. It's old, worn, suppressed. I know it at once. It's like pieces of a puzzle I can finally put together. The shivers turn to outright trembling, but I don't feel *unsafe*. Not with Kaladen so close.

"It started with my parents," I say, closing my eyes so I can see that scene once more. My heartrate skyrockets, but Kaladen's touch on my leg grounds me. Helps me differentiate between the past and the present. "When Jabir killed them, and there was so much blood, I ran to my baba to help him get back up. I knew he was gone, but I couldn't accept it. I was kneeling in blood, and all my body could think was that it was *so, so warm*."

I squeeze my eyes shut, suddenly terrified to touch that memory. But Kaladen is here, holding me tightly, as he murmurs, "I've got you. You can go there if you need to. I've got you."

Those words bring the floodgates of horror I suppressed in that moment, the sudden and shocking loneliness that hit me when I saw nothing but vacancy in my parents' gazes. The confusion and refusal to even understand what was happening. Tremors sweep through my body, from my jaw to my ribs to my calves. They leave me shaking so hard I feel I will break into pieces. Memories flash across my mind's eye, coming in fragments. The hem of my frock and my dirty, dark feet stained red. Jabir's scratchy beard and his gravelly voice as he carried me away, telling me to hush my crying. The emptiness of the room he left me in. Long hours of staring at a mud-smeared wall. Lying on my back with my ankles propped up on the wall, telling myself stories that Baba would come get me any minute and take me home. Humming my bedtime song when darkness sank into that room, and still no one had come for me.

They wash through me like the waterfall a few paces away, leaving nothing behind but the memory of their ravages.

I sag against Kaladen, my arms wrapped around his neck. He lifts me up and carries me out of the water. Our clothes are sopping wet, dripping on the ground. I cling closer to his neck as I sniffle and breathe.

Once upon a time, I never would have dreamed that the one to hold me while I unravel would be the Neverseen King.

At once, I'm dry. Skin, clothes, hair. Kaladen is dry, too. I lift my head slightly, surprised to not be so cold anymore, and then put it down when I realize he's dried us with magic.

"Where are we going?" I ask.

"Somewhere."

"I'm hungry."

His lips spread against my ear in a smile. "Good."

CHAPTER 24

THE MOURNER

KALADEN TAKES ME up a rickety wooden staircase that seems to appear out of nowhere. I am barely aware of where we're going. For once, that is fine with me. More than fine. I don't want to think right now.

He takes me over a doorless threshold into what appears to be a tiny house in a tree. I blink blearily as I take in the wooden beams of the walls and ceiling—which are only partially there.

He sets me on the floorboards, leaning against the smooth bark of a great tree, with my legs dangling over the edge. When I start to get up, curious to explore this treehouse, he tosses a thin, woven blanket onto my lap and orders, "Stay."

I watch from the edge of the platform as he makes his way across the room to a cabinet and opens it. He assembles something plate while my eyelids sag. I let more of my weight relax against the tree. Then he's beside me once more. "It's not food you're used to, but I hope it still tastes good. I need to change the spells to suit your taste."

I sit up eagerly. How am I suddenly a ravenous monster of a woman? Perhaps crying out my fears left new space in my body for food. My hands shake when I take a piece of fruit and bring it to my mouth.

The fruit is unusual. It has a red skin with black speckles of seeds and a tuft of stem green at the top. I pop the whole thing in my mouth. It's sweet and bright and I instantly love it.

"That is a strawberry. It's grown in another part of the human world. There are many more if you like them. This bread is dark wheat, and the cheese is called cheddar."

"Aren't you going to eat?" I ask around a full mouth.

"I suppose I should, shouldn't I?"

"Eat!" I cry, shoving the plate toward him. He smiles and takes a strawberry. He quickly loses his modesty, and we devour plate after plate of the simple meal. There is no end to the magical supply of the food, so we feast until we cannot eat anymore.

I slump against the tree, kicking my legs in utter satisfaction and rubbing the soft blanket between my fingers. "I know you said we need to train my magic, but I feel like napping."

Now that some clarity and strength has returned to my limbs—despite the exhaustion—I can look around the little treehouse. It's very plain, with one cabinet of food, a bed against the far wall, and another cabinet near the massive trunk of the tree we're in. The few walls that exist are only high enough to keep one from accidentally falling off the platform, the roof only covering enough to keep out rain. The rest is open to the cool air and wind.

"That can be arranged," he says with a smirk, nodding his head toward the bed. "But after that, I'm going to drill you in magic mastery until you're ready to drop dead."

I make a face at him, grab the blanket, and march over to the bed. My plan is to lie down, roll so my back is to him, and let my exhaustion claim me. But the moment I'm settled beneath the sheets, I sense Kaladen's gaze on me. I look up. "What?"

He seems to hesitate for just a moment. Then he gets up and motions to me. "Scoot over."

Instantly, my face turns to the temperature of an oven. My pulse skips five beats. But wordlessly, I scoot over.

He climbs into bed beside me. This bed isn't nearly so huge as his bed back in Arbasa. We can still lie side by side and not touch . . . but barely.

"I'm glad you're resting too," I say—as if that will make him not aware of how flushed I am. "You overwork yourself."

"I could say the same to you."

"It is good we are both resting." It sounds even stupider spoken out loud. I close my eyes, cursing myself inwardly for still being so rattled by his proximity. It's like each time we share a bed is new. Each time is terrifying and thrilling and so overwhelming.

Kaladen lets out a sigh. Then he turns toward me. I tilt my head to him and offer him the world's most awkward smile.

I'm not expecting him to reach out. To plant his big, square hand on my midsection—and *pull* me back against him. A tiny gasp escapes me as his familiar warmth once more becomes my cocoon.

"This is better," Kaladen murmurs into my ear.

I may be as red as the desert sands—and twice as hot—but I agree with him. I agree with him so emphatically that I twist and roll toward him. I throw caution to the wind and fling my arms around his neck, burrowing into his chest and pulling him as close to me as I can.

He lets out a low, short sound, and crushes me against him. "I've got you, Nadira. No matter what happens. I've got you."

A contented sound in the back of my throat escapes me. The instant it is out, I wish I could grab it and shove it back into my mouth. Because Kaladen has gone still. I can't let him suddenly decide to leave!

So I blurt the first thing I can think of asking: "Did you make this for Liliana?"

He lets out a long, deep breath. "I did."

"How did you meet her?"

"That is a long story."

I roll over so I can watch him expectantly. He lets go of me, and I mourn the loss—but I will gladly take this distance if it means he doesn't leave me altogether.

He chuckles, then rubs the bridge of his nose. "We were dealing with a troll rebellion. The High King sent the Wolf and me each with a company of warriors, but instead of us working together, it was to be a competition. To see which of us was more fit for leadership. We were only a few days into the campaign, and having successfully retaken control of a prominent city, Wolf decided it was time for celebration. Since we were near a door to the human realm, he used a loophole in the treaty and took the door when I had my back turned. I never would have known what he intended, except that the maiden he dragged back was raising hell and screaming our eardrums out.

"I confronted him at once. He replied that if I was jealous, I ought to just go get my own. So I fought him. And I won." Here, Kaladen lets out another exhale. "But I didn't kill him. Those were the days when I believed in mercy and hope. I took the girl and tried to take her back to her world, but the portal took us to the wrong time. In the end, I had no choice but to bring her with me on the campaign, with the promise that after it was finished, I would find out how to return her to her own age. She agreed and came along. It became quite an . . . *interesting* campaign after that. I was terrified that if I turned my back, the Wolf would take her again. But there was an unspoken agreement between Wolf and I in that day. I had won the girl, so I got to keep her. Eventually, we would all be eating around the fire, and she would be there too, rebuking us for '*eating like monsters.*'"

Here, he smiles and lets out another of his warm chuckles. It fades quickly to something more serious, more thoughtful. "By the end of the campaign, I think we were all a little in love with her spunk and fearlessness. But I was the one who'd rescued her, and it was my tent she stayed in. It was I who had first given her respect and dignity.

"When we finished the campaign and it was time to fulfill my promise to her, I worked hard to understand the nuances of portals. The Neverseen King before me was the one who showed me how to work portals with the precision that was necessary to send Liliana back. Finally, I took her home."

I lie still, listening. His voice grows quieter and quieter as he recounts the tale.

"I stood there, watching as she walked away from me, knowing I'd never see her again. I tried to be glad for it, that she would be where she belonged. Safe with her people. Yet I couldn't. It wasn't until that moment I realized just how devastated I was to lose her.

"Suddenly, she turned around and ran back to me. She said she loved me and that she wanted to stay with me. I couldn't believe it. We wed then and there, because I knew if she was to stay in Faerieland, she would need the protection of a marriage bond. The High King was furious that I'd wed a human instead of marrying his choice. But then the office of the Neverseen King came open, and the Wolf and I were once again rivals. I had never hated him until he dragged Liliana into our camp, but since that moment, I'd hated him with a vicious passion. On his side, the grudging respect I'd earned from Wolf was gone, replaced instead with bitterness and anger. He convinced the High King that whoever won the office of the Neverseen King should also get the human girl. So we fought once more, and you can imagine there was no version of reality where I was going to let Wolf take my wife from me. I won, yet again." He doesn't say it with pride. If anything, those words cause him to turn colder, and he speaks his next ones in that dry, rueful tone I used to know so well. "That was how I became the Neverseen King, married a human girl, and how the Wolf and I became enemies."

I furrow my brow, turning the story over in my mind. "So, when the Wolf is trying to get your position by undermining you before the High King . . . is he also trying to get me?"

Kaladen's nod is grim. "He wants to take you from me, to avenge how I took her from him and made a fool out of him."

Curiosity makes me shrug and climb out of bed, my energy renewed. There's more of this treehouse I haven't explored. "That makes sense. I would probably do the same in his position."

"Hardly!" Kaladen scoffs. "You would never be in the same position!"

At this point, I don't like to tempt fate with those kinds of words. I wander around the treehouse, ducking under low limbs, peering over the edge of the platform into the foliage below. Behind me, the bed creaks as Kaladen gets up as well. My bare feet make quiet pitter-patters on the smooth floor.

The treehouse curves around the trunk of the tree in an O shape, and as I follow it around to the other side, I discover another cabinet. It's like the one Kaladen got our food out of earlier.

I open it up, not sure what I'm expecting. Immediately, a tidal wave of energy and brilliant light forces me back several steps. The wave crashes against me and flows away until I can open my eyes and see what I have just uncovered.

Before me are shelves full of dozens upon dozens of small glowing orbs, like eggs, all arranged in neat rows, filling up the cabinet. They glow every color of the rainbow, reminding me of the portal doors.

"Kaladen," I say breathlessly.

He comes around to my side of the treehouse and stops the moment he sees the glows emanating on my face. "Oh. You found that."

"What is it?"

"That is . . . well . . . a project that Liliana and I were working on before she died."

"What sort of project?" I hold my hand over an orb the color of a robin's egg. It turns my skin a brilliant shade of turquoise.

Kaladen scratches the back of his neck. "There was this theory that the Neverseen King before me took very seriously. I've mentioned before that magic is all about finding balance and sustaining it. There is a legend that our many worlds were once all one, and then a great shattering took place, splitting fractions of the universe apart into separate pockets of reality. He theorized—and Liliana and I both thought this was very possible—that the reason the doors break down so often is because the worlds are striving, in a strange and very unhelpful way, to become one again."

He picks up an amethyst orb, rolling it over his palm, and drawing his thumb in a line down its smooth, glowing surface. "These are souls of the portals."

"They're *what*?"

"Souls. Essences of being. Taken from the portals and put here. The idea was that if we collected a soul from each portal and brought them together again, it would stabilize the Bridge such that the seals would never break down. My position as the Neverseen King would be far less perilous, and far more powerful. I was skeptical of it, I confess," he says. "But Liliana, ever the optimist, was very convinced it was true. And thus, we continued the prior Neverseen King's work to harvest the souls and bring them together."

That's when I notice, at the very bottom of the shelf, two empty slots. I point. "You didn't get them all."

He nods. "That was how she died. I told her . . ." His jaw hardens, flexes. He pauses for several minutes, as though he's not sure what he's going to say, or perhaps he knows what it is that he needs to say but doesn't know how to get the words out. "We had two portals left," he says finally. "Crenfyre was one of them, and the other was Roltwart. We were struggling to seal Roltwart on Lulythinar. She said she wanted to get its soul. I told her no; it was too risky. But she wouldn't listen. She wouldn't listen, and so she went to get it when I turned my back. And then . . . things went wrong."

"That's why you never finished?"

“Correct,” he replies, his tone growing firmer. “And I don’t intend to.”

“I understand that sentiment very well,” I say, even though part of me is instantly curious, instantly intrigued by those two empty spots on the shelf. I want to know how to find the soul of a portal. If we could do it before Lulythinar—

“I see what you're thinking, and no, we’re not finishing this. Even if we can get the soul for Roltwart, which is difficult enough, we cannot enter the Crenfyre portal. It’s impossible without dying, which is why we have to use an alternative method of sealing. The whole project is nothing but a suicide mission at this point.”

“But what if it isn’t?”

Kaladen’s voice turns cold. “There’s enough for us to worry about as it is. We’re not adding this.”

I nod slowly, acquiescing . . . for now.

We don’t talk the entire walk back to Arbasa, but my mind is so full of all the things I need to accomplish, I’m not sure I’ll ever be able to sleep again. When I pull on my shoes, I’m expecting to walk through that door, give a polite nod to Kaladen, and then hurry to Emin’s study to spend the afternoon researching markets and kingdom economics before it’s time for more portal work.

It isn’t quiet that greets me when he opens the door, however, but shrill, childlike laughter. It rips me from my contemplation. Beside me, Kaladen stands straighter, his gaze shooting to one side. “What is that?”

I follow the direction of his gaze to not one, not two, but five small children clad in filthy rags, fighting over a basket of naan bread. I recognize one of them as Abbi, with his too-large ears, and not far away, Zara—looking so thin a single gust could blow her over—holds that toddler in one arm and a piece of naan bread in the other. She doesn’t eat it herself, but feeds it piece by piece to the little one.

“What—” I start to say, but I’m interrupted by Eshe’s unmistakable shouting.

“You do as you’re told or you leave, understand?” She’s pointing one of her thin little fingers in the face of a boy at least six inches taller than her and twice as broad, though he must be ten years younger. He looks like he could knock her unconscious with a punch, and the tension filling his shoulders seems to indicate that he might do just that. But with an impatient huff, he turns around and walks the other way. "Well!" she cries, brushing her hands off and approaching where Kaladen and I stand, our mouths hanging open. "Hello!"

"What is this?" Fury lines Kaladen's voice. "Why are there all these . . . *children* in my palace?"

"Well," says Eshe, "they were starving, living on the street, and we have rooms and food here, and so I thought we should—"

Kaladen takes several aggressive steps toward Eshe. "You thought we should do what? This is *my* palace. You do not get to decide who lives here and who doesn't."

"True, but it's also Nadira's palace, considering that she is queen. And you cannot seriously intend to toss a bunch of homeless children back on the streets because you like your palace being as empty as a graveyard!"

I wince.

He whirls on me. "Did you know about this?"

"Of course not! I told her I was going to try to think of something, but I didn't mean for her to—"

"See?" Kaladen flings a hand back at me. "The queen didn't know about this. You cannot claim that it is her plan."

"I would have discussed it with you," Eshe says tartly, even though she and I both know it's a lie.

Kaladen stands there, his fists clenched at his side, fury emanating from the taut muscles of his back.

"Are you really going to make me send them away?" Eshe asks innocently, her eyes round, her long lashes blinking.

I stand there, shaking my head, half horrified and half amused. That little troublemaker! She never intended to ask permission. Her plan was to force Kaladen's hand because she knows he's not as heartless as he pretends.

He steps closer to her, dropping his voice so the children cannot overhear him. "*Eshe*. Have you already forgotten that dragon that nearly killed you all? Have you forgotten about Crenfyre? The goblins? Have you forgotten the women who died because they stayed here? Hulla, Mahja, and Gaya? You saw what happened to Emin! How could you possibly think this would be a safe place for *children* to stay? It isn't even safe enough for those with training in combat!"

She drops the innocent expression, her eyes flashing. "You think they're safer on the streets? Starving? Vulnerable to attack from both human and monster? Do you think they were safe when the *beechka* flooded the city?"

"*Beechka* don't kill."

"No, we were lucky on that count. But what about next time?"

Kaladen's face darkens. "There won't be a next time."

It's a lie, and if I didn't know better, I'd think his mouth twisted almost as if he could taste the sourness of his own words. Lulythinar is coming quickly. There will be more breakouts, despite our best efforts.

Eshe throws up her hands. "Then it's perfectly safe for them to be here! You have Nadira to help you contain everything, and they don't starve."

"*Perfectly safe*—are you out of your mind? The House is the barrier between the city and all the wild worlds beyond. The *only* barrier. They are safer on the *other side* of the barrier."

"Sultani, I grew up on the streets of Risya. You don't know what these orphans go through. I do. And *I* have felt safer in this monster-ridden palace than I ever did out there."

I watch the force of wills battling in front of me, not even sure where I stand in this argument. I see both sides, though I find Kaladen's point harder to overcome. How could we, in good conscience, keep children in a place like this? I find myself speaking before I even know what I intend to accomplish. "Is there some place on the palace grounds they can stay? Some place that isn't *in the palace*, to avoid them being hurt by the House's defenses? A place close to a gate where they could escape quickly if things went badly?"

"A compromise!" exclaims Eshe. "Such a thing didn't occur to me."

I ignore her and focus my attention on Kaladen, who has gone quiet. As if he knows exactly a place and doesn't want to admit it.

"You're supposed to take my side," he grumbles.

I smirk.

"There is one place," he says at last, giving up. "There are a few sheds where the groundkeepers store their tools. They're near the palace gates and separate from the House itself. They would need to be cleaned and cleared out—"

"Thank you!" cries Eshe, clapping her hands.

"You are in charge of this, not me or my staff. They have enough work to do as it is," says Kaladen darkly, pointing one finger at Eshe. "If any of them get hurt, they leave. If they cause trouble in my House, they leave. I refuse to take responsibility for this. You are in charge, and I will hold you responsible for any trouble caused."

Eshe grins. "Of course."

With that and nothing else, Kaladen marches off down the hallway, past the children who have stopped eating their naan to stare at him—crumbs plastered across their filthy faces. I sigh, my mind tripping over itself to try to understand all the implications of this new development.

"I'm going to go try to figure out how to feed all these mouths," I say. "And perhaps how to get enough water to wash everyone."

Even though I already know exactly where I'm finding water to wash them all.

I watch Kaladen's shadow disappear.

CHAPTER 25

THE NEVERSEEN KING

GETTING TO THE anchor of the Nallan Portal is easy enough. It's getting back out that always proves a challenge.

Three centaurs circle me slowly, their hooves splashing in the shallow water as I hold a full cup. One tosses his hairy head, red eyes blazing at me and brawny shoulders clenching as he grips his cudgel.

"You make this difficult every time," I growl.

The one with a shiny gray-blue coat growls a series of grunts, nickers, and clicks. My brain orients the sounds into something I understand. *Let us pass into the mortal world. Time has come for us to take dominion over the green grass of the human lands.*

I sidestep as the third one lunges toward me. "If you go out this door, the *green grass* you expect to find will sorely disappoint you."

Do not lie to us. We know the mortals claim rolling hills of green grass as far as the eye can see. You cannot dissuade us from our conquest.

I sigh. "Very well."

Then I spin around and throw a bolt of pure energy straight into the red-eyed one. He tries to dodge, but it pierces him through the heart. He falls.

The other two attack me.

One cudgel comes for my face. I grab it out of the air and yank hard. My opponent whinnies and plants his hind quarters, barely preventing me from smashing him in the chest with another bolt of magic. I dodge the second's blow, time a careful kick to his front legs. A crack resounds, and the horse-like scream would chill even the hardiest warrior. My bolt spears him through his chest before he hits the ground. Water sprays and sloshes over the edge of the cup that limits my motion.

Bare hands close around my throat from behind.

I clench my teeth hard, grabbing his forearm, and send my magic searing through my palm into his skin. He screams, but only one of his hands drops from my throat. I choke. My groping hand finds the knife in my belt and slams it backward. It pierces his hairy abdomen. Blood spurts and a cry goes up. The cudgel smashes into my brow.

I let out a fierce roar as I spin and shoot another blast of magic. It hits the third centaur, toppling him.

More are coming. The mist cannot hide their approaching shadows.

I break into a run. Air shifts around me, and I barely dodge the arrow that embeds deep into the door. "I hate this portal," I growl as I fling the door wide and throw myself through. I splash the water on the disintegrating seal and scrape open the cut on my finger.

My thumb throbs as I press my blood to the door. The seal flares bright red. *Renewed.*

I close my eyes and breathe.

My head pounds from the hit, but one quick step into the waking world fixes it. I slip back into the dream realm, where it's easier to ignore all the stray children working with Eshe to clear out the garden sheds. Easier to ignore the constant bark of Eshe's tone as she commands obedience while I work.

It's harder to ignore the constant humming of disintegrating seals. I can work all day and all night, and still never be done. Lulythinar creeps ever closer, threatening that if I don't teach Nadira everything I know, it'll cost her life. And yet, I am so attuned to her capacity for such magical exertion. I don't know if I can get her there in time without breaking her in the process. The treehouse will help, I hope, but even that brings back things I don't want to think about.

Like all those portal souls. It has been some time since I considered them. I so thoroughly dismissed that solution to the problem of the Bridge after Liliana's death that it is strange to encounter them once more.

I work hard the entire afternoon and evening, trying to create space for things to go wrong again tonight. Once, I take a short break to catch my breath, and just at that instant, my awareness of the rainforest portal prickles. I return to find Nadira hauling bucket after bucket of river water through the door, sternly instructing the children gathering around her to wash themselves. They make such a disastrous mess of the hallway and courtyard that the House shudders and groans irritably. Once she's seen to that, she shuts herself back in Emin's office.

My hand goes to my face. The thick ridge of a scar meets my fingertips.

I should have shown her my face while we were there. I should have let the glamours slide away.

With a sigh, I let my hand fall to my side.

It's best to focus on what is before me right this instant, which is the Adrell Portal. This one will be difficult and will likely keep me occupied until dusk. Best not to delay.

But I delay one more second, and glance at the door of Emin's study.

When I finally emerge from the Adrell Portal, exhausted and spent, pink splatters of fireflower nectar all along my forearms and the front of my tunic, the sun dips dangerously low on the horizon. I let out a long exhale. Has Nadira returned to our room already? I hurry, only to discover it empty. My frown deepens. She's usually very cognizant of the time, but then again, she was late for Emin's funeral.

The hallways are empty of every street urchin, but it's not quiet. A cacophony of shouting and stern, high-pitched orders from Eshe—*to settle down or be eaten by a monster*—are audible a shocking distance from the garden sheds they set up as bedrooms.

I find Nadira in Emin's office, still poring over heaps of books and scrolls. She has an empty book beside her, filled with her own precise handwriting. Notes? She hasn't lit a candle, despite how dark the room has grown. She isn't aware of me, not as I softly shut the door behind me and take a few steps into the room. Her head is bowed, her long hair falling uncovered to her waist, her head propped up on one fist, her foot tapping an anxious rhythm. I take a few more steps. How can she even see the words she's reading with how dark has gotten? It's not like she has fae sight.

"Your focus puts any diligent man to shame."

Nadira jumps three feet into the air and whirls. "You keep scaring me!"

"I'm not trying to!" Both of my hands go up in the air. "It's impossible not to scare you when you're in this deep study of yours! I've never seen anyone so engrossed in their work." I sidle up to her, trying to ignore the pulse of her heartbeat in the air as I glance down at her notes. "Basket weaving?"

She quickly covers the sheet of paper with her hand. "I'm exploring a few options," she says quickly. "Haven't decided on anything yet."

"Options for what?"

She sucks on her teeth, glancing back down at the piles of notes before her. "How to find a sustainable way to take care of these children. I was looking at the ledgers, and we've hardly had any money coming in for some time. Taxes aren't being collected. Trade is falling to pieces, decreasing the amount of tariff money we bring in. Eshe brought in some thirty children—but there's far more in the city. I've run multiple calculations. None of the results are promising." She takes the book and flips it back a few pages, showing me her estimated figures. I peruse them with interest. "And that's if we can even get our hands on the right suppliers, with prices increasing so much at the market. Clearly supply is low overall, so if we don't fix that, the entire kingdom's economy might crash. Then how to feed a few orphans will be the least of our concerns. I know I should be focused on Lulythinar, but I cannot ignore this."

My shoulders grow heavy as I listen to her. She keeps talking, explaining the problem to me, and I am mesmerized by the rising passion in her voice, the way her mind works so carefully and methodically, and yet, shame fills me. I have been so overwhelmed by the problem of the Bridge that I have not given Arbasa the time and attention that it needs. It needs so much more than I have been able to give it.

"I'm sorry," I say abruptly.

"What?"

"I'm sorry that I have neglected your people."

"Oh," she says, tucking a strand of hair around her head behind her ear. "You had far too much responsibility. I don't blame you at all. You've been trying to keep us alive for the last two hundred years. For that, I owe you thanks."

"You always try to make me sound more virtuous than I am," I say, and when she starts to roll her eyes, I interject: "But truly, I want things to be different moving forward. What do you need help with?"

She's quiet for several minutes, looking across the span of papers on the desk. When she speaks, her voice is cold and dark. "I need help with the city guard."

"What about them?"

"They have no accountability. The city is not safe for the orphans because of them. The guards . . . they do what they please to the urchins. Sometimes it is an overly severe punishment for theft. Other times, it is worse."

My eyes narrow, dark energy rising inside my chest. My words come out much calmer than I feel. "Did they ever touch you?"

"Me? No."

I nod once, understanding. "Eshe."

Her jaw flexes. "That was how we met. I was returning from one of my earliest jobs. I came upon her . . . and him. I remember being so upset from the job, feeling such deep shame, but when I saw Eshe, all of it was gone in an instant. To this day, I have never regretted that kill."

"Good." It comes out in a growl. "I will take care of the city guard."

"Thank you."

"Also." I lick my lips. "I want to crown you in front of the kingdom."

Her eyebrows lift a fraction, her lips parting.

"You're the queen of Arbasa. You deserve a coronation."

She grabs hold of the edge of the table for support. She opens her mouth to protest, but then draws her lips together. "If you think that is best."

I tilt my head to one side. "I do think it is best. Your people cannot see me, but they need to see you."

Her knuckles turn white. "It doesn't feel right."

I step closer to her, barely keeping my hand from drifting up to her cheek, barely keeping myself from making her look at me so I can drown once more in her dark eyes. "Why? Why doesn't it feel right?"

She squeezes her eyes shut. "Because I am the Mourner."

"You are Queen Nadira of Arbasa. You are no mourner. You need not hold that title any longer if you don't want it."

"I have enemies here," she insists. "You remember how Raha tried to kill me when she discovered I killed her father. There are more in this city, in this kingdom. People who would pay a fortune to see my body mounted on a spike at the city gates."

My blood flares red hot. I refuse to let my mind imagine that awful picture. "Then it is good you are the wife of a king who tolerates no harm of what belongs to him."

Her eyes finally meet mine. They are two glowing pools of stars in the dim light.

"I will plan your coronation," I say, turning to leave. "You have enough to manage already. Do you wish to come with me to our chamber?"

She blinks thrice, then glances around the growing darkness. "It's evening already!"

"Come," I say and hold out my hand to her. She casts a longing glance back at the work she's abandoning, then places her small hand in mine. I close my fingers around hers, gripping tightly. "Are you afraid?"

"A little," she admits.

"You don't have to do anything you don't want to."

She doesn't reply, but she meets my gaze and holds it.

When I open the door, however, the sun is much closer to dipping below the horizon than I expected. We don't even have a full minute to get back to our chambers. Grimly, I step back inside and shut the door.

"Are we stuck?" Nadira asks.

"It seems like it."

The study is very small, with bookshelves lining almost every wall, Emin's desk, with only that small cot shoved in the corner. The cot that smells very distinctly of Emin. I wrinkle my nose. There is also no way I can fit on that tiny thing.

Nadira must be thinking the same thing, because she smirks up at me. "You found the floor *very* comfortable yesterday. When you fainted."

"That's enough," I say.

She laughs, and I think I fall just a little bit more in love with her at the sound. It's not what I would like—to be sprawled out on the floor with a thin blanket that doesn't even cover my feet, while she takes the cot next to me. It reminds me of the campaigns the High King would send me on when I was younger. Most of those nights, we slept out under the stars with nothing but the clothes on our backs and the steel of our weapons in our hands.

When I think about it that way, and watch my wife's breathing even beside me, I decide this isn't so bad after all.

Then I think about Lulythinar approaching and the impossibility of the feat ahead of us, the almost insurmountable task just *tonight* of simultaneously training Nadira and sealing the growing number of unstable portals. It's been a hundred years since the last Lulythinar, but I still don't remember having this many breaking open, even without the High King's sabotage. And Liliana was a far more proficient aid than Nadira will be.

Everything was in our favor last Lulythinar, and it still wasn't enough.

I'm not even sure *I* will survive this one.

I cannot lose another wife. I cannot lose another wife. I cannot—I cannot.

I'm trying to be what Nadira needs. I'm trying to put aside my own fears of loss. I'm trying—trying—but I think I might drown in all that I'm trying to do. Her survival might not even be *possible*, yet here I am, thinking about her at every waking moment. Letting myself forget Lulythinar as if I can just pretend we'll have a normal life after it, as if every single Lulythinar to come isn't another death sentence for Nadira.

"What am I doing?" I breathe into the silence, running a hand down my face. "What am I even *doing*?"

I don't have the answer to that question, but I still have no choice but to join Nadira in the dream realm.

CHAPTER 26

THE MOURNER

"THE TRICK WITH this portal," Kaladen says to me, five hours into our nightly work, "is to be quiet enough to not wake the statues. They cannot kill you, but they can make you wish you were dead."

"So encouraging," I reply dryly, staring at the blue stone door we face.

"Are you sure you want to try this one? I can—"

"I've watched you do enough. It's my turn."

He doesn't try to dissuade me anymore. I step up to the door, breathing deeply. By habit, my counting starts.

One, two, three, four.

I ease the door open. A wave of cool wind, smelling of sulfur, washes over my face. I suppress a choke and press into the world beyond. My breath steals from my lungs, my counting momentarily forgotten.

I stand on a roughly hewn rock surface that continues as far as I can see in every direction. Massive stone pillars rise to the heavens above me, and I never would have realized they were carved statues if they didn't have gigantic feet and toes the size of my entire body. Eerie half-light reflects on the polished stone.

When I look back, Kaladen is right behind me, guarding the door. Silent as a corpse.

I'm good at being quiet too.

Five, six, seven, eight, nine, ten.

I move swiftly between stone feet, searching for the anchor. I count twelve paces and hunt in a circle around the door. Dodging around feet, I make my way around the entire circle, but find no glowing anchor.

Kaladen watches me. I fling up a hand, telling him to not help me. I want to figure this out myself.

Twenty, twenty-one, twenty-two.

I realize my mistake and would cover my face with my palm. Instead, I keep moving. Marching straight to one of the pairs of feet in the way, I breathe a prayer and then hoist myself up on the foot's arch. Nothing.

Kaladen's amusement carries silently across the distance. I shoot him a glare, expect to earn a grin in return but only receive a slightly curved lip instead, and then hurry to the next pair of feet.

This time, attached at the ankle, is a small glowing orb. Surrounding it is a cluster of rocks that seem very out of place. Kaladen put these here, didn't he? To keep from having to hew chunks out of the statue to use for the seal. I take the topmost rock, careful not to disturb the pile, and hop to the ground. I hurry back to the door, ignoring the enormous, clawed paws I pass, and the strange reptilian ones that remind me of the dragon Eshe and I used Crenfyre to kill.

Thirty.

We hurry out the door. I scratch open my cut and press it to the stone I hold against the seal. The seal flares bright red.

"Impressive," Kaladen says.

I whirl on him. "I did that! By myself!" The triumphant cry is out before I can help it, my grin stretching across my face. "I just sealed a portal!"

"You did, indeed. That stealth work was enough to make any fae jealous."

"Don't tease me!"

"I'm not."

I glare at him for all of three seconds before it washes away. "I want to do the next one too!"

"The next one is harder to—"

"I don't care! Tell me how to do it."

He stops. Leans a fraction closer to me. Something cuts through his uncharacteristic quiet; warmth and thrill emanate from him, curling in the air. Then he waves a hand and gestures that I follow him.

The back of my mind hums with fear that at any moment, the magic will catch up to us, rip me back to my past and force us to end our time together working. But hours have gone by, and still nothing has happened. I don't want to tempt fate, but part of me wonders if Kaladen was right: that bonding closer helped us.

I swallow as I stare at his back, his broad shoulders. It's almost terrifying to realize that I wouldn't choose to be anywhere in the world but right here, right now. I love using my skills for something good. This is like Eshe and I going on our old jobs, but this time, I have complete confidence that my partner won't suddenly do something stupid or unexpected, and I actually enjoy what I am doing. It's like all the good things with none of the bad.

I find myself wishing dawn will never come and we can stay in this intimate darkness, working together.

Kaladen's voice interrupts my thoughts. "This next one might challenge you."

My palms fall to the hilts of my knives. "Good."

But the way this one challenges me is not how I was hoping.

This portal, to Aufaamor, opens into a sea. The sea off the shore of Valehaven.

"I have not encountered issues with this portal in nearly a century," Kaladen tells me, pressing something into my hands. "But you must swim to the anchor. I keep this bottle to collect the water near the anchor for the seal." He takes one look at my pale face and adds: "You don't have to."

It *would* be easier to let him do it. I clench my jaw.

No.

I'm going to do this.

And I'm *not* going to pass out.

When I open the door, I half expect water to come rushing into the hallway and drown us. Instead, the water stays on its side of the door, and I find myself staring into a vibrant underwater world of brightly colored coral, swimming fish, and something in the distance that looks eerily like the legend of a mermaid.

"You must hold your breath. The entire time. It's too deep for you to swim up for air." Kaladen's hand lands on my shoulder, stopping me just as I reach for the wall of water. "I can teach you how to swim later, and we can come back to this one."

I don't want to come back later. Even though my blood pounds in my ears, I don't want to admit failure. I want to overcome this. Once and for all.

"Show me how to swim." I point to the water. "I'll practice holding my breath."

He studies me for a moment, as though to test if I'm serious. Then he draws a deep breath and steps through the door into the water. His clothes float around him, his cloak rising in the current. He looks back at me, waiting.

I can do this.

I fill my lungs and fall into the water before I can stop myself.

Cold encases me like ice, nearly freezing me immobile. My lungs immediately scream for air, and I nearly panic that I cannot inhale.

Kaladen gently kicks his feet and reaches for me. I grab the doorframe and pull myself halfway out so I can gasp for air.

He's there the next second, his hand on my back—the only warm thing in this frigid world.

"I'm fine," I say, breathing hard. "I'm going to try again."

The second time I submerge myself, it's still frightening, but it doesn't overwhelm me.

I grit my teeth and push further out into the water. My hair fans out behind me. It's a good thing the water is so cold. I can spend more time being miserable and less time passing out. Kaladen swims to my side and shows me how to kick my legs and move my arms. The panic flares again when I mimic him, but I push past it. I give a few futile kicks that get me nowhere.

Then, when I kick again, I move forward instead of floundering.

This time, it isn't panic that fills me, but excitement.

I pull myself back under the doorframe and stick my head out of the water to breathe. Only a second later, I push back out.

I can do this.

I'm *doing* this.

I'm shocked at how quickly I can move when I get my arms and legs working properly. Kaladen swims beside me, going slowly for me, but I don't want to need him. I want to get this.

The anchor glows in front of me, hovering in the water a few feet above the seafloor. Vegetation blooms and waves in the currents below me, and I almost get distracted by a lobster scurrying along the sand. A school of bright red fish swim near me. If Kaladen didn't reach out and squeeze my elbow, I might have used up all my air staring at this strange and beautiful world.

The thought of getting trapped without air makes me kick back into motion, fear flowing through my blood once more. I pull the vial from my pocket and hold it right up to the anchor. When I unstopper it, water fills it in a flash. I put the cap back on.

That's when my lungs squeeze so tightly I nearly gasp.

Holding the vial in my hand, I swim toward the door. Warm light and breathable air beckon. Kaladen casts me a worried glance. A few bubbles escape my lips.

I'm going to do this.

I push myself harder. My legs and arms kick, losing their potency. I had no idea how many muscles it takes to swim.

The urge to breathe grows stronger.

The panic sets in harder, reminding me of all the times I couldn't breathe. All the times I nearly suffocated. *Don't think about that.*

Too late.

Kaladen's hand closes around my elbow, about to pull me the rest of the way.

I yank back, even though everything inside me screams.

I'm doing this on my own. Maybe I shouldn't. I need his help. But somehow, in a way I cannot describe, this is important. I need to accomplish this.

I kick harder. My lungs nearly collapse.

And then my hand closes around a blessed doorframe, and I pull myself through.

We land in a pile on the threshold of the door. I gasp for air as Kaladen grabs my shoulder. "Are you alright? Did you swallow any water?"

I shake my head, trembling, and vaguely realize we're both dry. I shove to my feet, the vial clutched in one hand. The door swings shut. I splash the water onto the crumbling seal and press my bloody thumb to it. The seal flares to life.

"I did it," I gasp. Then, louder: "I *did* it! I felt like I was going to die in there—but I did it!"

My laughter rings out against the walls, the multicolored doors, the light that plays across Kaladen's shadows. I feel alive—so, so *alive*, like I did at our bonding. Kaladen's pride courses out from him, invisible and yet so tangible to me.

I'm acting on instinct, the heady pleasure of the moment. I grab the front of his tunic and pull him down to me, standing on my tiptoes to press my lips against his in a hot and fierce kiss.

His lips are soft, the shape of his mouth familiar to me. How I have *longed* for this, for him. He—

He's not moving.

Not kissing me back.

He's a statue beneath my hands, his mouth frozen against mine.

Is he just surprised? Maybe he's only acting in shock. I wait two seconds longer, keeping my lips pressed to his, hoping he'll suddenly kiss me back, waiting desperately for any shred of warmth.

It doesn't come.

I pull away immediately. My gut sinks so fast, so hard, I can barely keep myself from searching for some place to hide from the sudden, roiling confusion. I unclench my grip from his tunic. He retreats one step, and half turns his back. One of his hands scrapes hard at the back of his neck.

My mind cannot piece together what this means.

We've spent so much time working together. Weeping together. Laying together in the same bed. It wasn't like he tolerated me in those times. He pulled me against him. He touched me. Teased me. Comforted me. *Flirted* with me.

He's even already kissed me of his own accord. I wasn't pressing a knife to his throat demanding such a thing. He gave it of his own free will.

So what just happened?

He had told me this wasn't a real marriage, but then he turned around and treated it like it was real. He gave me *every* indication that he cared very deeply about me. Even now, I still cannot believe he doesn't.

Is he still lost in the memory of his first wife? Has he been leading me on all this time?

My triumph over the portal is instantly forgotten. I cannot make sense of this, but there is one thing I know. One thing he just made *very* clear.

He doesn't want my kiss.

I try to search the darkness shielding his eyes from me—the shadows he still wears and yet I forgot—but I am suddenly too ashamed to meet them. I step back and cough to clear the mortification from my throat. "Sorry."

My memory flashes back to when I was a child, proudly bringing my untied knot to Jabir, as if expecting him to love me because of it. *I'm such a fool*, I'd thought then.

I think it again now.

I'm *such* a fool.

I don't even know what makes me a fool in this moment. All I know is that it's true.

"Sorry," I say again, to fill the cavernous silence. I turn away, rub my hands down the front of my sirwal. "I was carried away by the moment. Shall we continue?"

I don't want to continue. I'd rather go die. But I don't want to sacrifice *all* of my dignity in the span of a minute.

His heartbeat is an erratic pulse in the air. His voice is lower, roughened. "The next portal isn't dangerous, but it is time consuming. It's this way."

He turns his back and strides down the hallway. I stare after him, horror only deepening in my gut. It's not anger that made him not kiss me back. I've *embarrassed* him. Kaladen, one of my only friends. Kaladen, who has cared for me better than anyone else has.

I don't think I've ever felt such deep shame as I do now.

It's like last night. There is no anger to keep me safe. I've let Kaladen in deeper than I should.

I close my eyes and reach inside me. There, waiting in my belly, is my ice. I tap into that source. Not much, just a tiny bit, like Kaladen taught me. I pull it up to my chest. I imagine it forming a shield around my heart. Suddenly, the ache softens. A twinge of anger returns—something I can grab onto.

If he doesn't love me, if he doesn't want us to be close, then he shouldn't flirt with me and hold me as if he does. It's his own fault if I misinterpreted the signals he was sending. And if he *does* love me—is that any way to treat someone you care about?

There.

I'm ready to continue our work. But this time, I don't rejoice after each seal. I keep the satisfaction deep inside me and say, "Next."

We barely speak a single word until dawn.

CHAPTER 27

THE NEVERSEEN KING

NADIRA'S KISS BURNS my lips for hours. I leave her to eat breakfast by herself the next morning and flee the palace altogether.

I cannot keep doing this.

I've been alive for half a millennium. I've fought monsters of all shapes and sizes and textures. I've been a warrior and emissary for the High King. And yet, it is this Great Kings cursed *woman* who never fails to flip my world upside down.

I swore not to love her. I swore not to care.

Well, that resolve flew out the window like a cageless bird! Then I resolved to love—but from a distance. And after that, I saw how much Nadira needed to be loved, so once again my resolve crumbled again.

This time I resolved to give her everything she needed, to not hide my care and affection.

But Lulythinar is only three weeks away, and the reality of its impending doom is turning me wild with madness. I was so optimistic only days ago, but with the number of breaking seals, I can no longer hide from the fact that this Lulythinar will be stronger and deadlier than the last. It'll be the worst I've ever seen. I scrape a hand over my face, the words wrenching from my clenched jaw: "I can't do this again. I can't lose my wife again. I can't. I can't. *I can't.* Not again. Please, not again."

I've condemned her to death, and I haven't even shown her my face. There is so much about me she doesn't know—things I have withheld from her.

How can I claim to care about her?

It felt like deceit to accept her kiss.

It *still* feels like deceit.

The rational part of my mind argues that I should have done in that moment whatever I needed to do to make Nadira feel safe. It's not as if I haven't frequently dreamed of kissing her—as if I haven't *hoped* she would break down that boundary and kiss me. I shouldn't have let her shut down and close off.

But I *cannot* kiss her while I wear shadows.

Not anymore.

She needs to see me for who I truly am.

Clenching my hands into fists, I march into the streets of Arbasa. I stay in the dream realm to not frighten random passersby, but I don't intend to stay here.

I reach my destination within minutes.

The main guardhouse boasts enough bunks to sleep two hundred city guards. I go straight to the mess hall, where the guards are eating their breakfast. No use going to their corrupt supervisor.

The raucous talk and laughter that immediately assaults me reminds me exactly why I have always found human men on the cusp of manhood to often be the worst among the entire race. They talk cavalierly of petty violence and disrespect toward women. I find a spot against a wall where I can lean and listen. None of them have Nadira's awareness and remain blissfully ignorant of my presence.

I wait until one young man pipes up at a table near me and boasts in vile language about the last urchin—a girl of eleven or twelve—that he'd molested. Several more chime in with similar stories. I make note of each of them. One young man, however, stops eating and says: "Have you not a shred of humanity?"

I make note of him too.

Then, while the first is still talking, I step behind him and leave the dream realm.

If I were Nadira, I would kill him before he knew what happened. But I am not Nadira.

I grab the long hair on the back of the man's head and yank hard. My blade fits just beneath his chin. Screams like those of a child's fill the room. *Pathetic*.

Eyes wild with fear search the shadows wreathing my face. He barely squeaks: "Neverseen King."

Half of the room has fallen to their knees. Others stare in shock, and I hear more than a few whispers of, *"He's real?"*

"Tell me again what you did to that little girl," I growl.

"I didn't do it!" he cries. "I was just fooling around—"

I tighten my grip on his hair, making him cry out. "I'll give you one more chance to go to your death with dignity."

He starts weeping, begging. I have no patience for such embarrassment. His body falls to the floor, his head still in my grip. The rest of the culprits, who already confessed to their crimes, quickly follow until I hold up five heads to the room. One of them happens to be the man Eshe was holding a knife to when I came upon them after the *beechka* outbreak.

It has gone as silent as the Mourner on the prowl.

Every knee bends.

"You are the protectors of this city," I spit. "To think that you take that privilege and wield it like a cudgel against those weaker than you! I do not know how you live with such shame."

Shoulders bow lower. Only one young man—the one who rebuked his fellow guards—doesn't crumple beneath my attention.

"This will go on no more," I announce. "I watch you, follow where you go and what you do, and I have seen enough. No more will you lay a hand on innocents." I hold up the five severed heads. "Unless you wish to join my collection."

"Long live the Neverseen King!" someone cries, before the entire room picks it up—shouting the anthem as if it will absolve them of guilt.

I turn my attention to the one young man who can look at me with no hidden shame. "What is your name?"

He crosses one arm over his chest and bows. "Tariq."

"Tariq is your new leader," I announce. "He will report directly to me."

Tariq's eyes widen.

"What about Commander Bashir?" someone asks.

"He is no longer your leader," I reply shortly. "Now, back to work. Breakfast is over."

I find this Commander Bashir in his office, laughing with a subordinate and drinking. When I march into the room, they drop the alcohol in a clash of broken pottery.

"To think," I growl, "that I was of a mind to spare you."

It takes all morning to straighten out the logistics of the guard and institute Tariq as the new commander. Ten worthless men are dead before noon, and I am glad for it.

When I return to the palace, Nadira is once more shut up in Emin's office, working hard. Eshe is wrangling a dizzying number of children to an afternoon meal, a toddler propped on her hip. A young girl, about fifteen, is at her side, helping her.

"You and you"—Eshe points to the two oldest boys—"are going to take the younger children scavenging this afternoon for rushes and long grass that can be woven into baskets. Keep your eyes out for clay deposits. We have use of those. The rest of you will help me try to decipher Nadira's pictures on weaving."

I leave them alone and, instead after checking the worst portals to ensure they will hold, I quietly return to my own office—one that I have not used in ages.

I promised Nadira a coronation.

What are you doing? I ask myself again. *Licking old wounds and hiding yet again?*

I firm my jaw. I will show her my face. Before Lulythinar. She must see the face of the one she will die for.

But until then, perhaps it's better if we keep our distance from each other.

CHAPTER 28

THE MOURNER

MY CORONATION ARRIVES much faster than I anticipated. The Neverseen King has planned much of it from the rainforest treehouse to avoid losing precious time, so I've had nothing to do with it. Not even when he needed to ensure the children didn't bother the foreign dignitaries he invited, did he bother me. He went straight to Eshe and worked something out with her.

I'm glad. The idea of being crowned in front of Arbasa and diplomats from other kingdoms is enough to nearly make me throw up.

Kaladen and I have stayed civil. We've worked together each night with no incident. Sometimes we go to the rainforest so he can coach me on controlling and honing my magic. I go there on my own every few days to catch up on sleep. He doesn't join me, and I am relieved.

This distance between us makes me more comfortable. We are exactly what we agreed to be: comrades. There are no kisses, no warm touches, no shared tears.

It's quite nice. I can focus better on my work for the children, city, and kingdom.

It's like I can better pretend Lulythinar isn't coming like a monster on the prowl.

During the day, I can lose myself in my frantic efforts to bring some life and stability back to this kingdom, and I can almost forget how much faster and harder we have to work to keep up with the portal instability the closer we get to Lulythinar.

Almost.

The day of the coronation is a flurry of activity. I bathe quickly, and just before I am about to dress in my regular clothes, a maid brings the most stunning red and gold robes. It's real gold thread embroidering the hems of the skirt and sleeves. Those are real cut gems on the waistband. The fabric is rich and sumptuous, a deep crimson that startles me with its resemblance to blood. There are sheaths sewn on for my knives at the hip.

"He wants me to appear a queen of vengeance," I mutter to myself. I don't like it for my own comfort, but I see exactly what a perfectly calculated move this is. Arbasa is weakened, but Kaladen intends for me, in my blood-red gown with my knives, to mark the beginning of a new age for my people.

I dress. Then I do something I have not done in weeks.

I turn toward the mirror.

For this first time, those dark eyes staring back at me don't feel like they belong to someone else. They look a little sad, but they aren't unfamiliar. The strong cheekbones, the full mouth, the stubborn, scarred jaw . . . The woman before me is strange, yes, but it's like I look upon a long-lost friend. Someone I knew long ago.

I turn my back to her, breathing hard. Still, my mouth twists up in the corner.

Eshe, always with at least one toddler on her hip or tied to her back, enters my room wearing a brilliant turquoise gown. "Look!" she cries, holding the little boy tightly as she spins so her sparkling skirts flare out. "The shadow freak got it for me! Who knew he'd have such good taste in fashion? First the gowns during the competition, and now these! And look at *you*. You look like a warrior queen come down from the heavens to slay your enemies!"

"I think Kaladen intends for me to strike fear in the hearts of our subjects," I say dryly.

"Not our subjects. The foreign dignitaries who are trying to ruin our trade."

We step into the hallway and head toward the throne room. A place I have been once before—and only in my dreams.

"Did the diplomat from Pur agree to the meeting following the ceremony?" I ask as sunlight streams into our eyes from the open windows. "And Offom?"

"Both agreed. Though we won't do the Ruby Hall—it's too big."

"And the children?"

"They are busy weaving baskets and foraging more materials. The oldest girl, Zara, is supervising the ones in the palace so they don't interrupt the coronation. They should stay busy with their work, but only a few have picked up the skill yet. Most of the baskets I have to pull apart for them to start over on. I don't want to waste materials."

I nod. "That's alright. It will take time. There's a renowned basket weaver in another city I'm in the process of hiring to instruct the more advanced children. Even if just a few children become skilled, it will be worth it. My next project is finding a source of cacao beans. The scrolls of history in Emin's office said cacao used to be a chief export of ours hundreds of years ago, but there was a war that—"

"Enough talk of economics!" Eshe laughs. "Just tell me what to do and I'll do it. The basket weaving keeps the children busy and out of trouble, if nothing else. *Most* of them, that is."

The door before us, the one leading to the courtyard, opens.

Eshe abruptly stops.

Because the tall young man who just walked through wears a city guard uniform.

Eshe's grip on the child tightens. Her stubbornness wars with sudden panic across her face, as though she is reminding herself that she is protected, that she does not need to immediately run for cover.

I step between them, giving Eshe a buffer. "Eshe, this is Commander Tariq. The Neverseen King just appointed him head of the city guard. He is in charge of bringing reform to their ranks."

"A pleasure to meet your acquaintance," Tariq says, bowing deeply to Eshe.

She shifts the toddler to her other hip, further away from him. She makes a valiant effort to reply, "Likewise," and it only sounds halfway strained.

Tariq glances at me, and perhaps he reads the reason behind Eshe's cold reception in my face, because he bows once more and turns to go.

"Before you leave, Commander Tariq," I say firmly, "report how many men of the guard have you executed in this last fortnight?"

"Nine, Your Highness."

"Nine men disobeyed the Neverseen King's direct orders?" I ask, even though I am well aware of the answer.

"No, my lady. I have been a city guard for five years. I knew already who had broken our code of conduct in grievous ways. Their bodies hang on the city gates now. No such breaches are tolerated henceforth."

Eshe's gaze snaps to his. Just as quickly, she looks away and says to the toddler on her hip, "Oooh, maybe we should go watch them rot later!"

She moves on toward the throne room. I smirk at her back, then nod to dismiss Tariq to his duty of ensuring order during the coronation.

Before we reach the back door to the throne room, a familiar presence fills my awareness. My first instinct is to tense, but I catch myself. Instead, I draw up a little bit of ice from my reserves, coat my heart one more time. Then I cast a sideways glance to the Neverseen King, who materializes beside me.

"I'll go on ahead," Eshe says, and scurries away.

Leaving me alone with my husband.

"Are you ready?" he asks in a low voice.

"They might riot and demand my head."

"They will do no such thing. And if they do, I give you permission to destroy them all with your ice."

It surprises a chuckle out of me, despite my determination to keep my distance from him.

He holds out his arm. I lean deeper into the coldness within me, so I feel nothing when I lift my hand and place it in the crook of his elbow. He loses much of his physicality, but enough remains that our people will see that I do, indeed, walk on the arm of the Neverseen King himself.

The doors open as a trumpet blares.

My heart leaps straight into my throat. It is the same throne room I remember—all awash in a fiery red glow, with rubies on strings dripping from the ceiling, and a polished floor that reflects the glorious arches above us. But when the Neverseen King summoned me in my dream, it was empty. Empty, save us.

Now it is so full the walls feel like they are caving in on me.

Lords and ladies of Arbasa, some from Risya, many from all over the kingdom. Foreign dignitaries, with their strange clothes and varying complexions. A grinning Eshe with a few small children clinging to her beautiful skirts. Tariq stands at attention at the back of the room, his men lining the walls and flanking the dais.

Gasps fill the room, punctuated by murmurs of, "The Neverseen King!"

Something about their shock emboldens me. I lift my chin a fraction higher and let my steps sound on the polished floor. The trumpet keeps playing as the Neverseen King walks me all the way down the aisle, straight to the throne. Beside the throne, on a small pedestal, is the crown I wore to Valehaven.

We reach the steps to the dais. The Neverseen King lets go of my arm, leaving me standing at the front of the room, facing the throne. His heavy cloak makes quiet swishes that carry through the entire silent room. He lifts the crown off his cushion and returns to me.

"Nadira al-Risya." His voice booms in the quiet, thunderous and terrifying. Many audience members shrink away, but I don't. "As the Neverseen King of Arbasa, I crown you Queen Nadira. I hereby name your enemies and allies as my own."

The crown descends heavily on my brow.

"May your arm be strong to rule in justice," he proclaims. "I henceforth grant you, Nadira al-Risya, full authority and all vestiges of the crown of Arbasa. You may now rise."

I force my hand to not touch the hilt of my knife as I stand. I meet Kaladen's nearly invisible gaze, and he gives me one single nod. My cue.

My long skirts drag behind me as I walk to the throne, flanked by massive stone lions. *His* throne, but now mine, too.

I face my people and sit.

Hundreds of eyes stare at me. Some of their gazes are rapturous, while others are less than pleased. My body is tight and tense, the weight of exposure almost dizzying. I keep waiting for that one person to declare that I am the Mourner, that I am the one who slaughtered their loved ones under the cover of darkness.

But no one does.

The Neverseen King sweeps his hand to the room. "Come forth, lords of Arbasa."

I try to hide the way I chew on the inside of my lip as over a dozen men rise and come to stand at the base of the staircase below me. Names fly to my memory—names like Lord Kishon, who would be standing here, had I not killed him.

"Swear your oaths," Kaladen orders.

One by one, each bows, his fist over his heart, as he recites the expected vow: "I hereby surrender my loyalty, my blade, and my very life to this throne that makes the sun to shine."

I dislike the vow tremendously, and I dislike hearing it more than fifteen times in a row even more. I'm very glad when the lords bow once more and return to their places.

"Long live Queen Nadira!" the Neverseen King declares.

Hundreds of voices join the chant. It spins around me, flooding my ears, my entire body. *This isn't real,* part of me demands. I draw more ice around me like a shield until my hands are colder than the golden armrests of the throne.

Then, suddenly, I spot a familiar face.

Not Eshe's. Not Tariq's.

No, this face is one from a nightmare.

Kanza.

One of the other eleven women from the Neverseen King's competition. The last time I saw her, she was bleeding out in a pitch-black maze from a wound Raha had dealt her. Kanza was not an enemy of mine, but she knew who I was. They'd all figured it out.

The world drowns out all sound as my mind spins to understand this. The Neverseen King rescued Kanza. I cannot remember if he told me her fate, but if she survived, I'm certain he did what he did to the first woman who fell: he returned her to her old life and wiped her memory of her time in his palace. He would have wiped her memory of *me*.

Which would explain why she now looks at me as the rest do—like a curiosity.

I force my gaze away from her. Who else survived the competition besides Eshe and I? The first girl, whose name I never knew. Then Kanza.

Mahja and Gaya were killed by Crenfyre. Fathuna and Dabria were killed by the Neverseen King after they betrayed him, working with Jabir and the Wolf. Itr was killed by Safya's blade. Safya was killed by Jabir's men when he led his attack on the palace. Hulla was killed when she left her room after dark.

That's only eleven of us. There was one more. One more who survived.

Horror fills my belly to the brim.

I immediately scan the room, searching for the last face I want to see right now.

There she is.

Raha.

Raha wears severe black, as she did during the competition. Her brow is hard, her scarf covering most of her face. But her eyes fix on mine, and while I cannot be sure if there is recognition in her gaze, there is certainly hatred.

It cannot be her father's murder that makes her look at me with so much hatred. It must be another reason. A reason that has something to do with the fact that I am queen and do not deserve to be. Or perhaps she is furious to discover the Neverseen King is real, and not a legend.

I clutch the armrests of my throne and force my gaze forward. *I will not be rattled.*

Kaladen erased both of their memories. They don't know me. They don't know what I've done. They cannot expose me.

The ceremony is not much longer, but I live in a tightly woven fog for the rest of it. When men and women come to pay their respects, I coat my heart in even more ice. Ice so cold the skin of my fingers turns blue.

Kanza comes forward. When she bows and says, "I wish you a prosperous reign, Your Majesty," I reply with a deep nod and nothing else.

Raha does not come. She slips out the back of the room like a phantom, and there is no relief in her absence.

Kaladen's invisible hand lands on my shoulder. I exhale hard. My first instinct is to lean into his touch, his support, his silent acknowledgement of what he knows is a hard moment for me. That would be the mature thing to do.

Instead, I hold still and let the ice overtake me a little more. Just until the end of the reception line. It slowly leaks out of me, despite my efforts to control it, and when it is finally over and I stand, ice coats the armrests I was just clutching. I feel Kaladen's gaze burning into me, into those twin patches of ice.

Then Eshe, without a child for the first time in a fortnight, runs up to the dais, dodging around Tariq without a single glance his way. "They're ready to meet!"

I don't look back at Kaladen. "Perfect. Lead the way."

If I die at Lulythinar, there is one thing I want to have done for my people.

"Can I get you some hot qahwa?" Eshe says brightly when we enter the small meeting chamber with great, arched windows facing the afternoon sun. Cut glass the color of rubies glints at us, inlaid in the stonework of those arches. "Or tea?"

I sweep into the chair at the head of the table, tenting my fingers beneath my chin as I regard the two men seated before me. One is old, with a long, graying beard beneath his turban. He is from Pur. The other—one with sharp black eyes, a blockish jaw, and even more blockish hands—keeps his crutch propped against the back of his chair. He is from Offom.

The first smiles at Eshe's sunny grin and accepts a cup of qahwa. The other keeps his focus fixed on me.

"We are *so* glad you took time to meet with us," Eshe says as she takes her own seat next to me. The older dignitary slurps his qahwa loudly.

I drill my attention into the two men. "I have a deal to propose to both of you."

"I have some questions about the Neverseen King," the dignitary from Pur says between sips.

"What sort of deal?" the one from Offom asks.

Eshe, having no understanding of the deal, tells him, "You'll love it."

The crown weighs heavily on my head, but I don't let intimidation hold me back. "We want all of your trade to come through our ports."

The Pur dignitary spits out his qahwa. Eshe hops up to clean it, all while laughing, "You're shocked, but just you wait!"

I keep myself from rolling my eyes. Then I continue, ignoring the dubious expressions before me. "I know what the Idameans are taxing you to use their port. Twelve percent. We are slashing our tariffs to three percent."

The Pur dignitary raises his eyebrow, leaning back in his chair. The Offom dignitary doesn't move a muscle.

"Three percent is on the condition that all your exports to the west and near east come through our ports. Yes, the Idamea port is closer, but that's why their tariffs are so high. I've run the numbers for you, based on my sources of how much sugar, molasses, and spices you export from Pur, and how much *you* export in textiles from Offom in a year." I slide several sheets of figures across the table. The two men accept them with interest. "I've calculated how much extra it would cost to sail your ships the rest of the way from Idamea to our nearest port, from manpower to supplies, to the increased chance of loss from a longer voyage. As you can see, your profits would still dramatically increase simply from the lower tariffs."

"How do I know these figures are done properly?" asks the older man.

I blink slowly. "Do them yourself."

Eshe leans over and whispers to him, "I can vouch for her. She is very good at arithmetic stuff. Figures and numbers and the sort."

"The numbers are solid," says the Offom dignitary. He lifts his sharp attention from the paper to me. "I suppose you want us to slash our own tariffs in return? If so, I'm afraid you'll be disappointed."

"That would be a separate negotiation," I reply. "We are open to discussions. At the moment, however, this deal is what we are discussing. You do not have to give your answer now. I have written up contracts for you to take back to your kingdoms." I slide them across the table to each of them. "These contracts are not up for negotiation. You will take them or leave them as is. I have worked to make them favorable to you in every capacity."

The Pur dignitary gets to his feet and collects the papers I've given him. "I will take these back and send word via courier of our decision."

Eshe grins. "Excellent! Here, come now. I'll show you to your room."

The two of them leave, and Eshe's bright chatter slowly fades to nothing. Leaving me alone with the diplomat from Offom.

"You seem very young," says the man.

I drum my fingers on the table at a leisurely pace, letting the echoes of his words fill the space.

"You seem young for a wife of the immortal Neverseen King."

I stop drumming my fingers. "Do you mean that as a question? Or a compliment?"

He lets out a long sigh and leans forward on his elbows. "Listen, Queen Nadira, I mean no disrespect to you. You seem to be a bright woman, and I'd wager the knives at your belt aren't decoration. But my people do not feel comfortable dealing with a kingdom wreathed in magic. Whether your sultan is truly some creature of magical origin or the scene in the throne room was a mere trick, I don't particularly care. All I know is that we want honest trade. Not dealings with magic."

I like his forthrightness.

"I'm proposing no dealings with magic," I reply. "It is nothing but honest trade. My husband had no part in these plans. I developed them myself, and I bleed as red as any other human. I understand your hesitation, but have you flipped to the last page I gave you? What I am proposing is pure profit. Because you have spoken plainly with me, I will speak plainly with you. Based on the calculations I've run, you would be a fool to let superstition keep you from this deal. If you do business with me, you will see your profits increase tenfold."

"A bold statement, Your Majesty."

I rise to my feet. "I stand by it."

For the first time since he entered the room, the diplomat's mouth curves upward.

CHAPTER 29

THE MOURNER

ONCE I'M FINALLY alone, walking the hallways of the palace toward Emin's office, a pair of murderous black eyes attacks my memory. I kept it together for the ceremony and for the meeting with the diplomats after, but now my hands shake. What was she *doing* here?

She doesn't remember you. She doesn't remember you. She doesn't remember you.

The air shifts.

I react before my rational mind catches up.

My blades are out, shooting toward who has just materialized in the air behind me.

Strong hands catch my wrists, force them back until I hit the wall. My knives clatter to the ground.

Kaladen's shadowed darkness hovers over me, pinning me in place. His knee presses into my thigh, keeping me from kicking him out of instinctive self-preservation. Breath steals from my lungs in a short gasp.

And then I'm staring up at him. At the sparks of his eyes.

I am acutely aware of the focus of his grim attention sliding up from my face, up my extended arms, to where he pins my hands above my head—to the ice coating my fingers. I give a halfhearted tug, but he doesn't release me.

"You're coming with me," he finally says.

I clench my hands into fists, breaking the thin sheen of ice. Fractured chips fall to the stone floor. "What if I don't *want* to?"

He leans closer to me until his breath stirs the hair falling in my face. "Don't make the mistake of believing you're the only stubborn one."

"Is this a competition?" I growl, my hands growing colder and colder as the ice spreads across my skin. "Do you want to fight, *Kaladen*?"

"I wanted to make sure you were alright. Judging by how quickly you pulled your knives on me, you are not."

I twist my face to one side, staring out a decorative window as the sun descends to evening. Anything to break the power of his gaze. But it doesn't stop my awareness of his hot breath tickling my ear, the column of my neck. Or the way he presses his weight into me to keep me restrained. "I never liked your patronization."

"I'm not patronizing you. I'm worried. Don't think I missed your ice slipping your control during the coronation. So are you done being stubborn? Or are you going to make me carry you over my shoulder?"

I turn hot. Anything would be preferred to that indignity. But I cannot let him know that. "All the better to stab you in the back."

He shifts his grip so he holds my wrists in one hand and, with the other, he takes my jaw and tilts my head so I have to look at him. I give him my darkest scowl. "You are so good at pretending you hate me."

"It doesn't feel very pretend right now."

Kaladen's eyes narrow. Abruptly, he releases me. But only for a moment. The next second, he twines his fingers in mine and holds my hand in an unbreakable grip. He sets off at a brisk pace, dragging me along behind him.

"What are you doing?" I demand, trying to pull my hand free of his.

He doesn't reply.

"I'll freeze your blood!" I threaten.

Still, he doesn't reply. Because—curse him—he knows it's an empty threat.

When he stops in front of the rainforest door, I dig my heels into the ground. "I'm not in the mood for the treehouse, Kaladen. Let me go back to my work."

"You've been hiding in your work for far too long."

"How dare you say that, when it is because of *you* that I—"

The words are cut off when I find myself suddenly exactly where I do *not* want to be.

Draped over Kaladen's shoulder, his hands pinning my kicking legs to his chest.

"Kaladen Ashrift Felladyr!" I shriek as he swings the door shut behind us. "You put me down right now!"

He takes my pummeling fists like they are nothing, even though my blows would have toppled most human men. He anticipates my maneuvers, and his strength remains unmatched. Still, I don't stop. I might not be able to break free, but I can make this difficult and unpleasant for him.

Then he tosses me to the ground beside the waterfall. I land on my backside with my hands splayed, but I roll and spring to my feet, putting distance between us.

I'm still wearing these too-fancy robes. They feel ridiculous right now.

"You're losing control of your ice," Kaladen says. "Get it all out."

"I don't want to train right now."

"Would you rather accidentally kill Eshe the next time you get spooked?"

My knives are all gone. So I do the next best thing to vent my fury. I hurl my flat palm like I hurl a knife, and ice shoots out of it. Straight at Kaladen.

Red flares suddenly in front of him. My ice sizzles out on his magic shield.

I grind my teeth and hurl harder, faster. This volley of ice is stronger and wider. Still, it sizzles up on his shield.

"I see you've been practicing!" Kaladen calls over the din of ice slashing against magic. "Look how controlled your blows are!"

"Don't patronize me!"

"I'm not. I'm genuinely impressed."

Clenching my jaw, I shoot a bigger blast, this one less targeted and more explosive. "Not that it does much against you."

He pushes forward against the onslaught of my magic, ice sizzling and burning into steam against the invisible shield he holds. "Is that why you're angry? Because I'm not letting you kill me?"

Cold fury fills my belly and spills out of my fingertips. The pressure inside me builds up, up, *up*. I refuse to back down as he advances on me. I won't let him intimidate me. The frozen lake of my soul I once visited flashes across my vision. An endless expanse of ice to protect me and imprison me.

"You know why I'm angry," I hiss.

Two knives land in the dark soil in front of my crimson robes. A scimitar follows it.

Kaladen lowers his palms. "Pick up your weapons, Mourner."

I gladly do as he bids, sheathing one knife while holding the scimitar in my right hand, the second knife in my left. He withdraws another scimitar and points it at me.

I prowl closer to where he stands, my blades up. "I know what you're doing. You're trying to work out my anger so I'm sweet and docile again."

A chuckle snorts out of him. "Sweet, yes. Docile? I don't believe you were that even as a child. That is not what I want for you. But you have much on your mind that I want you to release."

He wants me to let my emotions out?

Very well.

I'll show him *everything*.

My blade crashes against his. He blocks, parries my second attack, and then slips to my back to strike. I whirl to block. "You'd better not vanish!"

"I wouldn't dream of it," comes his arch reply.

Our blades collide once more. He comes at me in a series of attacks so violent I retreat several steps until my back hits the rock-and-clay cliffside. Water sprays my fine gown from the waterfall. His blade comes hacking for my throat.

I duck, and the blade sinks into clay. I dive under Kaladen's guard and force him back, regaining my lost ground. "Why was Raha here?"

"Her father was a lord. It wouldn't have been a good look to snub her."

"She tried to kill me!"

"I erased her memories. She continues her quest for the Mourner as if she never came to my palace."

I pelt him with attacks. He does not give an inch, meeting me blow for blow. "But word could get out that I am the Mourner, and now she knows my face!"

His voice drops to a low growl, his strikes turning more and more vicious, forcing me to retreat once more. "How many times have I promised to protect you? And why do you even consider Raha a threat? You beat her in a matter of minutes when the two of you fought!"

Fatigue ripples down my arm. I dip down into my stores of ice in my belly and let cold fill my blood, fueling me. If Kaladen thinks a few minutes of sparring is enough to work through the vast reserves of my anger, he will be sorely disappointed.

"You're not actually afraid of Raha, are you?" His blade sings dangerously close to my neck. I dodge and use my knife to deflect. "You're afraid of her exposing you. That she will reveal you as a murderer to all of Arbasa."

I stab straight for his heart. He deflects, as I knew he would, but that doesn't keep me from stabbing again.

"And even then, you're not afraid of being brought to justice," he continues, forcing me back, back, back, until I hit clay and rock once more. I block his blows, straining with all my might. "Because you are now above the law—and I would never allow you to be executed for your crimes. So what is it, Nadira?"

With one flashing movement, his blade flicks my knife out of my hand. I gasp, reaching to catch it—and he uses that moment to flick my scimitar away too. Snarling, I throw myself bodily against him to get to my weapons.

He catches me and slams me against the side of the cliff. He tosses his own scimitar away, and instead latches his iron grip on my wrists, holding me in place.

I bare my teeth at him, furious he should end our sparring so quickly. His face comes close to mine. My wet hair plasters against my scalp and gets in my mouth. I'm breathing hard, and so is he, the thunder of our heartbeats drowned out by the roar of the waterfall.

"You know what you are afraid of," he growls, bringing his lips to my ear. "And I know what you are afraid of. But will you admit it?"

"I want to keep fighting."

"Would you rather me tell you what *I* am afraid of?"

"That I will see your face and think you're ugly!"

He draws in a deep breath through his teeth. Seeing him frustrated satisfies a sense of justice inside me. He rejected my kiss after leading me to believe he wanted it. Seems fair that, at the very least, I can frustrate him in return.

He pins me in place with the force of his gaze. "You are *so smart*—probably the smartest person I know—and then you throw it all out the window when we have conflict! You become purposefully dense and difficult, but we both know exactly what is going on here, no matter if we admit it or not."

I lower my brows. "Then tell me, O Neverseen King. What is going on here?"

"I hurt you two weeks ago. You felt safe around me, and you acted—and I turned you away. And I'm *sorry,* Nadira. I've regretted it every moment since. Every single moment. I should have kissed you."

The heat that floods my cheeks is first shame, and then more fury. "No, you shouldn't have. I don't want condescending kisses, Kaladen! They are the *worst* kind, and I don't want them!"

"You think if I had kissed you, it would have been *condescending*?" For once, he stares at me, utterly baffled. His grip on my wrists slackens.

I glare at him. It's not as if our *entire relationship* has been me wanting more than he is willing to give. I'm sick of it.

"Nadira." He says my name in that way that makes me want to forgive and forget every cross word between us. But I'm done being baited because I'm just a stupid girl who chases love in any terrible place she can find it.

I hold my tongue.

He releases my wrists but keeps his hands flat against the cliffside at my back. I brace against the softness of his voice when he speaks. "Nadira, I know you fear being seen by your people for what you believe you truly are, deep down. You are afraid they will abandon you when they discover what you have done. And perhaps they would. But tell me, does it *really* matter if they hate you?"

"Of course it does!" I choke. "I couldn't stand it if they looked at me like . . . like I would kill their children if they left their guard down!"

"Have you ever killed a child?"

I shake my head. Emotion rises in my throat, thick and hot and unsettling. I want to escape it, but there is nowhere to run from myself.

"Then it would be foolish of them to be worried about that. Obviously, you have killed for two reasons: via assassination, for political motive, and in battle, against those who wish you and your loved ones harm."

I shake my head once more. "You cannot rationalize away my fear. I know it is stupid—"

He catches my chin. Forces my gaze up to his. "Fear is never stupid. It may not seem it at first, but fear is always rational. I don't like letting my own fear of loss dictate so many of my choices. But I have lost much. I have suffered much. It makes sense for me to be afraid of it. Just like it makes sense that after I turned you away, you would—"

"I don't want your lectures," I say, interrupting. Part of me wants to soften toward him. But there is a stronger, desperate part of me that turns frantic at the thought of trusting him again. "There's work I need to do, and—"

Suddenly, he takes my face in his hands. His calluses are rough against my cheeks. His touch is gentle and fervent, soft and demanding. "No, you're not leaving yet. Do you have a *clue* how long I have craved you? All the nights we have slept side by side, worked together for hours, when I have *longed* to take back every word of distance between us? When I wanted kisses and far more from you? Nadira al-Risya, you are determined to misunderstand me, so let me say this in no uncertain terms. I am captivated by you. I would do anything, go anywhere, sacrifice anything just for a chance to see you happy."

My stubbornness washes away like the last rainfall before the dry season. I stare up at him, at the darkness of his face, my breath quivering in my lungs. My voice nearly gives out. "Then why, Kaladen, *why* do you keep hiding from me? Why did you turn away from me?"

The darkness around his face shifts slightly.

Then, to my shock, it begins melting.

My hands fly backward, grabbing for purchase as my knees weaken. Fear stabs me hard in the chest, my eyes widening too large for their sockets. I've wanted this from the beginning—and yet now that it is happening, I'm suddenly terrified. I've grown used to reading his shadows, to discerning his expressions based on the shifts in the air. This is the last thing between us. The last veil.

It falls slowly. Layer by layer.

I've hated this barrier, but maybe I've needed it—this constant reminder that we can never be together in the way we may want. Maybe I don't want it gone. "Kaladen—"

He is fully corporeal, and his glamours fall away to reveal the tall, broad form I am familiar with. But it keeps falling, revealing the dark cloak fastened at his throat, the long black tunic he wears and how it is open almost to his waist. The luminescent, bronze skin of a muscular chest, threaded with thin scars, fills my vision. His tunic sleeves are short, revealing two thick, corded arms.

I swallow as I look up. Past his powerful shoulders, past his strong neck.

The last bits of glamour fight against the sunlight. The outline of shoulder-length, wavy hair gives way to brown with threads of gold through it.

My awareness of our surroundings completely vanishes. All I can hear is the pounding of his heart, tangling with mine. Afraid like mine.

And then, just like that, the Neverseen King stands before me.

Not breathing, I let my gaze devour his features.

His face is long, with a defined chin, nose, and a prominent jaw. A ropey scar extends across his right cheek, down through the shadow of facial hair to his full, downward-tilted mouth. His lashes are dark and thick. Pointed ears extend from his wild hair. His skin is smooth gold, reminding me at once of the High King.

His eyes are as blue as a pair of sapphires, as clear as a cloudless sky, as full and vast as the ocean. They arrest me like they have a hundred times before, only this time, I can see every miniscule play of emotion across those jewel-like irises. The hope, the vulnerability, the pain, the desperation.

Once upon a time, I see that he was heartbreakingly beautiful—as beautiful, or even more than the High King himself. That beauty has roughened to the scarred warrior's face before me, weathered with lines of deep loss.

He is still beautiful, but that is not what I see.

I see strength in every harsh line and angle of his face. In the deep wells of his eyes.

He is both not at all what I expected, and yet everything I imagined.

My hand reaches of its own accord. I touch my rounded knuckle against the ridge of his scar and trace it. His breath shudders out of his lips.

“Kaladen,” I breathe.

“Here I am, darling,” he whispers.

His knuckles are a murmur against my jaw, sliding to my chin. As though to tilt my face up to his. As though our eyes aren’t already locked, our mouths breathing the same air.

His thumb strokes the edge of my lower lip. A shiver cascades to my toes.

“Tell me,” he says softly, “am I as terrifying as you imagined?”

I give a shaky laugh. “Far worse.”

He presses his mouth to mine. It is not at all like last time—not at all like kissing a living statue. His lips are warm and soft and so alive. Where our other kisses have been forceful, desperate, all-consuming, this one is almost painfully slow and gentle. It’s like our lips are meeting for the first time. Like time itself has ceased and waits at our bidding.

He pulls back slightly, his eyes moving up from my mouth to meet my gaze. “I have held myself back from you for so long. No more, Nadira. My bride, my wife, my hope.”

No more.

No more hiding from each other. No more masks and glamours.

My heart cracks open, splitting and reknitting fissures in a kaleidoscope of color. I grab hold of his neck and pull him back down to me, kissing him harder and deeper, clinging to him as black sears across my vision.

But then it clears, and it doesn’t return as he cups my head, his long fingers tangling in my hair. I find the proof of his words as his kiss turns forceful, almost starved. It was *never* that he didn't want me. His desire for me has been the one constant through this wild time I've spent in his palace.

I have never felt so whole and free, so loved and safe.

He spins us, so his back is against the cliffside. Then, before I'm expecting it, he scoops me up against him so my legs straddle his waist. A breathy chuckle escapes me as he strides away from the waterfall. "Where are we going?"

"To the treehouse," he says, his voice deep and low as he climbs the steps. "There is something I must do."

My reply is muffled against his shoulder. "What?"

"Don't you wish you knew?"

I pinch his back. He chuckles.

CHAPTER 30

THE MOURNER

WHEN WE ENTER, he takes two steps into the space and tosses me onto the bed. I push up to my knees, both puzzled at his words and desperate to go back to kissing. He clearly has something else in mind, however, when he doesn't join me.

It's so strange to look at him—and see his face. To be able to run my eyes over him from head to toe. To be able to admire him in truth, and not just imagine.

"Lie down on your stomach," Kaladen instructs.

"Why?"

His mouth quirks—something I've imagined but not seen for so long. It's tinged in unexpected sadness. "If you do it, you'll find out."

"You never tell me what you're planning," I grumble to avoid giving away just how fast my heart beats. I do as he says, and it is not lost on me how terrifying this type of vulnerability used to be. Now, I only hum with curiosity.

Once I've settled comfortably on my stomach, he stands beside the bed and bends over me. His hot hands find the fabric of my gown at the shoulder and gently rip it open.

"What are you—" I gasp.

His grip on my shoulder tightens, pressing me down into the mattress. "Stay still." Then his thumb gives the side of my neck a long, soft caress. "I will not hurt you."

I relax into the bed, breathing in through my nose and out in a shuddering exhale. "I know."

He carefully tears away the garment to expose my back. Cool air flows across my skin. I force myself to relax. He stays where he is for a moment, then braces one knee on the opposite side of my hips, his gaze burning into my back.

My scars.

His finger traces along the length of a scar. I clench my shoulders, uncomfortable with how sensitive my skin is to his touch, and yet how insensitive the scar tissue is. My lungs clench when he lays both palms on my back.

"Breathe, Nadira," Kaladen whispers. "Breathe into my touch."

My hands fist in the sheets. "I'm trying."

"You're doing well. We are going to retrain your body to know that touch is love. It may take us a long time, but we will get there. Tell me if it ever becomes too much."

Tears prick the corners of my eyes. I squeeze them shut. "Alright."

My entire awareness focuses on his hands as he begins gently massaging my back and scars. He never lifts his hands away, keeping me grounded, but he slows his movement when I flinch. He pauses, waits for my heartrate to even, and then begins anew.

Slowly, my body relaxes. The random twitches of panic settle, and even though the discomfort of the strange insensitivity continues, it begins to come more under my control. I can breathe through it, and as his touch deepens past the skin to the muscles beneath, sparks of true enjoyment begin.

"I have seen the tips of these scars at the base of your neck sometimes," Kaladen whispers. "I knew they would be extensive, though just *how* extensive . . ." He trails into quiet, and his hands turn even gentler as he works.

I close my eyes and breathe deeply.

Then suddenly, my back gets warmer. I open my eyes and turn my head, only to find his long hair brushing my shoulder as he leans over me. I startle, but his hands brace my lower ribcage. Calming me, as he presses a kiss to the space between my shoulder blades.

"I'm sorry you carry these scars," he whispers. "I want to help you bear them."

I lick my lips. "There are a lot of them."

He lifts one hand from my ribs and plants it on the pillow beside my head. My eyes run up the length of a vein in his forearm, then widen as he leans further over me, his chest so close to my shoulder as his beautiful eyes find mine. I think I could stare into his eyes for an entire lifespan and never grow bored.

Then he leans even closer. His mouth descends to the side of my jaw. He presses a kiss to the mottled scars there.

"Kaladen," I cry, a tear leaking out of my eye. I try to turn my head away, but he places a gentle palm over my hair.

His voice is thick when he speaks, and for the first time, I can see the depth of his emotions written plain across his face. His face, which becomes dearer to me by the second. "Your scars are nothing to be ashamed of, Nadira. They are a testament to triumph." His lips move to my cheek, and then he tilts my head to claim my mouth in a kiss made of honey and saltwater. "Scars prove strength, not weakness."

"It doesn't feel that way, when they seem a burden I will never be free from."

He stretches his long body beside mine and lets the tension out of his shoulders with a deep breath. "I know. Believe me, I know."

I lift one hand and, after a moment of hesitation, touch one finger against his cheekbone. Slowly, I draw it in a line to his strong jaw. Then I trace the length of the scar down his face. His lashes flutter shut. "What was it like? Losing Liliana?"

He releases a short, low groan, as if this isn't what he wants to talk about right now. But I don't retract my question. I need to hear his answer—more than I realized.

"I didn't believe it at first," he says finally. "The Roltwart Portal has deep chasms, some so deep you cannot see the light of the burning lava at the bottom. I was fighting to keep the dracoli from pouring through the open portal. She was trying to get the soul of the portal—against my expressed wishes. I had this moment of sheer panic as I saw her disappear into the ground, only to realize she'd caught the edge of the rockface. I thought I could get to her in time. I thought—" His voice breaks. He shakes his head. Then he takes my palm, the one pressed to his cheek, and kisses my knuckles. "She fell. I've never known a moment more dreadful than when I screamed her name into that canyon. Counting the seconds while I still felt the raging rhythm of her heartbeat, knowing she was *alive, alive, alive*. And then, abruptly, it stopped. The tether between us snapped. I was left with emptiness. It was too sudden, too shocking. I didn't know what to do. And then a dracoli bit my leg so hard it almost broke. I usually avoid killing the denizens of the portals I guard. But not this time. So I got up. I slaughtered every dracoli in the vicinity. I dragged myself out of that portal and sealed it with the blood of its own creatures. That was the end of Lulythinar. The end of . . . almost everything for me."

"I don't know how you survived that," I whisper.

"I didn't think I would." He leans his head back on the pillow, eyes never leaving mine. "You are my saving grace."

Those words aren't a right description of me, but I let them go. Instead, I ask, "What was Liliana doing to get the soul of the portal?"

His brows immediately shutter. "Nadira—"

"Now listen," I say, shoving upright. "You don't get to decide what is too dangerous for me to know. I'm not asking to continue your *experiment*; I'm asking you to give me the information. I know that Lulythinar is fast approaching, and if I am not fully equipped, my life is at risk. So tell me, Kaladen."

He pushes himself up to a sitting position beside me.

"I know you don't want to," I continue, "but—wait, what are you—*oh*."

He has grabbed my face in both hands and instead of using his mouth to answer my question, uses it to thoroughly occupy mine. He kisses me all the way back down, so my head is pressed into the pillow.

"I'm kissing away your question," he says by way of explanation before he captures my lips once more—and I'm flushing too much to protest. Every time he kisses me is like the first time, intoxicating and mind-spinning. His touch brushing down my arm is infinitely gentle. There is nothing impatient about him, and it is that very tenderness that slowly melts away the tension in my limbs.

He pulls back. My lashes flutter open. He's smiling. "I love that expression on your face."

"What expression?" I demand self-consciously, pushing up on my elbow and fighting yet another blush.

"The one that says you trust me."

I blink and look away. "Oh." Then, refusing to be embarrassed, I say: "I asked you a question, Kal. So answer it or else—"

"*Kal?*" he repeats, drawing back as though from a plate of rotten food.

The grin is on my face before I can help it, though it wobbles a little when I try to stand—only to remember the back of my dress has been ripped open and if I'm not careful, it'll fall straight off me. I hold it in place and keep my spine straight as I stay seated. "I'll make you a deal. I won't call you Kal if you answer my question."

He levels a glare at me. It's so much better to see the detailed play of his irritation across his face rather than guessing at shadows. He opens his mouth to shoot some reply at me, but I beat him to it.

"I will even wear one of those nightgowns you had made for me. If, and only if, you answer my question."

He freezes, his mouth still open to speak. Color blooms bright on his golden cheeks. He snaps his jaw shut and looks away, scratching the back of his neck. His voice comes out a little strained as he says, "Fine."

Wicked satisfaction blooms in my gut. He may love to toy with me, but he's not the only one who can play games.

"Well?" I ask innocently. "What's the answer to my question?"

He clears his throat. "Every world has a beating heart at its core. Theoretically, a fragment of the greater world. For some portals, that heart is stationary. Other portals, like Roltwart, have a heart that moves throughout its expanse. That was why Liliana was so determined to get the soul when she died. Its heart had come near the portal. She heard its beat, and if you take a piece of that heart, as Neverseen King, I have the power to reduce it down to its essence."

"That doesn't sound feasible," I say.

"If we hadn't done it, I would agree with you. But I don't believe it's *always* feasible."

He means Crenfyre—Crenfyre is the one he cannot reduce to its soul essence. "Do you have to tunnel into the ground to get it?"

"A few times we had to, but not always. We had more spare time back then, when her blood kept the portals sealed longer." With that, he gets to his feet and gestures to the stairs leading out of the treehouse. "We should go back."

"Should we?" I ask, smiling. "We could stay another few hours before sunset."

The next instant, he's swept me up into his arms, grinning when I let out a squealing protest. I kick and cling to my dress, but he holds me close, and for all my protests, I secretly love it.

The sun dips dangerously low on the horizon when we return to Arbasa, and Kaladen hurries back to our room, where he unceremoniously dumps me in the bathing chamber to change.

Only now am I realizing that I should have worn one of these nightgowns the night after he didn't kiss me back. Then maybe we wouldn't have gone an entire two weeks without resolving the issue. A little spiteful torture might have been just as effective.

My smirk drifts away when I rummage through the wardrobe and find what I'm looking for. There are five different options, all made of fine imported silk. The fabric is butter beneath my fingers, and my courage falters at just how thin they are. I cannot remember wearing anything so thin and vulnerable in my entire life.

"You can do this," I whisper to myself.

I discard the black one, because it feels like the safest option, and to choose it would be cowardly. I likewise discard the scariest option—a light pink—and focus my attention on the remaining three.

The first is a green that reminds me of the magical vines around this palace. I toss that one back in the wardrobe. That leaves me with the final two: a luxurious purple, or a beautiful midnight blue. I stare at the two of them for several long minutes.

This shouldn't be hard.

I grab the purple one and throw the blue back into the wardrobe.

Putting it on, letting the cool fabric slide over my skin, reminds me exactly why I like having every inch of me covered when I dress. This dress has thin straps, no sleeves, leaving my shoulders and throat completely bare.

"There's nothing to be afraid of," I whisper to myself as I take a step and feel cool air around my limbs. "You aren't afraid of Kaladen. He isn't going to hurt you."

I know it rationally, but my body still shivers with vulnerability.

I take a few deep breaths and then force one foot before the other until I'm at the door. *You aren't afraid of Kaladen. You're not.* I turn the handle and push it open.

He isn't waiting outside the washroom, to my relief. The steady thump of his heartbeat comes from inside the bedroom, and it picks up its pace as I enter. My shyness overtakes my false confidence and I wrap my arms around my middle.

His gaze pierces me as I shut the door. He sits on the edge of the bed, his hand resting on his thigh. I feel the swift once-over he gives me as though it is a fire burning from my head to my toes. Then his eyes lock on mine.

"Hello," I say, because I don't know what else to do. I find somewhere else in the room to rest my attention. The tapestry on the far wall becomes my welcome distraction. I suddenly recognize the cerulean waterfall woven into its design as the same one from the rainforest portal.

He rises and comes toward me. The floating lumiral globes illuminate his progress until he stands before me. Shadowed, though not from any magicked glamours.

His warm hand slides around the back of my neck, slipping into my hair. He tilts my head back. A shuddering whimper escapes my lips.

"I know this is hard for you," he whispers as he leans his forehead against mine. "I want you to know two things. First, I admire your courage to do things that frighten you."

"I don't think this is called courage." It comes out in a breathy laugh.

"This is the very definition of courage, my little assassin."

His gaze is so intense, I look to one side, only to have him tilt my face back to his. I swallow hard as he brings his mouth to my ear.

"Second, I find you very lovely to look at."

My knees wobble. He pulls me against himself, one hand pressed into my low back as our mouths meet in a fervent kiss. My palms rest on the rapid rise and fall of his chest, and there is something viciously addicting to know that I am not the only one who has longed for this. He deepens the kiss, but only for a second, before he abruptly pulls away.

"I hate these portals," he growls, glancing over his shoulder.

"Is one breaking down?"

"It's been breaking down for the last few hours, but I thought we had a little more time." He runs a hand through his hair, still holding the back of my neck with his other. Then he looks down at me once more.

"That's unfortunate," I say.

He has my head in both hands the next second, pressing one last dizzying kiss to my mouth. "It is unfortunate, indeed, because I'd much rather kiss you until dawn than do portal work."

"Oh," I say stupidly, simultaneously pleased and flustered.

"We've got to get you to sleep. Otherwise, I'll have to go attend this portal by myself."

At that, I break out of his arms and hurl myself into the bed, pulling the covers over my head. "Do not fear! I'll be asleep in no time. You won't need to leave me behind!"

Kaladen laughs. "I'm not sure what fortune this is that I have married a woman who actually *enjoys* sealing portals. But I will not complain."

I keep my reply to myself as he slips into bed beside me, his weight shifting the mattress. And then his arms wrap around me from behind, pulling me against him. "Fall asleep fast, darling."

At first, I'm worried the hand he wraps around my waist will keep me wide awake. Instead, the soft strokes against my ribcage soothe me at once. I close my eyes and breathe in deeply of the sweetest warmth I have ever known.

The warmth, unfortunately, doesn't last long. The moment I enter the dream realm, Kaladen is already halfway out the door. "Quick! It's breaking down much faster than I thought!"

I match his fast pace. "Which one is it?"

"The goblin portal. I *hate* them so much."

We arrive at the Golden Hall. It takes me back to my first morning here at the palace. There's no time to admire the vast hall, the gilded paneling along the walls, or the great crystalline chandelier. Here, in the dream realm, I can see the otherwise invisible portal door floating a few inches off the floor, a cascading swirl of different shades of blue surrounding it. The red thumbprint is a dark brown, disintegrating as I watch.

"All those goblins are waiting on the other side, aren't they?" I groan.

"I thought you were excited to help me," he replies with a grin. It's gone a second later. "No, this *is* one of my most hated portals. You have to lead with your blade and squeeze into it without opening it all the way. And yes, this is one that often leads to injuries."

When he grabs the handle of the door, his other hand grips the hilt of a massive sword I've never seen before. I wish I had a scimitar with me. My knives will just have to suffice.

The second Kaladen turns the handle, he freezes. His head whipping to the right.

"Which one?" I ask, not taking my eyes off the flaking of this seal. It's barely holding together.

He curses. "Crenfyre. *Again*."

I search the room, as if looking for a solution engraved into the walls.

"We're going to have to let this one open," says Kaladen. His hand moves from the door handle to his belt, touching a small pouch I haven't noticed before. Does that have something to do with the alternative method of sealing he uses for Crenfyre?

"Or we split up," I say.

He head whips to mine. "Nadira, I don't think—"

Is he remembering how I fainted the first time I helped seal this portal? I firm my jaw. "We don't have another option. We cannot let these goblins free anymore than we can let Crenfyre free."

He suddenly has my face in both of his hands, his sword gone. His kiss is fierce—and brief. The next instant, he's gone. Leaving me to the goblins.

I send my awareness down into my belly. Ice already stirs there, responding to my adrenaline and fear as I grab hold of the door handle. I sense the shape of it, breathing deeply to stoke it and bring it to voracious life.

"You can do this," I tell myself.

Then I open the door.

Screeching nearly splits my eardrums.

Instead of leading with my blade, I stick my bare hand through. Immediately, sharp pain flares in my arm—a bite. It lasts only a second. I release my ice in a torrential flood. The effort sends my back arching and a cry ripping from deep inside my chest.

Then I squeeze through the door and slam it shut behind me.

It's a dim world, lit by three crescent moons hanging in the sky. My feet sink into something warm and gooey. I shudder.

But I'm not instantly flooded by goblins.

I look up.

There is a wide perimeter of ice surrounding me. Skewering bodies of strange, inky blue creatures with oversized fangs and bright yellow cat's eyes.

I hurry into motion, running as fast as I can through the sludge—which isn't fast at all. It grabs hold of my feet and I have to yank hard at each step. Ahead of me, I can make out more small, dark bodies coming, climbing over the ice.

I don't make ten paces before a heavy weight lands on my back, nearly yanking me to the ground. My knife finds its heart before its sledgehammer finds my brain. I sling the body aside before too much blood can slide down my skin and make me faint.

Another one launches itself at me. Then a blow to the back of my leg sends me to my knees in the murky green sludge.

"I hate you goblins!" I shriek—and explode.

My fury comes out in such a violent arc of ice, my vision starts to go black. "No, no, no," I growl at myself, shoving to my feet. This time, my ice coats the top of the sludge. Temporarily relieved of the goblins, I slide on my knees toward the little glow beyond the ice. The anchor floats in the sludge, a small iridescent ball. I swipe my sleeve in the goo right beside the anchor, then scramble to my feet.

At once, goblins flood me. Fangs tear into my sleeves, nicking my skin. I barely dodge tiny sledgehammers in every direction. Yellow eyes blink at me, filling my vision with their strange luminescence.

Clawed hands grab hold of my sirwal, climbing up my legs no matter how hard I kick.

"I—am—making—it—back!" Slices of my knives punctuate every word. "I *am*! The lot of you are worse than I remember! And I remembered you being very awful!"

If I have to kill hundreds of these creatures to survive, *I will*.

Another large blast of ice clears a slippery path ahead of me, but it does nothing for the ones clinging to my person. I stumble-run, hacking and stabbing as I go. A sledgehammer hits the small of my back. I buckle, breathing hard.

Then I'm back on my feet, snarling furiously. I throw two more off me and finally get enough purchase beneath me to run. Screeching follows close behind me. Still, I run. I fling another goblin off my back, leaving just one clinging to my left arm as I barrel through the door and slam it shut behind me.

The seal has only the faintest pulse remaining. I smear the sludge from my sleeve across the seal, scrape open the cut on my thumb, and press it to the door.

It flares bright red.

Then a bolt of blinding white heat smashes right next to me. I stumble backward, landing on my backside and somersaulting back up to my feet.

There's Kaladen, returned from Crenfyre, his palm upraised.

The creature who had come with me is nothing but a burned spot on the otherwise polished floor.

I stare at him, slightly dazed. Then I smile, lifting my filthy fist. I am . . . *utterly disgusting*. "I did it."

He stares at me. "I think I just fell a little more in love with you."

CHAPTER 31

THE MOURNER

"WELL, *YOU'RE* GLOWING this morning," Eshe chirps.

Kaladen had to leave early after our long night of portal work to help Tariq with more city guard logistics. Eshe has taken that opportunity to invade my breakfast with children.

"We accomplished very much in our work last night," I say, as if the rising flush in my cheeks isn't betraying every word out of my mouth. "I feel at ease this morning. I'm glad to be past the coronation."

"Take the baby," Eshe says to Zara, whose complexion has brightened in the time she's stayed here on the grounds, and sets a slobbering little boy—much bigger than a baby—in her arms. "Make sure the other children aren't fighting over their food."

Once the door shuts, and Eshe and I are alone in Kaladen's living room, she scoots across the settee to me, eyebrows almost to her hairline. I take a sip of my qahwa as if I don't know exactly what that expression means.

"Out with it," she says. "Should I prepare for shadow babies?"

I choke on my drink and barely avoid spewing it across the nice breakfast spread before me.

She claps her hands. "I'm going to be an aunt!"

I grab her wrist—still coughing. "No, no, no—no babies!"

She narrows one eye at me. "No babies? You're sure? Then explain the smiles when no one is looking and that pretty shade of pink in your cheeks."

"Maybe we just sealed a lot of portals!"

"Enough of the lies. Out with it. Otherwise, I will tell the children to spread the news in the streets of Risya that their new queen will soon have an heir."

"You are ruthless," I mutter.

"Never underestimate what I will do for a scrap of gossip."

My mouth twists at that. I lean back against the settee, trying to think of how to explain what happened last night. The memories flash before me again, of all the kisses we squeezed in between sealing portals. The three portals I sealed *completely* by myself.

"He showed me his face," I say quietly. "And we kissed. Not much else."

It didn't feel like those moments were lacking in any way. Kaladen is firm about taking things slowly. My instinct is still to guard against pain, and he said the unraveling of that instinct will take time. Instead of frustrating me, it makes me trust him more.

"He showed you his face?" Eshe shrieks, shooting up on the settee until she's literally *jumping* on the slightly cushioned seats. "Victory!"

"Get down!" I cry, forced to set down my cup so I don't spill hot liquid all over my lap. But I'm laughing despite myself, and maybe part of me enjoys feeling a little giggly and girlish. I remember something Dabria said so long ago it feels like forever:

Haven't you thought of what it would be like to be the one person in all Arbasa to discover the face of our Neverseen King?

"Is he handsome? You *must* tell me if he's handsome!"

"He is handsome, yes. It's just not in the way most fae are."

"I have absolutely no idea what that means."

Right, because she didn't go with us to Valehaven. I massage the bridge of my nose with two fingers. It's hard to describe the way he is both beautiful and roughened. "He is a rugged sort of handsome, rather than being exquisitely *beautiful*, as fae usually are."

Eshe grins. "So . . . exactly the sort of handsome you'd find tremendously compelling. Now, now, don't protest. Your blush gives you away. You'd be wasting your breath trying to convince me that you, in fact, find him hideous."

I drain my cup and set it down on the table. Then I get up and march out of the room.

"Wait!" Eshe yells, laughing and nearly tripping to chase after me. "Where are you going?"

"To get back to work," I reply, arching a brow at her. "Because apparently I'm wasting my breath trying to deny anything."

She breaks into a fresh hoot of laughter, and I barely withhold my own chuckle as I shut the door.

I do not go to my office.

Instead, keeping my senses on high alert for sign of Kaladen or servants or children, I take one of the back staircases, avoiding even my beloved banister.

With the sun shining and all I know about the House and the Bridge, the long, empty hallways full of locked doors shouldn't seem haunted. And yet, it is almost like they are more haunted than ever. Each door that I pass, with strange and different designs, is a door to an entirely new world.

Worlds of magic and malice.

It's like they have eyes, watching me as I walk past the unlit sconces. My feet make no sounds, my breath silent in the quiet stretch.

Finally, I come to my destination.

It's the last door on this hallway. It's larger than any of the other doors—the size of two of them put together. Cracked, gray wood is held together by wrought iron moldings. The hinges are rusted, ready to give way at any moment. But it isn't the hinges that keep this door closed.

I cannot see the seal in the waking realm, but I know it's there. Constantly breaking down this close to Lulythinar. Kaladen would kill me if he knew I came here unprotected. *You could end up like Mahja!* I can almost hear him shouting.

Somehow, I had hoped this door would shed its secrets to me, but it is like every other door here. Waiting. Silent.

Above the door is a stone placard with swirls engraved among skeletons.

"Crenfyre," I whisper.

It replies with a slight gust of wind that tangles into my hair.

CHAPTER 32

THE MOURNER

THE EVENING MEAL comes upon me unexpectedly fast. The diplomat from Pur gave me his answer before he left this morning—an affirmative—and the diplomat from Offom promised to write to me soon. There is so much to get done, so many possibilities I'm exploring to take care of these orphans and teach them trades to provide for themselves, so many possibilities to revive our dying economy. There's too much to do before Lulythinar, but if I wait, I fear I will never have the chance.

The things Kaladen told me yesterday about capturing the souls of portals rattle around in my brain. Constantly intriguing me. If I could get more information out of Kaladen, perhaps I could concoct a plan to get the last two souls—or at least fully understand why it's impossible and let the idea go.

None of it feels like work to me. I spend day after day poring over books, running figures and calculations, forming and tweaking and discarding plans. I don't like taking breaks to eat, but Kaladen promised to sup with Eshe and me at the end of the day.

And despite how engrossed I am in my work, I eagerly anticipate seeing him again.

When I emerge from my office, I head toward the banquet hall. But Zara intercepts me, and with a sweet smile, she says, "We're eating by the staircase."

I shrug and follow her.

Childlike shrieks are the first sound that reach my ears, followed by something unexpectedly familiar. *A burbling fountain.* I quicken my step until I round the corner and come upon a tableau that does strange things to my gut.

The doors to the courtyard are wide open. Shadows of waving palm trees cast against the grand staircase, which is covered with children of all ages. They string woven chains of flowers and grass and bits of ribbon along the banister. A rush of happy wind comes from the rafters, blowing dark curly hair back from sweet, laughing faces.

"No hair-pulling!" Eshe says, waving her finger in the face of a small boy, who has his fist tangled in his sister's thick hair. "Don't worry, you'll have your turn with the toy soon. You must ask nicely if you want your turn. Food is coming, everyone!"

A cheer goes up and the children scramble away from the staircase as servants come down the opposite hallway, bearing steaming baskets of stuffed naan. Zara hurries forward to help distribute the food to so many hungry mouths. I reach the banister and lay my hand on its warm wood.

Hello, my friend, it says.

Look at how beautiful you are! I reply, tapping the strings of flowers and grass. *Your decorations are fabulous.*

Beautiful! it cries back with pure joy. *Fabulous!*

You put kings to shame, I reply with a grin. *I love it.*

I love it!

I laugh and give it a good long scratch before the children rush back and plop on the stairs to eat their lunches. I look up, through the open doors, out to the sunny courtyard, and my heart fills when I behold the restored fountain, the burbling water and warbling birds bathing in its crystalline surface. The vegetation is restored too, with tall palm trees and flowering shrubs and every good thing I missed after Crenfyre.

Zara sits surrounded by the youngest children, ensuring each one has help eating. Eshe sits cross-legged on the floor, the toddler splayed in her lap as he stuffs his face with naan. I take my seat on the bottom step of the staircase, and one curly-haired girl named Aya scoots to my side. Not at all afraid of me. I smile at her. Then I peek at Eshe, and even when she's snapping for Abbi and his friends to behave and sit still for their lunch, I cannot remember ever seeing her happier.

I'm sure she's plotting how she's going to sneak more children in from the streets the moment Kaladen isn't looking.

Two long shadows fall over us. Aya next to me looks up, and her mouth drops open in fear. But instead of running, she glances at Eshe, then at me, and scoots closer. I lightly touch her shoulder, trying to reassure her that, of course, I will protect her.

It's Kaladen and Tariq, come for food.

Kaladen wears his shadows once more, but they're not nearly as deep as usual. Tariq looks smart and dashing in his captain's uniform, and he bows to Eshe and me the moment he enters.

Eshe feigns interest in wiping the toddler's mouth.

"Sorry we're a little late," says Kaladen. His gaze finds me immediately, and there is something about his weighted attention that immediately makes me recall his touch on my back, his mouth on mine. My hands turn moist, and I look away—but not before I catch the edges of a smirk emerging from his shadows.

He sits on the ground near to me, though not near enough to frighten the girl at my side who eyes him curiously. Tariq sits beside him. The two of them bring such a contrast to our strange little meal. At first, all is quiet as the children watch the Neverseen King and city guard eat. As though trying to decide if either of the two men will suddenly dart forward to grab them.

After several long minutes in which no one is grabbed, and Tariq and Kaladen prove themselves rather boring, the usual chaos of children breaks out once more. One of Zara's younger charges topples forward, hits his nose on the floor, and starts screaming. The older boys finish their food and run into the courtyard to find sticks to fight with.

Aya beside me stares long and hard at Tariq, who has captured her particular interest. Eventually, she stands and marches over to where he quietly eats. He looks up at her, pausing before he takes another bite of his food.

"Can I play with your hair?" she asks.

He blinks.

"You can play with mine!" Eshe interjects a little shrilly. She yanks her scarf off her head and pulls her long, beautiful hair free. "See!"

Tariq watches Eshe's hair tumble down to her waist. Then he returns his attention to the girl, who also studies Eshe's offering. "I like his more," she announces. She doesn't even wait for an answer before marching behind him and pulling the tie out of his hair. He sits as still as a rocky cliff face as her tiny fingers weave messy braids.

My mouth twists upward at Eshe's scowl. That scowl only deepens when more of the children rush to braid Tariq's hair. Abbi announces, "I'm going to see if I can weave hair like a basket!"

Tariq casts me a helpless look, and I cannot help but chuckle in return. Kaladen radiates amusement as he says dryly, "These little basket weavers better not be too good, otherwise shaving might be the only remedy once they're through with you."

It's not long before he, too, is swarmed by children who deem his broad shoulders the perfect climbing equipment.

The older boys come rushing back in, armed with sticks. "Tariq!" they call, heedless of propriety. "Show us how to fight!"

"I want to fight, too!" Aya cries. She immediately drops what she's doing and her big eyes fill with tears. "They never let me fight with them, but I want to learn too!"

"I'll show you," Tariq assures gently, patting the girl's shoulder in an attempt to calm her tears. "Don't worry. You won't be left out."

She sniffles, swallowing her tears, and nodding.

"Hold still!" Abbi demands.

"Basket weave my hair instead," Kaladen says. "If you will not be content without destroying someone's hair."

Tariq gets up, his hair a mess of half-finished braids, but he pays it no heed as he takes the girl to find a proper stick before they commence with fighting lessons. When I steal another glance at Eshe, she watches him carefully. Her expression is one of conflict—fear that she shouldn't let the children trust a city guard, and the realization that she might have misjudged him. She catches me looking and sticks out her tongue.

I mouth: *"You'd be wasting your breath trying to convince me that you, in fact, find him hideous."*

She grabs a stuffed naan from the nearest half-empty basket and hurls it straight at me. I catch it, laughing so hard my core hurts.

"Food fight!" Abbi cries.

"No!" Eshe, Zara, Kaladen, and I all yell at once. "No food fights!"

I shake my head at Eshe and take a bite of the naan. "You are such a bad influence on these children."

She glares at me.

Then something taps my ankle. I look down and see sinuous green—and let out a shriek. I barely remember not to whip out my knives in front of a passel of small children and, instead, scoot up several stairs.

It's a vine.

"Badh-a," I groan, pressing a hand to my chest as the vine draws back from me. "Why do you always scare me like this?"

Kaladen holds his hand out to the vine, and it immediately rubs the curl of its . . . *head-thing* on his wrist. "This isn't Badh-a. That was the one who strung you up in the courtyard and worked with Safya. This is Badh-o. She's much sweeter than Badh-a."

I blink, my hands gripping the stair I'm sitting on. Several of the children laugh at me for being so startled—apparently, they think nothing of magical vines—but the pieces are fitting together in my mind. "Badh-o. Then is this one . . ."

Kaladen lets the vine wrap around his thick forearm, listening to its pops and squeaks. He nods once. "I see. She says you kept thinking she was Badh-a and being suspicious of her. She wants to be your friend and means you no harm."

The vine unwinds from him. She approaches me slowly, but eagerly, and when she is only a foot away from me, she bursts forward a beautiful flower. I relax. I offer my hand out as a peace offering. She slides her blossom into my palm.

"My apologies, Badh-o, for being suspicious of you," I say. "Are we friends now?"

Squee! it replies, twirling its flower.

I laugh. "You should go meet Eshe. You'll probably like her more, anyway."

At once, the vine shoots to Eshe, who tries to hide her hesitancy. The child in her lap, however, bursts into a full-bellied laugh at the beautiful vine.

Then I'm sitting there, watching a magical vine perform tricks to make an orphaned little one laugh, the Neverseen King sitting on the floor letting a boy weave his hair like a basket, and a city guard with braids show thrusts and parries with a stick to his army of enthusiastic urchins.

Suddenly, I realize just how sacred this moment is.

So I let go of my own itch to get back to my work. I stay on the stairs of my favorite staircase, and I sit with my favorite people. The people who have made me hope again.

Kaladen's back straightens, like a dog coming to sudden attention. My gaze shoots to him and clueless Abbi. Then I feel it too.

A shift deep inside me. Not *my* magic . . . but magic connected to me.

A portal.

"Tariq," Kaladen barks, shooting to his feet. The commander immediately ducks inside, ignoring the protests of his little army. "Help Eshe get the children upstairs and locked in a room at once."

Upstairs. Not in the sheds they've turned into rooms. Not away from the palace grounds. Is he afraid the children wouldn't make it without interception?

Bile burns in the back of my throat.

The vine folds up its blossom and vanishes like it was never here. Eshe's grin dissolves into something much more serious as she shifts the little one in her arms. "What's wrong?"

"Hopefully nothing," Kaladen replies. "But we must not be careless. Tariq will stay with you and the children just to be safe."

Eshe lowers a stubborn brow. "We'll be fine. We don't need him. You can send him back to the guard."

Tariq, who isn't exactly out of earshot, shoots a look at Eshe, and then drags in a deep breath as he herds children up the staircase.

Kaladen takes one more step closer to Eshe. His voice drops to a low simmer. "He will not hurt you or the children. He is a good man, principled and strong."

I catch up to them and add my equally quiet voice to the conversation. "He doesn't have to be in the same room with you. He and Zara can take some of—"

"No, if he's coming," Eshe replies fiercely, "then I need to keep my eyes on him. I'm not leaving him alone with *any* of the children."

"Fair enough." Kaladen nods toward the staircase where Tariq and most of the children are disappearing. "Hurry now."

Once they're gone, Kaladen and I exchange a look.

"Valehaven Portal," he tells me grimly.

I flip out my knives. "I suppose that means the High King sent visitors."

CHAPTER 33

KALADEN

WE FIND THE Valehaven door swinging listlessly on its hinges, the great tree portal closed . . . but recently opened. The scent in the air is unmistakable. I clench my fists tight and whirl on my heels, tracing the direction of that scent—just as I feel the shift at the palace gates. *Cursed Great Kings.* I shut the Valehaven door.

I'm so glad I didn't order Tariq to take the children away from the palace. "The Wolf has gone into the city."

"What?" Nadira turns a horrified gaze to mine.

"I'll go after him. You stay here with Eshe and the children. It might be a trick, so be prepared for anything. Call my name—my full name—if you need me. I'll hear you, and I will come."

She gives a single nod.

Then she turns and hurries back the way we came. I slip into the dream realm, losing my physicality, and rush as fast as I can after the Wolf. I curse his name with every second that goes by. There is no end to my frustration that while I am here, serving the High King exactly as he bids, there is one bent on undermining me behind my back. I cannot spend all my days in Valehaven ensuring the Wolf does not tickle Faradir's ears with tales of my shortcomings.

I am forced to slow down and step out of the dream realm to ensure I'm still on the right trail. Then I continue on foot, glamouring myself to invisibility as I hurry into the depths of Risya, searching for my nemesis.

I reach the abandoned belltower. His scent ends here.

There is no reek of blood in the air. That should comfort me, yet it doesn't.

I push open the broken door. Its rusted hinges snap, and it falls to the ground in a cloud of dust. "Wolf! You have no business in this city. Come out of hiding."

He's not on the ground floor of the tower, and the stairs are broken. But the stairs won't be a hindrance to him.

When silence remains his only reply, I call again, louder: "Come down, Wolf! Or I will bring this tower down on your head."

I slide out of the way as a heavy body lands—exactly where I was just standing. In the darkness of the dusty tower floor, a great creature on four legs, with massive claws and a dripping snout, faces me. His coat is shaggy, his overlong legs sinewy and powerful.

"I come on the business of the High King," comes the Wolf's growling response from between his protruding fangs. He shows his teeth in a nightmarish grin. "Will you not receive me as a guest, dear Kaladen?"

"What does the High King want?" I snap. "And what does it have to do with this city?"

"It was just a simple errand. You can escort me back if it would make you feel better."

And give the poor people of Risya a heart attack when they see the creature from hell I lead through its streets? My frustration rumbles in my throat and I take two aggressive steps toward the Wolf. He snaps at me, but I evade his teeth and grab his neck.

His great paw swipes at my face. I dodge again, narrowly avoiding a deep bite into my forearm. I let go of him, but keep my hands outstretched. Ready to fight. "Tell me what you did. Tell me before I kill you and drop your sorry corpse before the High King."

He bares his teeth at me and growls low in his hideous throat.

"Tell me!"

He pounces. I shift to the side, but his claw catches my shoulder and scores a deep line into my flesh. The scent of my own blood rises to my nostrils. Thick, tangy, and metallic. "This is how you want to play?" I roll up my sleeves and widen my stance. "*Fine.*"

I charge him, shooting bolts of magic from both of my open palms. He leaps unnaturally high in the air to dodge them—toward me.

We hit the ground. I roll, forcing him into the dirt. I grab his neck with one hand, and with the other I summon another bolt of magic. His slavering jaw narrowly misses my shoulder. He claws straight for my heart, making my bolt fire wide. I lose my advantage as he forces another roll, slamming me into the wall of the belltower.

My head spins. I rip a blade from my belt. A savage cry rips from my lips as I throw my weight toward him. His claws rip down my back as I stab the knife between his ribs. A doglike whimper of pain escapes the Wolf, but it is quickly suppressed by a deep, rumbling growl.

I need to finish this. I need to get back to the palace. But I need to know what the Wolf has done. *I need to know.*

I get my legs up and kick him so hard he hits the opposite side of the belltower. Dust and debris rain down from above us. But I'm already in motion, forcing the Wolf to the ground, straddling his back and pinning his limbs so he cannot hurt me. "Tell me what you've done," I order, breathing hard. "Tell me or else I will kill you and find out myself."

That's when the string fastened to my heart pulls taut, and a desperate voice rings in my head.

"Kaladen Ashrift Felladyr!"

CHAPTER 34

THE MOURNER

I WISH I had Kaladen's invisibility. Then I could stalk up and down the hallways of the palace without worrying about being seen.

Still, I find a shadowed nook near the base of the staircase. I rest my hand on the polished wood of the banister. *Tell me if you sense anyone entering the palace. Or if you sense something escaping a portal.*

Tell me, it replies.

I will tell you, I say, giving it the proper response to my request.

I will tell you, it says.

I give it a quick scratch as a thank you and let the shadows claim me. My spot gives me a good view out of the courtyard, down both hallways in either direction, and a view up the staircase. It's also close enough that if someone made it to the rooms where Eshe and the children are before I sensed them, I can hear a door being broken down.

My breathing steadies. Instinctively, the counting starts in my mind.

One, two, three, four.

When I hit sixty-two, a quiet breeze from the rafters flows down the staircase. I reach out and touch the wood.

Entering the palace, the banister says.

My muscles brace. *Fae, human, or portal?*

Human.

I blink. *Servant? Yes or no?*

No.

Friend or enemy?

Enemy.

Is the enemy on this floor?

Yes.

Coming toward me?

Yes.

Good job, I tell it. I draw my knives and stay in my hiding spot. And wait.

And wait.

Several minutes slip by, and still no sign of another living being. I frown. Premonition trickles down my spine, my belly turning colder and colder. I slip out of my spot.

There's no one in either long stretch of hallway.

Maybe the House was confused when it answered my questions. I touch the banister again.

Is the enemy on this floor?

No, it says at once.

The floor above me?

Yes. Enemy, enemy, enemy!

I curse under my breath and silently run up the staircase. Nothing bad could have happened because I still hear nothing. But I don't know if I've ever heard the banister this frightened.

When I reach the second floor, I duck against the banister and peek around the corner. My eyes widen instantly.

Because Eshe isn't in the room like she promised. She is sitting just outside one of the doors, a scowl contorting her pretty features, and her arms crossed stubbornly over her chest.

"Eshe!" I hiss. "Get back in the room!"

She doesn't even startle when she looks up at me. "I'm not putting up with that city guard and his city guard-sized ego!"

Slight movement past Eshe catches the tail of my eye.

A crossbow, resting on the long arm of a black-wreathed intruder, points from a nearby cracked door—

Points straight at Eshe.

Everything inside me turns to dread-laced ice. I barely have the mental clarity with which to whisper: *"Kaladen Ashrift Felladyr!"*

But, as fast as he can move, he cannot stop this.

Pure, unadulterated rage fills me to the brim.

How *dare* someone lift a hand against Eshe?

I don't have time to be afraid. I don't have time to wonder if I might accidentally kill Eshe. There is nothing but a split second and the whistle of an arrow through space.

My arm cuts the air in a violent arc. Ice shoots from my fingertips and embeds deep in the wall right next to Eshe.

The bare tip of the arrow punctures the ice. The tip pierces Eshe's temple.

My whole world stops.

Just as the arrow stops.

Only the barest prick of its deadly point breaks her skin. A single drop of blood beads at the small wound. Slides down her cheekbone, all the way to her jaw.

My entire existence narrows to that drop of blood.

An undignified "uhh!" escapes Eshe's horrified lips just as the door swings open and Tariq's strong hand grabs her upper arm and yanks her to safety. I'm on my feet in an instant, pursuing the hooded figure. Over and over again, that image of Eshe's blood plays in my mind. Tariq follows, but I bellow: "Stay with the children!"

This is *my* quarry.

Because I know who this is, and I know why she's here.

The way my enemies move and fight is seared into my brain.

The door slams behind the intruder and a bolt clicks just before I throw my shoulder into the door. Pain radiates through my body. I hardly feel it beyond the cold rush of my fury. I dig deep into my belly, gathering as much latent magic as I can without exploding from the sheer force of it.

With a savage cry, I release the magic straight at the door.

It blows out with hardly a scrap of resistance.

Sunlight glitters on the refracting tips of enormous ice crystals inside the vacant bedroom.

The black form leaps over the windowsill. Out of view.

I run as fast as I can, dodging around the lethal tips of my own ice, and jump out the window after the intruder. I roll when I hit the ground. But before I'm even back on my feet, air whistles as the shadow of a long scimitar comes straight for the back of my head. I roll out of the way. The blade hits the flagstone with a force that sends vibrations through the ground and into my body.

I throw my worst blade by instinct as I leap to my feet.

My assailant lets out a grunt and bends over slightly. I've hit her in the gut. Satisfaction and an unfamiliar, wild sort of pleasure bursts through me.

I brace my legs, standing opposite my enemy as she lifts her black gaze from the wound I've dealt her. Poisonous hatred shoots like her crossbow's arrows. If her memory was indeed wiped, someone must have restored it—because there is no denying the exact source of her hatred.

"Raha," I growl.

She straightens, letting go of the knife still in her gut. She's not idiotic enough to pull it out. A humorless snort slips free of her severe mouth. As though she realizes she has only minutes left, and she has nothing left to lose. A slow smile splits the shadow of her hood. "How did it feel—that moment when you thought Eshe was going to die?"

I hurl a powerful blast of ice straight at her face. She dodges, laughing and gasping in pain. Then she yanks her crossbow off her belt and fires it at my eye. She moves so fast, so liquid, with such precision, I barely have time to duck.

Enough games.

I rush her, a violence of hatred filling my movements, turning my vision black. But I don't need my vision to kill. My rage guides me, guides the strokes of my knife as I parry her scimitar's slashes. Her blows are fast and heavy. I barely block them, my wrists nearly buckling under the force of blocking her larger weapon with my much smaller ones.

She might be fast, but I'm still faster.

Suddenly my vision clears, and I have her pinned against the palace wall. My knife is buried in her chest, hot blood flowing over my fist clenched around the hilt. Raha gasps, her mouth falling open in pain, her empty hands shaking. Still, her gaze is murderous. Still, she refuses to bend.

"You didn't come here to kill me," I snarl through my teeth. Our faces are so close together, and I have her completely at my mercy—as I once did before.

But this time, there is not a stitch of mercy in my soul.

"You came"—the words shake with rage, with fury, with a deep, fathomless well of hatred I did not know I possessed—"to exact your vengeance on an innocent soul who only ever showed you kindness."

It is so black an intention I can hardly fathom it.

Blood stains Raha's teeth. "Death is too kind a mercy for one like you. I used to want you dead. But now I want you to live, and live, and live—forever. I want you to live knowing that it was because of you that your friend died."

My brows narrow. "You are going to pay for those words."

I grab the blade in her gut and twist.

She screams.

"Nadira!" a loud, masculine voice booms across the courtyard.

Kaladen.

Something inside me fractures.

I can't let him see this. I can't let him see *me* like this.

But that means letting Raha go. Or finishing her off. It means not dragging out her death like I should have dragged out Jabir's. It means not funneling my rage into punishing Raha for the loss I almost experienced just now.

"Step away from her right now!" Kaladen demands. "We need to question her!"

Memory of his gentle hands against my back assaults me. It almost—*almost*—breaks me.

But it's the memory of Eshe's blood that overwhelms Kaladen's voice. It's that single drop of sliding blood that turns everything inside me to pure ice.

"No one touches those I love," I whisper to Raha. "If you had kept this between you and me—"

"This never was just between you and me. And you know it."

I've heard *enough.*

"Nadira!" Kaladen bellows.

I feel him behind me, rushing to stop me. But it's time he saw the truth of what I am, what I have always told him I am, what he refuses to believe.

I yank the blade out of Raha's stomach. She lets out a pained groan.

And then I stab her again.

And again.

And again.

And again.

A fist like iron grabs my wrist and hurls me to the ground. My palms hit the flagstone so hard the skin rips open and bleeds.

"What have you done?" Kaladen cries.

I twist just as he catches Raha's limp corpse before it collapses.

"We needed to question her!"

My brow lowers. "She needed to die."

"You didn't wonder how she got her memories back?" Kaladen sets the corpse down much gentler, then kneels beside me. He's bleeding, but it doesn't temper his anger at me. "The Wolf is trying to destroy us all, and she was a piece—"

"She tried to kill Eshe!" I scream into his face. "Don't try to tell me I shouldn't have killed her. I *loved* killing her. I wish I could have killed her longer and slower. I don't care about questioning! I care about how satisfying it was to feel my knife find resistance against her breastbone and to shove all my fury against it. To feel it crack. To feel the blood on my hands, to see the stain of crimson. It felt *so good,* Kaladen. I don't regret it. You cannot *make* me regret it."

He's wearing his shadows again, and it makes it easier to direct my hatred at him.

"Nadira." His voice softens to concern, his hand landing on my shoulder. "Can you hear yourself? This isn't you."

I fling away his touch, scooting away from him and scrambling to my feet. "It *is* me. Can't you see?" I throw my hands wide, my voice choking on a hysterical sob. Then I point at my own chest. "*This* is me. You're shocked, aren't you? You thought I was just a tortured soul who needed love, just a sweet girl who fell into the wrong hands, and you made me believe it for a short while. But now I see the truth. I'm not the victim. I couldn't punish Jabir like he deserved, and I thought it was because I wasn't truly a monster. That wasn't true at all. I *am* a monster. It was just hiding too deep for me to find it." I laugh—the sound broken and wild, as tears shred my cheeks. "I found it now."

Kaladen casts a look over his shoulder. I'm shocked to see a great, slavering beast lying on his side and bound on the far side of the courtyard.

The Wolf.

But Kaladen doesn't return to the Wolf to kill him. He follows my retreat, approaching with such force, a prickle of fear runs down my spine. I cannot hold my ground, so I stumble backward until he reaches out and snatches my arm to stop me. "Nadira—"

"Don't *touch* me!"

He holds up both hands at once, releasing me. The next second, his glamoured shadows are gone, revealing a dirt-smeared face, his kind blue eyes, and the fierce set of his jaw. Revealing that dear and desperate face I've so long hoped for. "Watching a loved one come to harm will make monsters out of any of us."

I point my shaking finger at him. "Stop pitying me. Stop trying to see the good in me. You know you were horrified by what I just did. I heard it in your voice. I *felt it*. Stop treating me like a broken doll. You never know when I might turn on you. My love will always be poisoned by hatred."

He doesn't take another step toward me. Wind blows his sweaty hair away from his face, and without his shadows, I can see more clearly the blood staining his garments, the patches of torn skin. My first instinct is to be worried, but just as quickly, I dismiss it behind the cold wall of ice behind me. His magic is likely healing those wounds as we speak.

"I hate watching you lie to yourself," he says. "But I do understand it. We lie to ourselves because we cannot stomach the truth."

"And what is the truth I cannot stomach?" I growl. My hands haven't stopped shaking, no matter the fierce shield of anger I cling to. "Tell me what it is, *Kaladen*."

His jaw ticks, his eyes flashing. There is that fearsome stubbornness that I both love and hate. He won't just *walk away*. He won't just leave me alone. Ever since the first time I laid eyes on his shadows, he has tormented me.

"You are frightened by what you just did." His soft voice carries on the wind as the sun begins to set. "So you deflect the true gravity of it by claiming to be a monster. Monsters ruthlessly torture and murder.

But a monster did not just gut Raha. You did. A rational human being with a tremendous amount of self-control. *All of us,* every single person in this world and every other, is capable of heinous crimes. Most of us do not find ourselves in a situation where that desperate part of us emerges. But now you have. So the question becomes: what will you do now? Now that you've seen this part of yourself?"

I shake my head. My teeth sink into my tongue, the sting of copper filling my mouth.

"You want me to turn away from you in disgust," he continues, mercilessly. "You are frightened by love. Because Nadira, *I love you*, and I have for much longer than I wanted to admit. What just happened does not change that. Not for me. But I have always held you with open hands, knowing you may not want this. That you may not want *me* enough to stay, even in the struggle and the pain. I have made peace with that."

"Please stop," I beg. My body throbs with ice, as though from a thousand fresh cuts. "Please stop talking."

His roar sends me back a step. "*I will not!* Not until I say this. I love you, and I will not leave you. You are free to go. I have never wanted you as my prisoner. You may leave and run to the ends of this world and every other. But I will stay, and I will love you, and if you return, I will always, *always* open my arms to you."

"*Please.* Please stop."

His tone drops, emotion choking his words. "You are my wife. I will have no other."

I turn away, unable to look at him. Unable to think. Unable to even breathe. The ice inside me fills every crevice, every inch of my body.

Kaladen's head whips to one side. "Valehaven."

That cuts through the frigid fog. It clears enough of a path for a cohesive, panicked thought to ricochet into my mind. "Someone else just came from Valehaven?"

His violent curse stands the hair of my neck on end. His eyes are a horribly darkened cast of midnight.

I turn around—

And find that the Wolf is gone, his bonds lying in a pile on the flagstone.

"Oh sands," I breathe.

It clicks for both of us in the same terrible heartbeat.

Wolf ran into the city to find Raha. To restore her memories. To create a diversion—an *emergency*. And then his accomplice came.

To help him take the Bridge from Kaladen.

We're already running.

Kaladen vanishes. My legs pump as fast as I can.

That's when the screaming begins.

CHAPTER 35

THE MOURNER

MY FEAR DRIVES me blindly through the courtyard. I careen through the open doors and I'm about to barrel up the grand staircase—

But at the curve of the staircase is an enormously tall fae form. One with towering antlers and a massive, billowing cloak. His cloven hooves click on the stairs.

Eldreth of the Star City.

His long fingers are wrapped around Zara's throat, dragging her down the staircase. She whimpers. Her whole body quakes. So this was what Wolf promised him if he helped: a fresh human girl to add to his collection.

My fury could set a forest ablaze.

I widen my feet at the base of the staircase and yell, "Release the girl, Eldreth!"

Eldreth tosses a disinterested glance my way. He ignores me and the screaming coming from the upper floor.

I throw my hands forward and unleash the wrath inside me in a flood of ice. I aim straight for his face and neck, which are high enough above Zara's head that I won't risk hitting her. Eldreth's arm slashes upward, and my ice careens off his shield of flashing light—piercing the walls of the House.

He pushes the girl further down the steps. "I claim only what I am due."

"That girl belongs to no one but herself," I snarl. My next blast of ice embeds into the staircase next to Eldreth. I don't have time to feel sorry for my banister before Eldreth shoots a white-hot bolt of pure magic at me.

I throw myself to the side, somersaulting back up to my feet and countering with another blast of ice. "Let. Her. *Go!*"

"Enough with you!" Eldreth cries. His fingers tighten around Zara's throat. She chokes. "I will damage her if you keep fighting me!"

"*Eshe!*" Tariq's strong voice screams from above the stairs. "No!"

Eshe—Eshe—where is Eshe?

I cast around frantically for her. I maintain my stream of ice against Eldreth, and much of my brain is forcibly occupied on dodging his obliterating bolts. Where is she?

Then, suddenly, I spot her.

Right behind Eldreth. Hidden in the sweep of his long cloak. Raising a knife above his head.

My world slows.

Halts completely.

Everything around me is frozen in pristine clarity. Zara clutching the hand around her throat, her mouth open and her face knotted in pain. Eldreth focused on me, a blast of magic paused midway through the air between us. Tariq running down the stairs with a raised sword. His expression contorted with horror. And Eshe.

My beloved Eshe.

My beautiful friend.

A mixture of concentration and fury draws her brow together. The last light of day burns through the courtyard, turning the bleached highlights of her hair a fiery red. Illuminating her lips twisted to reveal her crooked front teeth. The knife she holds in both hands.

No.

Eshe stabs Eldreth in the back of the head. I throw myself to the ground, the heat of his magic singeing my garments. Zara screams. Another bolt of magic flies wide. It explodes against Tariq's sword and sends shattering pieces of metal hurtling in every direction.

I know it is going to happen even before it happens.

Because Eshe may be quiet on her feet. She may be fast and clever and nimble.

But no matter how careful Eshe is, no matter how distracted Eldreth is, she cannot stop his retaliating blow.

And Eshe knows it.

His arm is swinging back, and even after the light fades from his eyes, his magic-filled palm continues its momentum.

And strikes Eshe in the gut.

They both fall.

I cannot scream.

I cannot call her name.

I cannot move.

Not as Zara pulls free and scrambles away, sobbing uncontrollably. Not as Tariq catches Eshe before she hits the stairs, screaming her name. In a strange, hazy moment of disbelief, I think suddenly how right Kaladen was to trust Tariq. He barely knows Eshe, and she never gave him a single polite word—but here he is. Trying to protect her. Trying to save her. *Caring* for her.

He lifts her up. Her entire torso is blackened. Half her right arm is gone.

I have no voice. My tongue sticks to the roof of my mouth.

My heart pounding inside my chest screams: *Kaladen! Kaladen Ashrift Felladyr! Help me before I die!*

"We need to get her help!" Tariq shouts at me, pulling me out of my stupor. He leaps over Eldreth's fallen corpse, holding Eshe close, and brings her to me. "Tell me where the Neverseen King is, and I will get him!"

"He's coming!" I say, knowing it without a single doubt. Whatever battle he is fighting against the Wolf, I know he will come. He will leave everything and come.

I fall to my knees. Tariq gently leans Eshe against my chest, her good side pressing into me. She gasps for air, trembling hard.

"Eshe, Eshe, Eshe," I breathe, pressing my hand against her sweaty face, brushing away her hair. "Can you hear me? We're getting help. Kaladen is going to heal you."

She wheezes, her eyes wide and unseeing as she stares at the ceiling.

"What can I do?" cries Zara, tears streaming down her filthy cheeks and bruised neck. "Tell me what I can do!"

"Go to the children," Tariq answers at once. He grips her upper arm. "Are you alright?" She nods—a brave lie. "Stay with them. Tell them I will come back shortly. Call if you need me."

She leaps to her feet, still crying, and runs up the stairs past the enormous fae body.

I look down at Eshe in my arms. I'm still stuck in denial. Still believing this is a nightmare I will wake up from. "I've got you; I've got you," I whisper to her. Each of her wheezing breaths kills me a little more. "Kaladen is coming. He will heal you. You just have to hold on a few more minutes."

The stump of her arm quivers.

Her eyes roll toward Tariq, her brows drawing together in pain. "I'm sorry," she gets out. "For not trusting you. I wish . . . I wish I could have known you better."

"It's alright," he says at once, gently touching her shoulder. "You had good reason not to trust me. And you *will* get to know me better. Just as I've hoped to get to know you better."

Because Kaladen is coming. He will fix this.

She tilts her head back toward me. I know that look in her eye.

"No," I stay sternly, choking on the lump in my throat. "You don't give up. Remember how you always get out of the worst scrapes? Remember how you escaped with Lord Kishon's stupid egg even after they'd caught you?"

Her mouth pulls into a smile. But her breathing grows harder and harder.

Kaladen! Get here now!

She tries to cough. A pained whimper escapes her instead, and her voice comes out crackled and ragged. "Nadira. I know you don't like this, but there are two things you need to know. I love you, and your friendship has been my dearest gift on this earth. Second"—her smile redoubles, stronger, braver, and that signature sparkle returns to her eye—"this was *absolutely* worth it."

What do you want? I once asked her. I'll never forget her reply:

Not much, in truth. A full belly, a comfortable place to sleep, at least one friend. And I want to do things that make me feel alive. I also want to help the street orphans. I want them to be fed . . . and protected.

Eshe's lip quirks, as though remembering it, too. "Tell the shadow freak thank you for the kidnapping and the food and the epic palace."

"Don't give up," I growl at her, holding her closer. "You have got to hold on just a little bit longer. He'll be here any minute."

"I can go look for him," Tariq says, a quiet urgency in his voice.

"You won't be able to find him. He's coming. He'll be here any second." My heart pounds frantically in my chest. As loud as I can, I yell: "Kaladen Ashrift Felladyr! *Please* come!"

I look down.

Eshe's eyes are open. She has gone still.

Tariq's hands are suddenly there, cupping her face, pressing his thumbs to her pulse. "Eshe. Can you hear me?"

My heart has stopped beating.

Tariq tries to keep the urgency out of his voice, tries to keep himself level and calm. Maybe because he senses I am slowly fracturing into tiny pieces. "I can try to resuscitate her."

When I don't reply, he forcibly takes Eshe from my arms. I don't have the strength to fight him. He leans her battered and burned body carefully on the ground. He pulls open her mouth, covers it with his, and blows air into her lungs. He pumps her chest with his hands, then returns to her mouth.

This isn't happening. I'm dreaming. I'll wake up soon. It'll be over. She's fine. She's alive and well and with all the crazy children she rescued.

The longer we sit there, the lower the sun descends on the horizon, the darker it gets, the more it sinks in. Tariq doesn't stop trying to revive Eshe. He keeps going and going and going.

And then my heart constricts.

She's gone.

Kaladen didn't come.

My friend is dead.

CHAPTER 36

KALADEN

WOLF'S SHARP TEETH tear into my shoulder. I throw us backward, slamming his body into the wall of the children's sheds—the place he ran the moment he was free, following the scent of easy prey. His teeth come for my throat. I dodge hard to one side, barely enough that he misses my jugular.

Wild animal snarls fill my ears. The stench of flowing blood clogs my nostrils.

Only a minute ago, I finally understood why Wolf is fighting me the way he is. He isn't trying to kill me. He is trying to wound me. Over and over and over again.

Because then my magic—and the House's magic—floods my body to heal the wounds.

Weakening me.

I throw a bolt of magic behind me. The sizzle of fur tells me I've only grazed him. I try again to throw him off me, to stab him with my sword, but he barely dodges.

Nadira's frantic voice yanks hard at the tether between us. *Again. Kaladen! Get here now!*

I'm coming! I call back, even though she cannot hear me. *I'm coming!*

I throw my elbow back, stab hard with my sword. A wolfish cry of pain tells me I hit something. It's enough to throw him off, to burst into a run. I shift into the dream realm to move faster, but he follows me. He launches himself at me, and I duck back into the waking world before his teeth sink into the back of my neck.

Kaladen Ashrift Felladyr! Please come!

A stab of agony in my chest makes me pull back sharply. But I'm not wounded.

That came from Nadira.

A burst of strength comes from nowhere, overcoming the weariness sunken into my bones, and I grab the Wolf by his scruff, lift him up, and hurl him into the wall. Plaster cracks and crumbles.

"Go back to Valehaven!" I demand.

He tries to come for me once more, but I have just enough time to slip once more into the dream realm and chase the pulse of that agony before he can follow. I try to reason away my fear, telling myself that Nadira is fine—that I would feel it if she died.

But something is desperately wrong.

The agony doesn't let up.

It only grows stronger.

I know before I arrive at that cursed scene that the emotion throbbing against the tethers linking our souls is heartbreak. I know too well the echoes of loss.

Nadira sits slumped on the ground. Staring at Tariq, who tries to revive a burned body lying on the floor. *Eshe*. She's not the only dead—a fae sprawls face down on the ground. Eldreth came through the Valehaven portal while I was fighting the Wolf.

My strength flags. Still, I run forward, falling to my knees between my wife and her dead friend. *My* dead friend. "Nadira! What—what has happened?"

She doesn't look at me. Her empty, tear-filled eyes fix on Eshe.

I shift my focus to Tariq. "What *happened*?"

Tariq, breathless, pulls his mouth back from Eshe's as he pumps her chest. "That creature broke into the room we were hiding in. I tried to fight him, but he was *so fast*. He grabbed one of the orphan girls and left. Eshe chased him down the stairs—and I followed. But I wasn't fast enough to prevent her from killing the creature. He . . . did this. Can you do anything?"

"You've got to save her," Nadira whispers.

I look helplessly at Eshe—at the burn that spreads from the side of her hip up to her ribs. At the stub of her arm. At her very still chest. I don't have to check. She's gone. She's been gone for some while now.

Nadira's voice is stronger, more desperate, even though her gaze still doesn't shift from Eshe. "You've got to save her."

The agony pulsing in my chest feels like my own. Stabbing and relentless and overwhelming. It floods my weakened limbs, floods the fast-healing wounds that only drain more of my strength.

But I reach out my hand. I press one to Eshe's shoulder above her heart, the other to the good side of her waist. I summon what power I have left, and I pour every last shred of it into Eshe's body.

It's not going to work.

I knew it, and yet a tiny part of me hoped. I feel it the moment my magic surges. It is like I pour it into an empty chasm. Eshe's burned flesh reknits together. The ripped tissue of her arm heals over. But there remains no soul in this husk of a person.

I cannot bring Eshe back.

But for Nadira, I will give her what I have. I shouldn't—because the Wolf is on my tail. I know I shouldn't, and yet I cannot look at the emptiness in my wife's gaze, cannot feel the sundering pulse of heartbreak in my chest, and do nothing.

I'm sorry I couldn't come sooner. I'm sorry I couldn't stop this.

At last, I pull back my hands. Except for her severed arm, Eshe's body is restored. She lies on the ground as though she is asleep. Her kind face is satisfied.

"I will take her," Tariq says quietly. He lifts Eshe into his arms and makes to carry her upstairs.

My vision swims into black. My limbs are as heavy as lead. I fight hard not to lose consciousness. "Get the children," I manage to order. "Get them out of the palace. Take them somewhere safe. Immediately."

He hears the fear in my voice and nods. Then he's in motion and out of my sight.

Carefully, weakly, I turn. "Nadira."

Her hollow gaze shifts to me. It's like I look upon the death of a dozen stars.

"Nadira," I say again. It comes out in a wheeze. I want to comfort her, but I know there is no comfort from a loss like this. "You're not safe here. You must go with Tariq."

"The Eye knew," she replies, a whisper on the wind.

The darkness tries to take me once more. I hold still, blinking hard until it clears.

"The Eye knew she was going to die. That is why it tried to bargain with me for her life. And I didn't take it."

"Because you shouldn't have taken it."

Her gaze suddenly comes into frightening focus, and her empty voice fills, slamming against the walls around us. "So I'm supposed to *live* with this now?"

Oh Nadira.

I understand so well what she feels. Except to say so would diminish her suffering. I want to give her hope. I want to give her everything in my heart—every hard-won lesson I learned through Liliana's loss.

But I cannot.

Some truths are impossible to believe until you experience them.

She will not believe my assurances that she will recover from this. She will not believe anything I say. And that is fine.

I stay where I am, sitting beside her. My strength continues draining as magic rebinds the wounds the Wolf gave me. I'm not sure how much longer I will be conscious. Somehow, I know when I come to again, she will not be with me. The pulse of her agony grows fainter, as though she draws away from me even now.

So I say the one thing I need her to know. "I love you, Nadira."

I love her so much that I have done the one thing I swore never to do.

I have given up the Bridge—the one Liliana died protecting—because I loved again.

She stares at me, tears slipping down her cheeks. The agony renews in my chest, but this time I do not know if it is mine or hers. "You didn't come. I needed you, Kaladen, and you didn't come."

Her beautiful, stricken face fills my vision.

"I cannot do this anymore," she breathes. She gets to her feet, turns on her heel, and flees into the courtyard.

Her running form is the last thing I see before an entirely new voice consumes my darkening awareness.

"Finally. I have overpowered you at last. The Bridge and the bride arc *mine*."

Nadira's name is the last thing that screams through my mind.

CHAPTER 37

THE MOURNER

IT IS JABIR chasing me. It is the High King of Valehaven. It is Eldreth and Yirmuth and the Eye of Baltor and Prince Trenian. It is the ghosts of my mama and baba and my dear Eshe. They reach for me, trying to grab my hair, my garments, my pumping legs.

I cannot outrun them.

No matter how far or how fast I run, I cannot escape this nightmarish reality. I cannot make it stop. I cannot wash away that image of Eshe's lifeless body. She joins the pool of blood where my baba fell. It is her blood dripping down my back like sweat, coating me, covering me, drowning me.

"Get *away* from me!" I scream, scraping desperately at my arms, legs, and torso. "Get off! Get *off*!"

I cannot breathe. I don't *want* to breathe.

Why won't the dark streets of Risya swallow me whole? Why won't the sky come down and devour me? Why won't the earth open and consume me?

It's my fault Eshe is dead. I believed Kaladen would come. I didn't bargain with the Eye—I could have bargained for something other than her immortality. Protection against those who would hurt her, perhaps.

If I hadn't let her bring those children into the palace, she wouldn't have died protecting them. If I hadn't been so consumed with killing Raha, I wouldn't have been distracted when Eldreth came. I wouldn't have distracted Kaladen at a crucial moment. If I had just—

Not fallen in love with him.

I could have taken Eshe and left the palace. He could have taken Safya for his bride. She could have been the one to be killed by Eldreth.

I trip on a pothole and sprawl flat on the road. Panic nearly overtakes me, that Jabir will catch me. I scramble back to my feet. A furtive glance over my shoulder reveals nothing but empty street. But I know he's there. He's always there. He lurks in every haunting corner.

When I try to run again, my balance is thrown. I stagger against the wall of an alley.

"You there!" calls a voice that unmistakably belongs to a city guard.

I turn, my fingernails digging into the crumbling plaster. "Get away from me or I'll kill you."

"Baki, Ghulam, Nur!" the first guard calls, stepping away from me and my threat. To me, he holds up his torch and one hand. "This doesn't need to get violent. You only need to answer a few questions—"

"That's the queen!" one of the running reinforcements cries. He sounds so young. So much younger than me. "Your Majesty, what is the matter?"

I stay where I am, cornered like a thief. Like a criminal. I don't withdraw my knife. Not a single rational thought can compute in my brain. Instead, I'm wondering how long it would take me to kill all four of these guards standing before me.

Guards hurt Eshe. She never would have had to stay in the palace if the city guard hadn't been so corrupt.

The last guard pulls up short. My attention snags on him, on the way his dark face suddenly turns pale in the moonlight. "Is that the queen?"

"Yes! Something's wrong!" cries the young one.

The other guard, standing very still, says, "*That* . . . is the Mourner."

All five of us freeze.

I don't say a word. I don't breathe.

The young one is the first to move, looking back at me. "No, that is Queen Nadira. I saw her at the coronation."

I clench my fingernails into the plaster so hard they ache.

"She is the Mourner. A woman just tipped the guard off that the queen is the Mourner less than an hour ago. Your Majesty, please don't fight us. We don't want this to be difficult for you or for us."

"I don't think we can arrest the queen?" the youngest one says nervously.

I give a quiet snort, and the icy rage filling me eases the excruciating stab in my chest. "I'm afraid if you want to bring me to justice, you'll have to catch me."

With that, I plunge into the black-as-night alley.

Their footsteps are fast on my trail. I lead them through the city, embracing the temporary distraction. I leap and grab hold of the edge of a roof, brace my core, and pull myself up to the top. Then I turn around. I face the guards as they run and catch the edge of the roof . . . only to fall back down.

"Tell them all!" I cry. "Tell everyone in the city that the Mourner is their queen! Try to catch me. Try to kill me. I will come to justice one of these days. My body will hang from the city gates. But I swear it on the grave of my baba, it will *not* be by your hands."

I dodge a crossbow arrow just as the strongest of the group pulls himself up. I turn on my heel and run. The wind catches my hair, rips away my scarf. I leap from one roof to the next and the next, then catch a beam and swing myself back to the ground.

I've lost the guards.

But I have not lost Jabir. I have not lost Kaladen's voice.

I love you, Nadira.

Those words were lies—paltry attempts to tame the monster inside me. But I am not docile, and I never have been.

I will not be tamed.

The forces around me have shaped me enough. It is time to break the chains that have always bound me. It is time to overcome the fear that has been my greatest shame.

I reach the belltower in no time. I anchor my rope and climb it in less than a minute.

Then I pull myself onto the beam holding the great bell. At last, I stop.

My feet dangle over the drop.

So far to the ground.

My blood pumps wildly in my veins. The rising moon illuminates the expansive city beneath me—and the knife that I draw in my shaking hand. Separator, my best and sharpest knife. The knife I save for assassinations.

It doesn't feel like giving up to press the tip of that knife against my beating heart.

I will conquer this.

This is what I should have done years ago. I shouldn't have let Jabir turn me into a monster. I shouldn't have ruined Eshe's life. I shouldn't have opened myself up to the Neverseen King.

I should not have been a coward.

I should have ended my life before I could have amassed this mountain of guilt.

Before I lost Eshe.

I tighten my grip on Separator. Fear flips my belly. My whole body trembles.

It'll be over in a second, I tell myself. And then my body will fall, hit the bell, and the entire city will know the Mourner is finally dead.

My mind flashes to the first time I tried to do this. It was after my first kill when I was eleven. Jabir had tied a man to a chair. He'd tried to make me kill the day prior by beating me when I refused. But I had held my ground. I refused to kill.

The next day, he brought me again into the room where he had the man tied to a chair. I could barely move from the lashes I'd taken. That time, he gave me the same assignment: *kill the man*.

But instead of torturing me, he began torturing the man.

The longer I resisted, the more severe the torture for the man. The echoes of those screams come back to haunt me now, turning my hand clammy.

I threw up after it was done, and I didn't stop for over a week. I could keep nothing down—to the point Jabir truly became afraid I would die.

I wanted to die. I wanted to die so much.

But Jabir forced medicine down my throat. He forced food and drink after it. Bit by bit, I recovered. I didn't want to. I did anyway.

When I finally got my knives back, I tried to end things myself.

The stinging cold of that memory returns to me. The way I shivered, wrapped up in the threadbare quilt Jabir gave me, as I picked up my largest knife. It was dark then, as it is now, and only the moon watched as I moved the knife from my chest to my throat—unsure which would be better. It wasn't the fear of pain that stayed my hand.

I didn't know how to kill without drawing blood, and I couldn't bear the thought of lying in a pool of my own blood. Like Baba. Like Mama. Lying there while it devoured me.

My hands shake. The tip of my knife pricks against my skin. One thrust, and it will all be over. My pain, my haunting memories of Jabir and Eshe and Kaladen. The guilt that followed me from the day

I couldn't stop my parents from being slaughtered, all the way through my assassinations, up until Raha's murder. The blood on my hands is a weight that will drag me to the depths of hell.

"You can do this," I tell myself. "You couldn't do it then, but you can do it now. Don't hesitate. Put all your strength into it. You won't even feel it."

I don't realize how deep my teeth have sunk into my lip until I taste copper.

One thrust, and it'll be over.

Will death even bring me the oblivion and peace I long for?

My knife pauses, trembling. What if I endure this fear of my own death, then the pain of it, only to find it doesn't free me from my bondage? What if I become a shadowless ghost, floating through the world, searching for rest and finding none? What if I give up everything good—the sunshine, the gurgling fountains, the singing birds, Kaladen's voice—in exchange for an eternity of torment?

"I can't do it."

The broken words are out before I can stop them.

My hand with my knife falls into my lap.

The tears flow, then. Hot and weighty.

"I *can't do it.*"

A sob rips from my throat. I let my knife fall—until it hits the ground below with a thump. Then my mouth opens in a violent scream.

"I cannot do it!"

I'm a fool. A coward. A murderer. A broken shell of a monster. A creature, most of all, to be pitied. My tears turn to agonizing laughter. "I cannot even take my own life! I am an assassin and I cannot take my own life!"

I draw my knees up on the narrow beam and bury my face in them. *Oh Eshe.* My beloved Eshe. How can she be gone? The world will never be the same without her smiles, her laughter, her ridiculousness, her stubbornness, her goodness.

I don't know how to go on from here.

I don't know how to free myself from these crushing burdens of loss, guilt, and fear.

So what do I do?

I stare up at the rafters of the belltower, the stars and moon in the sky around me.

Maybe Kaladen was right. That I choose to call myself a monster because I am afraid of what it would mean if I wasn't just a broken woman who has lost everything she ever loved. Who lost everyone who ever loved her.

Maybe it was never about choosing love over hate.

Maybe this world, this world that holds both the good and the twisted, the kind and the evil, was never about love and hate.

Maybe it was always about choosing love over hurt.

A fresh wave of tears washes over me, bowing my shoulders. I don't know how to love. The wounds go so, so deep.

But then a memory resurfaces.

Of warm hands gently working the scars on my back. A rich low voice.

I love you, Nadira.

I love you, and I will not leave you. You may leave and run to the ends of this world and every other. But I will stay, and I will love you, and if you return, I will always, always open my arms to you.

"Why do you love me?" I weep. "Why don't you free yourself from this—from me?"

You are my wife, and I will have no other.

Kaladen was right. I am so deeply frightened by his love, even as I crave it. I don't know what to do with it—whether to hide from it or run toward it.

I have taught myself to be hard. To be unfeeling and cold, even with the few people I love. That was the only way to cope with the pain. The ice in my gut stirs in response.

Everything Kaladen has taught me, however, has been the opposite. Softening. Releasing. Moving through the storms and the waves.

Maybe what I need to do isn't to run from this guilt and the ravages of loss. Maybe I need to open myself up to it, to let myself really feel in a way I haven't felt before.

Kaladen isn't here to hold me through the storm. But maybe I don't need his help. Maybe I can hold myself.

I reach out one hand and brace it against the crossbeam. Then I close my eyes.

And I let myself shatter into a million pieces.

It's like I'm watching myself—watching the tiny girl scream for her parents. I weep for her. For the tragedy no child should ever witness. I watch her grow older as she is torn between hating Jabir and longing for a fragment of his love. I watch as she suffers abuse after abuse, getting back up again, fighting to hold on to herself. The way she collected the names of those she killed. How she switched from struggling against Jabir to working hard to learn all he wanted to teach her . . . so she could make it fast and painless for her victims. For the first time, a flood of compassion fills me. Compassion for this *child,* who was put in an impossible situation. Compassion for the eleven-year-old girl who killed because her soft heart couldn't handle watching someone suffer.

"Oh sands," I gasp. My teeth bite hard around my knuckles. I brace myself so I don't tip off my beam and fall. Kaladen kept saying it—but it was like I never heard him.

Nadira, I don't think you realize how terrible the things were that you endured.

I run my fingers along the scars of my jaw. The ones at the back of my ribs. The countless others marking my body.

These do not mark me as weak—and they never did.

They prove that I survived.

I survived my parents' deaths. I survived Jabir's abuse. I *survived.*

The tears come harder.

I will survive Eshe's loss.

I will.

That doesn't ease the ache in my chest. It doesn't fix how much I desperately long to see her face again and tell her how much she meant to me—even if she already knew she was my entire world.

But the ache doesn't need to go away.

With the heel of my palm, I dry my tears.

It is like a tremendous weight, an overwhelming burden, has vanished into the night without a trace. I am left with nothing but the surety of my love for Kaladen and the unrelenting pain of Eshe's death.

I cradle that love and that pain in my heart—the loss that I will carry with me to the end of my days—and I rise.

CHAPTER 38

NADIRA

I KEEP MY voice quiet as I call into the empty courtyard of the palace: *"Kaladen Ashrift Felladyr!"*

I don't know what Kaladen's full name in the Wolf's hands might mean, but I don't intend to give him that power. Whatever power that might be.

There is no response.

The healing magic.

Something dark trickles down my spine. Strangely enough, it's not fear. No, this is something entirely different.

I lick my lips and try once more, but this time I speak even softer than before. "Kaladen Ashrift Felladyr. I'm sorry I left you. I'm sorry I blamed you for Eshe's death. And—and I love you."

Nothing.

It's after dark. I dare not enter the palace hallways. I cannot enter the dream realm without Kaladen—which means my options are to stay outside the palace, or to climb through windows in hopes of discovering a room where he might be.

I flick my knives into my palms, brace my legs wide, and shout at the top of my lungs: "*Wolf!*"

I whirl and sidestep by instinct—and barely miss the violent scrape of a taloned claw down my back.

A beast snarls before me. He is almost as big as a horse, with long, sinewy legs of pure muscle. The slavering mouth dripping with sharp fangs twists into a smile, and massive paws the size of my face drag his claws in a shivering line down the flagstone.

I sheath both knives and instead hold up my bare palms. Ice floods my body—not overwhelming, but forceful. Ready at my beck and call.

"Where is my husband?" I demand.

The Wolf's maw widens in a terrifying grin. "I am your husband now."

Then he pounces.

My ice careens wide as I hit the ground hard. I try to roll, but his claws slam down on my chest, pinning me with his tremendous weight. Two of his claws frame my throat. His other paw slams into my wrist just before I blast him in the face with my ice. I twist and barely manage to stab my one free hand—coated in ice shards—into the side of the Wolf's neck.

His jaw clamps down on my arm. I scream.

Then he roars in my face.

I roar back at him. There is not a single ounce of fear in me. It is nothing but pure rage.

The Wolf chuckles. "I like you. You're going to be such fun."

Keeping me pinned, he tilts his jaw away from my face, even as I demand: "Where is Kaladen? What did you do to him?"

His long, doglike tongue emerges from between his lethal teeth. He drags it across my forearm—licking up the blood from where he bit me.

I go still.

He pulls back, licking his chops. He smiles at me. "Beautiful."

The Wolf hurt *my* Kaladen. And now he licks my blood and claims me as his prize.

Hatred runs like water through my veins. Still, I restrain it.

I cannot fight or struggle my way out of my current position. The Wolf clearly does not intend to kill me. I will comply with him for now. I will not fight him—*for now*.

He has done something to Kaladen. I don't know what, but when I reach inside myself, I find one solid, unbreakable assurance.

My husband is alive.

I cling to that with everything inside me.

"This iron should make you a little more docile," says the Wolf. His front leg shifts to a long, powerful fae arm and hand. I try not to be surprised by the incongruous sight, try to focus on struggling against whatever he is trying to clamp around my neck.

The pain hits me the moment something cold touches my skin. It radiates through my body like a throbbing headache. At once, my magic shuts down. A bolt of fear hits me as I reach frantically for that well of power—and find nothing.

It throws off my balance, enough that the Wolf slams me to one side. My face hits flagstone. The collar around my neck pulses with blinding hot pain. My whole world becomes nothing but that agonizing pounding.

When my awareness finally clears, the world is no longer dark as midnight.

It is awash in the golden glow of many torches.

CHAPTER 39

NADIRA

NO ONE PINS me. I try to shoot to my feet.

But my feet are bound.

My hands, too.

That's when I realize that much of the surrounding gold isn't just the torches . . . but that I am literally in a golden cage, suspended above the ground.

What?

Just when I look up, the door slams shut. There is the Wolf, in fae form, locking it with a golden key and a gleaming, toothy grin. Then he turns his back to me and shouts: "It is the era of a new Neverseen King!"

A cheer goes up.

A *cheer?*

The throbbing in my body does not ease, but I shift on the floor of the golden cage, lifting myself up with my core to peer out between golden bars.

I almost don't recognize the courtyard of Kaladen's palace.

It's *full* of creatures.

They carry torches and *lumiral* globes. They stream out of a palace window on the first floor—*the Valehaven portal.*

"Thank you for coming to celebrate with me!" the Wolf cries. "We shall celebrate the conquering of Kaladen Ashrift and the Bridge!"

Another cheer goes up, this one more violent than the first. My eyes are wide as I try to take in the scene before me. Are these creatures about to set into Risya? Will they ravage my people and land for their sport?

"Kaladen," I breathe.

That single word sends lightning shooting from my iron collar. One minute, I am upright. The next, I'm collapsed once more on the floor of the cage. How long have I been lying here? My mind fogs with pain.

It clears the instant the Wolf's leering grin fills my vision once more. I try to scramble back in the cage, but he catches my upper arm and drags me to him.

His eyes flash. "This won't hurt that much."

He rakes a claw down my arm. I refuse to let my cry of pain escape my teeth, glaring at him while my blood flows into his open palm.

"I am going to kill you," I growl to him. "As you take my blood, so I will take yours."

"Challenge accepted," he says with a wink, and fists his hand around my blood.

Then he flings me back against the wall of my cage.

"I have the human bride's blood!" he cries, holding up his fist to the crowd. "Now it is time to celebrate. Eat, drink, and be merry, my friends! Stay within the confines of the palace grounds for now and do whatever you please until dawn."

With that, his form vanishes to glamoured shadow. As if he truly is the Neverseen King now.

Did the children get out? Is Tariq protecting them somewhere? I dearly hope so. I watch the crowd for any sign of a human child, but to my relief, there is none.

I hold still for hours. Watching silently as darkness and torchlight fight in an unending battle. My cage is suspended off the ground, giving me a view of the entire macabre celebration, but not a good perspective on the individual creatures. Some seem fae like Kaladen, but others are strange in ways I cannot describe. My blood is not the only shed tonight. I watch countless fights break out amid the merrymaking, and countless heads roll.

When I prove boring, they quickly forget about me.

That is when I begin working on my bonds.

At dawn, once the celebration is over, I will break out of this cage.

The problem isn't my bonds, but the lock. I never was good at picking locks like Eshe, and I have nothing on me I could use. Not even my knives. The Wolf must have taken them the first time I fainted.

The key is with the Wolf, and at some point, I lost track of his shadowy form. I make my moves as though he watches me this entire time. When I finally work my bonds loose, I don't move. I don't even let the rope fall to the floor. I grip it in my fist, and I wait.

The night only grows darker and heavier around me. I pretend to try to sleep by lying down. I close my eyes and keep my movements subtle as I work the bonds of my feet. Once I have worked that knot, I let my body loosen like I truly am asleep.

And I wait.

At some point, the Wolf bids several of his minions enter the city. I force myself not to react, to hold still. When they return dragging a city guard, I dare not betray my awareness by throwing up.

Not even as they bring him to the Wolf, and I shut my eyes just before his teeth rip out the man's throat.

He's going to destroy the city. The entire kingdom.

Nevertheless, I wait.

Above me, the stars wink at me. As if they too are part of the celebration. Only one group of stars, one constellation I've never seen before, seems to darken at the sight in the courtyard.

Emin's constellation.

When I dare, I look at those stars. They look back at me, and I can almost see the steward's steely gaze coming through. Willing me to not give up.

At last, the sky begins to lighten. At first, it's so subtle I don't notice it. Then, I cannot deny it—the sky turns purple, then lavender.

I keep my pulse steady. Around me, the raucous sounds of the revelry die down. I listen carefully to the screams of pain and pleasure, the crush of goblets on stone, the clip clop of hooves on the ground.

Until *finally,* there is the sound I've been searching for.

The clamoring of feet and knees over a windowsill.

They're leaving.

They're going back to Valehaven.

I wait until the courtyard is silent.

Then, slowly, I lift myself up.

Blood and wine stain the flagstone as far as I can see. The fountain flows red. Broken goblets and crushed fruit litter the ground.

But as the sun crests the horizon, not a single soul is visible to me.

Not even the Wolf remains. He is probably wreaking havoc on our carefully contained portals. I grit my teeth. The portals are a problem for another day.

I let my bonds fall off as I get to my feet. The collar around my throat throbs, but so long as I do not try to work magic, the pain is manageable. I feel for a latch, for anything to remove it. There is nothing. It feels like a solid link of iron.

I face the lock and swallow.

Then I drag my fingernail down the barely healing cut the Wolf left on my arm. Blood wells. I smear it on my finger and face the lock once more, bracing myself.

For Eshe.

I press my finger to that lock.

White hot electricity explodes through my body.

I do not know how long I remain unconscious. But eventually, I come to, and the sun hasn't even finished rising.

The door to my prison swings listlessly on its hinges.

I pick myself up, ignoring the agony of each movement. The sunshine blurs in my vision. *Lulythinar is only a few days away.*

My left arm quivers from its many wounds, but I don't let that stop me as I lower myself out of the cage, then drop to my feet and roll into a crouch.

I don't have time to find my knives, so I make do searching the fallen fae bodies in the courtyard for weapons. I come up with a dagger that is clearly more decorative than functional and an arrow—without a bow.

This, along with my sheer determination, will have to do.

I'm going to Valehaven to find my husband.

The sun casts my shadow before me as I sprint for the window all the rest of the creatures disappeared into. I slip into the dimness, clutching my dagger in one hand and trying to ignore the pulse of my iron collar.

The room is empty, save for a wilted tree trunk in the center.

I press my bloodied finger to that trunk and watch as emerald green and gold burst to life and unfold into a magnificent, towering tree. As leaves shake and branches rustle, something bumps my bent knee. I look down to find a long vine curled against me. "Badh-o?" She rubs against me, sliding a curled leaf under my palm. As though to comfort me. "You'll come with me?"

Badh-o nods. I purse my bruised lips together, then stroke her stem. A dagger, an arrow . . . and a magical vine.

I rise to my feet.

"My name is Nadira Ashrift Felladyr," I growl under my breath. "I may not be a monster, but for the sake of those I love, I will not be afraid to become one."

For Kaladen. For my beloved Eshe.

I open the door and plunge into another world.

THANK YOU FOR READING THIS BOOK!
IF YOU ENJOYED IT, PLEASE CONSIDER
LEAVING A REVIEW ON AMAZON.

COMING SOON:

I will be assassin, queen, and monster to reclaim what is mine.

MORE FROM ANASTASIS BLYTHE

THE ZHENINGHAI CHRONICLES

Maiden of Candlelight and Lotuses
Guardian of Talons and Snares
Warrior of Blade and Dusk
Princess of Shadows and Starlight
Captive of Twilight and Treachery
Daughter of Darkness and Dreams

THE KING AND THE ASSASSIN

The Assassin Bride
The Neverseen King
The Nightmare Queen (Coming Soon)

BRIDES OF THE FAE

Bride of the Fae Prince
Bride of the Midnight Prince (Coming Soon)

ABOUT THE AUTHOR

Anastasis Blythe makes her home in central Texas with her husband. When she's not writing, she gardens, accompanies local bands and choirs on piano, rescues feral cats, and tries to keep up with the laundry. She loves exploring the world through reading, walks in nature, and thoughtful conversations.

To stay connected with her, be sure to sign up for her newsletter at AnastasisBlythe.com/Nadira.

Connect with Anastasis online at:
Website - AnastasisBlythe.com
Instagram - @AnastasisBlythe
Facebook - Anastasis Blythe
Goodreads - Anastasis Blythe

www.ingramcontent.com/pod-product-compliance
Lightning Source LLC
Chambersburg PA
CBHW020339310726
48979CB00015B/2424/J

* 9 7 8 1 9 6 0 6 0 6 1 0 5 *